Stay Alive

SIMON KERNICK

CENTURY

Published by Century, 2014

2 4 6 8 10 9 7 5 3 1

First published in Great Britain in 2014 by
Century
Random House, 20 Vauxhall Bridge Road,
London SW1V 2SA

www.randomhouse.co.uk

Addresses for companies within The Random House Group Limited can be
found at: www.randomhouse.co.uk/offices.htm

The Random House Group Limited Reg. No. 954009

A CIP catalogue record for this book
is available from the British Library

Hardback ISBN 9781780890753
Trade paperback ISBN 9781780890760

The Random House Group Limited supports the Forest Stewardship Council®
(FSC®), the leading international forest-certification organisation. Our books
carrying the FSC label are printed on FSC®-certified paper. FSC is the only
forest-certification scheme supported by the leading environmental organisations,
including Greenpeace. Our paper procurement policy can be found at:
www.randomhouse.co.uk/environment

Typeset in Times New Roman by Palimpsest Book Production Limited,
Falkirk, Stirlingshire
Printed and bound in Great Britain by CPI Group (UK) Ltd, Croydon, CR0 4YY

For my daughters, Amy and Rachel

One

Amanda Rowan had just stepped inside her front door, a shopping bag containing a pair of new shoes in one hand, her keys in the other, when she heard a sound that stopped her dead.

It was a faint, sudden gasp. Like air escaping from a tyre. Coming from somewhere upstairs.

Amanda listened intently, but all that came back at her was thick silence, interspersed with the ticking of the grandfather clock further down the hallway and, for a few seconds, she wondered if she'd imagined it.

The lights were on all over the house, and her husband's Porsche was in the driveway, which meant he was home. He shouldn't have been. He was supposed to be away on business in Manchester until the following afternoon. She'd seen him leave in the car early that morning, and had even spoken to him three hours earlier, just as he was about to go off to a client dinner. Except he hadn't been going to a client dinner, because his car was here, two hundred miles away from Manchester.

Something had brought him back home early. And she knew exactly what it was.

George had been having an affair for months now. She'd found out about it purely by accident a few weeks earlier. One evening he'd forgotten to sign out of his Hotmail account on one of the two iPads they had in the house, and when she'd picked it up and tried to log into her own account, a long list of messages to George from an Annie Mac – a woman she'd never heard of – with subject titles like 'I need you, darling' and 'Missing you desperately', had appeared. Feeling numb, but not altogether surprised, Amanda had opened the first one and read it through. She didn't need to read through any of the others. She got the gist.

Even so, it still rankled that he was so blasé about the whole thing that he'd bring his lover back here to the marital home. Maybe it had been her who'd made that strange noise, although it hadn't sounded like anything she'd associate with lovemaking.

Amanda put down the shopping bag and closed the door quietly. Like her husband, she wasn't meant to be coming back tonight. She'd arranged to stay overnight in London at her dad's house, but her dad was a cantankerous old sod, and they'd had one of their inevitable arguments. Rather than let his angry barbs wash over her, as she usually did on the few occasions she visited him, Amanda had lost her temper, stormed out the door with a curse for a goodbye, and driven straight home.

It was weird though. No music was playing in the house, and the TV wasn't on, which wasn't like George. He needed background noise.

Upstairs, one of the floorboards creaked. Someone was creeping around up there and, even though she knew who it would be, Amanda tensed. That's what happened when you lived in a three-hundred-year-old cottage in the middle of the woods, she thought. She loved this place. It had character, beauty, and desperately needed solitude, but it was also only a few miles from the M3, and barely an hour from the bright lights of London. And yet at night, when the only sounds were the hooting of owls, and the occasional drone of aircraft passing high overhead, it made her feel vulnerable. Especially without George's background noise.

A floorboard creaked again. It was coming from one of the bedrooms. Amanda frowned. George was a big man who'd usually downed a bottle of red wine by this time of night, regardless of who he was with, and he tended to make a lot of noise moving about, even when he was trying to be quiet. He also had an irritating habit of loudly clearing his throat, especially when he'd had a drink.

But the creaking had stopped, and there was nothing coming from up there now.

The obvious conclusion was that he was trying to hide, because he knew he'd done something wrong. Like bringing his lover home while his wife was away.

Amanda stood in the hallway. Her heart was beating loudly and her mouth was dry. She wasn't the sort of person who enjoyed furious confrontation. She preferred just to walk away when things went wrong. And she'd already lost her temper once tonight.

Pull yourself together, she told herself. This is *your* home.

Bracing herself, she called his name, her voice loud, but with just a hint of nervousness in it as it cracked through the dead silence.

No answer.

'George? Are you up there? It's me. Amanda.'

Still no answer.

'Look, I know you're there. Your car's outside.'

Slipping off her heels and taking a deep breath, she slowly made her way up the staircase and onto the long narrow landing that ran the width of the house. The lights were on but it was empty. To her left, the door to the master bedroom – the room she shared with George, at least when he wasn't snoring like a chainsaw – was wide open. It was dark inside but she could see that the bed was unmade, the sheets piled up and ruffled. There was no doubt there'd been action in there today.

Turning away, she saw that the light was on in the guest bedroom at the opposite end of the landing, and the door was ajar.

She took a step towards it, then another, before pausing and taking a deep breath that seemed loud in the silence. The house was suddenly utterly still. She kept walking towards the guest bedroom, her bare feet silent on the varnished floor, and stopped a foot away.

She couldn't hear anything behind the door. Not even a breath. It was as if the whole world had stopped moving.

Reaching out a hand that was ever so slightly shaking, she gave the door a push, and as it creaked open a few inches, Amanda caught the pungent stink of blood and faeces, and saw the naked, bloodied foot sticking out on the carpet. The foot belonged to a woman. It was small and dainty, and the toenails were painted a bright, confident red, several shades lighter than the thick pool of blood forming on the carpet several feet further in.

Was that the noise she'd heard when she'd first come into the house? The final gasp of a dying woman?

If so, it could only mean one thing. The killer was still in the house.

Behind her, the floorboard creaked once again, and it felt as if icy fingers crawled up her spine.

Amanda swung round fast just as a man in dark clothing and a balaclava, taller and leaner than George, appeared in the doorway to their bedroom, barely twenty feet away.

For a long second, she didn't move as her eyes focused on the hunting knife in his hand. Blood – fresh blood – ran down the groove and pooled at the tip, forming beads that dripped onto the floor.

She swallowed. There was no way she would reach the staircase before he did.

And then the intruder was coming towards her with long, confident strides, his boots banging hard and purposefully on the floor.

Acting entirely on instinct, Amanda scrambled over the landing stair rail, jumping the six feet down onto the staircase and falling down painfully on her behind, before scrambling to her feet again and bolting down the remainder of the steps, jumping the last five in one go as she heard him coming down behind her, moving just as fast as she was.

As her feet hit the floor at the bottom, she slipped on the floor and went down hard on her side, losing a precious second as the intruder charged down the staircase right behind her.

In one rapid movement, she jumped to her feet just as he threw himself down the last of the steps and landed barely a yard away from her.

Amanda had a choice of two exits – out of the back of the house or through the front – and only a split second to make her decision. Knowing that she hadn't double-locked the front door behind her, as she usually did, she ran through the front hallway, trying desperately to keep her balance in her bare feet. She could hear his heavy breathing – he was that close – and it took all her willpower to slow up just enough to grab both handles of the door and yank it open, before throwing herself through the gap and into the cool outside air.

But she'd barely gone two yards when she felt a hand grab her jacket from behind, and she was yanked backwards into a tight embrace as his arm encircled her neck, the grip immediately tightening. Screaming as loudly as she could, Amanda thrashed wildly with a strength born of pure adrenalin, her arms flailing as she tried to fight her way out of his grip. She felt a surge of pure, hot pain as one arm collided with his knife, the blade slicing through the light jacket and shirt she was wearing, ripping through the flesh. But somehow she managed to drive an elbow into the side of his head with enough force for him to loosen his grip. Amanda went to the gym five times a week, and the previous year she'd done a boxing course. She was fit and she was strong and, right then, it counted in her favour. Wriggling free from his grip and dodging the knife, she threw a wild punch at him – something he clearly wasn't expecting, the blow catching him full in the face.

He stumbled back, cursing and putting a hand to his nose, but still keeping the knife held out in front of him. Already he was beginning to right himself, and Amanda knew that she only had a few moments' respite. Reaching down in one movement, she grabbed a handful of gravel from the driveway and flung it at him, before taking off in a run towards the thick wall of beech trees that bordered their property on three sides, ignoring the painful grind of the gravel on the soles of her feet.

Their nearest neighbour was Mrs Naseby, an elderly widow whose tiny cottage was about a hundred yards away. Other than exchanging Christmas cards, and occasional polite conversations if they crossed paths in the woods, she and George didn't have much to do with Mrs Naseby, but Amanda was counting on the fact that she was home tonight as she sprinted through the trees, trying to put as much distance between herself and her house as possible. She stole a glance over her shoulder, but the dark space behind her was empty.

Mrs Naseby's cottage loomed up out of the darkness in front of her, a dim light glowing from inside.

'Be in,' she hissed through gritted teeth. 'Be in.'

She vaulted the wooden trellis at the end of Mrs Naseby's ramshackle garden and continued up to the front door without pause. Glancing once more behind her, she hammered on it hard and then bent down and shouted through the letterbox. 'Mrs Naseby, are you there? It's Amanda Rowan from next door. Can you let me in? Please! It's very urgent.'

Amanda could hear the sound of talking on the TV, but nothing else. She hammered on the door again, looking round at the same time to check that her assailant wasn't following. She couldn't see anything, and all she could hear was the pounding in her chest. The gash on her right arm was a good four inches long, and bleeding profusely, but there was no longer any pain. The adrenalin was taking care of that.

'Come on, come on,' she called out, banging on the door again.

'Who's there?' came an uncertain voice.

Amanda leaned back down to the letterbox again, speaking rapidly, the fear in her voice obvious. 'It's me, Amanda, from next door. There's been an accident. I need to call the police urgently. Can you let me in?'

There was a brief hesitation, and then the door slowly opened on a chain, and Mrs Naseby's face appeared. She looked nervous but as soon as she saw the terrified expression on Amanda's face, her nervousness turned immediately to concern. 'Oh my goodness,' she gasped. 'You're hurt. Come in quickly. Let's call you a doctor.' She removed the chain – her movements slow and awkward, the result of arthritis – and shuffled aside to let Amanda in out of the cold.

Amanda almost knocked her over in her haste to get inside the house. 'Lock the door quickly,' she shouted. 'There's someone out there.'

Mrs Naseby's eyes widened in shock as she got a better look at the huge tear in Amanda's jacket and the blood staining it red as it seeped out of the wound. She had one hand on the door handle, the other on her walking stick, but she didn't seem to be making any effort to close the door.

Knowing the urgency of her situation, Amanda reached over to slam it shut but, before she could get there, it flew open, knocking Mrs Naseby against the wall and sending Amanda stumbling backwards. Mrs Naseby cried out, trying but failing to keep a grip on her stick. As the stick clattered to the floor, and her legs went from under her, she fell onto her side, just as the man came storming into the hallway, a renewed urgency about him.

Ignoring the old lady completely, he lunged at Amanda, knife first, his dark eyes burning beneath his balaclava.

Dodging him, she ran for the staircase, bounding up it as it whined and creaked beneath her feet, not sure where the hell she was going, but knowing she had to put as much distance between herself and her assailant as possible.

A door was open in front of her and she ran through it and into Mrs Naseby's bedroom, noticing with huge relief as she slammed it behind her that there was a key in the lock. Pressing her whole body against the door, she locked it with shaking hands. She could hear him outside, his breathing calm and steady as he tried and failed to turn the handle.

A split second later, the door reverberated on its hinges as he slammed into it. It was only a flimsy lock and Amanda knew it wasn't going to hold for long.

Shit. She was trapped. The door reverberated again and she heard the sound of wood splitting.

Looking round desperately, she spotted the half-open bedroom window. Running over, she forced it fully open, then clambered out through the gap just as the door flew open and he came striding in the room, making straight for her with the bloodied knife raised, like something out of one of her worst nightmares.

Gripping the window ledge with both hands, she turned herself round and slid down the wall. Then, just as she let go to jump the rest of the way, a gloved hand grabbed her wrist, and suddenly she was dangling helpless in mid-air.

As his sleeve rode up, she just had time to see the tattoo on his arm.

With his free hand, he brought the knife down towards her wrist. But as she pulled and wriggled with all her might, his grip loosened, and then she was falling through the air.

She hit the tarmac feet first and a stinging pain shot up her Achilles tendons as she rolled over and leapt to her feet, running again, making for the trees and freedom, tearing through the foliage. She felt a stinging pain in her right ankle but ignored it and kept running, running, running, making for the road, and anywhere where there might be people who could help her.

The hole appeared without warning and, as her foot ploughed straight into it, she tripped and went sprawling, landing painfully on the hard ground.

For a moment, she didn't move, concentrating instead on quietening her breathing.

And then she heard it. The sound of a twig breaking, followed by undergrowth being pushed aside.

He was still following her.

Using her hands, she pushed herself into the lee of a holly bush, trying to get as far under it as possible. Finally, she lay still and held her breath.

Don't move. Don't speak. Don't breathe. Don't move.

In those moments, she thought about her own vulnerability, and the fact that a person's world could change in the blink of an eye, or the deep, painful slash of a knife. One minute, she was a married woman living an easy life in idyllic surroundings, with few if any worries; the next she'd discovered a murder in her own home, and suddenly she was alone in the woods while the man who'd committed it hunted her with a knife.

She seemed to lie there for a long time. A minute? Two? Five? It was difficult to tell, and she didn't dare look at her watch. But however long it was, she heard no further sound from her pursuer.

It seemed that he might have given up and gone.

And that was when she saw the glow of headlights coming from the road that ran through the woods, no more than fifty yards away. She had no idea who it could be. Very few cars used this route, especially at this time of night, because the road didn't go anywhere, and there were only a handful of houses up here.

But in the end, none of that mattered. What mattered was that it couldn't be the man chasing her because the car was coming from the wrong direction, which meant the headlights represented safety.

A twig cracked loudly a few feet away, and Amanda's heart lurched. In the next instant, she was on her feet and sprinting through the woods, desperately trying to get to the car before it passed by. Screaming, too. Screaming at the top of her lungs, knowing that she must look a terrible sight to anyone driving through this lonely place at night, but no longer caring.

Her lungs felt as if they were bursting as she tore out of the trees and onto the road barely ten yards in front of the car, with its blinding headlights.

'Help me!' she yelled, waving her arms, hardly hearing the

screech of brakes as the driver tried to stop, realizing at the last second that he wasn't going to be able to manage it in time.

Amanda dived out of the way, crashing painfully into the tarmac, as the car passed by, inches away from her.

And then finally, mercifully, everything went black.

Two

The wound on Amanda Rowan's left forearm still throbbed. It was a good four inches long, running in a near dead straight line to just above the wrist and, even though the stitches had long since been removed, the cut was still deep and raw – a permanent reminder of the events of that bloody night. She examined it in the mirror as she did every morning and evening – a symbol of her vanity – but, once again, there was no discernible improvement.

She turned away from the mirror and went over to the window, looking over the sprinkling of houses that made up the village she'd made her temporary home, hundreds of miles from the house she'd shared with her husband, which was now tainted beyond repair.

The police had said that George and his lover – a woman fifteen years his junior – had been the victims of a serial killer known as The Disciple who'd been terrorizing the south of England for most of the previous year. Amanda had been the first person to have confronted him and lived, and as everyone, including friends, family and the police had been keen to tell her, she was extremely lucky to have escaped a killer who'd built a reputation for ruthless efficiency in his work.

The twenty-four hours after the attack had been frenetic. First at the hospital, where they'd treated her, not only for shock and the stab wound on her forearm, but also the extensive bruising she'd received during her ordeal. After that it had been the exhaustive police interviews, when she'd had to go over and over what had happened, even though her first instinct was to bury it deep in the recesses of her brain. And then, finally, the inevitable media storm. Amanda's case had an extremely compelling storyline. Not only was there the infidelity angle, the wronged wife returning home unexpectedly, but the fact that The Disciple had been so determined to kill Amanda that he'd chased her right through her neighbour's house (thankfully, Mrs Naseby had been unhurt), forcing her to jump from a first-floor window, and that she'd only just missed being hit by a car during her escape, and still survived, was the stuff of media dreams. Everyone wanted to interview her. The *Sun* had even offered her a hundred grand for her exclusive story.

But all Amanda wanted to do was get as far away as possible from what had happened. The police hadn't been keen for her to go. Instead they'd offered her twenty-four-hour protection at a local safe house until they had The Disciple in custody, but Amanda was insistent. She was escaping the media – at least for the time being – and she didn't want a police officer living with her either. She'd given the lead detective on the case – a big, good-looking DCS called Mike Bolt – her new address, and promised to keep it secret, even from her immediate family, until The Disciple was in custody. The consultant psychiatrist working with the police on the case had also suggested it might not be a bad idea for Amanda to get well away from the scene of her trauma, so Mike Bolt had reluctantly agreed (not that he had much choice), and had arranged for the local police to keep an eye on her. She also had a panic button, with a direct line to the nearest police station, installed at the property.

'You don't think The Disciple's going to come after me, do you?' Amanda had asked Bolt. 'There's no way I could ID him, so I can't represent any sort of threat.'

'I wouldn't have thought so,' he'd told her, in a way that suggested it was possible he might, 'but it's always best to stay on the safe side.'

And stay on the safe side she had. She'd picked a location deep in the Scottish Highlands, in a village miles away from the nearest town, paying three months' rent upfront. Only one person outside the police knew she was here, an old friend she trusted with her life – someone she knew would never betray her, either deliberately or otherwise.

She kept a low profile in the village, staying out of the pub and exchanging nothing more than brief formalities with her neighbours, none of whom recognized her, thanks to the fact they'd kept her picture out of the newspapers. Occasionally, one of the villagers would ask what a pretty young thing like her was doing living alone in the middle of nowhere, and Amanda would reply that she was writing a book, and wanted to be in a place that would give her the necessary inspiration. Further questions were fended off politely but firmly, and it hadn't taken long for people to get the message.

As it happened, Amanda had told them at least part of the truth. She *was* writing a book. Or planning one, anyway. It was something she'd wanted to do since childhood, but had never got round to doing, and she'd been working on the plan until late the previous evening, which was why she'd risen so late today.

Amanda's semi-detached stone cottage was the only house with two floors amongst the sprinkling of ugly, chalet-style, 1960s bungalows that made up the village of Sprey, and she loved to stand at her bedroom window looking out at the thick pine forest that started just beyond the tiny Presbyterian church. It was late October, and though winter was fast approaching, a watery sun was shining in a sky patchy with white clouds, and it looked as though it was going to be a nice afternoon. For Amanda, it was a toss-up between actually starting the first draft of her novel – something she kept putting off – or going for a nice long walk in the hills and woodland round her temporary home, or down by the river that ran beneath the village.

It wasn't much of a decision really, and she was just about to go and make herself some brunch and a decent pot of coffee to give her sustenance for the walk ahead, when she saw something that made her stop.

A car she didn't recognize – a black four-wheel drive too clean to have been out here long – was slowly passing her front gate, and the driver was looking right up at her. It was hard to see what he looked like because of the distance between her house and the road, but she was certain he wasn't one of the local cops, and she didn't like the way he turned away from her just a second too quickly.

As the car disappeared behind the hedge at the end of her front garden, a knot of tension formed in Amanda's gut, and she realized she was grinding her teeth, a habit that she seemed to have picked up in the three weeks since George's murder, and one she knew she had to stop as it was already beginning to drive her mad.

Taking a deep breath, she turned away from the window, telling herself not to get so paranoid. There was no way that The Disciple could know where she was staying and, even if by some incredible accident of fate he did, there was no way he'd risk coming all the way up here to kill her. He was a hunted man. It was just a matter of time before he was caught.

No, she told herself. She was safe. Nothing like that was ever going to happen to her again.

Three

Right from childhood, it had always been Frank Keogh's ambition to be a police officer, and there was never any danger that he wouldn't achieve it. He worked hard at school, did well at sport, and the stubborn, single-minded streak he possessed – the one that often drove his family and friends mad – meant that he got in at the first attempt, aged eighteen, coming second highest in his class at Hendon.

Keogh didn't just want to be any old cop. He wanted to be a detective, and bring the really serious criminals to justice. It was no surprise to anyone that he was in plainclothes by twenty-one, and a detective sergeant by twenty-five. The bosses up top liked him. He was tough, tenacious and patient, and they were already talking about him being DCI-level by the age of thirty.

The problem for Keogh was the rulebook. He'd always had a strong sense of natural justice. He wanted to see the bad guys suffer and the good guys win, and it offended him that this often didn't seem to happen. The good guys – the police – were stymied by an ever-increasing set of rules. The bad guys often escaped justice because their lawyers were good, and the law was on their side. This injustice drove him mad, as did the fact that, in the end, the criminals were so easy to catch. It wasn't like in the books or the movies, as he'd imagined it to be when he'd joined up. These people were idiots. They left a trail of evidence in their wake, meaning that most of the detective work was building a case to go to court and then filling out a load of paperwork.

Disillusioned, Keogh decided on a change in direction. He'd always had a thing about guns. There was something about their sheer power that fascinated him, and there'd been more than the occasional moment when he'd fantasized about putting one against the head of some cocky low-life thug and pulling the trigger. He never would have done, of course – he had far too much to lose for that – but he decided on the next best thing, by joining the Metropolitan Police's elite CO19 firearms unit. He figured it would give him a new challenge, and a much-needed adrenalin rush now and again. His plan was always to go back into plainclothes eventually, work himself higher up the greasy pole, then retire and write a book about his experiences, which he was positive he could turn into a real success.

It surprised no one, least of all Keogh himself, that he got into CO19 at the first attempt. He remembered thinking when he went out on that first patrol, a gun at his hip as he and his colleagues drove through the mean streets of Lewisham, that this was as good as life got. He was young; he was good-looking; he had a beautiful fiancée. The world was his to dominate.

Except it wasn't, because fate has a way of intervening when it's least expected, and leaving the best-laid plans in ruins. And fate really had it in for Frank Keogh.

It was three months into his time in CO19 when the Armed Response Vehicle he was travelling in received an urgent call from Dispatch about a group of youths from a well-known local street gang travelling in a stolen vehicle, one of whom was reported to have brandished a gun at passers-by. They got a dozen calls like this every day, and rarely did they come across anyone who was actually armed, but each call had to be taken on its own merits and, because they were very close by, they'd raced to where the vehicle had last been sighted, intercepting it at some traffic lights.

All three of them had been out of the ARV in seconds, pistols drawn and shouting at the men inside the vehicle to put their hands above their heads. It looked as if the three of them were complying but, as Keogh approached the car from the side, the man in the back pulled something from his pocket. It was ten o'clock at night and dark, and Keogh had no idea what it was the man had in his hand, but Keogh remembered vividly him turning round rapidly in his seat and bringing up an object that looked a lot like a gun.

Keogh had pulled the trigger then, shooting him twice through the window at a distance of no more than five feet. One of the bullets caught him in the neck, the other hit him in the eye as the pistol kicked, and it was this one that was fatal.

It turned out that twenty-year-old Derrick 'Slugs' Foster had been holding a mobile phone when Keogh had shot him, and that none of the three men in the car was armed, not even with a knife. As far as Keogh was concerned, none of that mattered. He'd done his job, and he'd done it properly. The guy had pulled something that could have been a gun from his pocket and he'd looked as if he was going to fire it. In those situations, you have maybe a second and a half to make the choice of whether to fire or not. Make the wrong choice and you get shot, and Keogh was not the kind of guy who got shot because he was too scared to react.

But the bosses – those men who'd been so supportive of him when he was on the way up – didn't see it like that. Neither did the local community. The following night, the estate where the dead man had lived was the scene of the worst rioting that London had witnessed in years, and within days a 'Justice for Derrick' campaign had been set up by local community leaders, backed by several sympathetic human rights lawyers, calling for charges of murder to be laid against the man who'd pulled the trigger.

Keogh was suspended from firearms duty, as was routine in such incidents. Then, as the furore mounted, and further street disturbances broke out in several other London boroughs, he was suspended from duty altogether. Then came the bombshell. The establishment had decided to bend to the power of the mob and the special interest groups. He was going to be charged with manslaughter. No one was above the law, said the well-groomed ex-public schoolboy from the CPS as he'd announced the charges at a news conference that was shown as the top story on every news channel.

During the run-up to the trial, Keogh's fiancée left him, citing the pressure of the situation. He'd really had a thing for Kirsty. She was the one. They were going to have a family and grow old together. Losing her had been like a massive and continuous kick in the balls. He couldn't get it out of his head that she'd rejected him. But, even then, Keogh hadn't lost his self-belief. He still had support from his colleagues past and present, and he was certain that no jury would convict a serving police officer with an unblemished record for shooting dead a low-life like Derrick Foster in a spur-of-the-moment, high-pressure incident.

Unfortunately, he was wrong. Found guilty, he was sentenced to three years in prison. And it was hard time that he did, segregated from the main prison population for his own safety, and made to spend his days with rapists, paedophiles, and all the other assorted scum of the earth. The guards warned him to be careful even there because members of Derrick Foster's gang inside the prison had put a contract out on Keogh's head, and within two weeks he'd been attacked by a fellow con wielding a sharpened piece of plastic. He'd been slashed twice in the face and neck, and though he'd managed to fend off his attacker until help arrived, the good looks he'd prided himself on were ruined forever by the scars left behind.

They were the worst, darkest times of Keogh's life. Brought as low as he'd ever been, he even contemplated suicide. But then, slowly but surely, that single-minded determination that had served him so well in the past came back into play. He forced himself to adapt to prison life and bide his time until release, and all the time his bitterness grew. He'd get his own back. On the bosses who'd hung him out to dry; on the public who'd done nothing to stop him being put behind bars. On every last one of them.

He got out in two years, already forgotten by the rest of the world, but it had only been a matter of time before his bitterness found an outlet, and so began a journey that had got him here today, driving slowly past Amanda Rowan's rented cottage in a four-by-four.

She'd noticed him looking at her, he was pretty sure of that. He cursed, but kept driving. He was used to taking risks. It was all part of the job description, and at least now he knew she was where she was supposed to be. When he'd first arrived here in the darkness of the early hours, he'd considered breaking into the house, but she'd had at least half a dozen locks on the back door, and the brand-new PVC windows were locked and secure, with no sign of keys anywhere convenient. He'd also considered knocking on the door and showing his fake police ID, but had dismissed it as too risky. Amanda Rowan was no fool. There was no guarantee she'd let him in – the scars were always a problem like that – and, if she didn't, then it would have blown everything.

Now that he knew she was at home, all he had to do was be patient. By coming to an isolated spot like this one, she'd made it far easier for him.

When he was about two hundred yards past her cottage, and the village had given way to fields with trees beyond, he made a right turn up a narrow lane. He followed the lane as it went straight for about fifty yards, passing a couple of barns, before swinging a sharp right back in the direction of the village. He stopped the Land Rover in a spot he'd recce'd earlier, and parked up on the verge amidst a copse of trees. From this position he could see the rear of Amanda's cottage. Its rear garden backed directly onto a fallow field, and he could see a couple of kids playing on a trampoline in the garden next door.

If Amanda Rowan came out the back way, cutting across the field, he'd see her easily. If she went out the front, the tiny, sensor-operated camera that he'd planted in the undergrowth just inside her front gate would pick up the movement and start recording. Whatever happened, as soon as she left the house, he'd know about it.

And they'd finally be able to get to work.

Four

Jess Grainger had never been in a canoe before, mainly because it had never crossed her mind to get in one. She wasn't a big fan of water, unless it was steaming hot and pouring out of a showerhead. She could swim okay, but only because they'd made her learn at school – and she still wasn't that great at it – and right now the thought of falling into a cold, grey Scottish river (which she was sure she would do by the end of the day) filled her with a mixture of dread, and resentment that she'd agreed to come along on this trip in the first place.

Uncle Tim must have read her thoughts because he clapped her hard on the back, his hand lingering for just a second too long. 'You're going to love it, Jessie,' he said, giving her a big toothy smile as he took a deep breath of the fresh country air. 'Just look at it.' He took his hand away – thank God – and swung it round expansively as he admired the view of the gently running river, with the forest stretching up the hills that rose gently on each side of it.

'Some of the best countryside in the world up here,' the old guy who ran the place they were hiring the canoes from announced as he pushed one of them into the water, turning it round so that it rested in the shallows parallel to the bank. 'And I've been to a hell of a lot of places, I'm telling you.'

Jess was sure he had. Thin and wizened beneath his beanie cap, with a face full of cracks and lines, the old guy looked just like an Arctic explorer. But his words didn't make her feel any more enthusiastic as she clambered unsteadily into the front of the canoe, almost toppling out of the other side in the process, and lowered herself onto the hard wooden seat.

The old guy handed her a wooden paddle while Aunt Jean got in the back with all the grace of a rhino, landing heavily in her own seat.

'I'll do the steering, Jessie,' announced Aunt Jean. 'You just paddle. One side then the other. You'll get used to it soon enough. It's easy.' Her tone wasn't unfriendly, but it wasn't too cheery either, and Jess could tell she didn't really want her there, but was trying to make an effort for Casey's sake.

Casey was Jess's little sister and she lived with Uncle Tim and Aunt Jean up here in the middle of the Scottish wilderness, having moved up a few months ago after Dad had died. They weren't real sisters. Jess had been fostered, then adopted, aged seven, by the couple she came to know as Mum and Dad, when they didn't think they could have children of their own. Then, less than a year later, Casey had turned up. By rights, Jess should have been jealous, but from the start she'd adored her little sister, and felt hugely protective of her, a feeling that had grown even stronger when first Mum, then Dad, had died.

The whole reason Jess had come up here from London was to see Casey and make sure she was settling in okay. And to be fair, it seemed she was. Unlike Jess herself, Casey was really excited about this canoeing trip, and she jumped into the front of the other canoe, taking her paddle excitedly from the old guy, while Uncle Tim got in the back.

The old guy grinned at Casey, his eyes twinkling. It was, Jess thought, the same old story. Everyone fell in love with Casey. She was just that kind of girl. She was blonde, bubbly, with a sweet cherubic face, a cute button nose, and a lively personality, but also enough smarts to know how to get round people, and make them do what she wanted without them realizing they were doing it. Although more than seven years separated them, Jess had always grown up in her shadow. Sometimes it surprised her that she wasn't more envious of Casey, but only a few times had the fact that her sister got all the attention ever irritated her, and in truth, she loved her sister just as everyone else did. And now, with Dad gone, Casey was all she had left.

'Okay, you've got my phone number,' said the old guy, standing above them. 'The mobile reception's patchy along the river, but you'll be able to get it in parts. The river's running pretty slow at the moment, so you shouldn't run into any problems but, if you do, just give us a call. Otherwise, we'll meet you at the bridge near Tayleigh at five o'clock. That should give you plenty of time.'

Five o'clock? That was almost four hours away and Jess felt her heart sink. There were a hundred things she'd rather be doing than this. When she'd come up, she'd envisaged taking Casey shopping in Inverness, not hauling ass down some Godforsaken river in the back of beyond.

'Have you got everything, Tim?' yelled Aunt Jean from behind her, her voice loud in Jess's ear.

Tim patted the rucksack beside him. 'Food, drink, the lot,' he replied, sounding as excited as Casey. 'Are we all ready?'

25

'I'm ready,' shouted Casey, lifting the paddle above her head, two-handed, making the old guy laugh.

'You're going to have a great time, wee lassie,' he told her, and gave their canoe a push so it drifted into the deeper water. 'And you will too, lassie, if you let yourself,' he said to Jess.

'She's from London,' said Jean, as if this explained everything. 'She's not used to the great outdoors.'

'I'll be fine,' said Jess wearily, forcing a smile as she sank her paddle in the water, while the old guy gave their canoe a push and they drifted slowly out onto the river.

And right into the beginning of a nightmare.

Five

Mike Bolt was dreaming about his dead wife.

It was something he did more and more these days. The fact was he'd pretty much deified her. In death, she could do no wrong, which was why he'd never been able to hold down a serious relationship in the almost ten years since she'd passed away. He'd been engaged a couple of years back for a while to a CPS lawyer called Claire. He'd even moved her in to his place in Clerkenwell, and for a while he'd thought that she might finally be the one to get him over Mikaela. But in the end it hadn't worked either. Claire did things that irritated him, things that Mikaela would never have done. She talked about her work all the time; she obsessed about her weight and kept going on strange, masochistic diets; and she didn't like children. Bolt wasn't a huge fan of kids either, but Mikaela had been, and she'd also been two months pregnant when she'd died. So, as far as Bolt was concerned, it reflected badly on Claire, and was yet another reason to end his relationship with her.

Since Claire had gone, Bolt had had a couple of other flings, including a recent one with a former colleague of his, Tina Boyd, which had been doomed from the start (Tina was far too much of a handful for him, and probably any man), but for the last few months he'd been resolutely single, giving him ample opportunity to fixate on Mikaela – something that he'd lost no time in doing.

In this particular dream Bolt was having, he and Mikaela were riding horses across a long lonely stretch of beach somewhere in France. Mikaela's horse was galloping away into the distance, and looked to Bolt to be out of control, but Mikaela didn't seem to care. The wind was blowing through her long blonde hair and he could hear her laughter fading away as she got further and further from his horse, which refused to go any faster than at a gentle trot even though he was yelling at it to get a move on. And then, as he watched, Mikaela disappeared from view altogether.

Which was the moment the windswept beach began to fade as an incessant ringing in his head drowned out everything else.

Bolt's eyes snapped open and he sat up in the bed. His mobile was vibrating and bouncing round the bedside table. The clock said 05.46. As he reached over to pick up the phone, he paused to look at the photo of him and Mikaela that stood next to it. It was a shot from their holiday in Corfu two summers before she died, both of them tanned and grinning at the camera. Whenever he was in a relationship, Bolt would hide the photo away, sneaking only the occasional peek at it, but the moment he was single, it would be back on the bedside table so that he could wake up every morning to his memories. He knew it was bad for him to dwell as much as he did, but he seemed incapable of doing anything about it. Emotionally, he was trapped in a past that had ended almost a decade earlier, and the sad thing was, he probably always would be. Only one thing kept his mind off Mikaela, and that was work.

And it was work calling him now. Specifically, his long-time colleague, Mo Khan. And, even before he picked up the phone, Bolt knew what it was going to be about, because there'd only be one reason why Mo would be phoning at this time in the morning, although he hoped to God he was wrong.

Yawning, he pressed the Call Receive button. 'You woke me from a beautiful dream.'

'I'm truly sorry about that, boss, but right now that's the least of our problems.'

Bolt felt his heart sink. 'There's been another one, hasn't there?'

'It looks that way. I've just had a call from a DCI Matt Black of Thames Valley CID. They've got a murder scene up in some woods between Reading and Basingstoke. A home invasion. Two dead, one injured. They think it might be the work of The Disciple.'

'That's three casualties. He usually only targets couples.'

'It looks like he attacked the husband and his mistress, and the wife turned up and disturbed him. She made a dash for it, and although she got cut up a bit, and almost got hit by a car while she was running, she's conscious.'

'Is there anything specific that makes Thames Valley think it's The Disciple?'

'The MO's definitely his, boss. No question about it.'

Bolt sighed and got out of bed, looking for some clean clothes. 'Christ, this is all we need. The pressure's going to be even more intense now. Who's driving, me or you?'

'I'm just about to get in my car now. I'll be with you in twenty. You can sleep on the way down, have some more beautiful dreams.'

Bolt grunted. 'Somehow I doubt it.'

Six

For the last fifteen months, a brutal serial killer dubbed The Disciple had kept the south of England in the grip of fear, and the media in the grip of excitement. Before the previous night's attack, he'd committed six murders in three previous incidents. His modus operandi was always the same. He picked isolated detached properties occupied by professional couples, all of which so far had been to the west of London. He would break in at night, disable the male partner with a non-fatal stab wound to the leg, before overpowering and binding the female partner. He'd then torture and sexually assault the woman, and on one occasion the man as well, before finally killing them both with a knife, using their blood to daub Satanic signs on the walls of the room in which he carried out the attacks. On each occasion the left-hand little finger of the female victim had been cut off, and was subsequently missing from the crime scene, suggesting The Disciple was taking them as trophies.

Bolt had been brought in to lead the inquiry four months earlier, after the previous senior investigating officer – a good solid cop called Mason, whom Bolt had met a couple of times before – had had a massive heart attack and dropped dead. That should have told Bolt everything he needed to know about this case. It was a nightmare for any SIO. Not only was the pressure for a result enormous, and seemingly continuously building, but leads on the ground were desperately scarce. The Disciple might have been a sick, deranged individual, but he was also clever enough not to leave any DNA behind at the scene of his crimes. So far, the only possible clue they had to his identity was a witness description of a man in dark clothing and a woollen cap seen by a male dog walker hanging round near the house of the final two victims the day before they were killed. The description of the man himself was fairly basic – tall, well-built, somewhere in his thirties – but the witness had noticed a dark green tattoo on his left forearm, where his sleeve had been rolled up. It wasn't much to reassure an increasingly concerned public that they were making progress on the case, especially considering the number of detectives working on it, but Bolt had learned in more than twenty-five years as a police officer that sometimes you simply had to be patient and wait for the break, although in recent weeks he too had grown intensely frustrated with the lack of leads.

Now, though, it looked like they might have one, in the form of a survivor. Bolt wasn't going to get his hopes up too much, but when he'd taken the case he'd always known that, as long as he kept killing, The Disciple was going to make a mistake eventually. Maybe, just maybe, this was it.

It was 7.10 a.m. and night had given way to an overcast morning when they arrived. The murder scene was a large detached house in the middle of a stretch of beech wood – the kind of place that estate agents would claim had character – surrounded by a high brick wall, which was possible but not easy to scale, set on a quiet, heavily wooded back road not far from the A33. The road in front of the house was lined on both sides with police vehicles, and a group of uniformed PCs were drinking coffee and eating sandwiches.

'It's a perfect location for The Disciple,' said Mo, as they parked up behind a police van and got out of the car. 'He could have watched the house to his heart's content and no one would have spotted him.'

'I don't understand what makes people live out in places like this,' said Bolt. 'It's so damn lonely. I need people around me. I need to hear, I don't know . . . Noise.'

'You're a city boy. So am I. But I reckon my wife would love it out here.' Mo stood staring at the house, leaning back so his belly stuck out. He'd always been a short, stout little guy, the very antithesis of Bolt, who was tall and broad-shouldered, but he'd put on a fair bit of weight of late, and with his thick head of almost-silver hair, he was now beginning to resemble a middle-aged Hobbit. 'How much do you reckon this place costs?' he asked vaguely.

'God knows. A million. Two million. A lot more than you or I could ever afford.' Bolt reckoned that Mikaela would have liked a place like this too. She'd always wanted to move out of the city and start a new life and family in the countryside. For a moment, he wondered how they would have coped: them living out here and him still a city cop, commuting into town. Pretty well, he imagined.

She'd liked fresh air. Bolt could take it or leave it.

They climbed under the police tape, showed their IDs to the group of cops eating their breakfast, then made their way over to the van containing the coveralls that they needed to put on before they could enter the crime scene. Bolt felt mildly nauseous at the prospect of going inside. He hated the sight of any dead body, and always had done, ever since he'd seen his first one back in the early days in the job. He'd seen plenty since and, every time, it reminded him far too much of his own mortality – the knowledge that one day he would end up a lifeless husk like all of them.

Death depressed Bolt. The needless, violent deaths of those whose time should have still been far away depressed him even more, and there were few killings more violent and needless than those committed by The Disciple. At the home of the last two victims, he'd been almost overcome with emotion as he'd walked through the house, seen the photos on the wall of the young couple – both barely thirty – and then gone into the bedroom and seen the terrible things that had been done to their naked bodies. *Almost* overcome, but not quite. Ultimately, he was still professional enough to hold himself together in front of his colleagues, but more and more these days he wondered if he was becoming too affected by his job; whether it was time to pull back from the tough, high-profile cases and finish the last four years of his thirty with a whimper rather than a bang.

'DCS Bolt?'

Bolt turned to see a short, prematurely bald guy with a kindly, boyish face and chubby cheeks, dressed in coveralls. 'Yes?'

'I'm DCI Matt Black. Thames Valley CID. I'm in charge of securing the scene.' He spoke matter-of-factly in a slight West Country burr that reminded Bolt of the guy who'd played Inspector Wexford in the old TV series. He also looked too young to be a DCI, but maybe that was just Bolt showing his age.

'Pleased to meet you, Matt.' He put out a hand and shook, before introducing Mo to him. 'We'd appreciate it if you could show us around the scene.'

'Of course. Come this way.'

They followed Black as he led them through the police vehicles and along a path lined with fluorescent markers towards the house. An imposing set of wooden security gates with a curving line of wrought-iron spikes along the top announced the entrance. The gates were open, revealing a gravel driveway and turning circle in front of the house, and a separate two-car garage to the left. A red Porsche Turbo – the kind beloved of middle-aged men wanting to impress the girls – was parked in front of it, and Bolt assumed that it belonged to the male victim. As they passed through the gates, he asked if they'd been open when the first officers had arrived at the scene.

Black shook his head. 'No. They were closed and locked. We think the suspect came over the wall round the back, and picked the lock on the back door. It's only got a single five-bar lock, along with two bolts that weren't pulled across, so if someone knew what they were doing, it wouldn't be that hard to get in.'

'You'd think they'd have a state-of-the-art security system living round here,' said Mo.

'They do. And CCTV cameras covering the back and the front of the property. But the alarm wasn't on, and it looks like the CCTV camera round the back was tampered with.'

'How?' asked Bolt.

'The lens has been spray-painted black. The camera itself is about ten feet up an apple tree in the garden, facing the back door. My guess is the suspect shinned up the tree and did it.'

'Can we take a look?'

Black nodded. 'Sure. Follow me.'

As they walked down the driveway and round the side of the house, Bolt noticed a pool of vomit congealing on the front doorstep.

'That came out of the first officer on the scene,' Black told them matter-of-factly. 'Apparently, the two upstairs were his first murder victims. And, as I'm sure you can imagine, it's not very pretty up there.'

Bolt flashed back to the last Disciple murder scene. The blood and the horror. 'Poor sod,' he said. 'I don't think you ever get used to that kind of thing.' But he noticed that Black didn't seem unduly concerned by what he'd witnessed. Maybe some cops did get used to it after all, and he was the exception rather than the rule.

The rear garden was several hundred feet long and about half as wide, and was enclosed by the same high brick wall that lined the front of the property. Mature bushes and foliage ran along the borders, while beech trees from the encroaching woods loomed up beyond the wall. Apart from the occasional birdsong and the faint hum of rush-hour traffic from the nearby A33, the woods were silent.

'The camera's up on this tree here.'

Bolt followed the angle of Black's finger to a point about halfway up an apple tree that stood a couple of yards beyond the patio at the back of the house. There was still plenty of foliage on it, and even a few mouldy-looking apples. 'I can't see a thing,' he said.

Mo shook his head. 'Neither can I.'

The two of them approached the tree, and only when he was at the bottom looking up could Bolt make out the black box partly concealed by a branch. It would have been easy enough for the suspect to have got up there and spray-painted it, but only if he knew where he was looking. He turned to Black. 'How the hell did he know it was there?'

Black shrugged. 'He's your killer, DCS Bolt. Not ours. I thought he was meant to spend a lot of time casing the homes of his victims before he went in. If he knew what he was looking for, he would have found it eventually.'

It was a fair point, and once again it made Bolt realize how carefully their killer picked his targets and planned his attacks. 'Can you take us through what happened here?' he asked.

'We haven't interviewed the woman who survived the attack, but her name's Amanda Rowan and she's the wife of the male victim, George Rowan. From what we can piece together, she came home and disturbed the killer, who was in the process, or had just finished, murdering George Rowan and a woman we've tentatively identified as 29-year-old Ivana Hanzha. Miss Hanzha is listed on the payroll of the investment bank that Mr Rowan works for.'

'So we can assume she was Mr Rowan's lover.'

'It looks that way. Anyway, we think Mrs Rowan's arrival wasn't expected, either by the victims or the killer. There was some sort of confrontation and then the killer chased her out of the house.'

'You said there was CCTV at the front,' said Mo. 'Did that capture anything, or was that tampered with too?'

'No it wasn't, and yes it did,' answered Black. 'We examined the footage a couple of hours ago and it clearly shows Amanda Rowan entering the property at nine fifty-three p.m. last night, and then exiting again through the front door at nine fifty-six, being chased by a man dressed entirely in black and wearing a black ski mask. He grabs her and slashes her on the arm with a knife, but she manages to wriggle out of his grip and then disappears from shot. After that, it seems she ran to the nearest neighbour – an old lady called Vera Naseby, who lives about a hundred metres away. We haven't interviewed her yet, but she was the one who called 999 and alerted us to what was going on.'

'It looks like Mrs Rowan had an incredibly lucky escape,' said Bolt.

Black nodded. 'Even luckier than you think, because the killer continued to chase her. When Mrs Naseby answered the door, he was right behind her. He followed her into the house and up the stairs. She had to jump out of Mrs Naseby's bedroom window to get away from him.'

Bolt and Mo exchanged puzzled glances. The Disciple might have been deranged but he'd always shown himself to be an efficient operator. 'Maybe he's more hot-headed than we thought,' said Bolt slowly.

'Maybe he just doesn't like leaving witnesses,' said Black.

'You said in the footage that the suspect was wearing a ski mask. So why risk chasing a witness through a neighbour's house, especially if she hasn't seen your face? It just seems unduly reckless.'

Nobody had an answer to that one, but Bolt was hoping the reason was because The Disciple was becoming caught up in his own hype, and now believed he was untouchable. It was a reasonable enough explanation. Sociopathic killers experience a real sense of power from ending the lives of their victims. If they get too much of it, and think they're more powerful than they really are, they end up doing stupid things.

'Come on,' said Black. 'Let me show you inside.'

They stopped at the open back door – a standard half-glass PVC design – and checked the lock. It was undamaged, but this didn't tell them anything. They already knew that The Disciple had housebreaking expertise, since he'd got into the other three properties through locked doors.

'So we reckon he must have been watching the place a while, seen that the couple were inside. Then, when the coast was clear, he came in this way.' Black led them into a huge, spacious, open-plan kitchen, where a couple of white-suited SOCO were dusting for prints. Even downstairs, the smell hit Bolt immediately – a sour, pungent stink of turned meat – and he tensed. He would have given a month's wages then not to see the bodies, but knew he was going to have to. He needed to be sure that this was the work of the man he was after.

They followed a line of red markers on the floor through the kitchen and into an even bigger lounge with three separate sofas and a huge plasma TV taking up the majority of one wall. Ahead of them was the front door, next to which was a pair of high-heeled court shoes, one of which was on its side. Amanda Rowan would have kicked them off as she came in the door, presumably having no idea what was about to happen to her. A staircase ran up to the next floor and, as Bolt followed Black up it, he imagined The Disciple creeping up here, knife in hand, listening for sounds of life. It took an amazing amount of self-confidence to enter a home like this, not knowing your way around it, and hunt down your prey, knowing that you were always one against two.

The smell grew stronger.

'I've got Vicks if you need it,' said Black, taking out a handkerchief and putting it to his nose as he reached the top of the stairs. He motioned to an open door at the end of the landing, behind which a couple of white-uniformed SOCO were working.

Bolt shook his head and moved past Black, wanting to get this over and done with, Mo following him. The two SOCO looked up as Bolt walked into the bedroom, then turned back to what they were doing as he inspected the scene grimly.

It was a bloody mess like all the others, the bodies still lying where they'd fallen for the last time. The male victim – George Rowan – was tied to a chair at the foot of a large iron-framed double bed, facing towards it. He was naked, and there was a deep knife wound in his lower thigh just above the knee, which had bled profusely. There were other wounds to his abdomen, face and groin too, where he'd been deliberately cut by his attacker. But it was the thigh wound that Bolt was most interested in, because this was the typical first strike of The Disciple. It was how he liked to operate – sneaking in and disabling the male half of the couple by stabbing him in the thigh, before restraining them both. Rowan's head was slumped forward, his grey-black hair obscuring his face, but Bolt could clearly see that his throat had been cut.

The woman – Ivana Hanzha – was lying on her back on the double bed, her naked body drenched in blood from a number of different stab wounds, several of which had been aimed at her genitals. She was young, and even now Bolt could see she'd been pretty. Her eyes were closed and there was a peaceful expression on her face that belied the savagery that must have invaded her last few minutes. Her arms had been pulled up above her head, the wrists handcuffed to the wrought-iron bedstead. The handcuffs used were the old-fashioned, chain-link style – the same type that The Disciple had used in his second attack six months earlier. The roll of duct tape used to restrain Mr Rowan was also similar to that used by The Disciple, but it was the two long lines of blood smeared on the far wall, meeting at one end like the sides of a triangle – as if the killer had been trying to paint something but had been disturbed – that confirmed it for Bolt. He knew exactly what it was the killer had been trying to paint. The Disciple left a bloody pentacle on the wall of every murder scene; it was his grim calling card, and he would have done it here if Amanda Rowan hadn't come home when she had. He also noticed that the little finger on Ivana Hanzha's left hand was still there, meaning he hadn't had a chance to remove it as a trophy.

Bolt took one last look at the bodies, thinking that this was the indignity of violent death. You were left on display while the living worked around you. You were photographed and inspected, then finally cut up on a pathologist's table. You were no longer human. Instead you were little more than a puzzle to be solved by those who didn't know you, and a slowly fading memory to be kept, and possibly treasured, by those who did. The sight left him feeling deeply depressed. Here were two people who'd been making love and enjoying each other's company without a care in the world. There was even a bottle of red wine and two half-full glasses. They might have been committing an infidelity but, even so, they'd been alive. Excited. Now they were nothing.

He turned away. 'It's our man,' he said to Mo as he walked back onto the landing, wanting to get some fresh air before nausea joined the depression.

'We think he came up here and waited until they were in bed together before he carried out the attack,' said Black.

Bolt nodded; usually The Disciple waited until his victims were asleep before striking. Once again, it seemed as if he was getting braver, and potentially more foolish. 'We're going to need to see the CCTV footage, Matt, and I'd also like to know what time the camera out the back was tampered with.'

'We can do that, no problem. Are you sure this is him?'

'Oh yeah,' said Bolt. 'It's him all right.'

When he and Mo were outside the back door, Bolt took a series of deep breaths, trying to cleanse himself of the stink of death.

'Are you all right, boss?' asked Mo who, like DCI Black,

didn't seem to be that badly affected by the sight of murder victims.

Bolt sighed. 'Yeah, I'm okay.'

Mo looked around. 'You know, he took a big risk last night, chasing Amanda Rowan like that. He was lucky. He won't always be so lucky, and he may well have left clues behind this time.'

'I want to be the one who nicks this bastard,' said Bolt. But, in truth, he wanted to kill him. Someone as savage as this man simply didn't deserve to live. He didn't deserve to grow old in a relatively comfortable prison with a TV in his cell and access to the Internet, funded by the taxpayer. Bolt had never been a supporter of the death penalty, but in the case of The Disciple, he'd make an exception.

'You can't let it get to you, boss,' said Mo quietly. 'I know it's hard and I know we're under a lot of pressure, but we'll get him. And I reckon this might be the turning point.'

Seven

The first thing Mike Bolt thought when he saw Amanda Rowan in her hospital bed a few hours later was that she was a very attractive woman, especially considering what she'd been through. He'd already been told that she was thirty-eight – nine years younger than her husband – but she could easily have passed for five years younger than that. She had the slender, healthy appearance of someone who keeps fit but doesn't have to try too hard at it, with tanned, unblemished skin, and shoulder-length black hair that looked like something out of a shampoo advert. She had nice eyes too. Big and brown, the kind that a certain type of man always falls for.

Bolt stopped, feeling bad suddenly for even thinking about what she looked like. She'd already been told that her husband was dead, and it was clear that she'd been crying, but when she looked at him and Mo, it was also clear that she was in full control of her emotions.

Bolt introduced them both, and they took seats next to her bed. 'The doctor said you were okay to speak with us,' he began. 'I'd just like to say on behalf of us all that I'm very sorry for your loss, and we really appreciate the fact that you're willing to speak with us. We want to arrest whoever did this, and we will.'

Amanda Rowan managed a weak smile. 'Thank you. Have you any idea who it might have been?' Her accent was well-educated Home Counties and there was an underlying lightness to her voice that gave Bolt the impression that, in normal times, she laughed a lot.

'It's too early to draw firm conclusions,' said Bolt, 'but the killing bears certain similarities to those carried out by The Disciple. I'm assuming you've heard of him?'

The colour drained from Amanda's face, and she ran a hand across her brow. 'Yes . . . Yes, I have. Jesus.'

'You were very lucky, Mrs Rowan,' said Mo. 'If it was The Disciple, then you're the first person to survive one of his attacks.'

'I saw a woman when I went upstairs . . . Was she . . . with my husband?'

'We believe your husband was at home with a woman, yes,' said Bolt without hesitation, wanting to soften the blow but knowing he couldn't. 'She's been tentatively identified as a Miss Ivana Hanzha. Did you know her?'

Amanda shook her head. 'No, but I knew George was having an affair. I found out by accident a few weeks ago. I was going to confront him about it.' She sighed. 'But I suppose I was just waiting for the right opportunity. He was meant to be away on business in Manchester last night.'

Bolt wondered what it was like for her not only to have lost her husband, but also to know that he'd spent his last hours with another woman – and then to have almost died in a savage attack. Under the circumstances, she was holding herself together incredibly well.

He asked her to give them a detailed account of what had happened from the moment she'd arrived back to when she'd nearly been hit by the car, letting her speak without interruption. It made for a chilling story, but the lengths to which the killer had gone to try to catch her still bugged him. Why take such a huge risk when he'd already had his fun with George Rowan and Ivana Hanzha?

'Can you tell us anything about your attacker that might help us identify him?' asked Mo when Amanda had finished speaking.

She thought about it for a moment. 'A tattoo. He had a tattoo on his left forearm. I saw it when I was hanging from Mrs Naseby's window. She's okay, isn't she? Mrs Naseby?'

Bolt nodded. 'She's very shaken, obviously, but otherwise unhurt. She's a feisty woman.'

'Poor thing. Thank God she's okay.' Amanda looked down at her hands and Bolt could tell she was struggling hard not to cry again.

'Can you describe the tattoo, Mrs Rowan?' asked Mo. 'Take your time. It could be very important.'

Amanda swallowed and looked up. 'Well I . . . I didn't really get a good look at it. Obviously I was concentrating on trying to escape. It was dark green, I think, and sort of a curved pattern.' She paused and frowned. 'That's about as much as I can tell you. I'm sorry.'

But it was something. Their one witness description of a potential suspect had mentioned that he had a tattoo on his left forearm. Bolt leaned forward in his seat. 'And you can't tell us anything else about him? You didn't catch a glimpse of his face? Any other features? Did he speak at all?'

Amanda shook her head. 'I've told you everything I know. As I said, I was desperate to escape. Did the CCTV camera catch him on film? We've got cameras at the back and the front of the house.'

'We've got him captured on film, yes, but at the time he was wearing a mask and dark clothing, which isn't a huge help.'

'I'm sorry. I haven't really got anything else.'

'And you didn't see anyone acting suspiciously near your home in the days, even the weeks, leading up to the incident?'

Again she shook her head, but Bolt was leaning forward, impatient suddenly. 'You say he chased you through the house, and even through your neighbour's house, even though she was there at the time . . .'

'He did. Ask her if you don't believe me.'

'I'm sorry, Mrs Rowan, it's not that I don't believe you, but I'm struggling to understand – if there was no way you could identify him – why the killer took the time and trouble to chase you into a neighbour's house, risking everything, when by rights he should have been thinking of escape. If this is the work of The Disciple, then it's showing a reckless side to him we haven't seen before.'

'I don't know what to say.' She shrugged. 'Maybe it wasn't him, but you seemed to think it was.'

Bolt and Mo exchanged glances. They'd discussed the apparent recklessness of the killer's actions before they'd come in to interview Amanda. Mo had been convinced it was The Disciple, and he'd be even more convinced now; Bolt had thought it highly likely. He still thought it was highly likely. But he wasn't certain.

'Are you aware of any reason why someone might want to hurt you?'

Amanda looked puzzled, as if she couldn't believe he'd ask her a question like this. 'No. I don't have any enemies. I'm just an ordinary person.'

'What about your husband? Do you know why anyone might target him?'

'No.' Her tone was tinged with just the faintest hint of exasperation. 'We're ordinary – sorry, we *were* ordinary people. We've got money, yes. My husband has – God, I've got to stop doing that – *had* a very good job. We've done well, and we've put money aside, but we're not billionaires. And his job's boring . . . He doesn't have any enemies, as far as I'm aware.'

Bolt knew this was true. Before they'd come here, he and Mo had checked up on Amanda and her husband, and there was indeed nothing in either of their backgrounds to suggest that they had any enemies at all.

They asked a few more questions, went over events once more, before Bolt finally brought the interview to a close. Amanda looked exhausted, and he thanked her for her time, and put his business card down on the bedside table, wanting to tell her that she'd get over her loss, but just managing to stop himself. It had been ten years since Mikaela had died, but he still hadn't got over his loss, and he doubted he ever would.

When they were back in the hospital car park, Mo turned to him. 'I know we've got to cover every angle, boss, but this has got to be the work of The Disciple. You agree with me, don't you?'

Bolt nodded slowly. 'Yeah, I think it is, but we've got to look at the possibility that it might be a copycat killing. It's in the public domain that The Disciple tortures and murders his victims. It's also known that he's likely to have tattoos. So someone could be wanting to make it look like the work of The Disciple. It's happened before. Remember that case of The Night Creeper? He killed four women, and they thought he'd

47

murdered a fifth, but it turned out to be someone trying to make it look like his work.'

'Course I remember, but let's be honest. Under the circumstances, it's unlikely. Firstly, this fits his MO perfectly. I know there are some aspects of it out in the public domain, but not that many. No one knows he paints Satanic symbols on the walls, or that he disables his male victim with a knife wound, like he did to George Rowan. They don't know he ties the male victim to a chair – usually with duct tape – and makes him watch. The point is, I don't think a copycat killer could possibly have faked it that well, not unless he had inside knowledge of the investigation, and that's hardly likely, is it? Just because the killer acted recklessly, that doesn't mean it's not The Disciple. He may be less in control than we think. Which is a good thing.'

Bolt smiled as they reached the car. As was often the case, Mo had convinced him. They'd worked together a long time and he trusted his colleague's judgement. 'I know, you're right,' he said, getting in the passenger side. 'And I really hope he is out of control, because after this we're definitely going to need to get a break soon.'

Their break came two hours later at the end of a tense press conference at Reading Police Station, jointly chaired by Bolt and DCI Black. Like Mo Khan, the media were already convinced that the latest killings were the work of The Disciple, and the reporters wanted to know how close the investigating team were to catching him, now that he'd struck on four separate occasions. Bolt hadn't wanted to give too much away, and his answers had been carefully worded. But they were clearly too non-committal, because the questions from the floor became steadily more hostile. What were the police actually doing to find The Disciple? Why were there so few clues to his identity in an age when there'd been so many technological advances in crime fighting? Was it time to change the people at the top of the investigation?

Eventually, mercifully, it ended, and as Bolt left the room with Black, Black's mobile rang. He took the call, motioning for Bolt to hang on, his whole demeanour growing steadily more excited as he spoke to the person at the other end.

'What is it?' asked Bolt as Black came off the phone.

'The SOCO team have found traces of two different blood types in the bedroom where the murders took place,' explained Black, 'both reasonably fresh. Which wouldn't normally mean anything, except for the fact that Mr Rowan and Miss Hanzha share the same blood type. So someone else bled in there in the last twenty-four hours.'

Bolt smiled. 'And since Mrs Rowan was out all day, it's likely to be the intruder.'

Which, for the first time, meant they had DNA.

Eight

Amanda was just putting on her jacket when there was a knock on her front door.

She didn't get many visitors and there was no way she was going to open the door without knowing who was on the other side of it, so she crept back upstairs and peered down from her bedroom window like a suspicious old lady.

A short young man with neatly trimmed red hair stood on the doorstep. It was DC Andy Baxter, her liaison officer from Highlands CID, who lived a few miles up the road, and who liked to come by to check all was well with her more often than Amanda thought was strictly necessary. Today – probably because it was a Saturday – he was dressed in jeans and a windproof jacket, rather than his usual suit and tie.

Amanda moved back out of sight. Although she liked Andy – he was an easy-going enough character – she'd only seen him yesterday, and she was beginning to think he was developing a crush on her; not that he'd ever show such a thing, with her husband dead only a few weeks. But the point was, she didn't think she could handle sitting with him drinking tea while he made small talk. It was possible, of course, that he had some news, but if it was that important, he'd almost certainly have phoned ahead. She'd wasted enough time today already, trying and failing to start her book, and she needed to get out and breathe some fresh air. Andy was an unwelcome delay.

She waited in the silence of the bedroom. He knocked on the door again, then for a third time a minute after that, before finally conceding defeat. Even so, Amanda waited a good minute before she looked back out of the window to check that he'd definitely gone, and saw him walking back to the road to where his car was parked and getting inside. He drove for twenty yards and turned round in the front car park of the local pub – a dank little place that looked like a scout hut called The Crooked Ship, which she'd never been inside – before driving back towards the road up to Inverness.

Moving quickly, Amanda hurried back downstairs and over to the front door. It took her a good thirty seconds to release all the dead bolts, locks and the two chains that ran up the frame and kept her barricaded and safe in the cottage. The locksmith had thought her mad when he'd come round to fit them all, but then he hadn't known her story. Being attacked by a killer with a knife in your own home is going to make anyone paranoid, especially a single woman living by herself.

When she was outside, Amanda took a deep breath. It was a mild afternoon and the sun was trying to come out from behind a cluster of light clouds, and she suddenly felt good about the world for the first time in what seemed like a long while. She crossed the road, nodding at an old lady in a head-scarf who was posting a letter, before joining the footpath that ran round the back of the pub, which would take her in the direction of the river.

The camera Keogh had planted in Amanda Rowan's garden was motion-sensitive, and it kicked into life for the second time in three minutes, the feed on his laptop showing her opening her front door as she emerged from her house. He'd been thinking she wasn't there, because a few minutes earlier a red-headed guy, whom Keogh could tell straight away was a copper, had knocked on the door several times and got no answer. But it seemed she was trying to avoid the guy, because she looked about quickly, as if she was checking the coast was clear, before triple-locking the door behind her and walking past the camera and through her front gate.

She was a good-looking woman, Keogh had to admit. Slim and lithe, with shoulder-length jet-black hair and a lean, angular face that suggested a mix of good breeding and plenty of time down at the gym. He would have gone for someone like her once, and she would probably have gone for him. No longer. Not with his face all cut up. Still, it seemed a shame that she had to die, and for just a quick second he experienced a twinge of guilt as some long-ago conscience came back to haunt him. He ruthlessly forced the guilt from his mind. This was business. And it was a business he was good at.

Keogh picked up the VH1 radio and spoke into the mouth-piece. 'The target's on the move. Get ready.'

Feeling a small but perceptible twinge of excitement, he switched on the Land Rover's engine and pulled away.

Nine

Today 16.03

Walking relaxed Amanda. It gave her space to think and, as she made her way down the footpath that would take her through thick pine forest down to the nearby river, she thought of her experience with The Disciple, and the dramatic effect he'd had on her life. She could picture her husband vividly, tied naked to the tub chair in the spare room, drenched seemingly from head to foot in blood, the ruined, tortured body of his lover lying almost at his feet. It was an image that would be etched on her brain for as long as she lived.

If she was brutally honest, she and George had never had a good marriage. They'd met online on a dating website. Amanda had always sworn blind that she'd never resort to online dating but, after a long period of single life, followed by a rocky five-year relationship, which had gone on at least four years too long, she'd finally relented. She'd had a good dozen dates, most of whom had been totally unsuitable, before she and George had hooked up. He wasn't particularly good-looking. A big man, running to fat, with a ruddy complexion that owed more to good than clean living, and thinning hair, the first impressions weren't good, particularly as – like so many men on those dating websites – he didn't look a great deal like his photo, and was almost ten years older than her. But he had kind eyes, and a strong demeanour, and he'd made her feel good.

For the first date, they'd gone for a drink in his local in Old Street, and in spite of Amanda's misgivings, they'd quickly hit it off. A second date had followed, this time in the far plusher surroundings of BamBou in Charlotte Street (she'd told him she liked Thai food), and a month later he'd proposed to her. He called her the best thing that had ever happened to him – the woman he'd been seeking the whole of his adult life.

Amanda should never have said yes. She didn't love him. She liked him – he made her feel secure – and, she had to admit, the fact that he was an investment banker with plenty of money didn't hurt either. But there was no passion, no desire. No hunger.

However, after years and years of trying to find the right man and failing, she wanted to settle down. She wanted to have children, too, and knew that at thirty-five the clock was beginning to tick loudly. George would make a good father and a solid husband. He was long-term material.

But it hadn't worked out like that. George hadn't been able to get her pregnant. He had a low sperm count. So they'd tried IVF and that hadn't worked either. He'd also turned out to be a boring workaholic who wanted her to be a homemaker rather than a career woman, even if there was no one there to make a home for. They'd ended up moving out to the country, and she'd given up her job as a market research analyst in the West End. To be fair, she hadn't been too bothered about that, but country life – especially country life in the middle of the woods, with none of her friends around – had bored her senseless. And when the dream of children had disappeared, followed closely by the discovery of his affair, so too had any hopes of saving the marriage.

And now there was no marriage to save. George was gone. And, though she could never admit it to anyone, she felt a guilty sense of liberation.

It was when she came out on the road a couple of hundred yards west of the village, just before the start of the forest, that Amanda saw it. The black four-by-four that had driven past her cottage a couple of hours earlier parked twenty yards ahead of her. There was another car parked behind it, and a uniformed police officer was leaning in the Land Rover's window talking to the driver. It was clear he'd been stopped, and she wondered why, although she was relieved that he had been. She didn't like the idea of suspicious-looking men driving round the area, not after everything that had happened to her.

To reach the footpath at the beginning of the forest, she needed to pass both cars and, as she approached them, she experienced a feeling of unease. Something didn't feel quite right, and for a moment she considered simply turning round, heading back home, and triple-locking the door behind her. Even though this was the main road to Tayleigh, the nearest town, very little traffic passed along this way. It made her suddenly feel very vulnerable.

But Amanda didn't turn round. Instead, she told herself to stop being so paranoid. There was no way The Disciple knew she was here and, whoever it was in the four-by-four, he wasn't going to do anything with a police officer breathing down his neck.

As she drew level with the cars, the police officer turned round and smiled at her. He had a chubby baby face that didn't quite sit right on his broad muscular shoulders, and there was something about his smile she didn't like. It looked almost like a leer.

Working hard to hide the tension she was feeling, Amanda smiled back and continued walking, keeping her head down and deliberately avoiding looking over at the four-by-four's driver, wanting to get off this road as soon as possible. The moment she was out of sight, she'd run down to the river. Her ankle was still a little tender from where she'd jumped out of Mrs Naseby's window, trying to escape the man who'd murdered her husband, but she was still quick enough on her feet to put some real distance between her and the four-by-four.

'Don't move an inch.'

The voice – hard, aggressive and foreign – came from the bushes off to the side of her. Turning, Amanda saw a man emerge from the bushes, barely five feet away. He was small and wiry with olive skin and jet-black hair, and he held a gun out in front of him, pointing it directly at her ribs. Bar the incident three weeks earlier, Amanda had very little experience of criminals, but she could tell immediately that this man was the type who'd pull the trigger without hesitation, and from this distance he wouldn't miss.

'Turn away from me, and walk across the road to the cars,' he continued, his voice far too calm, as if he accosted people like this every day. 'Hurry.'

Amanda did as she was told, the shock of what was happening, and the knowledge she was trapped, stopping her from making a run for it. At the same time, the big police officer turned away from the driver's window, his smile replaced by a cold, dead-eyed expression. Grabbing her violently by the arm, he pulled her towards him, at the same time producing a set of wrist restraints from his pocket.

'Do as you're told and you won't get hurt,' he said in a thick Scottish accent, yanking Amanda's arm behind her back as he manoeuvred her towards the back of the four-by-four.

'Who are you?' she asked, conscious of the quiver in her voice. 'This must be some mistake.'

'There's no mistake, Mrs Rowan,' said the driver, who was getting out of the car now. He was in his late thirties, and spoke with a London accent, and he would have been strikingly good-looking if it weren't for the two long thin scars running almost dead straight across his face and neck, one of which ended in a tangle of uneven tissue at his nose. But it was the syringe in his gloved hand that grabbed Amanda's attention. They were going to drug her with something and abduct her, and the terrifying reality was that she had absolutely no idea why.

'We just want a quiet chat, that's all,' said the driver, who had the air of a man in charge. He walked over to her, holding up the needle, while the big policeman expertly flicked the first of the restraints round her wrist before pulling her other arm behind her back. The third man – the one with the gun – walked over to the four-by-four's boot and pulled it open.

Which was the moment Amanda heard another car coming round the corner towards them.

The others heard it too and turned in its direction.

Amanda knew instantly that she had just one chance to break free and that, if she didn't take it, she was as good as dead, because whoever these men were, they meant her serious harm.

Feeling the policeman's grip loosen ever so slightly, she yanked herself free in one single, sudden movement, catching him completely by surprise. Fuelled by adrenalin and panic, she kicked out at the driver, her walking boot connecting with his upper thigh and unbalancing him. He lunged at her with the syringe, but she was already pulling away, dropping into a crouch to make herself as difficult a target as possible.

She wasn't quick enough. The policeman grabbed her by the collar of her jacket and yanked her back towards him with such force that he cut off her breath. But this time Amanda wasn't coming quietly. She kicked and struggled, screaming, desperately fending off the needle as the driver tried to stab her with it, hearing the car screech to a halt only a few yards away.

The driver's door flew open and Andy – her liaison officer – jumped out, his face a mask of indignation. 'What the hell's going on here?' he yelled.

'This lady's under arrest,' the policeman shouted back, pulling her round so they were both facing him.

Andy produced his warrant card, and held it up high, coming towards them calmly and confidently 'And I'm a police officer as well. Highlands CID. What the hell have you arrested her for?'

Out of the corner of her eye, Amanda saw the guy with the gun move away from the car and shouted a desperate warning. 'Andy, watch out! He's got a gun!'

Almost in slow motion, Andy turned towards the car, the confidence seeping out of his expression as he saw the gunman striding confidently towards him from the other side of the road, gun arm outstretched as he took aim. For the first time Amanda saw that the gun had a long, cigar-shaped silencer on the end, like something out of a movie.

Andy lifted a hand in surrender, his voice rising higher as he spoke. 'Please, I'm a police officer . . .'

The gunman smiled. Then, when he was only five feet away, he pulled the trigger.

A fine cloud of blood sprayed out of the side of Andy's head, and his eyes squeezed shut, almost as if he was counting in a game of hide and seek. For an interminably long moment, he tottered unsteadily on his feet, then collapsed to the ground.

The whole drama, from Andy getting out of the car, to having his life snuffed out, had taken barely five seconds, but it had given Amanda enough time to work out her next move, and in the sudden silence that often comes after a single act of terrible violence, she reached behind her with her free hand and grabbed the police officer by his balls through the material of his trousers, twisting them round with an intensity born of desperation.

It worked. He let go of her immediately, crying out in pain, and Amanda tore free from his grasp, sprinting past the front of the four-by-four, trying to keep the driver and the cop between her and the gunman.

A shot rang out, whistling somewhere past her head as, crouching low, Amanda swung a hard left into the welcoming embrace of the forest, sprinting for her life.

'No!' she heard the scar-faced driver scream. 'She's got to be taken alive! Get after her!'

And as she tore through the thick undergrowth, hearing the sounds of pursuit all too close behind her, knowing she had to keep her balance or she was dead, two questions ripped through her fear.

What have I done? And why do these people want me?

Ten

Jess had to admit she'd enjoyed the trip so far, although her arms were beginning to ache now.

The river was beautiful. It meandered gently through thick patches of woodland and rolling green fields, with majestic mountains rising up in the distance behind, and with just the occasional isolated house appearing amidst the silent, natural beauty. Because that was the amazing thing about this place. The silence. Jess had never experienced anything like it before, coming from London where there was always some kind of street noise, even in the dead of night. Here, you could hear literally nothing, bar the call of the occasional bird and the soothing flow of the river, for ages at a time. So far, they hadn't seen another soul. There'd been a couple of minor rapids earlier and, though she'd never admit it to anyone, Jess had been nervous going through them, imagining the canoe capsizing and her having to swim for shore. Or, even worse, Casey and Tim's canoe capsizing, and Casey being lost beneath the water. But of course, everything had been fine, and now the two canoes cut through the flat, still water, side by side, while Jess marvelled at how isolated it was out here.

She turned to Casey, who was taking a rest from paddling the other canoe, and letting their Uncle Tim do the work. 'Having fun?' she asked her sister.

'I love it,' grinned Casey, her whole face lighting up. 'How about you, Jess? Are you having fun?'

'Course I am. I'm spending time with you, aren't I?' She winked at her sister.

'I liked the rapids earlier the most,' continued Casey. 'They were like the flume ride at Thorpe Park, only better.'

'That's because they're real,' said Tim. 'We've got another one coming soon. That's the last one, then it's just an easy run into Tayleigh, and hopefully a quick pint at The Farmer's.'

'I don't think so,' said Jean. 'We're being picked up by the canoe owner. I'm sure he won't want to hang about while you have a beer.'

'He might if I buy him one,' said Tim, who liked a drink.

'No,' said Jean, with a finality that brooked no further argument. But there was a lightness to her tone that told anyone listening that she was just bantering with her husband, and loved him really.

Jess had a boyfriend, Joe. They'd been together four months and had had numerous ups and downs. Jess thought she loved him, although she wasn't sure, and when she heard the easy way Jean and Tim talked to each other, it made her vaguely jealous.

'I don't want this to end,' said Casey, looking round at the scenery, her eyes lighting up.

'We can come back any time you like,' said Jean.

'Tomorrow?'

Jean laughed. 'Maybe not tomorrow, but I'm sure we can come next weekend if the weather's good. Right Tim?'

'Course we can,' he answered, turning round in his seat and smiling back at Casey.

Jess felt happy then, for the first time in a while. Things finally seemed to be working out. Casey had left all her friends behind in London, and Jess had been so worried that she wouldn't settle in up here, but she should have known better. People warmed to Casey. She could settle in anywhere, which meant Jess could now concentrate on getting her own life together, finishing college, and hopefully going off to uni.

'Tim, can we pull into shore up here? I need the toilet,' said Jean, who'd had to stop for toilet breaks twice already today. 'Sorry girls, I'm a slave to my bladder,' she added, giving Jess a little bit more detail than she actually needed.

'There's a spot just up here, look,' said Tim, pointing to a small sandy strip a few yards across, just upstream on the right.

As they rowed the two canoes over, bringing the noses to a halt in the sand, Jess heard a popping sound coming from somewhere up in the trees ahead. She frowned, wondering what it was, but nobody else seemed to hear it and Jean clearly had more important things to worry about as she scrambled out the back of the canoe and disappeared behind a nearby tree.

'Does anyone else need to go?' asked Tim. 'We're still a good hour from Tayleigh.'

Casey said she was okay, but Jess was feeling a bit of a twinge and didn't fancy getting uncomfortable later. 'I do,' she said, getting up unsteadily in the canoe and jumping off the end onto the sand, careful not to get her Converses wet. Stretching, she walked up the bank, looking for a tree as far away from Jean as possible.

Which was when she heard the sound of someone coming fast through the trees and turned to see a woman in dark clothing running down the hill towards her, barely twenty yards away, a look of utter panic on her face.

For a moment, Jess couldn't believe what she was seeing. But the woman kept coming, getting closer and closer, if anything her pace quickening as she caught sight of Jess.

Five yards separated them now.

'Run!' the woman snapped, making no attempt to stop, her voice like the staccato crack of a branch. 'Now!'

Jess wasn't used to taking orders from someone she'd never met before, especially one who'd appeared out of nowhere, but as the woman ran past her in the direction of the boats, Jess caught sight of two more figures coming through the trees further up the hill, and it looked like one of them was carrying—

Jesus. It was a gun.

Jess had always been a fast runner. At school, she'd excelled in the sprints, and had always been quick off the mark. She was quick off the mark now. Turning in one rapid movement, she sprinted for the boats, already a good few yards behind the mystery woman.

Jean, meanwhile, appeared from behind the tree she'd been using, still pulling up her baggy shorts, a surprised expression on her face.

'We need to go!' Jess yelled at her. 'There are men with guns in the woods!'

'Oh my God!' cried Jean, but she didn't need telling twice, running for the canoe at a good pace for a big woman.

The mystery woman reached Jess and Jean's canoe first and, as Tim and Casey looked on aghast, she pushed it back into the water, then jumped in, grabbed one of the oars and began paddling wildly. Jean jumped in after her, grabbing another paddle, while Jess, realizing that Tim and Casey were making no effort to paddle backwards into the water, grabbed the nose of their canoe and shoved it into the river as hard as she could.

'What's going on?' Casey cried out, clearly terrified.

'We've got to get out of here, okay,' Jess answered, trying and failing to stay calm, wanting to pick Casey up and hug her tight, but continuing to push the canoe, which was still hardly moving at all. 'Paddle, Tim, for God's sake!' she yelled.

'What the hell's happening?' he demanded.

'Just do it.' With a last big heave, Jess jumped in the boat, pushing Casey down between the seats so she was out of sight and grabbing her oar.

'Jess, what are you doing?' she sobbed.

Jess didn't answer. She was paddling backwards like crazy and looking towards the bank where the two men she'd seen earlier had now appeared on the sand, no more than twenty yards away. One of them, a small guy dressed in black, definitely had a gun in his hand, but the other – a much bigger guy – looked as if he was wearing a police uniform, and didn't appear to be armed.

'It's the coppers,' shouted Tim, indignation in his voice. 'She's running from the coppers.'

'They're not policemen!' shouted the woman in the other canoe, still paddling wildly, and for the first time Jess noticed she had an English accent. 'They've just killed a policeman.'

Tim didn't sound convinced. 'What the hell are you talking about? You're running from them, lass, and no mistake.'

And then the gunman on the bank raised his weapon and pointed it in the mystery woman's direction.

'Get down everyone!' yelled Tim, panic in his voice.

Out of the corner of her eye, Jess saw Jean scramble down in the other boat, almost upending it in the process, while the mystery woman continued to paddle backwards, keeping her head down. Jess didn't hesitate: she rolled back in her seat, grabbed Casey in a bear hug and the two of them fell to the bottom of the canoe as a shot whistled somewhere overhead.

A second shot rang out but Tim was still in his seat, paddling wildly, managing to turn the boat round so it was facing down-river, and then he too scrambled onto the floor, keeping his head down as a third shot cracked across the river. Except this time it sounded as if it was further away, and Jess let out a very small sigh of relief as she hugged Casey close, feeling the wetness of her sister's tears in the crook of her neck.

Eleven

Keogh closed his eyes and shook his head angrily. They'd lost Amanda Rowan and now he was in a lot of trouble.

He'd driven the dead cop's car off the road and concealed it in undergrowth where it was unlikely to be seen unless someone was looking for it. The cop himself was scrunched up in the boot, and by the time anyone found him, they'd be long gone.

Now, as he jogged back up to the four-by-four, keeping his head down, the radio in his jacket pocket crackled into life. It was MacLean, the big cop who'd let go of Amanda when she'd whacked him in the balls. 'Have you got her?' Keogh demanded, the frustration obvious in his voice.

'There were some canoeists down by the river,' answered MacLean, sounding out of breath. 'She jumped in one of the canoes with them.'

Keogh cursed. 'How many canoeists?'

'Four of them, I think. A family.'

This was the problem when you worked with someone you hadn't chosen, thought Keogh. Things went wrong that much more easily. MacLean worked directly for Keogh's employer, and Keogh had only known him a week. The guy was supposedly good but he'd messed up by letting the girl go. Still, there was nothing to gain by dwelling on that now. It was time to think fast. 'How far have they got?'

'Not far. We can still see them, and there's no mobile reception down there, so they won't be able to phone for help. There's a lookout point about half a mile downriver on this side, called Eagles Reach. If we get there in front of them, we can cut them off.'

'Okay, leave it to me,' said Keogh, jumping in the four-by-four and reaching down behind the driver's seat for the rifle as he started the engine.

*

'Who the hell do you think you are, charging into our boat like this?' demanded Jean, a real anger in her voice. 'You could have got us killed.'

The two canoes were side by side, on the other side of the river and out of sight of where the two men had emerged, and they were all sitting upright again now. The river was a good fifty yards wide here, and Jess took a deep breath, feeling safe and shocked at the same time. She took a close look at the mystery woman. She was slim and pretty, and she had that well-off look about her that was only slightly marred by the fact that her hair was all over the place, and a pair of plastic handcuffs hung accusingly from her right wrist. She was paddling fast, while Jean sat glaring at her back, waiting for an answer to her question. From behind her, Jess could hear Casey crying. Turning round, she leaned down and lifted her sister into a sitting position, feeling an intense burst of protective love for her as she wiped the tears from her face.

'It's all right, baby. It's all right. No one's going to hurt you.'

'But who were they?' Casey asked Jess, her voice small and quavering.

Tim grunted from his position in the back of the canoe, where he too was paddling. 'We still need an answer to that,' he said, looking over at the woman in Jean's canoe who was facing them all, an apologetic expression on her face.

'I'm sorry,' she said, her voice breathless, but calmer now that the immediate danger had passed. 'I was out walking. I live up in the village on the other side of the hill. And those men just tried to abduct me.'

'No one abducts anyone up here,' snapped Jean. 'I've lived in these parts all my life and I've never heard of such a thing. Have we, Tim?'

'Never,' said Tim firmly.

'I'm telling you the truth. Why would I lie?'

'Because you're on the run from the police.'

'I told you: they weren't police.'

'They didn't look much like police,' said Jess, feeling the need to stand up for the woman, because one thing was for sure, she didn't look much like a criminal. 'One definitely had a gun and it had a silencer on the end. How many police do you see with them?'

That quietened everyone for a few seconds, but Jean still didn't look convinced. 'We'll drop you off on the opposite bank and then you can be on your way. Those men can't cross the river here, so you'll be safe. You'll be able to call the police.'

'That's a good idea,' said Tim. 'Calling the police.'

'Shit, I didn't even think about that,' said the woman, pulling a mobile from the pocket of her jeans.

Jess did the same, hoping that one of them had reception. She was still pretty pumped up herself from what had happened. She wouldn't say she was scared, though. If anything, she'd just experienced a real adventure. Escaping from men with a gun. It would be one to tell Joe and her friends when she got back to the civilization of Clapham. She was just sorry that Casey had been involved. Jess gave her hand a squeeze as she examined her phone.

No service. Jess frowned and shook her head, then looked across at the mystery woman, who was also shaking her head. 'I've got nothing on mine either,' she said. 'This is a bad place for reception. It gets better a couple of miles downriver. We can call for help then.'

'That's convenient,' muttered Tim.

'It's true,' said Jess. 'I can't get reception.'

'Let's just get across the river and drop this lassie off before we hit the rapids,' said Auntie Jean, calmer now, 'then we can all be on our—'

The shot exploded out of nowhere, cracking across the still of the water, making Jess jump in her seat. The next second, she felt a warm splash on her face. She shut her eyes reflexively and, when they opened again, Jean was tottering in her seat in the adjacent canoe, a gaping red hole in the side of her head, blood pouring down her face and onto her neck. Jess would never forget the slightly confused expression in Jean's eyes in the half-second before they closed and she toppled heavily in her seat, falling sideways so that her ruined head hung over the side of the canoe, grey hair hanging down towards the water as if she was leaning in to wash her hair, barely touching distance from Jess.

Then everything happened at once. Casey screamed; Tim cried out like an animal in terrible pain; and the mystery woman dropped her phone and jumped into the water, keeping Jean's canoe between her and where the shot had come from on the opposite bank. A second shot rang out and Jess's canoe lurched hard to the left as she and Tim instinctively tried to dive for cover in the same direction.

Their canoe was capsizing as more shots shattered the silence, and suddenly Jess was in the water, flapping wildly, unable to touch the bottom, her clothes already feeling like dead weights as she reached across and grabbed a screaming Casey, pulling her close. But she was already struggling to keep the two of them afloat, even with the life jackets on, as she swam desperately for the bank, still a good twenty yards away, hoping that the upturned canoe would give them some kind of cover from the shooter.

'Get back here!' shouted the mystery woman from somewhere behind her. 'We need to use the canoe as cover!'

Jess felt something whistle past her head, causing a big splash in the water no more than a few feet away. It could only mean one thing. Whoever was shooting wasn't just aiming at the woman. He was aiming at Jess herself, and Casey too, and for the first time she felt truly scared. She was a target. Someone she'd never met before wanted to kill her.

At that moment, she came as close to panic as she'd been on that fateful night eleven years before, when she'd been just a child, and had witnessed things that no child should ever see. But she'd refused to buckle then, and she couldn't afford to do so now.

Still hanging onto Casey, Jess turned round in the water and saw the woman hanging onto their canoe as it continued to float down the river. A few yards away, Tim was swimming out towards the other canoe, where Jean still lay with her head hanging over the side. He was trying to reach her, and even in the midst of the drama happening all around them, Jess felt a pang of sorrow for him. But Tim was struggling and he had to grab the empty canoe for support as it came past him.

Jess's face dipped underwater as she tried to swim towards the woman, and she took in an involuntary gulp of cold river water, making her choke. Holding onto Casey was making progress worryingly slow. Casey was trying to help by swimming, but all she was doing was making it harder for them both.

'Don't move, Case, I've got you,' sputtered Jess. 'Just stay still.'

'Here, grab my hand,' called the mystery woman, reaching out towards them.

Taking a deep breath, Jess kicked with her legs with everything she had, grabbing the woman's hand and hauling Casey over to the canoe. 'Take hold of the boat, babe,' she gasped at her sister, but when Casey tried to get a grip on the top of it, she couldn't reach and slipped back into the water, bobbing upright thanks to the flotation device she was wearing. 'Just hang onto me,' Jess told her, her voice an exhausted gasp. She wasn't as fit as she should be, and she could feel her energy levels sapping fast.

'I can hold her,' said the woman. 'Give her to me.'

Jess turned round and looked at the woman who, though clearly tired, appeared in far better shape. She was tempted to do it too, she was that tired, but in the end, she couldn't risk it. This woman had brought all this down on them out of nowhere, and she wasn't going to entrust her with the care of the one person in the world she truly loved. She gave Casey a reassuring smile. 'I'm going to let you float for a bit, okay, Case? But I won't let go of you, I promise.'

Casey nodded but, as Jess untangled her from the crook of her arm, a shot exploded out of nowhere, blowing a hole in the canoe up near the front where Uncle Tim was clinging on. A split second later, he cried out in pain and clutched at the side of his face. Blood poured through his fingers, and Casey screamed, forcing her way back into Jess's grip.

'It's okay!' shouted Tim, looking at the hand. His cheek was bleeding quite heavily but – unlike Jean had been – he didn't look seriously hurt, and there was actually an expression of relief on his face. 'I think it only grazed me.'

A second bullet exploded out of the boat only a foot in front of Casey, leaving a golf-ball-sized hole in its wake.

'Jesus Christ!' yelled Jess. 'We can't stay here. It's a death trap.'

'We need to pull the boat towards the shore!' shouted the woman, a calm authority in her voice that made Jess listen. 'It's giving us better cover than swimming for it. Everyone keep as low as you can in the water and kick as hard as you can.'

'I can't hold you much longer, babe,' hissed Jess through gritted teeth, feeling Casey getting ever heavier in her free arm.

Up ahead the river eddied and rippled, its noise growing louder, as the canoes approached the next set of rapids. Jess could see an exposed rock sticking up ahead of them and she knew that the moment it got shallower they'd be easy targets again.

Another shot ricocheted off the top of the canoe and Jess felt the vibrations in the wood close to her hand. Suddenly she could feel the bottom of the river beneath her feet as they sank into silt. They were only about five yards away from shore now and it was getting shallower all the time. The water ran up to a small muddy spit backing onto woodland. There'd be no scrambling up a bank. It was a straight run, tantalizingly close now, and already Jess was having to crouch down as she waded through the mud. The water went down to barely three feet deep. Any second now they would no longer be able to conceal themselves behind the canoe, and already Uncle Tim's head was poking over.

The next shot was way above their heads. They were finally putting some distance between themselves and their attackers.

'All right,' shouted the woman, 'this is our best chance. On the count of three, run for the bank. And don't stop for anything. One, two—'

'They'll kill us!' screamed Tim.

'Three.'

The woman let go of the canoe and dashed through the water, and Jess immediately gave Casey a shove. 'Go baby, go. I'm right behind you. Run!'

But it was still waist-deep for Casey and she could only wade, so, with a last burst of strength, Jess picked her up under the arms and staggered through the water with her, thinking that any second now her life could be ended by a single bullet.

More shots rang out. One after the other, but Jess kept going as if in a daze, the shore seeming to take forever before it was beneath her feet.

And then Tim was by her side, helping to lift up Casey, and together the three of them ran out of the water and into the undergrowth after the woman, out of sight of the men who wished to kill them.

Twelve

Keogh stood at the lookout point watching the river curve away beneath him into the distance through the binoculars, the .303 rifle he'd been using propped up against a litter bin. The two canoes, each marked with the name of the canoe hire company, had come to a rest in the shallows two hundred metres away, their progress impeded by a sand spit sticking out from the trees on the other side. The woman's body lay sprawled out in the nearest canoe for the whole world to see.

He swung the binoculars to his left, looking upriver, just in case another boat was coming down it. But, thankfully, there was nothing. At this time of the year, already deep into autumn, there would be few people using the river, and Keogh was surprised that the canoe hire company was still even renting out boats. He lowered the binoculars and sighed loudly. 'Jesus, what a disaster! Why didn't you take her out earlier?'

He was addressing the man standing next to him. The Algerian, Mehdi. The one who'd shot the local policeman a few minutes earlier and who, in Keogh's opinion, should have managed to intercept Amanda Rowan, before she ran into whoever these day-trippers were and messed up everything. Keogh had worked with Mehdi on and off for several years. An ex-military policeman in the Algerian army, he'd always been as reliable as he was ruthless. Unfortunately, he'd picked a very bad time to make a mistake, and now they had the kind of damage limitation exercise on their hands that was going to be fraught with risks and complications. Not to mention a dead police officer.

Mehdi stared at him, his dark, heavily lined features twisted into a defiant frown. 'You said the orders were to take her alive. I didn't have a choice.'

'You could have shot her in the leg. We need her alive, but she doesn't have to be walking.'

'I tried, but it's hard getting a good shot in when you're running down a hill in the middle of the woods.'

Which Keogh had to admit was true. Ultimately, as leader of the operation to capture Amanda Rowan, the failure was his responsibility. The question was: what did he do about it?

He turned to the man on the other side of him: the big cop, MacLean. MacLean was their local contact, although he was based over forty miles away which, to Keogh's mind, meant he wasn't local at all, and therefore of little use to him. But Keogh's employer had insisted he come along, so Keogh had had no choice but to use him. 'We need to secure those canoes and get them out of sight,' he told MacLean. 'Where's the nearest river crossing?'

MacLean fixed him with a bovine stare. He had a very round, slightly pudgy baby face, and thin sullen eyes that made him look untrustworthy. God alone knew how he passed his police entrance exams, thought Keogh. They must be pretty desperate for recruits up here.

'Tayleigh,' he said. 'It's the first town, about five miles down the road from here.'

'Is the road good?'

'Good enough. It won't take that long to get back to the canoes if we drive fast.'

'How well do you know the area?'

'Well enough. I used to have a girl out this way a few years back.'

A short-sighted one, thought Keogh, but he was secretly pleased. It seemed MacLean might be some help after all. 'So, we should assume the target knows the area a bit too. She's been up here a few weeks now. Where will she be heading?'

'Tayleigh as well. There's nowhere else round here really.'

Keogh looked down towards the trees where Amanda Rowan and the people she was now with were hidden.

'Which way will they go?'

'There's a footpath that mainly follows the river all the way into the town. If they start walking now and go fast, I reckon it'll take them two hours. We could easily cut them off. The path's not well used.'

Keogh nodded, thinking about his resources. He had MacLean and Mehdi with him now, and Sayenko, the cadaverous, chain-smoking Ukrainian, who'd been keeping watch on the other side of the village, and was now en route back to them. That was four in total. It should have been a perfect number to snatch an unarmed woman, but it wasn't many for a full-scale manhunt. 'I think they'll suspect we'll try and cut them off on the path. Amanda Rowan's no fool. She's done pretty well so far. But we'll send someone down there, just in case. What other routes could they take?'

MacLean squinted in the afternoon sunlight, the movement making his face look even chubbier. 'The only other way would be across country. Once you get through those woods, you head over those hills over there, into the valley, take a right, and keep going.'

Keogh looked to where MacLean was pointing. The line of hills in the distance were bare and rolling, but not particularly high, and looked as though they'd be easily climbable, even for kids. 'Is there plenty of cover?' he asked.

MacLean shook his head. 'Not really.'

'And what about houses? Could they get to a house?'

'There's one or two up there, but not many.'

Keogh grunted. 'They don't need many. They just need one with a phone, and then the whole op's compromised.' He walked over to the four-by-four and pulled a local Ordnance Survey map from the glove compartment, opening it up on the bonnet. MacLean and Mehdi joined him, and MacLean pointed a meaty finger down at a spot on the map where the river curved through thick woodland on its winding route into Tayleigh.

'The canoes are here,' he said. 'Like I said, they could either follow the path along the river or, if not, they'd probably go this way.' He ran his finger up through the thick sweep of green on the map that represented forest, then swung it right through a mixture of woodland and exposed hills until he was at the small town of Tayleigh, which straddled the river. From its scale on the map, it looked pretty small – a couple of thousand people at most, thought Keogh – but the point was, if their target got there, the op was over and Keogh would be out of a job. Or worse.

'How long do you reckon it'll take them to go that way?' he asked MacLean.

'A lot longer. There's a lot of climbing involved. It depends if she travels with those canoeists or not. There were a couple of kids there, weren't there? They'd slow her down a fair bit. But I still reckon they're more likely to go that way.'

Keogh thought about that. He suspected Amanda Rowan would leave the canoeists behind, and make her own way back. If she did that, though, she'd be far harder to track. It might make the whole thing messier if she stayed with the rest, but probably easier for them to deal with. He scanned the route MacLean had suggested they'd take: up through the forest then over the hill and across the valley. It made sense for them to go that way, but, worryingly, there were at least three houses that he could see dotted randomly along the way. Thankfully, the first of them was several miles at least from where they'd abandoned the canoes.

'I've got a couple of hunting dogs back at my place,' said MacLean suddenly. 'They can track anyone.'

Keogh smiled. This made things a lot easier. 'How long will it take to get back here with them?'

'If I go fast, an hour.'

'Do it. As soon as you're fifteen minutes away, call me.'

MacLean nodded and turned away, while Keogh folded up the map, not looking forward to the inevitable conversation he was going to have to have with his boss about the way things were going, but knowing too that he couldn't put it off. As he was walking back to the driver's seat, Mehdi, who was back at the lookout point, called out.

'Hey, look at this. I think we might be getting lucky here.'

Thirteen

'Are you okay, Case?' Jess asked. She was kneeling down, holding her sister in her arms, while trying to stop her own shivering. Never had Jesse felt so protective of her as she did now.

'I'm scared,' said Casey, looking up at her with big frightened eyes. 'What's going on?'

It was a hard question to answer, but Jess tried. 'Some bad men want to hurt us.'

'Is Auntie Jean okay?' The hesitation in Casey's voice suggested she already knew the answer, but desperately wanted to be told she was wrong.

Jess swallowed. 'No. I don't think she is.'

'We don't know that,' snapped Tim, his voice a potent combination of anger and despair. He was standing a few feet away, soaked to the core like the rest of them as he looked out through the undergrowth to where the two canoes had come to rest on the sand spit sticking out into the river, barely ten yards away. The top half of Auntie Jean was just about visible slumped over one of the canoe's sides. She wasn't moving. 'I'm going to go and bring her in here,' he continued. 'If she's hurt, she needs help.'

'For Christ's sake, don't go near her!' It was the mystery woman speaking. She was standing a few yards away, hands on thighs, slowly getting her breath back. 'You'll be shot.'

Tim turned and glared at her. 'What's it got to do with you, eh?'

'I'm just trying to help you.'

'No you're not. You're not helping at all. All you've done is bring trouble down on us. If it hadn't been for ye, none of this would have happened, so keep out of it, okay?' His voice was harsh and loud, and cut through the quiet of the woods like a blunt hatchet. He was clenching and unclenching his fists as he spat out his words.

'Look,' said Jess, trying to defuse the situation, 'they could still be out there. You don't want to get killed too.'

The moment the words were out of her mouth, she regretted them. She was certain Jean was dead – she'd seen the way she'd toppled over in the canoe as the bullet had hit her – but, even so, she shouldn't have said it.

'And ye can shut up too!' he yelled. 'It's nothing to do with ye either. She's *my* wife. My wife!' His voice contorted with pain as he tried to bring himself under control.

'I'm sorry,' said the mystery woman, undeterred. 'God, I am, but don't go out there. If your wife's hurt, we can get her help some other way.'

'How? The phones are ruined now.' He pulled out his mobile, pressed a few buttons, then flung it on the ground disgustedly. 'Now, if you'll excuse me, I'm going to go and see how my wife is. I'm sorry ye had to hear that, wee lass,' he said to Casey, who was staring at him wide-eyed. 'This is . . .' He stopped, as if he no longer knew what else to say, then turned and walked purposefully towards the break in the trees that led out onto the sand spit.

None of the rest of them said anything. Jess thought about calling out but concluded there'd be no point. Tim had made up his mind to go to his wife, and who could blame him? They'd been together for years and years, and though Jess herself wouldn't say she got on particularly well with either of them, she could tell they loved each other very much, and there weren't many people you could say that about.

No shot rang out as Tim strode out onto the spit and leaned over the body of his wife. He was in that position for a good few seconds, and Jess stared at him intently, wondering what he thought he was doing. But then she saw his shoulders heaving silently and knew, with a final certainty, that Jean was dead. Tim lifted his wife out of the boat and turned back towards them, holding her in his bloodstained arms, tears streaming down his face.

Jess held Casey close to her, and looked over to the mystery woman, catching her eye. Even soaking wet, she still had poise, and Jess was suddenly furious at her, not for putting Jess herself in danger, but for destroying poor Casey's life all over again. She'd lost her mother, her father, and now her aunt. Who was going to have her now?

There was only one chink of hope in all this. And that was if the men were gone, they could get back in the canoes, and maybe try to float downriver to the town where they were meant to be meeting the guy from the canoe place.

It was all she could think of as Tim walked towards them.

Far above them on the other side of the river, Keogh rested his rifle on the stone wall bordering the lookout point and took aim at the figure walking along the sand spit with the dead woman in his arms, following his movement through the sights, thinking that finally something was going right for them. Now that the woman was no longer on display for any passer-by to see, it made their task just that little bit less urgent. Keogh had a simple choice. Did he let the man live, or did he take him out as well? If he let him live, the man would report everything, which could lead the police straight back to Keogh and his boss. All the canoeists had seen Mehdi and MacLean's faces. Mehdi had a record. MacLean was a cop. It was too much of a risk.

Keogh hesitated. It might be better to wait a few seconds. If Amanda and the canoeists thought they'd gone, they might come back out to the canoes, and he could put a bullet in her leg. He didn't want to have to kill the kids. He was pretty certain he could have taken at least one of them out earlier, but he'd deliberately avoided them. After all, he wasn't an animal, although he was pretty sure Mehdi, and probably even MacLean, wouldn't hesitate to do them. But they were less important targets than the adults, because they were always going to be less reliable witnesses.

Squinting down the sights, taking his time now that his target was moving nice and slowly, Keogh made his decision. Business was business.

He lowered the rifle ever so slightly as the man reached the trees, his dead wife in his arms, then pulled the trigger and watched him fall.

It was a perfect shot.

Fourteen

The shot cracked across the water, shattering the silence, and Tim fell to the ground like a stone, dropping Jean in the process. Casey cried out and Jess pulled her close, shielding her eyes.

There was a long second of silence and then Tim cried out in pain, grabbing his leg. He was lying on his side facing Jean's body, gritting his teeth. Only his head was inside the tree line, but he was trying to crawl further in.

'Uncle Tim!' cried Casey, struggling to get out of Jess's grip.

'Stay where you are,' hissed the mystery woman, who was crouching down a few feet away. 'They've wounded him deliberately. If we try to pull him in, they'll shoot us too.'

Jess turned to her. 'But why? What do they want us for?'

The woman put a finger to her lips, motioning towards Casey, who was still struggling in Jess's grip. 'It's just too dangerous. Please. Trust me.'

Tim inched forward on his belly, his progress painfully slow. 'Ah Jesus,' he hissed, through clenched teeth. 'Girls, you've got to get out of here. Get to Tayleigh. Now . . .'

'We're not going to leave you, Uncle Tim!' cried Casey, tears streaming down her face. 'We're not going to leave you!'

His face contorted in pain. 'You've got to.'

But then suddenly Casey had broken free, and she was on her feet and running over to her uncle.

'No!' yelled the woman, jumping up from her crouch and sprinting forward in a single movement to cut her off, before Jess even had time to react.

Casey was only a yard from Tim when the shot rang out.

And then she was flying through the air as the mystery woman caught her in a sideways rugby tackle, and the two of them landed together in the dirt, rolling away as a third shot cracked through the air.

Tim's body kicked wildly as the bullet struck him somewhere in the back, and he lifted his head, his mouth open in an expression of surprise, before he slumped forward and lay still.

But it wasn't Tim Jess was interested in. It was Casey. Where was she? Had she been hurt?

Another shot rang out, and another, and Jess had to lie flat on her front as the woman and Casey rolled along the ground towards her and out of the line of fire.

Just as suddenly as it had begun, the shooting stopped, and Jess scrambled over to where the woman lay on top of her sister. Casey's eyes were closed and Jess felt a terrible, gut-wrenching panic. 'Casey, Casey, baby. Are you okay? Please tell me you're okay.'

For a second nothing happened, and a strangled sob rose up in Jess's throat. She couldn't lose her sister. Not Casey. Anyone but her. Anyone . . .

And then her eyes opened and she was staring up at Jess. 'I'm scared,' Casey said simply.

Jess sobbed with relief and pushed the woman aside as she took her sister in her arms, holding her close.

For a few seconds, the girls clung to each other, both shivering from the shock and the cold. Then slowly Jess got to her feet and looked over to where the woman stood looking at them, an expression of regret in her eyes.

'I'm sorry to have got you involved in this, I really am,' she said.

Keeping Casey's face pressed into her shoulder, Jess looked across at the bodies of her adoptive aunt and uncle, as still as ghosts, then back at the woman. 'Why the hell do these people want to kill you?'

The woman sighed. 'I have no idea. But I do know one thing. We can't stay here. They're going to be coming after us and we're still a long way from help.' She looked at Casey, and then at Jess, and Jess was once again struck by the way she held herself and the calm manner in which she took charge. 'My name's Amanda,' the woman continued, 'and I'm going to get you both to safety, get you some warm, dry clothes, and then everything's going to be okay.' Her voice was soothing in its tones, almost patronizing, and Jess could tell that she'd never had kids. She didn't really know how to handle them.

'It won't be,' said Casey, looking over towards the bodies of Tim and Jean. 'My new mum and dad are dead.'

'I know, and I'm sorry. But we've got to protect ourselves now. You both saw the faces of two of those men. That means you're in danger too.' She turned and looked up into the thick, dark forest. 'Let's go. We need to get to Tayleigh before dark.' Without another word, she turned and headed into the trees.

Casey looked up at Jess, her big blue eyes still wet with tears. 'I don't want to leave Uncle Tim and Auntie Jean,' she said. 'It doesn't seem right.'

But Jess knew it was a time for hard decisions. 'Neither do I,' she answered, stroking her sister's wet hair. 'But we've got no choice. You've got to be strong for me, okay?'

Casey nodded, managing a weak smile. 'I'll try.'

'I know you will.' Jess helped her to her feet and together, hand in hand, they started after the woman who'd got them into this nightmare.

Fifteen

16.35

Keogh lowered the rifle, wondering if he'd hit either Amanda or one of the kids with his last shots. He hoped he hadn't killed a kid, but he knew he'd be able to handle it as long as he didn't actually have to see his handiwork. He also knew he'd be in a lot of trouble if one of the shots had accidentally killed Amanda. He didn't think it had, but you never knew, and he cursed himself for being so reckless.

Turning away from the lookout point, he made the call he'd been dreading on the satellite phone he was carrying.

His employer answered after three rings. 'Is the situation resolved?' he asked brusquely.

'Not quite, sir,' said Keogh, and briefly explained what had happened. As he spoke, he realized how bad it must be sounding.

'I don't pay you to fuck up,' growled his employer, 'but that's exactly what you've done. If you want to live to see another job, you'd better deal with this and get hold of this woman.'

Keogh was only too aware that such a threat from his employer wasn't idle. He had the type of money, power and resources to kill almost anyone he wanted to. He had the ruthlessness too. 'I will, sir,' he answered, 'but I can't guarantee that we'll take her alive. That's what's been the problem so far.'

'I pay you very well to resolve problems like that. She has information I need very badly, you know that. You need to find her now, and if anyone else gets in the way, kill them too. Kill anyone you have to kill. It doesn't matter, as long as you get her back to me tonight. Do you understand me? And I mean alive.'

Keogh fought down his irritation at being talked to like a servant. 'Yes, sir.'

'Then do it. Otherwise I'll have to find someone who can. Call me when you have news.'

Keogh put the phone away, knowing now that his life depended on what happened in the next few hours. It was time to be ruthless. He'd already sent MacLean off to get the dogs, which would give them a much better chance of successfully hunting her down. In the meantime, they needed to make sure the canoe company didn't raise the alarm. It was inconvenient that both the canoes were currently stuck on the sand spit over the other side of the river in full view, but now that the afternoon was moving inexorably towards dusk, Keogh considered it highly unlikely that any other boats would come down here.

The Ukrainian, Sayenko, had arrived in his vehicle – an old Defender – and he and Mehdi were standing beside him awaiting instructions. Sayenko was a lean, wiry individual with tightly cropped grey hair and a dried-out, heavily lined face that looked in dire need of rehydrating. According to the boss, he had more than twenty years' experience in the Russian military and had served in combat operations in Chechnya twice, and he wasn't afraid of killing when it was necessary. He didn't say a lot, but he spoke good enough English, and was capable of taking orders, although of the two men, Keogh considered Mehdi, who'd been living in the UK for more than a decade and a half, and whom Keogh knew far better, the more reliable. It was Mehdi he addressed now.

'I need you to visit the canoe centre that rented out those canoes. The place is called Calvey Canoe Hire and, according to MacLean, it's on the Inverness Road, about five miles northeast of here. There's unlikely to be more than one person there, and it may be that he's further downriver waiting to pick up the canoeists, but I want you to check it out.'

Mehdi nodded casually, seemingly unworried by the assignment. 'And if there is anyone there?'

'Talk to them. Find out how many canoes they've got out, and whether there's anyone else working there today. Then call me straight away.'

'And after that?'

'Kill whoever's there and hide the bodies. We need to close . down this thing as fast as possible. When you've done that, we'll join up again and get hold of that woman. Any questions?'

Mehdi shook his head, and Keogh fished a set of keys out of his pocket and threw them over. 'Take the four-by-four. And move fast. We're running low on time.'

Mehdi didn't need asking twice and, as Keogh watched him jog back up towards the four-by-four, he was pleased he had men with him who weren't squeamish about killing in cold blood.

Because, one way or another, there was going to be a lot of killing tonight.

Sixteen

Two weeks ago

Mike Bolt leaned forward in his seat. 'We brought you on board to get a handle on the man we're hunting. You're supposedly the best criminal behavioural psychologist in the business but, with all due respect, I'm struggling to find anything you've told us that isn't blindingly obvious to everyone.' He paused, hugely aware of the urgency of the situation. 'I need something better. Something insightful.'

'I'm not a miracle worker, DCS Bolt,' answered Dr Thom Folkestone.

'No,' said Bolt. 'I can see that.'

Dr Folkestone looked mildly put out by Bolt's comment, and even managed a small pout. He was a handsome, if very boyish-looking man of thirty-eight, with foppish blond hair and twinkling eyes, who looked far too young and carefree to be the eminent psychiatrist he was. But, as Bolt had pointed out, however ironically, he was supposed to be the best.

As a general rule, Bolt avoided using behavioural psychologists. It wasn't that they couldn't provide useful information to aid an inquiry – sometimes (though not always) they did. But in his experience, some senior investigating officers became almost in thrall to the profiling techniques used by behavioural psychologists for narrowing down the list of suspects, thanks to the influence of TV and film. In the past, this had led to some notable injustices, and Bolt wasn't keen to repeat the mistakes of past murder inquiries. But at the same time, with leads scarce and The Disciple's body count steadily rising, the pressure for a result meant exploring every avenue possible; although, right at this moment, sitting in Dr Folkestone's expansive central London office, Bolt was beginning to think they were wasting their time.

'All I can do is give you an insight into The Disciple's character,' continued Folkestone, who was dressed in an expensive three-piece suit with the waistcoat done up – a look that, for some reason, annoyed Bolt. 'We're talking about a physically fit white male – I would say almost certainly between the ages of 35 and 45 – who's of above-average intelligence. However, I don't believe he'll have a mentally demanding job. I don't see him as a hard worker. He saves his planning for his crimes. I think his job involves driving long distances, which is why he's able to spend time targeting his victims, and he lives alone somewhere in the west London area.'

'Do you think he's killed before this current spate of attacks?' put in Mo.

'It's possible. Although, if he has, it would almost certainly not have been as well planned as the current killings.'

'I'm glad you said that,' said Bolt.

Folkestone leaned back in his leather swivel chair and raised an eyebrow. 'Why?'

'Because we know he has killed before. Fifteen years ago.'

'Why didn't you tell me?'

'We've only just found out ourselves. The forensic team discovered a trace amount of blood at the scene of the last Disciple killings that didn't match that of either of the two victims: George Rowan and Ivana Hanzha, or that of Mr Rowan's wife, Amanda. The DNA extracted from the blood matched that of the killer of a young Frenchwoman called Beatrice Magret, who was sexually assaulted and murdered in Hampshire in 1998.'

Folkestone nodded slowly, as if deep in thought. 'That's interesting. Can you give me the details?'

Mo Khan got out his notebook. 'She was a twenty-one-year-old student studying at University College London, and she was on her way to the Isle of Wight Festival with two other students – one female, one male – when the car they were in broke down on the A31. There was some sort of argument and Ms Magret stormed off on her own. She was seen by a witness walking at the side of the road towards the village of Soldridge about twenty minutes later, but that was the last sighting of her alive. Her body was found two days later, ten miles away near Alton, partially concealed in woodland. She'd been beaten, tortured and sexually assaulted.'

Mo paused. Although he was as professional as any copper Bolt had worked with, the fact remained he had three kids of his own, including a seventeen-year-old daughter, so it was difficult not to get affected by the senseless waste of Beatrice Magret's murder. 'According to the coroner, the assault was prolonged and brutal,' he said slowly, 'and then her skull was caved in with a blunt instrument. The scene-of-crime photos make pretty grisly viewing.'

'But no knife?' asked Folkestone, with a professional's dispassionate tone.

Mo shook his head. 'No. No knife.'

'And any Satanic symbols on the corpse?'

Again, Mo shook his head.

'Needless to say, the case was unsolved,' said Bolt, 'with very few leads generated, even though there was quite a lot of publicity at the time.'

'Yes, I seem to remember something about it,' said Folkestone, 'but I'm surprised it's the same person. Not so much because of the different modus operandi – it stands to reason that this would develop over time, and certainly it bears other hallmarks of The Disciple's MO – but the timescale between that killing and the start of the current crop feels too long. Have you looked to see if there were any similar unsolved killings in between?'

'I've got a dozen detectives scouring the PNC right now, but nothing's standing out.' When Bolt had first heard about this new murder earlier that morning, he'd thought it might represent a significant breakthrough, but already his enthusiasm was beginning to fade. If the murder of Beatrice Magret was The Disciple's handiwork, and it clearly looked as if it was, then once again it seemed his luck had held. The case, though still technically open, had been wound down many years back.

'What do you make of The Disciple's attack on Amanda Rowan?' he asked Folkestone. 'When we last spoke before the Rowan/Hanzha murders, you said the man we're looking for is highly organized, forensically aware, and extremely careful. And yet he takes a huge, and potentially fatal, risk to try to kill a woman who hasn't seen his face, and after he's already got his rocks off with her husband and his lover. What do you think makes him do something like that?' A week on, this still bugged Bolt, although given the often and impulsive irrational behaviour of even the most successful criminals, it really shouldn't have done.

But Folkestone didn't seem to find this puzzling at all, which shouldn't have surprised Bolt either. Like most people who valued their own opinions, he had an answer to everything. 'He's all those things, DCS Bolt, and he's also a perfectionist. But at the same time he's also, in layman's terms, a control freak. He controls his victims; he controls the scene of the crime by leaving behind virtually no evidence; he even thinks he controls the police inquiry by being the one who chooses when and where he strikes. That makes him much harder to catch than what we'd call a normal killer. But it also makes him prone to mistakes. I don't believe he was expecting Amanda Rowan to turn up and, when she did, he had to think fast. He decided to kill her, but when she proved a harder proposition than he was expecting, it seems he couldn't handle the affront of her disturbing *his* crime. Rather than give up, as his perfectionist instincts would have told him to do, he became extremely reckless in his efforts to kill her. He still wanted to retain control, even though he no longer did. And this may well be how you catch him.'

'How do you mean?'

'He might be a perfectionist, but he's clearly got a streak of recklessness. You need to take advantage of that. Push his buttons. Encourage him to make contact with you, and explain why he's committing these crimes. He's a narcissist and he clearly loves the notoriety. It'll also make him think he's in control once again.'

It sounded like a daft idea to Bolt. Anyone as careful as The Disciple wasn't going to respond to such an obvious ploy. Mo looked sceptical too.

Folkestone gave an expansive shrug. 'I can see you don't agree, but I think it's got to be worth a try. What have you got to lose?'

Which Bolt had to admit was a fair point. 'We'll consider it, Doctor,' he said, getting to his feet. 'Thanks, as always, for your time.'

'How is Amanda Rowan, by the way?' asked Folkestone as the three of them shook hands. 'Has she recovered from her ordeal?'

'She's a very resilient lady,' said Bolt, remembering that Folkestone had been the one who'd agreed to her decision to go to Scotland and rent a house. 'She's doing well.'

'I'm glad to hear it. She's a very lucky woman.'

'Well, it depends on your version of luck, doesn't it? She's lost her husband, found out he's having an affair, had her home turned into a charnel house, and been slashed with a knife by a man who came very close to killing her. That's definitely the kind of luck I could do without.'

'But she's alive, DCS Bolt,' said Folkestone. 'She's alive. And it seems, with The Disciple, that's a first. I imagine it must be irritating him immensely.'

'You don't think he'll try to locate her, though, do you?'

Folkestone smiled broadly. 'Reckless he may be, but not that reckless. And I'm sure you've got her tucked away safe and sound.'

'Absolutely,' said Bolt, heading for the door.

Seventeen

Today

Glenn Scopeland, better known to those who knew him as Scope, sat in the minibus watching the river flow by towards the stone, three-arched bridge that spanned the small Highland town of Tayleigh. He looked at his watch. It was gone five. In less than an hour it would be dark, and there was no sign of the family of canoeists he was here to pick up. Jock, the owner of the canoe hire company, had given him two mobile contact numbers for the group, and he called them each in turn.

It didn't surprise him when they both went straight to message. Reception was patchy on this stretch of the river at the best of times. He left two separate messages asking to be called back as soon as possible, then settled back in the seat to wait. He didn't think there'd be any problem with them. Customers were often late. The scenery was gorgeous and they often just dawdled. The river wasn't particularly high at the moment – it had been a fairly dry summer and autumn so far, so it was unlikely there'd been any capsizing. He decided to give it fifteen minutes, then he'd call Jock and see what he wanted him to do.

Scope had worked for Jock for a few months now, ever since he'd arrived in Scotland. The work was irregular and poorly paid, but he enjoyed it, and he got on well with Jock, which in the end counted more than most things. Scope had some money set aside, so for the moment at least he didn't have to worry.

By his own admission, he was something of a drifter. Ever since he'd left the army more than ten years earlier, he'd held down a variety of jobs – never anything too serious, or for too long – and he'd moved round, both in the UK and Europe. His wife, Jennifer, had divorced him when he was still in the army. Things had been a bit of a mess domestically and his daughter, Mary Ann, had ended up going off the rails. She'd died of a drugs overdose, aged barely eighteen, and then Jennifer had died in a car crash that might have been an accident but was, thought Scope, probably suicide, six months later. Now he was the last member of his immediate family still alive. Sometimes that made him feel guilty. Other times, it made him rail against the injustices of the world. But up here in the lonely wilds of Scotland, he was finally coming to terms with his loss, and his place in the world. In truth, this was the first time he'd been even mildly content in a long time. He'd even begun to enjoy his own company, now that he'd escaped a past that in recent years had become increasingly violent.

Four years ago, he'd gone after the men he believed were responsible for the death of his daughter, starting with the dealer who'd sold her the fatal dose of unusually pure heroin, and working his way up the chain until he'd finally reached the corrupt businessman who'd grown rich by importing the drugs direct from Turkey and Afghanistan. Scope had killed the businessman and his two bodyguards with a lot less emotion than he'd been expecting, which worried him. He didn't consider himself a bad man, and yet he'd done bad things.

And just when he was hoping that his killing days were behind him, he'd received a call six months ago from his wife's brother-in-law, begging him for help in looking for her kidnapped son. Scope wasn't a detective, but it seemed he had a knack for finding people, because he'd rescued his nephew and killed the kidnappers, somehow avoiding the attention of the authorities in the process. It was after this that he'd decided to get well away from civilization, while his luck still held, and now all he wanted to do was clear his head and try to work towards some kind of future.

He looked at his watch again. 5.15. Frowning, he got out of the minibus and walked the few steps down to the narrow strip of shingle, which was the usual exit point for the canoes at the end of the day trips, and looked back up the river. It ran straight, wide and shallow for about a quarter of a mile into Tayleigh, but there was still no sign of his family of canoeists. The sun was coming down fast and the light fading. Scope couldn't imagine that anything was wrong, but he still didn't like it.

Pulling out the mobile, he called the office landline.

The phone rang for more than two minutes but there was no answer, which struck him as odd. If Jock was out, he'd have left the answering machine on. He always did that, never wanting to miss out on a potential booking, and the office was attached to the cottage where he'd lived for the best part of thirty years, so he couldn't be in there. There was also a speaker attached to one of the outside walls, which amplified the ringing, so even if he was down by the canoe put-in point, he'd have heard it.

For the first time, Scope began to feel concerned. Had

something bad happened to the canoeists, and had Jock gone to their aid? But, if so, surely he'd have called. After all, he wasn't in the best shape.

And then, just as he got back in the minibus, he saw him: a man walking on the opposite bank of the river, a mobile to his ear. Scope squinted to see him better. The man was in profile and a good fifty yards away but, even from this distance, Scope could tell he wasn't a local. Wanting to get a better look at him, he reached into the glove compartment and rummaged round until he found a pair of binoculars that Jock liked to use for birdwatching.

The man had his back to Scope now as he mounted a flight of steps on the other side of the bridge, but as he reached the top and climbed into a four-by-four that was illegally parked on the side of the road, his face came back into view again, and Scope noticed two things. One, he was using a satellite phone rather than a mobile, which was extremely unusual in these parts, and two, he had two faded scars, which looked like knife wounds, on his face.

Scope watched him drive away, wondering who he was, because there was something about him he didn't like.

He put the binoculars away and, as he picked up the mobile, it rang in his hand.

It was the office and he smiled at his own paranoia. Bad things didn't happen up here in this stretch of the Highlands. It was one of the reasons he was here.

'Hey Jock, I've been trying to get hold of you. The canoeists haven't turned up.'

'That's why I'm calling,' said Jock. 'They came out early.'
'Where?'
'Down near Cawler Rapids. Can you get back here?'
Scope frowned. 'Are you all right, Jock? You don't sound

too good.' He didn't. His words were being delivered slowly and with effort, as if he was in pain. Scope knew he'd had some trouble with his heart a couple of years back, and he had to watch his health.

'I'm okay, but I need some help here. Now.'

'But what about the canoeists?'

'They're here. We'll get the canoes later.'

'They're all right, though?'

'Yeah. Fine.' It was clear he wanted to get off the phone.

'Sure,' said Scope, wondering what was wrong with him. 'I'm on my way.'

Eighteen

The receiver fell from Jock Calvey's hand, and the intruder replaced it in its cradle on the desk.

'How long will it take him to get back here?' the intruder demanded in a thick Middle Eastern accent.

'Fifteen minutes,' whispered Jock. He felt sick. He'd tried so hard not to betray Scope. The man was a friend more than an employee. Scope didn't give a lot away in conversations, and Jock could tell he had a past that was tinged with tragedy, but he was a good man – the type who would do anything for you if it was within his power. And now he was bringing him here to his death.

In a life spent entirely as part of a small, close-knit rural community, Jock had never been in a situation anything like as terrifying as this; never once thought that violence would come knocking on his door as it had done today.

'You did the right thing. And now your family are protected. That is good, yes?'

The intruder was smiling, looking pleased with himself. He'd been smiling when he'd arrived at the office too, trying to look friendly as he pointed to an Ordnance Survey map in his hand, but straight away Jock hadn't liked the look of him. The smile looked fake. And it had been. As soon as he'd opened the door, the intruder had punched him hard in the face, knocking him over.

Jock wasn't a big man, and at 64 his best years were a good way behind him, so he'd been in no state to resist as the intruder had dragged him to his feet, holding him with one hand while punching him in the face and gut with the other – the whole time never making a sound. Finally, he'd been flung back down in his office chair, and the intruder had handcuffed him by the wrist to one of the chair legs so that he was sitting at an extremely uncomfortable angle. The whole thing had lasted barely twenty seconds.

And then the questions had started. Who else was here? Who else had he hired canoes to today, aside from the family with the two girls? Who was meant to be picking them up at the other end of their trip?

Jock had no idea why he could possibly want all this information. And he certainly couldn't imagine what anyone could want with Tim and Jean Robinson, and the two girls with them. The little blonde one reminded him of an older version of his only grandchild, Grace, and he prayed nothing had happened to her. She'd seemed so sweet and full of life.

Although Jock was in no state to mount physical resistance, he was a lot tougher inside than he looked, and at first he refused to answer the questions, telling the intruder to take what he wanted but leave him alone, silently thanking God that his daughter and his granddaughter weren't visiting, and that, whatever happened, he was the only one who was going to get harmed.

But his bravery hadn't worked. The intruder had produced a knife. And that was when the torture had begun.

Jock felt faint now. His left thumb was missing, as was part of his right ear. His nose had been slit down the middle, and it was still dripping blood down his chin and onto his throat. The pain from his nose was excruciating, much worse than from his ear and the jagged stump where his thumb had been, but it hadn't been this that had made him betray Scope, a man he'd been determined to protect if he possibly could. It was when the intruder had picked up the photo of Grace, taken by Jock himself on her fourth birthday, that he knew it was over. The bastard had smashed the photo on the floor and told him calmly and matter-of-factly that he worked for a large organization full of men as heartless as him, and it would only be a matter of time before they found his granddaughter and cut her head off. Unless Jock started answering the questions fully and frankly, that was exactly what was going to happen, he explained, while all the time grinding the ruined photo into the floor with his boot.

The terrible thing was, sitting there in the little office he'd always loved so much, with its view out to the river, Jock had known that whether the man was telling the truth or not, he simply couldn't risk anything happening to Grace, or to his daughter, Mary, who was bringing her up alone.

So he'd told the intruder everything. And now, by phoning Scope and getting him to come back here, it looked as if he'd condemned an innocent man to death.

Jock looked up at the intruder. He was a young man, early thirties at most, not even that bad looking if you ignored the coldness of his features, and yet there was a blackness in his heart that seemed to have come straight from Hell. Jock knew, just as he'd known right from the beginning of the attack, that he was going to die. His time had almost come two years ago when he'd had a massive heart attack while sitting at the bar of The Farmer's Arms. He'd been revived then by a junior doctor – up from Glasgow on a walking holiday – who'd been in the pub at the time, and ever since he'd appreciated every day that God gave him.

And now those days had come to a sudden and bloody end, and Jock felt an overwhelming sense of loss.

The intruder looked back at him. He was smiling, the knife still in his hand.

Jock thought about begging for his life. But he knew it would do no good. In twenty minutes he'd learned a great deal about the evil that existed in the hearts of certain men.

Instead he closed his eyes and prayed the end would be quick.

Nineteen

Today 17.44

It was beginning to get dark and Scope was on his guard as he drove through the open gate into the yard and parked next to Jock's battered old Nissan Micra.

The office of Calvey Canoe Hire was a wooden, single-storey extension sticking out from the front of Jock's rambling brick cottage. The light was on but Jock wasn't sitting at his desk, which was unusual, given that he wasn't in the yard either. But the lights were on in the cottage and Scope remembered that he hadn't sounded too good, so maybe he'd gone back inside to rest.

Even so, something wasn't right. The way Jock had said the canoeists had abandoned their canoes halfway down the river but hadn't told him where; and the fact that there was no sign of them now, even though there was a four-door Toyota Rav parked on the other side of Jock's Nissan that almost certainly belonged to them.

Scope had an antenna for trouble. It was what came from

fourteen years in the British infantry, serving first in Northern Ireland at the tail end of the Troubles, then in the killing fields of Bosnia, and finally in Basra in southern Iraq where, along with the rest of his battalion, he'd spent six months being shot at, bombed, and abused by people who'd smile and wave at you one minute, then walk round the corner out of sight the next and detonate a shrapnel-filled IED aimed at ripping your whole patrol to pieces. It made a man cautious, and Scope had long ago learned that being cautious could save your life.

First he had a look inside the Rav – the kids' books and sweet wrappers on the back seat confirming that this was the canoeing family's car; then he crossed the yard and peered in the office window. Nothing looked out of place, and Jock's A4 diary, in which he wrote down pretty much everything to do with the business, was open on the desk at today's date. Scope tried the door. It was unlocked and he stepped inside, closing it very slowly behind him so that it didn't make the whine it usually did.

The first thing he noticed was the silence. He couldn't hear anything, which was a surprise if Jock and a family of four were in residence. He took a couple of steps further into the room, moving as quietly as possible, and stopped next to the door that led into the cottage's living room. He put his ear to the wood, but still couldn't hear anything. It was as if no one was here.

But if they weren't here, where were they? And why had Jock insisted he come back?

He reached down to open the door into the cottage, which was when he saw it on the carpet. A dark, penny-sized stain that he didn't remember being there last time he'd been in the office. Crouching down, he touched it with the tip of his middle finger.

It was blood. And it was fresh.

Scope tensed. Jock had called him back here. Jock had sounded under duress. There was no sign of the canoeists. Now there was blood on the floor.

Scope had made enemies in his past, some of whom were very powerful. It was possible that they'd tracked him all the way to here, and that this was an ambush.

He thought fast. If people were here waiting for him, they'd have heard the minibus pull in a couple of minutes earlier, which meant they'd be suspicious if he didn't put in an appearance soon. Retreating the way he'd come, he opened the office door and shut it again, loudly this time. 'Jock, it's me,' he called out, keeping his eyes trained on the door leading into the cottage, just in case someone came rushing through. 'I've just got a couple of things from the van to put away, then I'll be through, okay?'

There was no sound or movement from behind the door to the cottage, and for a second Scope wondered if this time his paranoia might be misplaced, but he quickly discounted this. Something was definitely wrong; even if it wasn't as bad as he was suspecting, it didn't matter. It was always better to be safe than sorry.

He went back out through the office door again, as if he was going back to the minibus, then ducked down low and raced round the side of the cottage out of sight. The logical course of action would have been for him to take off out of here and call the police, but he couldn't do that without at least some evidence that some wrongdoing had occurred. And there was something else too. He was fond of Jock. The old man had been good to him. If someone had hurt him, then Scope wasn't going to let whoever it was get away with it.

He continued round to the back of the cottage, listening for the sound of anyone coming out looking for him, but could hear nothing. The whole place remained silent, except for the occasional noise of the night animals that lived in the woods surrounding the yard as they came out to hunt in the gathering darkness.

Scope fished in his jeans pocket until he found the spare keys to the cottage, which Jock had given him a couple of weeks earlier, in case of an emergency. He'd been touched that the old man had entrusted him with a set of keys when they'd only known each other a matter of months. It wasn't often that Scope got close to people. He tended to keep his distance, a result of the fact that the two closest relationships of his adult life – those with his wife, and his beloved Mary Ann – had ended in tragedy. But he'd seen a kindness and a vulnerability in Jock that had drawn him in. Like Scope, Jock was lonely, having been on his own since his wife had left him for the bright lights of Edinburgh more than twenty years earlier. The two of them had talked over a bottle of decent whisky on more than one long night, and though Scope had never really opened up about his own past on those occasions, he'd always felt that he could have done if he'd needed to – even the darkest parts – and the old man would have understood, and not condemned him. And for that he was thankful.

He owed Jock. And he owed anyone who might have hurt him.

The back of the cottage was dark but, as Scope peered through the frosted glass in the back door, he could see the living-room lights were on. He carefully unlocked the door and crept inside, conscious that he was unarmed and acting with a complete disregard for his own safety. But that was Scope all over. He'd never been able to turn his back on danger, even though he was always trying to convince himself that his days of walking into the lion's den were firmly behind him.

The back door opened directly into a narrow hallway that led past the stairs and into the living room, with a kitchen on one side, and a spare room where Jock liked to hoard all kinds of junk, on the other. Scope couldn't see the door that led through to the office from the angle he was at, nor could he hear a thing from anywhere inside. Slowly, and making as little noise as possible, he made his way through the hallway, past the staircase, being careful not to trip on the boxes that littered the floor like obstacles, containing everything from boat engines to old paperbacks. Jock was a hoarder. He seemed incapable of chucking anything away, unlike Scope, whose possessions tended to be few and temporary.

The living room opened up in front of him as he reached the end of the hallway, revealing a scene that made him retreat into the shadows.

Jock lay dead on his front in the middle of the floor about ten feet away, next to the two easy chairs where he and Scope had sat when they'd shared those bottles of whisky. His face was pressed into the carpet, his arms down by his side, and the beanie hat he always wore – indoors and out – was missing. Somehow its absence made him seem much smaller and more diminished than he had in life. He was no longer Jock. He was just a corpse, and the sight of him, hollowed out like this, filled Scope with an intense emotion that he couldn't quite define. It wasn't sadness. It wasn't even anger. It was something darker and more hopeless than that, and he had to force himself to suppress it as he took in the injuries that the old man had suffered.

A thin rivulet of blood had run from a deep cut on his nose onto the multicoloured, 1970s-style carpet that had always given Scope a headache, and there was a gaping, messy hole where one ear had been. More blood was clustered round Jock's right hand, although Scope couldn't see the cause of it, nor did he want to. One thing was certain, though. Jock had suffered terribly before he'd died, and the man responsible for that suffering was leaning against the far wall next to the door leading out to the office, a pistol with suppressor in one gloved hand. He was short and well built, with the cool poise of a professional killer, and it was clear that he was waiting for Scope to come walking through the door from the office, so he could put a bullet in him.

So it seemed he *had* been the intended target of the ambush, which meant two things. One, Jock would still be alive if it hadn't been for him. Two, his days up here in Scotland – days that he'd grown to enjoy – were over, and once again it was time to move on.

There were, however, more immediate concerns. The killer hadn't seen Scope yet, but he would as soon as he looked round. It looked as if he was working alone, too, since there was no sign of anyone else. Roughly fifteen feet separated them. Scope was unarmed. He didn't even have his lock knife on him. If he rushed the guy now, he'd never make it, and it was too dangerous to try to creep up on him. There wasn't enough furniture to cover his approach, and if he were spotted halfway across the room, he'd be an easy target. The killer struck him as the sort who would neither hesitate, nor miss from close range. His whole demeanour was too confident for that.

It left Scope with a simple choice. Go back the way he'd come in, and when he was out of earshot, call the cops and leave it to them. Or deal with it himself. The advantage of calling the cops was obvious. He wouldn't have to risk his neck, nor would he run the other risk of getting himself into trouble. He could just take off and that would be the end of it.

But there was also a major disadvantage. Round here, miles from the nearest town of any size, it could take hours before an armed response unit turned up, and by that time the man who'd killed Jock would have long since disappeared, leaving few if any clues behind. Jock's death would go unavenged. And, in the end, Scope just couldn't have that.

He took a step backwards into the hallway, wanting to get to the kitchen and find a knife, but as he did so his foot hit one of the boxes of junk. Not hard. In fact it barely touched it, but in the heavy silence of the cottage, it was enough to attract the attention of the killer, who swung round fast, gun outstretched, catching sight of Scope immediately.

Even as he pulled the trigger, Scope was turning and diving headfirst into the semi-darkness of the hallway. A second shot rang out as he rolled across the floor, hitting another box. He jumped to his feet, keeping low and trying to make himself as hard a target as possible, as two more rounds flew past him, putting holes in the frosted glass of the cottage's ancient front door. He could hear the guy coming behind him now and he swung a hard left at the bottom of the staircase, almost tripping up on a box full of oil paintings, and ran headlong into the darkness of the kitchen, slamming the door shut behind him.

He was trapped now. There was no way he'd make it out of the window before the guy caught him, but he didn't panic. In situations like these, his subconscious always dragged up the words of wisdom he'd been given by a drill instructor during his first days of military training. '*As long as you're still fighting, you haven't lost.*' It had sounded like cheap bullshit at the time, but they'd always served him well. And they did now.

Grabbing a couple of plates and a frying pan still full of congealed fat from the stove, he leaned against a kitchen unit and waited the two seconds it took for the door to come flying open, before flinging the plates straight at the guy, followed a split second later by the frying pan.

Surprised by the ferocity of the assault, the killer managed to fend off the two flying plates, while getting off a wild shot that rattled one of the window frames. But the frying pan caught him under the chin, sending him staggering as he tried to right himself and pick out his target.

Scope didn't give him time. Crouching down, he sprinted the ten feet across the kitchen and dived into the killer, grabbing his gun hand and forcing it straight upwards as the two of them staggered backwards into the hallway. Scope tried to drive his head into the killer's face, using his momentum to land a telling blow, but the killer had quick reactions and he turned his head away, so that Scope's forehead slammed into the side of his head, hitting hard skull. The two of them went crashing to the floor, upending the box of paintings in the process, Scope ignoring the pain as he concentrated on slamming the killer's gun hand repeatedly into the floor as he tried to get him to release the weapon.

But this guy was good. He was clearly winded by the fall, but he wasn't letting go of the weapon. Instead, he shoved a knee into Scope's groin and reared upwards, slamming a fist into his right cheek. Scope's head reverberated from the pain and he felt a flash of nausea as the killer came close to knocking him off altogether. But then, in one sudden movement, he counter-attacked. Grabbing the killer's other arm by the wrist, and forcing it back down to the floor so he had him temporarily pinned down, he waited the half-second it took for the killer to rear up again, and in that moment he drove his forehead into the bridge of his nose with every bit of strength and anger he could muster. The killer yelled in pain as his nose broke, and Scope butted him again in the same place. Then, changing tactics, he jumped up, dragging the other man to his feet, and smashed his gun hand into one of the kitchen units. This time the gun went off, sending a shot into a cupboard, before clattering to the floor when the man's grip on it weakened. But, if Scope thought his opponent was finished, he was mistaken, because in the same moment the killer pulled his other arm free, reached inside his jacket and yanked out a bloodied stiletto with a six-inch blade.

Scope leapt backwards as the stiletto sliced through the air, narrowly missing his stomach, then threw himself to the floor, grabbed the gun from where it lay a couple of feet away, and swung back round, his finger on the trigger just as the killer fell upon him, knife raised for the death blow.

There was no hesitation. Scope pulled the trigger three times in quick succession, every shot hitting his opponent in the upper body at point-blank range.

The knife clattered to the floor as the killer let out a heavy grunt and rolled over onto his side. He lifted one gloved hand weakly as his body was racked with spasms.

Slowly, Scope got to his feet, still holding the gun. He looked round. There was no other noise coming from inside the cottage, so he'd been right about the killer being the only one here. But he needed to find out who else was after him and where they were, and there was only one person who could provide him with that information.

Kicking the stiletto well out of the way, Scope reached down and turned the killer over onto his back. He looked in a bad way. Two of the bullets had punctured his chest, the other had hit him in the belly, and there was blood dribbling down from his mouth. His eyes were wide with a mixture of fear and shock, but the most important thing was that he was still alive and conscious. Once again he tried to lift an arm, but Scope kicked it down again and pointed the gun between his eyes.

'Why did you want to kill me?' he demanded.

The killer started choking and rolled back onto his side, spitting out a thick glob of blood onto the floor, but Scope wasn't about to show him any mercy, and he pulled him back round, this time pushing the suppressor into his cheek.

'I asked you a question. Why did you want to kill me? Did someone pay you to hunt me down?'

The killer looked confused.

'Answer me, you piece of shit. Were you paid to hunt me down?'

The killer gave a slight, almost imperceptible, shake of his head. 'I don't even know who you are,' he managed to say, his words little more than a strained hiss.

Scope frowned, caught out by his answer. 'You're lying.'

'No.'

'Then why the hell are you here?'

But he never got a reply. The killer started to choke, and his whole body went into spasm. This time it was Scope who turned him on his side so that he could cough up the blood blocking his airways, but it was too late. After a couple of seconds, the coughing, like everything else, just stopped. Scope grabbed him by his jacket collar, lifting him up, wanting to glean any last bit of information that could tell him what was going on, but the guy was gone.

Scope let him go and stood back up, concentrating on steadying his breathing, as he came to terms with the cold, hard fact that violence had come knocking on his door once again, and he'd responded in kind. He'd never gained any real satisfaction from killing, even when those he killed deserved everything that was coming to them, and he felt none now.

Jock's murder might have been avenged, but it wasn't going to help him or his family, and Scope just felt empty.

Empty and confused.

The man he'd just killed had had no idea who Scope was, and Scope was sure he hadn't been lying. There'd have been no point when he was that close to death. And yet he'd obviously tortured Jock to make him call Scope to get him back to the office so that he too could be killed. It didn't make sense.

He sighed. He was missing something here. And where were the family of canoeists? Jock had claimed on the phone that they'd cut short their trip, but he'd been under duress then, and there was no way they'd have just got out and abandoned their canoes. And yet they'd never arrived in Tayleigh either. Scope thought about this. According to Jock, they were an ordinary local family, so it seemed unlikely they'd be targeted by a professional killer, like the man he'd just killed. But if Scope wasn't the target, and neither was Jock, then they had to be. And it seemed the killer was determined to cover up any trace of their journey, even going so far as to kill the people who'd hired them the canoes.

Scope needed to locate the family, especially as they had kids with them. There was a chance they were dead already, of course, but he couldn't assume that. Once again he contemplated calling the police. But things had changed now. He'd killed a man and, regardless of whether the killing was justified or not, he'd still be arrested and questioned, maybe even charged with murder. And all the time that family were out there somewhere. The police would have more chance of finding them, of course, but resources up here were scarce and it would be hours before they could set up a full-scale operation, particularly as Scope had no actual evidence that anything bad had happened to them.

He checked the killer's pistol. It was a Browning with a ten-round magazine, and there were four rounds left in it. Crouching down, he searched the dead man, trying hard not to think too much about what he was doing. For Scope, there were few grimmer experiences than running your hands over a dead body, especially when it was still warm. The killer had no ID on him, which was no surprise, and he was carrying a spare magazine in one of his pockets, but the magazine was empty, making Scope think he'd already used the gun today.

And then he found the satellite phone.

He remembered the guy he'd seen on the bridge. The scar-faced one, who'd looked out of place, who'd also had a satellite phone. There was no way this was a coincidence. Whatever was going on here, it was a lot bigger than he'd originally thought.

He pocketed the phone, knowing it could prove highly useful where there was no mobile reception and, after rummaging round until he found a small lock knife in one of the kitchen drawers, he left the room and walked back through the house, stopping only briefly next to Jock to say a last goodbye, before emerging into the cool night air.

He didn't return to the minibus, though. Instead, he walked down to the storage shed and pulled out a one-man kayak. The canoeists, he was sure, had never left the river.

So that was where he'd start looking for them.

Twenty

They'd been walking for a long time, hours probably; and now that darkness had almost fallen, and it was becoming harder to see where they were going, Jess's unease was growing. She was trying incredibly hard not to think about what had happened that afternoon – the fact that she'd witnessed two murders, and almost died herself. Instead, she put all her concentration into encouraging Casey to keep going. Her sister was exhausted, freezing and terrified, but she hadn't complained. Not once. She'd followed Jess because she believed Jess would protect her, and Jess would. She'd protect Casey with her life. No question.

The mystery woman, Amanda, had found a trail she recognized some time earlier (it was difficult to tell how long for sure, because the water from the river had made Jess's watch stop), and it was now leading them up a hill. None of them had talked much during the journey, even though Jess was desperate to ask her why the men had been after her. But, for the moment, they were all too busy trying to save energy and put as much distance between themselves and the river as possible. Jess knew she was taking a chance by relying on Amanda to get them out of here, but for the moment she didn't feel as if she had much choice, since she had no idea where they were, and at least Amanda did. While they stuck together, they had a chance.

Jess turned round and saw that Casey was beginning to lag behind. She was shivering, too, but still soldiering on without complaint. Jess had done everything she could to encourage her little sister, but she could see that Casey wasn't going to be able to carry on for much longer.

'How are you doing?' asked Jess, slowing up to wait for her.

Casey managed a weak smile. 'I'm really cold, Jess,' she said, sounding so tired that Jess could barely hear her. 'I don't know how much more I can walk.'

'We'll stop soon, I promise.' She turned to Amanda, who was still marching ahead. 'How much further is it?' she called out.

Amanda swung round quickly, and walked back to them. 'Keep quiet for Christ's sake,' she hissed. 'We don't know who's out here.'

'Casey can't keep going much longer,' Jess hit back, looking the other woman in the eye to show she wasn't intimidated. 'She's shattered, and she needs a change of clothes. So do I. I'm freezing.'

Amanda's expression softened. 'It's still a good two hours to Tayleigh, but there's a holiday home round here somewhere. I've passed it a couple of times on my walks. It's always been empty—'

'That doesn't matter. We can always break in. How far is it?'

'I'm not sure. I don't know the area that well, and it's hard to see where we are in the dark, but I'm pretty sure it's off this trail. There's a waterfall up here somewhere, and there's a path near the top that leads down to it.'

They all stopped and listened, and Jess thought she could hear the sound of running water coming from further up the hill, but it might just have been the wind through the trees. She shivered and looked up at the sky where only a small piece of moon shone down through the thick canopy of trees, giving them just enough light to walk by.

'Come on,' said Amanda, starting off again. 'We need to keep going. I don't think it's that far.'

Jess looked down at Casey, who was staring up at her forlornly. Even in the darkness, her big blue eyes gleamed with life. Jess gave a mock sigh and winked at her. 'I'm going to carry you for a bit now, Case, but don't get any ideas, okay? This is definitely a one-off.'

Casey's face lit up and she fell into Jess's arms. Jess hugged her tight, wanting to warm her up, then lifted her up like she had when Casey had been a little girl. Together they started after Amanda. It was hard work. Jess wasn't as fit as she had once been. At school she'd been a promising middle-distance runner and had even competed for the local athletics club at 800 metres, but since she'd started sixth form and discovered boys, bars, and the fun of just hanging out and doing nothing, she'd let things go. Before today, the last time she'd run more than fifty yards was when she'd been late for the bus, and that had been a good three months back. But she was determined to help Casey, however exhausted it made her, and she trudged along in silence, forcing herself to imagine a nice warm fire and a cup of tea.

But the hill was getting steeper and, after only a few minutes, she was panting heavily. Casey had stopped talking, and her head was resting against Jess's shoulder. Jess wondered if she was asleep and hoped she was. She'd faced far more today than a girl her age should ever have to face. The problem was that she was going to wake up very soon because Jess couldn't keep going like this for much longer.

Up ahead, Amanda turned round and, seeing Jess struggling with Casey, she walked back to them. 'I think the waterfall's just up here,' she whispered, seeing that Casey was asleep. 'Look. Can you hear that stream there?' She pointed into the thick wall of pine trees.

Jess listened, and now she could definitely hear running water.

'It's not that far now,' continued Amanda. 'Why don't you let me carry her for a bit? You look exhausted.'

'I don't know,' said Jess, reluctant to let Casey go. 'I don't know anything about you.'

'I'm not a bad person, I promise.'

'Then why are those men chasing you?'

Amanda shook her head wearily. 'I really don't know.'

'They must have a reason.'

'Well, I don't know what it is. I promise.'

Jess wasn't sure she liked Amanda, but the more she thought about it, the less she looked like a criminal on the run. She looked too well off, and her clothes were expensive. 'Be careful with her,' she said, a hardness in her tone. 'She's all I've got.'

'Don't worry, she'll be okay. I'm not going anywhere without you.' Amanda smiled a pretty smile that for some reason really annoyed Jess, but she handed Casey over, feeling a guilty sense of relief.

Taking her gently, Amanda continued climbing the hill, her pace not slowing at all, and Jess had to walk fast just to keep up with her. Jess wondered if she was some kind of political refugee or whistle-blower who held some big secret that could bring down a whole government, and had to be stopped before she blurted it out. But whatever it was she'd done, she wasn't talking. So, for the moment at least, Jess had no choice but to accept her story.

The waterfall appeared out of the gloom. It was about the height of a big house, and pretty narrow, running down between two rocks before forming a round pool at the bottom that on a hot, sunny day would have been nice to swim in, but right now just made Jess feel cold. A set of steep wooden steps had been dug into the soil, each spaced several feet apart, and they led to the top. It was more of a climb than a walk, and Jess had to help Amanda with Casey as they made their way slowly upwards.

'If I remember rightly, the path's up here on the left some-where,' said Amanda, breathing more heavily now.

Jess was panting too, although she was pleased that Casey still appeared to be asleep. Amanda started up the path with renewed purpose and Jess felt a real rush of excitement. If they got to this house, they could call the police and this whole thing would be over. She could take Casey back to London with her, and they could be together again properly. It was awful about Jean and Tim, but Casey would get over it, with her help. There'd be practical issues, of course. Jess had no money and was living with temporary foster parents until her eighteenth birthday, but they could sort something out. She knew they could.

'Here it is,' announced Amanda, stopping between two pine trees just up ahead.

It didn't look much like a path to Jess, and there were no lights in the distance that she could see, which tempered her excitement a little. 'How far is it?' she asked.

'I can't remember exactly, but not too far.'

'Can you still manage Casey?'

'For a bit longer, yes.' She motioned for Jess to follow. 'Come on.'

They walked in silence until the path became more obvious. Finally, Amanda broke the silence. 'I'm sorry about your parents,' she said.

'They're not – they weren't – my parents,' said Jess quietly, not wanting Casey to hear this conversation. 'It was our aunt and uncle. Our parents are both dead.'

Amanda frowned. 'I'm still sorry.' She sighed. 'I didn't mean to get you involved.'

'I know. It's okay.' And then, for some reason she couldn't quite fathom, she added: 'I'm adopted.'

'I guessed that.' She didn't add anything but then she didn't need to. Jess was mixed race, and quite clearly not Casey's real sister.

'My parents, the ones I called Mum and Dad, adopted me when I was seven.'

'What happened to them?'

'Dad had a heart attack two years ago. A massive one, while he was at work. Apparently, he died pretty much instantly. I don't think Mum ever really got over it. They doted on each other, you know. It was almost sickly.' Jess smiled at the memory of the two of them snuggling up together on the sofa, whispering and laughing in each other's ears, then forced it aside, knowing there was no point languishing in a past that was never coming back. 'Anyway, she got breast cancer last year. We thought she'd beaten it but it came back everywhere, and she died in June. That's when Case came up here to live with Tim and Jean.'

'You've had it tough,' said Amanda, without sounding all syrupy sympathetic like a lot of people did.

You don't know the half of it, thought Jess. She'd had it tough right from the very beginning. And what she'd seen in those years before she'd been adopted still haunted her nightmares, even to this day. Life, in Jess's experience, was hard. You either accepted that fact and lived with it, or you ended up wallowing in self-pity, and Jess had never been a one for that.

The house loomed up out of nowhere behind a thick tangled hedge. It was modern-looking, with a long sloping roof like a Swiss chalet, and looked totally out of place in the middle of the woods. A gate led into a small front garden that needed work doing to it and, as Amanda stood aside holding Casey, Jess opened it and walked through. The house was in darkness. It looked empty and unloved, with grubby windows and paint peeling from the walls where the ivy was stretching up in tangled, invading fingers.

'I didn't think there was anyone here,' said Amanda, coming in behind her. 'But they might have a phone.'

Casey stirred on Amanda's shoulder and shook herself free of her grip. 'Where are we?' she asked, turning to Jess and rubbing her eyes.

'We've found a house,' said Jess, putting a protective arm round her shoulder. 'We're going to let ourselves in so we can get some dry clothes and food.'

'But isn't that like burgling?'

Jess smiled. Casey had always had a real sense of right and wrong. 'No,' she said. 'It'll be more like borrowing.'

There were no keys in obvious places, but the windows were old and single-glazed, and they found one round the back that faced directly into the kitchen, and which looked easy to break. Cold, wet and thirsty, Jess didn't hang around. She found a clay plant pot and, while Amanda stood back with Casey, she heaved it into the glass. It didn't break the first time, or the second, but on the third attempt, she put everything into the swing, and a piece of glass the size of a football exploded, sending shards all over the kitchen worktop. Feeling a grim sense of satisfaction, Jess put her hand through the hole and turned the handle, opening the window. She leant in and used the still-intact plant pot to sweep the glass onto the floor, then climbed through the open window and helped Casey in.

'Won't the people whose house this is mind you've smashed their window?' asked Casey.

'Course they won't. They'll just be happy we're safe.' She took Casey's hand. 'Come on, let's see if we can find you some warm clothes.'

'I'll have a look for a phone,' said Amanda, climbing through the open window and shutting it behind her.

But Jess didn't see a phone as she moved through the empty house, finding a couple of towels in an airing cupboard in the hallway. There was a small single bedroom on the ground floor with long out-of-date *Toy Story* wallpaper covering the walls and a wardrobe opposite the bed. The only thing hanging up inside was a navy blue dressing gown with a picture of Buzz Lightyear on the back, which looked as if it had been designed for a six year old. 'Okay, Case, get those clothes off,' said Jess, pulling it out.

Casey pulled a face. 'Do I have to wear that?'

'Unless you want to freeze to death, yes.'

Reluctantly, Casey started removing her clothes, and as Jess wrapped one of the towels round her, the door opened and Amanda walked in, wearing a concerned expression. 'There's no landline,' she said simply.

'No mobiles lying around?' asked Jess, knowing there wouldn't be.

Amanda shook her head. 'Nothing.'

The implication was obvious. They might have found shelter but, in the end, they were still trapped out here in the woods.

Twenty-one

Today 18.25

Keogh was agitated. He hadn't heard from Mehdi for over an hour and hadn't been able to raise him on the satellite phone. The Algerian was reliable, which meant that either he'd mislaid the phone or, more likely, something had happened to him. It was a problem. He needed Mehdi to guard the path along the river that led into the town of Tayleigh, in case Amanda Rowan had decided to risk trying to get there that way. Now they were just going to have to hope that she hadn't, and had opted for the cross-country route that MacLean had predicted she would. Otherwise, the whole op was finished.

He was parked in a sheltered lay-by with a thick line of forest on one side and a long, rolling, gorse-covered hill on the other. Next to him, in the four-by-four's passenger seat, sat Sayenko, the tall, cadaverous Ukrainian. Keogh hadn't allowed him to smoke in the car, and had warned him against smoking outside and leaving cigarette butts with DNA on them where they could later be found in the police search of the area that would inevitably follow, but Sayenko had been insistent. He needed his cigarettes, and he made it clear that he was going to have them. So they'd come to a compromise. Sayenko would smoke outside and then dispose of his butts in the four-by-four. Now both it and he stank of stale smoke, making Keogh's mood even darker than it had been already.

He disliked having men under his command who were prepared to defy him, but the problem was that Sayenko was a longstanding colleague of the boss's, and the boss rated him highly, so he didn't have a lot of choice. He looked a cold bastard too, thought Keogh, with his tight, heavily lined face set naturally in an undertaker's frown, and narrow, flint-like eyes that poked out from the bony contours of his skin like malignant probes. Sayenko didn't say much, which suited Keogh just fine. He wasn't the kind of man who enjoyed small talk, nor was he interested in other people. Instead, he stared out of the window into the darkness. It was rugged, hard country out here, with far too many hiding places. But it also meant there were very few people around. In the ten minutes they'd been sitting here, not a single car had driven past, which meant they were unlikely to be disturbed in their work.

For a moment Keogh thought back to how he'd got himself in this position, leading a team of killers on a manhunt through the Scottish wilderness.

It had begun three months after he'd got out of prison for manslaughter. He'd still been on parole, living in a shitty little bedsit in an even shittier part of London, with no money, no prospects, and only a heart full of bitterness, when one day he got a knock on his front door. The visitor was an old detective colleague of his – a guy he hadn't seen nor heard from in more than five years – called Jerry Johnson. The thing was, Keogh had never liked Johnson, who was a seedy bastard with a reputation for using prostitutes, and who was married to a stone-faced Thai bride who looked more like a man than he did. He didn't think Johnson cared much for him either. He'd never been in contact in those months when Keogh had been awaiting trial, so it had been a real shock seeing him standing in the grimy hallway outside his door.

'I've got a proposition for you,' Johnson had said simply, not bothering with any niceties. 'Something I think you'll like.'

Keogh had been intrigued enough to invite him in, not knowing what to expect. Without bothering to sit down, Johnson had told him he was acting as a middleman for an unnamed individual who wanted to give Keogh a job.

Keogh had asked what the job entailed.

'You're going to be a fixer,' Johnson explained. 'A man who does what it takes to make the boss's problems go away.'

'And what does the boss do that he needs his problems fixing by an ex-con like me?'

'He makes money,' said Johnson. 'Lots of it. Sometimes people try to get it off him. Other times they stand in the way of him making it and need to be moved out of the way.'

The inference was obvious. Johnson represented some kind of gangster, which surprised Keogh. He might have been sleazy, but Keogh had never taken him as corrupt. Johnson had told him that the pay would be good, the work ongoing, and that he had twenty-four hours to think about it.

'I don't need twenty-four hours,' Keogh had replied. 'I'll tell you right now. I'm in.'

Johnson had given him one of his leering smiles. 'I knew you would be,' he said. And then he'd turned and left, and Keogh had never seen him again. The boss, it turned out, liked to keep the cops on his payroll away from the other workers.

The rest, though, was history. Keogh had come on board and

had taken to his new role like a duck to water. Before today, he'd killed three times in cold blood on behalf of his boss, and had never felt an ounce of regret, although he was beginning to wonder if, by taking on this particular assignment, he'd bitten off more than he could chew.

He looked at his watch. Almost half past six. MacLean should be here with the dogs any time now; then they could begin the pursuit of Amanda Rowan. The important thing was to extract the target, get rid of any witnesses, and get out fast.

The passenger door opened and Sayenko started to get out.

'Where are you going?'

The Ukrainian held up an unlit cigarette as he slipped off his seat, shutting the door behind him, and Keogh wondered if he was going to be fit enough to take part in the hunt, given that he was close to being a chain smoker.

At that moment, headlights appeared on the horizon, the first ones they'd seen since they'd parked up. Keogh looked for Sayenko but he'd slipped into the undergrowth, and all that was visible was the glowing ember of his cigarette. Keogh slid down in his seat, not wanting to be seen either. Thanks to the deaths so far, there was going to be a major police investigation into what had gone on here today. The four-by-four had false plates and would be at the bottom of a loch somewhere in twenty-four hours, but Keogh had a criminal record and, though his scars were faded, they still made him stand out.

As the headlights came closer, Keogh's satellite phone rang.

'It's me,' said MacLean as the Toyota Land Cruiser he was driving pulled up opposite the Land Rover.

Replacing the phone in his jacket, Keogh sat back up in the seat and got out of the car. He could see two big dogs moving about behind a mesh barrier in the back of the Land Cruiser. There was also someone else in the car, sitting behind MacLean. As Keogh approached the driver's side door, he peered in and got a better look at the shadowy figure of the second occupant. He immediately turned away, suppressing the faintest hint of a shudder. People didn't tend to scare Keogh. You could deal with most men one way or another, if you kept your wits about you, but occasionally you came across an individual with a darkness about them that was so potent and twisted that even the strongest men held them in some awe. The woman in the back of the Land Cruiser was MacLean's mother and, though she was pushing seventy and looked just like any other old lady, Keogh had heard stories about her that made his skin crawl.

'How's the boss?' he asked, as MacLean clambered out of the Toyota. MacLean had changed out of his police officer's uniform now and, like Keogh and Sayenko, was dressed in dark clothing.

'Not happy at all,' he answered, his hulking figure towering over Keogh. 'He wants this thing sorted out quickly. And he definitely wants the girl alive.'

'Why did you bring her?' Keogh motioned ever so slightly towards the car, his voice trailing off.

MacLean smiled, clearly pleased with the doubt in Keogh's eyes. 'In case everything else fails. Like I say, the boss wants this girl. And he wants her badly. Ma can watch the road while we go into the woods, and if they turn up here, she'll be able to keep them occupied until we get back. People trust Ma. They think she's harmless.'

More fool them, thought Keogh as MacLean walked round to the Land Cruiser's boot and released the dogs, putting them on tight leashes. They were young-looking Dobermans and looked as if they were raring to go.

Keogh turned away and took the weapons from the back of the four-by-four.

It was time to begin the hunt.

Twenty-two

Five days ago

They got their big break on The Disciple case purely by chance. In Mike Bolt's experience, this was often the way it happened. Good old-fashioned detective work counted for a lot, as did the huge advances in technology that made committing a crime so much harder than it had been even a few years back. But sometimes it was just luck that made the difference.

A month earlier, Bolt had set up a hotline for members of the public to call in with any information they had on the identity of The Disciple. Such was the high profile of the case, that the hotline had been taking an average of more than a hundred calls a day. Many of them had been from people giving the names of individuals they didn't like, or were suspicious of in some way, and all these names had to be checked out, which took time and effort, and almost invariably turned into dead ends. Because of this, Bolt had made it clear that top priority was to be given to any name that appeared twice from separate sources, and this had finally happened a week earlier.

Leonard Philip Hope had been named first by a former girlfriend who'd had a short but violent relationship with him. She claimed he'd tied her up and beaten her on several occasions and, the last time he'd done it, he'd strangled her unconscious. He was also tattooed on his left forearm. On its own, this information wasn't particularly useful. Sadly, there were many men who beat their girlfriends, just as there were plenty who were tattooed, but when Hope had been named by a clinical psychologist who'd treated him for post-traumatic stress disorder eight years earlier, and who described him as an incredibly damaged individual with a frightening obsession with the occult and sexual violence, Bolt had taken an immediate interest.

Hope was a forty-one-year-old former soldier who'd spent five years in the army before being dishonourably discharged for insubordination. He had no previous convictions, but had been given a police caution aged seventeen for indecent exposure after he'd flashed at a group of schoolgirls. He lived alone in the house he'd grown up in, in Ealing, which he'd shared with his widowed mother until her death, and for the last eighteen months he'd been working for a local courier firm as a driver, a job that took him across southeast England. In this respect, he perfectly fitted the psychological profile that Dr Thom Folkestone had suggested for the suspect. Hope had also filled up the company van he used for deliveries with petrol at a garage five miles from the scene of the first murders the day before they'd been carried out, putting him in the area at a crucial time.

But, of course, none of this made him guilty. Bolt remembered all too well the case of Colin Stagg, the man wrongly accused of the brutal murder of Rachel Nickell on Wimbledon Common twenty years earlier, who'd been targeted because he seemed to fit the psychological profile, only for the murderer to turn out to be someone else entirely. Bolt wasn't going to make that mistake. But the more his team looked into Leonard Hope's background, the more they liked him as a suspect. His school reports suggested a quiet boy of higher-than-average intelligence, but one who was also disruptive. He'd been suspended from secondary school on two occasions – once for an assault on a younger pupil; the second time for a more serious assault on a female teacher that had involved him touching her inappropriately. He'd been fourteen at the time. How Hope had managed to stay on at the school while avoiding criminal charges was beyond Bolt, but somehow he had. More interestingly was an incident that had happened while Hope had been in the army, stationed in Cyprus, in 1999. A young Dutch couple, tourists on the island, had been walking back to their hotel from a nightclub in the early hours of the morning, past a quiet stretch of waste ground, when they'd been attacked from behind by a masked man. The attacker had struck the man on the back of the head with a blunt object, knocking him unconscious, before dragging the girl into some bushes and exposing her to a short but very violent sexual assault. He'd then beaten her unconscious with the same blunt object, and fled.

Both tourists recovered from their ordeal, and although neither had been able to give much of a description of their attacker, the young woman remembered him uttering the word 'bitch' during the assault, in what she described as a British accent. Soldiers at the base were questioned, including Hope, but because no DNA had been recovered from the scene of the crime, and no trace was ever found of the weapon used, no one was arrested. Hope had been off duty and off the base at the time, but he had an alibi. He was visiting a prostitute several miles away and she claimed he'd spent the night with her. Bolt could see why this had eliminated him at the time, but in hindsight, with everything else they'd found out about Hope, he now thought it was all far too convenient. It wouldn't, Bolt suspected, have been that hard for a reasonably intelligent man to have bought an alibi from the prostitute; maybe he'd even sneaked out without her knowing to carry out the attack and then returned. Either way, Bolt now knew they had more than enough to justify a full-scale surveillance operation.

That surveillance had been going on for two days now. Like all twenty-four-hour surveillance ops, it was resource-heavy, using three separate teams of ten officers each. So far, Hope hadn't done anything remotely suspicious, which was no great surprise. His habits were fairly mundane. He went to work, drove round most of the day delivering parcels, then returned alone to his flat at night. The problem was that there tended to be as long as six months between his killings, and since he'd only killed George Rowan and Ivana Hanzha two weeks previously, it was unlikely he'd be stalking new victims for some time to come yet. Their great hope lay in matching Leonard Hope's DNA to the murder scene at the Rowans' house, and the killing of the French student, Beatrice Magret, back in 1998. That way they'd have enough to arrest him and press charges. Unfortunately, because he had no actual convictions, Hope's DNA wasn't on the national DNA database, so one of the surveillance teams had had to take possession of a disposable coffee cup he'd dropped in a rubbish bin after one of his deliveries, so that SOCO could take a sample from it. But the results of any DNA test wouldn't be known for at least five days, and meanwhile the pressure for a result remained absolutely intense.

Bolt tried not to let it get to him, but it wasn't easy. Including Beatrice Magret, The Disciple had been linked to a total of nine murders, and Bolt was finding it incredibly frustrating having to fend off criticism about the investigation, while at the same time having to wait to find out whether or not Hope was their man.

'He's got to be,' said Mo as they turned into the driveway, and pulled up in front of the large mock-Tudor house belonging to Richard Oldham – the witness who'd seen a man outside the house of two of The Disciple's victims shortly before they were attacked and murdered. 'He fits the bill perfectly. Not just because he's everything that quack Folkestone says he is – loner, history of violence, above-average intelligence; but the key's the Cyprus thing. That's just too coincidental.'

Bolt sighed, switching off the engine. 'I agree, but I still wish we had more on him.'

'We'll get it eventually. It's going to be Hope's DNA at the Rowan house murder scene. Then we can just nick him.'

'That's going to be another five days. I just want this thing cut and dried. Then we can wind up this investigation, and get involved in something less heart-attack-inducing.'

Mo looked concerned. 'You sound weary of the job, boss.'

Bolt thought about it for a moment. 'I guess I am. It's been twenty-seven years now. Can you believe that? Twenty-seven years as a copper dealing with the dregs of society, and the criminals are still committing plenty of crime.'

'But if they weren't, we wouldn't be in a job. And, anyway, what else would you do?'

Bolt groaned. 'I really don't know.' It was true. He didn't have any outside interests. He had no girlfriend to share his time with. He didn't even have many friends outside the Force. It struck him then that he'd become almost as much of a loner as Leonard Hope, which wasn't a particularly encouraging thought.

'It's this case, boss,' said Mo. 'It's getting us all down.'

He motioned towards the house. 'Maybe Mr Oldham can help us.'

'Let's hope so,' said Bolt as they got out of the car, but he wasn't so sure. It had been five months since Richard Oldham had seen a man in dark clothing and tattoos hanging round in woodland behind the home of John and Kathy Morris, two days before they were brutally murdered, and barely four hundred metres from where they were now, just outside the village of Tilford in the Surrey countryside. At the time, Oldham's description of the suspect had been basic in the extreme, and the e-fit he'd helped create had, by his own admission, not been a great likeness, so Bolt wasn't at all sure he'd be much help now, but they'd come out here anyway with surveillance photos of Leonard Hope on the off-chance that Oldham would recognize him. It wasn't a job that Bolt needed to do as head of the investigation. He could easily have left it to a DS, or even a DC, but it was a rare sunny day, and both he and Mo had been keen to get out of the incident room and do something.

They'd called to let Oldham know they were coming and he'd answered the door straight away. He was a small man in his late sixties, with a few white strands of hair on an otherwise bald and suntanned head, dressed in a paisley tank top and neatly pressed trousers, the kind of gear Bolt imagined you'd wear on a golf course.

Bolt introduced himself and Mo, and Oldham gave them a broad welcoming smile and invited them in.

'You said on the phone that you had some photos for me to look at,' he said as he led them through a hallway not much smaller than a hotel foyer, and into a traditionally furnished living room with views onto a well-kept back garden. 'Does that mean you have a suspect in mind?'

Bolt wasn't keen to give Oldham any more information than he had to, although there seemed little point in denying the obvious. 'We've got an individual of some interest, yes.'

'Thank goodness for that. It hasn't been the same round here since the murders. They were a lovely couple as well. And now to hear he's killed again.' Oldham gave a visible shudder, motioning for them to sit down on one of the two leather sofas facing each other. 'Can I get you a drink of anything?'

'No, we're fine, thanks.' Bolt took an A4-sized envelope from his jacket and, as Oldham sat down, he removed three surveillance photos taken of Hope the previous day. One was a full-frontal shot of his top half as he emerged from his house. He was just over six foot tall and well built, and there was a confidence about the way he held himself, but even Bolt had to admit his face was pretty ordinary, with no obvious standout features. In the photo he was wearing a T-shirt, exposing the tattoo that covered most of his left arm. The second photo was a close-up of the tattoo itself – an intricate design that appeared to show two dark green dragons locked in an embrace, with the tails starting a few inches above the wrist, and the upper part of the bodies disappearing beneath the shirtsleeve. The third one was a close-up of Hope's face in full profile. Again, nothing stood out on it, other than the fact that he had dark bags under both eyes, and a small mole on his left cheek. The photos had been scanned to Highlands CID the previous day so that Amanda Rowan could look at them but, as she hadn't seen her attacker's face, she hadn't been much help. All she'd managed to give them was that the tattoo looked similar to the one she'd seen on her attacker's arm.

So now Oldham was their best chance of moving the case along, and as he inspected each of the photos in turn, taking his time, Bolt realized he was nervous. Bolt didn't want to wait five days for the results of the DNA test. He wanted to know now that Hope was his man so that he could get the bastard off the street and the pressure on him would finally ease.

'I didn't really get a look at the tattoo as such,' said Oldham, 'although it's the right colour. But . . .' He paused, looking again at the close-up of Hope's face. 'This definitely looks like the man I saw.'

'Are you absolutely sure, Mr Oldham?' asked Mo.

'Not absolutely, but pretty sure, yes.'

'That's very helpful,' said Bolt, taking the photo. Oldham's ID was good enough for him, even though it wasn't exactly a definitive yes, and almost certainly wouldn't stand up in court. Right now, though, that didn't matter. Bolt just needed enough evidence for a search warrant.

'Does this mean you'll be able to arrest him?' asked Oldham.

'We can't comment on that, sir, but I'd ask you not to say anything to anyone about seeing these photos. We'll let you know any developments on the case as soon as we can.'

When they got outside, Bolt grinned at Mo. 'Right, that's enough for a warrant.'

Mo looked less convinced. 'Are you sure? It wasn't exactly a concrete ID.'

'It's good enough for me,' said Bolt. He'd been around long enough to know that sometimes it was easier to take the initiative than wait for the wheels of justice to turn. 'With a bit of luck he'll be in custody by the end of the day.'

Twenty-three

Five hours later they were parking thirty yards down from Leonard Hope's house, on a quiet residential street of interwar terraced houses, many of which looked like they needed updating. After a lot of pushing and a full-scale row, they'd been granted the search warrant Bolt had been so keen to get hold of, and with Hope himself currently three miles west of them making a delivery in Hounslow, and under the watchful eye of one of the ten-man surveillance teams, they were taking the opportunity to look inside his house for clues. It wasn't going to be a full-scale search, even though they had permission for one; nor was it going to be done publicly. The plan was simply to hunt round for clues, without alerting Hope to what they were doing.

'I don't like this,' said Mo, who'd already said this several times that day.

Bolt turned to him, surprised by his long-time partner's reticence. 'I don't understand why not. We've got plenty of circumstantial evidence, and now we've got a positive ID. What more do we need?'

'It wasn't that positive, and this is a sixty-eight-year-old guy remembering someone he saw months ago. Someone who, even at the time, he could barely describe. But when you were in court this afternoon getting the warrant, you swore to the judge that Oldham was certain that it was Hope.'

Mo was right. In court, Bolt had exaggerated the strength of Oldham's ID of the photo, but he was sure it had been the right thing to do. 'You said yourself you believe Hope's guilty. I think he is too. So what do you suggest we do?'

'Wait for the DNA results. Then we'll have our proof one way or the other. In the meantime, we've got him locked down with surveillance, so it's not as if he's going anywhere. If we go charging in there now, boss, and it later turns out in court that we obtained the search warrant under questionable circumstances, the case might be thrown out.'

'Not this time. No judge is going to dare chuck out the case against Hope on a technicality, not when he's killed that many people. Come on, Mo. We're doing the right thing.'

Mo sighed. It was clear he wasn't convinced, which surprised Bolt. He wasn't usually a by-the-book man, but then he had a family to support and mouths to feed. He couldn't afford a blemish on his record, whereas for Bolt it was a different story. He'd become more fatalistic of late. If he had to risk his own career to put down serious criminals, then so be it.

Knowing there was no point continuing the discussion, he opened the car door. 'Let's get this over with before he gets back.'

They crossed the road and walked to Hope's front door in silence. His house was one of the more cared-for of those in the street. The door and windows looked new, and the small front garden was neatly tended, with the grass on either side of the path freshly mowed. It was a warm autumn day, and plenty of houses had their windows open, including the ones on either side of Hope's, suggesting that – although the street was empty – his neighbours were at home. This meant they were going to have to be very careful. The last thing they needed was for someone to spot them breaking in and either call the police, or alert Hope to what was going on.

Both Bolt and Mo Khan were experienced housebreakers. During their time in the National Crime Squad, the Serious and Organized Crime Agency, and most recently attached to Counter Terrorism Command, they'd had to make more than their fair share of covert entries into the homes of suspects, usually to plant bugs in them. Hope's front door had three separate locks, all of which were on, but it still only took Bolt about a minute and a half to pick them. As Bolt worked, trying to look as casual as possible, Mo stood slightly behind him, obscuring the view from the street. They were both banking on the fact that because they were dressed in suits and didn't look like burglars, they wouldn't attract attention. But they needn't have worried. As Bolt opened the door and stood back, he gave a quick glance left and right. The street was still empty and no one appeared to be at their window. It was clear they hadn't been noticed.

The house was just as neat and tidy inside as out, which, in Bolt's experience, was a rarity with criminals, who tended to be a slovenly bunch. 'Blimey, I wish my place was as well-kept as this,' he said, walking through the hallway into a narrow kitchen with worktops running down one side. A single, half-drunk cup of tea by the sink was the only thing out of place. The surfaces were spotless and a number of pots and pans hung down from hooks on either side of an old gas cooker. Bolt checked the cupboards and saw that they were well stocked with a variety of ingredients and condiments. Leonard Hope was clearly interested in cooking. Bolt shook his head. Even after years as a police officer, he always found it hard to reconcile the fact that sadistic, sociopathic killers like The Disciple – individuals who thought nothing of torturing their fellow human beings to death for pleasure – could have harmless, mundane interests like everyone else. But, of course, it was this apparent ordinariness that often made them so hard to identify.

While Mo started in the living room, Bolt went through every cupboard and drawer in the kitchen. According to the pathologist who'd carried out the autopsies on all The Disciple's victims since he'd started his current round of killings, the same weapon had been used in three of the attacks, and it was this that Bolt was most interested in finding. The weapon he was looking for was a knife with a serrated edge and an eight-inch blade. Two of the teeth about an inch down from the tip were slightly bent to the left, which meant it shouldn't be too difficult to identify it if it was here. Bolt had once done a search of the flat of a young gang member who lived with his mother, after they'd arrested him for stabbing a rival to death, and he'd found the murder weapon, which turned out to be the kid's mother's carving knife, in the kitchen knife rack. He'd washed it clean of blood and simply put it back. When asked later why he hadn't tried to get rid of it, he'd replied that his mum would have killed him. Apparently, she liked that knife and was always on at him for borrowing it. But he had a feeling that Hope would be a lot more careful than that.

They worked through the house, moving quickly. Because the place was so tidy, it didn't have a very lived-in feel, but it didn't look much like a show home either. The furniture was old-fashioned and worn, and most of it had probably belonged to Hope's mother. It was the same with the pictures on the wall. They were old prints of animals and country scenes and reminded Bolt of the ones in his grandparents' old house. There were no photographs on display anywhere. In fact, there wasn't much of anything – no books; a handful of CDs and DVDs; a few stacks of old utility bills – and certainly nothing that might suggest that Leonard Hope was a prolific and extremely dangerous serial killer. The only computer equipment he owned was an Acer laptop in his bedroom, and there was nothing untoward in the recent Internet history. He liked to visit news sites, and several of the pages he'd viewed referred to the police hunt for The Disciple, and the murders of George Rowan and Ivana Hanzha, but then he also liked to visit cookery and DIY sites. Officially, the terms of the search warrant didn't allow for a search of the hard drives of any computer on the premises, but Bolt made a copy of the hard drive anyway, figuring he could at least trawl through it unofficially.

Every five minutes, he received a radio update from the DS running the current surveillance team. Hope was still making deliveries, and none of the team knew how many more he had to make, but in the two days they'd been following him, he'd been back at 6.01 and 6.06 p.m. respectively, which meant they had to keep an eye on the time.

As it happened, it took Mo and Bolt barely half an hour to cover the whole house. As well as searching in every available bit of storage space, they'd also checked for any false walls, loose pieces of carpet and floorboards, under which a knife could be concealed, but without success.

'Nothing,' said Mo, joining Bolt at the top of the stairs. 'Either he's very careful, or he's innocent.'

'He's not innocent,' said Bolt, who was having difficulty keeping a lid on his frustration. He'd been expecting to find at least some clue to Hope's guilt, even if it was just a few books on devil worship, or some perverted porn in the Internet history of his laptop. Very few serious criminals hid all traces of their guilt, especially those who had no obvious reason to expect a visit from the law. He exhaled loudly. 'There's still one place left to look.' He pointed to the hatch above their heads that led into the loft.

Mo looked at his watch. 'Have we got time? It's 5.15. He's not going to be that much longer.'

'He's in Hayes at the moment, according to Grier, so even if he turned round and came straight back here, he'd be a good half hour. We've got time.'

'Did you see a ladder in here anywhere? Because I didn't.'

Bolt frowned. 'No, I didn't. And we searched the place well enough.'

'So he probably never goes up there.'

'Or he doesn't want anyone else going up there.' He grinned at Mo. 'Come on. Jump on my shoulders. I'll get you up there.'

Mo pulled a face. 'You're joking, aren't you?'

Bolt shrugged. 'Well, it's either that or I get on your shoulders.' At six foot three and weighing just short of fifteen stone, he was a lot bigger and heavier than Mo, who stood barely five foot eight.

'This is going to look very silly, boss.'

'Then it's a good thing no one's going to see us then, isn't it?' He went down on one knee and leaned forward.

With a shake of his head, Mo came over and gingerly sat down on his shoulders, while Bolt got slowly to his feet directly beneath the hatch. 'Christ, I think you need to lose some weight,' he muttered.

'I have. You obviously need to get to the gym more.' Mo hauled the hatch open with a grunt.

There was a sudden sound of something falling, and Mo

yelled out and threw himself backwards off Bolt's shoulders, sending the two of them crashing to the landing floor.

Bolt landed badly, the side of his head striking the corner of one of the walls. He turned round and saw that Mo had actually fallen back through the open door into Hope's bedroom, and was in the process of sitting up unsteadily and rubbing the back of his head. 'What the hell was that all about?'

Mo pointed. 'Look.'

Which was when Bolt saw the two-foot metal spike impaled in the landing carpet directly beneath the hatch, and barely an inch from the sole of his foot. Two lead dive weights had been tied to the spike to make it fall faster, and the whole contraption was attached to a taut length of cable that ran back into the darkness of the loft. What was certain was that it could easily have killed either of them if Mo hadn't reacted when he did. 'Jesus Christ, he booby-trapped it.'

Through the shock of their near miss, Bolt felt a sense of elation, because now he knew for certain that Leonard Hope was their man. No innocent person would install a device designed to kill anyone who tried to break into their loft. He had to be hiding something up there.

At that moment, the VHF radio in Bolt's jacket crackled into life. It was DS Dan Grier, the head of the surveillance team. 'Bravo One to Omega. Target X is now heading west on the A40, just passing the Polish War Memorial.'

Bolt sat up, wondering if Hope was on his way back home. 'Omega to Bravo One. What's the traffic like?'

'Thinner than usual, and he's making good time. I've got him going about fifty at the moment. Have you found anything useful yet?'

Bolt looked at the spike again. 'Not sure,' he answered, 'but whatever you do, don't lose him. I repeat: Do not lose him.

146

And keep us posted of his progress. We're going to be in here a few minutes yet.'

'Come on, boss, let's just get out of here,' said Mo as they got to their feet. 'We've got enough to charge him with now thanks to that bloody thing, and we can send the specialists up there later to check for any booby traps.'

Bolt could see that Mo was shaken up, and he couldn't blame him. He was shaken up too. But he was also curious. 'I want to know what he's hiding. I'm going up. I'll have to get on your shoulders.'

'But boss . . .'

'Look, I've sweated this case for six months now – we both have. If this is our man, I want to know now.'

Seeing that he wasn't going to persuade him otherwise, Mo reluctantly bent down and waited while Bolt clambered onto his shoulders and slowly lifted his head into the gloom of the loft.

'Well, well, well,' he said, shining his torch inside and seeing the crudely painted pentacles lining the walls. 'We've got him.'

Twenty-four

'Omega to Bravo One. Give me the target's current location.'

Bolt could hear the sound of his heart beating as he stood on the landing next to the metal spike still impaled on the floor. In his free hand, he was holding a clear plastic bag containing a still-bloodied hunting knife with a serrated edge, and what appeared to be two bent teeth on the blade where the pathologist had suggested they'd be. The chances of it not being the murder weapon in at least three of the murders had to be as close to zero as you were going to get. Bolt had found the knife within a couple of minutes of clambering into the loft. It was taped to the inside of the water tank, where Hope had made only a cursory attempt to hide it.

There was almost certainly plenty of other evidence against him up there as well. There'd been a desktop computer on a desk in one corner, and Bolt was certain it would provide a wealth of information. The loft – festooned as it was with Satanic symbols, and scrawled messages celebrating violence and death carved into the walls and supporting beams – was clearly the place where Leonard Hope relived his bloody crimes, and Bolt didn't want to spend any more time up there than he had to. A SOCO team could deal with all that. The important thing now was simply to get this bastard into custody, and fast.

'Bravo One to Omega. Target is proceeding south on Hangar Lane, just passing the turning to Beaufort Road now. At this rate and in this traffic, ETA is somewhere between five and seven minutes. Are you still inside? Over.'

'We are, and we're coming out now. We now have definite evidence that Hope's our man. I repeat: definite evidence, and we need to make an arrest ASAP. I want your whole team to follow him back here. We'll be waiting in our car on the street. As soon as he parks up, we take him down. Is that clear?'

'Bravo One to Omega. Clear as a bell. We're on him like glue.'

'Just make sure he doesn't spot the tail. We can't afford to mess this up.'

Bolt replaced the radio in his jacket pocket, keeping the mike open so he could hear the chatter of the surveillance team as they escorted an unsuspecting Leonard Hope right into the trap that they were laying for him, then turned to Mo. 'Right, are you ready?'

'Don't you think it would be best if we get a TSG team down here?' asked Mo, who was still looking a little pale as he followed his boss down the stairs.

Bolt smiled grimly. 'The bastard's caused me more sleepless nights than I care to remember, and that booby trap of his almost killed us, so I think we deserve to be the ones to make the collar.'

'To be honest, I'd just as happily leave it to the TSG. I'm a lover not a fighter.'

'As I've heard many times, my friend, but don't worry. I wouldn't put a Lothario like you at risk. You can hang back until we've got him safely under control, then join in. That way you can pretend you're both.' Bolt felt a sense of elation as they walked back to the car. They'd finally got the man who'd haunted his dreams, and made his life a misery these past few months.

But as they got back to the car, the surveillance chatter took on a renewed urgency. As Bolt yanked the radio out of his jacket, he heard Bravo One, DS Grier, shout that the target was making a break for it.

'Omega to Bravo One,' Bolt yelled into the handset, 'what the hell's going on?'

'Bravo One to Omega, suspect has just made a sharp turn into Woodville Gardens and is now heading west. He's going fast. I think he must have spotted the tail, although I can't see how.'

'Omega to Bravo One. Take him down now. We're on our way to meet you. Confirm the vehicle he's driving.'

'White Ford Ka van with Speedy Mail Couriers written on the side.'

As DS Grier reeled off the registration number, Mo started punching keys on the car's satnav.

'Find Woodville Gardens,' Bolt told him as Grier's voice came over the radio again, telling them that Hope had now made another turn, narrowly missing a woman pedestrian. 'He's driving like a lunatic,' shouted Grier. 'We may have to abandon the pursuit.'

'Omega to Bravo One, stick with him!' Bolt shouted into the radio as he pulled away from the kerb. 'We can't afford to lose this guy.'

'Up to the end of the street and turn right,' said Mo. 'We might be able to intercept him.'

'Call backup. I want this whole place flooded with coppers, plus helicopters. If he escapes, we've had it.'

Bolt barely stopped at the end of the street before swinging a hard right, and accelerating away. He couldn't believe that Hope had spotted the tail five minutes from home after it had been glued to him for the previous forty-eight hours. It was bad luck in the extreme, but that no longer mattered. The important thing was to stop him, but Bolt knew full well that if Hope continued to drive like a lunatic, especially in winding residential streets like this, and with darkness beginning to fall, they'd have to abandon the chase. The rules of police pursuits in the UK are some of the strictest in the world, and Bolt knew it wouldn't just be him who suffered if something went wrong – like a civilian getting injured, or even killed – but every other copper involved as well. But he wasn't prepared to give up now, not when they were this close to a man who'd murdered nine people.

'Next left,' hissed Mo, interrupting his conversation with the emergency dispatcher.

Bolt yanked the wheel, making the turn, imagining what the media would say if The Disciple escaped now. There'd be a firestorm, and he'd be right in the middle of it.

'Bravo One to all cars!' shouted Grier over the radio. 'He's just turned into Hillcroft Crescent, now heading north. He must be going sixty! Oh shit—'

'Omega to Bravo One, what's going on?'

'A car's just pulled out in front of us . . . He's blocking the road . . . We're trying to pass.' Bolt heard the sound of horns, and cursing. 'Bravo One to all cars, we've lost the eyeball. We think he might have turned into Park Hill.'

'All right, boss, we're near,' said Mo. 'Make a left here.'

Bolt barely slowed up as he turned into yet another residential street, the tyres of the Audi A4 he was driving wailing angrily. It was almost dark now and he knew he was going to have to be careful not to get in an accident. A primary school loomed up on the left, then a church. He saw a mother walking hand in hand with two young children and, hearing his rapid approach, she turned and gave him an angry look, motioning for him to slow down, although he wondered if she'd be quite so annoyed if she knew the identity of the man he was after. On the radio, the different cars of the surveillance team were communicating in short, urgent bursts, but it was clear that none of them had Hope's van in their sights.

'Okay, boss, left again up here. I think we may be able to cut him off.'

Gritting his teeth, Bolt made the turn.

'Park Hill's just up here on the right. It's about another fifty yards.'

But Mo had barely finished speaking when a white van came hurtling out of a side road, clipping a car parked on the other side, before righting itself and driving up the street away from them.

Bolt didn't even bother to read the registration number. He knew it was Hope and he slammed his foot hard on the accelerator, giving chase.

Up ahead, a car was coming down on the other side of the road, but it was veering out towards the middle. Hope, who was rapidly picking up speed, swerved to avoid it, hit another parked car and lost control of the van completely, scraping another couple of cars before mounting the pavement and smacking into a wall.

'Right we've got you now!' yelled Bolt triumphantly. Only fifty metres separated him from Hope's van and the speed he was going he'd cover the ground in a few seconds, and then finally they'd be able to take him down.

Up ahead, a figure jumped out of the van and sprinted away from it, while the car that had been coming the other way pulled up on some double yellow lines, its driver opening the door to get out.

Bolt sounded his horn to warn the driver to stay in the car, making no attempt to slow down.

'Careful, boss,' said Mo, gripping his seat, as Bolt raced towards the stricken van.

And then, as they drew level with the turning from which Hope's van had emerged only a few seconds earlier, a sudden glare of headlights loomed up out of nowhere as a car came flying out far too fast, shunting the Audi in the side like a bumper car and sending it spinning round a hundred and eighty degrees in a sickening shriek of metal. Bolt didn't have time to react before they hit a parked car sideways-on and came to a crunching halt.

For a second, neither he nor Mo moved. The other car was a few yards away, smoke rising from its ruined bonnet. Both occupants – a man and a woman – looked shocked but otherwise unhurt, and Bolt recognized them instantly as two of the surveillance team.

Then his instincts kicked in. Jumping out of the car, he shouted for Mo to follow him, and took off after Hope at a sprint. He could make out the faint wail of sirens coming from more than one direction, but they were still too far away to be of any help, and there was no immediate sign of the rest of the surveillance team. Grabbing his radio, he was about to shout his current location, but realized he didn't know the street name, so pocketed it. Right now he was on his own. And, full to the brim with adrenalin and aggression, that suited him just fine.

He couldn't see Hope any more, but there was no way he'd be hiding behind one of the cars. He'd be trying to put as much distance between himself and his pursuers as possible. There was a left turning up ahead and Bolt took it at a sprint. He didn't have time to look for a road sign but just kept running. Unlike Mo, he not only liked to keep fit, but also to make his own collars. Too many times these days, the detectives left it to the TSG, the Territorial Support Group (the Met's version of the Riot Police), to arrest the suspects, but for Bolt there was nothing better than taking down the person you'd been hunting. It was one of the great joys of the job and he felt a real exhilaration now as he ran alone down the cool, night street, ignoring the pain in his side from the impact of the crash.

Hope was in his sights now, thirty yards away and running, which was when Bolt noticed something strange. It looked as if he was on the phone. They'd always been convinced he was working alone, but it suddenly struck Bolt that maybe they were wrong. Maybe he had an accomplice. Serial killers had worked together before. It was rare but not unheard of, and, in this case, it made sense. It was no easy task to control and restrain a couple, but if there were two of you . . .

Bolt redoubled his pace, his footfalls heavy on the pavement. Hope was a big man and well built, but Bolt felt sure he could take him alone if he had to.

Hope must have heard his pursuit because he pocketed the phone and looked back over his shoulder, suddenly increasing his own pace, but he was nowhere near as fast as Bolt, and barely fifteen yards separated them now. Bolt felt his excitement growing. Hope was running like a desperate man, his gait ungainly, and there was no way he could keep it up for much longer.

When there were only ten yards between them, Hope turned into another side street, almost tripping over his feet in the process, and Bolt sensed victory. So much so that he didn't even slow down as he followed his quarry round the corner, and was subsequently completely surprised to see Hope right in front of him, swinging an arm through the air.

Bolt just had time to see that he was holding something big and solid in his hand, and then he felt a sudden excruciating pain in his cheek as the blow struck him, the force of it sending him falling sideways into the road. He landed next to a parked car and rolled over, temporarily dazed, his vision blurring.

He thought he heard a car starting nearby, but couldn't say for sure, because the next thing he knew, Mo Khan was kneeling next to him, asking if he was all right.

'Get after him,' he managed to say, although his voice sounded muffled, as if he'd just been anaesthetized.

Mo frowned, and then he said the words that Bolt had been dreading. 'He's gone, boss.'

And he had gone too. Within twenty minutes of Mo's first call for backup, a blanket cordon had been placed round an area of more than a square mile, and a full-scale house-by-house search was in progress, involving more than four hundred officers. It was widely believed that there was no way Leonard Hope could have left the area on foot without being apprehended, and yet twenty-four hours later, when the search ended, there was still no sign of him. There were no witness sightings; there was no footage of him on any of the many CCTV cameras surrounding the area; and there were no reports of stolen vehicles.

It was as if he'd disappeared into thin air.

Twenty-five

Today 19.00

Scope kayaked fast through the darkness, making good progress. The distance from Jock's place to Tayleigh along the river was just over 11 miles. It was a lot of ground to cover, but the wind had picked up from the east, and was helping to push him along as it whistled down the natural tunnel made by the river. Pine- and beech-covered hills rose up majestically on both sides of the water, and above him the first stars were beginning to appear, joining the thin slither of moon, and providing just enough light to see by, as Scope scanned both banks for any sign of the canoeists or the canoes.

He was no longer wondering why a local family of four had been targeted by professional thugs, including the scar-faced man he'd seen earlier. The simple fact was that they *had* been and, if it wasn't too late, then it was his duty to help them. What was really preying on his mind, though, was the fact that once again his life had been disrupted by violence. Sometimes it felt as if death stalked him like a relentless hunter. He could escape for a while – weeks; months; years sometimes – but it always caught up in the end, even here in one of the quietest, wildest parts of the country.

Scope considered himself a quiet, reasonable man. He preferred to turn his back on trouble. He liked people. Sometimes he even dreamed of meeting someone special again, and starting another family. Living happily ever after, as they did at the end of the movies. But it never worked out like that. And, whichever way he chose to look at it, he was fully prepared to use violence to achieve his ends. He'd killed six men in cold blood to avenge the death of his daughter, even though none of them had been directly responsible for Mary Ann's death. In the end, she'd voluntarily injected the heroin herself. Only one of the six he'd killed had even met her. And yet even when one of them – a young, mid-ranking dealer – had been on his knees begging and crying for mercy, Scope had put a bullet in his head, and only occasionally had he lost sleep over what he'd done. Other people would have gone to the police, let them deal with it, but Scope hadn't. He'd taken the law into his own hands.

It was the same when his nephew had been kidnapped six months earlier by men trying to blackmail the boy's father. He'd gone after the kidnappers himself and kept the police out of it. And now, here he was, paddling like a madman down a lonely river, far from the place he'd once called home, a gun in his waistband, his heart pumping, not just from the exertion of the last hour and a half, or from the intensity of killing a man, but from something else. The excitement of what he was doing. A part of Scope – a very primitive part – was actually enjoying this.

He was going to miss Jock. He was going to miss this place too. He stopped paddling for a moment, getting his breath back, and looked up at the vast night sky as it stretched over towards the west, where just the faintest hint of pink glowing light still lingered. Sometimes, at night, Scope would sit outside the tiny cottage he rented, and watch the stars that swarmed across the night sky, wondering if his wife and daughter were up there, watching him. The air up here was sharp and fresh and, as he sat in the kayak, he took a long deep breath, thinking that the scene in front of him – the tar-black river vaguely shimmering in the light of the moon, and the forest rising up on either side of it – was much the same as it would have been a thousand, even a million years ago. It made him feel insignificant, a tiny intruder in a tiny boat who would soon be gone, while this would remain here forever. Right now, knowing that he was about to risk his life to help people he'd never met, it was a comforting thought.

Somewhere amidst the greenery came the plaintive call of a heron, breaking the silence, and Scope began paddling again, keeping close to the bank as he rode a series of shallow rapids, enjoying the sensation of the kayak bouncing up and down in the water.

And then, as he rounded a bend in the river, he saw the two Canadian canoes sitting on a sand spit that jutted out from the left-hand bank thirty yards in front of him. He rode the kayak onto the spit and climbed out, looking around. The two canoes were about five yards apart, and straight away Scope noticed there was no sign of any paddles, which struck him as odd. There was something else too. A long dark stain running down the inside of one of them, next to the back seat. He'd picked up a mini-Maglite torch at Jock's and he shone it at the stain, tensing as he realized it was blood. Then he saw the golf-ball-sized holes at various points in the canoe. He counted five of them on one side, and a corresponding number on the other.

There was no doubt in Scope's mind that they'd been caused by bullets, and from a high-calibre weapon as well. The entry holes appeared to be on the right side of the canoe, suggesting someone had been shooting at the canoeists from somewhere on the other side of the river. Looking in that direction, Scope saw a small gap in the trees at the top of the hill, and recognized the lookout point. So the shooter had been up there and, for whatever reason, he'd ambushed the canoeists as they'd paddled downriver.

He'd clearly hit at least one of them, and yet there was no sign of any bodies.

Turning away, Scope walked slowly into the trees that ran down to the bank, which was where he found the bodies of the man and the woman. Their names, Scope remembered Jock as saying, were Tim and Jean Robinson, a local couple from somewhere up between Tayleigh and Inverness. Tim Robinson was lying sprawled over the top of his wife and, as Scope shone the torch down, he could see that he'd been shot in the back, roughly between the shoulder blades, by someone who knew what they were doing when it came to high-velocity rifles. Jean Robinson was lying on her back beneath her husband, staring upwards. Her eyes were open and a thin trail of dried blood ran from one corner of her mouth.

Scope wasn't sure how long they'd been dead, but it looked as though it had been a while. Although he was wearing gloves, he didn't want to touch the bodies and contaminate the scene. He was in enough trouble as it was, and it would be far better if no one knew he'd ever been here. According to Jock, the Robinsons had been with their two nieces who were up from London. One was only a young girl, whom Jock had described as a real sweetheart, and Scope didn't know how he'd handle finding her body, if it was round here. Ever since he'd become a father, aged only nineteen himself, he'd been hugely protective of young children. He hated the idea of them suffering violence. He'd done two tours in Iraq during his decade in the army, and during the second tour, an IED meant for the patrol he was a part of, had been detonated prematurely by the insurgents who'd been lying in wait for them, killing two boys riding past on a rusty old bicycle instead. The boys had only ridden past the patrol a few seconds earlier. They'd been smiling and laughing as they balanced precariously on the bike, and Scope remembered smiling back at them, thinking at the time that – wherever you went in the world – kids were always kids. They'd been no more than twelve, those boys, and the impact from the blast had flung their bodies more than fifty feet through the hot desert air. They'd landed in the dirt just in front of the lead soldier in the patrol, and Scope remembered vividly the scene of chaos as, deafened by the blast, they'd all dived for cover at the side of the road, several of the men letting off bursts of gunfire into the surrounding uninhabited scrubland in a vain attempt to flush out the insurgents.

He also remembered the moment he and some of the others had rushed over to the two injured boys who lay writhing on the road. They'd been torn apart by the pieces of shrapnel that had been packed into the bomb. The smaller of the two was missing a leg and half an arm, and there was a gaping hole in his throat that smoked and sizzled. As the medic – a guy called Sherman who killed himself two years later – bent down to administer some kind of first aid, the boy had stared up at Scope, his eyes wide with fear and shock, and Scope had had to look away because all he could see was his own daughter lying there in place of the boy, with limbs missing and body burned, bloody and smoking. As the boy succumbed to his terrible injuries, along with his friend, Scope had stood at the side of the road, eyes clamped shut, his whole body shaking as he tried to force the nightmarish images from his mind.

He'd never been able to understand how anyone could hurt innocent kids, and yet he knew there were people out there who were fully prepared to. As he stood amongst the trees now, he wondered if whoever had shot up these canoes had already killed the two he was looking for.

But when he shone his torch round, there was no sign of any other bodies. He tried to work out what had happened here. The shooter had been firing from the other side of the river. Clearly, he'd killed the two adults but, since there was no sign of the children, either the shooter had had accomplices on this side of the river to pick them up, which seemed unlikely since they were a good few miles from the road here, or, more likely, they'd escaped. But if the children were up from London it was unlikely they knew the area. If Scope were them, he'd try and put as much distance between himself and the river as possible. He didn't know the area that well himself, but he was fairly certain that the path that ran roughly parallel to the river for about twenty miles, and eventually led back into Tayleigh, was a few hundred metres south of him through the trees. If the children had kept in a roughly straight line, they'd have got to it eventually, although they might have missed it, or chosen to make their way further into the forest.

Deciding it was the best place just to start looking for them, and for the men who were hunting them, Scope zipped up his jacket, took a deep breath, and began running through the trees, not sure what the hell he was getting involved with, but determined to see it through.

After all, what else would he be doing tonight?

Twenty-six

Today 19.10

'Look, I haven't been entirely honest with you,' said Amanda.

'No,' said Jess. 'I thought not.'

They were standing in the living room of the house where they'd found shelter. Next door, Casey was flat out in the single bedroom. Jess was amazed that she was able to sleep after everything that had happened today, but she was thankful she was. The less she dwelt on the deaths of Tim and Jean, the better. They'd searched the house from top to bottom just in case there was a phone hidden anywhere, but there wasn't. They had, however, found some women's clothes in the upstairs bedroom. It was mainly walking gear and Jess was now dressed in a woollen jumper that was at least two sizes too big for her, and which itched, and a pair of waterproof trousers that crinkled when she walked. But at least she was dry now, and with the heating clanking away in the house, she was also warm for the first time since she'd fallen in the river.

They'd kept the lights off so as not to attract attention, and

Jess eyed Amanda coolly through the darkness, feeling a flash of anger. She'd always had a hot temper, it was one of her downfalls, and she needed to keep a lid on it now. 'So what's really happening? And why are these people after you?'

Amanda sighed. 'You've heard about The Disciple, haven't you?'

Jess nodded. You'd have to have been living at the bottom of a mineshaft for the last year not to know about The Disciple. 'Yeah, I've heard of him. He's meant to be on the run, isn't he?'

'That's right.' She paused. 'Well, he murdered a couple three weeks ago – a man and his lover who were together in the man's home.'

'I heard about that. Didn't the wife walk in on it?'

'Yes, she did.'

The truth dawned on Jess then. 'And the wife was you?'

Amanda smiled grimly. 'They managed to keep my photo out of the papers. The police wanted me to stay down south until they'd arrested the killer, but I wanted to get as far away from what happened as possible, which is how I ended up here.'

Jess looked at her carefully, still not entirely sure whether to believe her or not. 'And you think it's The Disciple chasing us now?'

Amanda shook her head firmly. 'No. I was ambushed today by three men, and I saw all their faces. A few days ago, I was shown a photo of the Disciple suspect, Leonard Hope, and he definitely wasn't one of them. And this is where I really was telling the truth. I have no idea who these men are, or why they want me.'

'Why should I believe you?'

'Because I've got no reason to lie, Jess. Look, I've involved you both enough already, and I regret that, I honestly do. Just like I regret what happened to your aunt and uncle. But the point is, it's me they want, not you and Casey. Without me you'll be safe, so the best thing is if I leave you here and make my own way back to the nearest town.'

Jess felt a flash of panic at the thought of being left here alone with Casey.

Amanda must have seen the look on her face because she gave Jess a reassuring smile. 'As soon as I get to civilization, I'll send the police back here for you, I promise.'

'How far is it?'

'About five miles across country. Alone, I could probably make it in an hour and a half, and have help back here in two.'

Jess wasn't convinced. 'Don't you think we should stick together?'

'It'll take too long with Casey, and we'll be too exposed. It's best if I go alone. They won't come looking for you here.' She stepped forward and put a hand on Jess's shoulder, giving it a squeeze. It was a curiously intimate gesture.

Jess thought about it. Amanda was right. Casey would slow them all down if they tried to cross country, but the idea of the two of them stuck here alone and vulnerable in a place they didn't know, didn't make her feel much better either.

'What happens if you don't make it?' she asked Amanda.

Amanda took her hand away from Jess's shoulder and frowned. 'If I don't make it, you're better off staying put, anyway, but I'm pretty sure I will. I don't think these guys know the area that well. It's dark now and there's a lot of country out there. Just keep the lights out and stay hidden. If I send help back, I'll come with them, and I'll knock on the door four times in quick succession, then pause. Then one more knock. That way you'll know it's me. Don't let anyone else in, no matter who they say they are. If no one comes out back tonight, it means they've got me, which means they won't be interested in looking for you, but – either way – make sure you wait until daylight before looking for help. Do you understand?'

Jess nodded, knowing there was no point in trying to persuade Amanda to stay with them. 'I understand.' She paused a moment before asking the next question. 'But if they want to get you so badly, why didn't they just shoot you when you were in the canoe?'

'Because they want me alive. Don't ask me why, but whatever the reason is, it's not a nice one.' Amanda took a deep breath. 'I've got to go. Look after your little sister, and stay calm. Okay?'

'Okay.' Jess watched as Amanda went out through the back door, then bolted it behind her, before retreating into the darkness of the house, suddenly feeling very alone.

Twenty-seven

The three men made a menacing sight as they moved purposefully down the forest path in a tight line, the two Dobermans
that MacLean had brought back with him straining at their
leashes. Each of them was armed with a pistol with suppressor
attached, while Keogh also carried the Remington .303 rifle
he'd used to shoot at the canoeists earlier, and the big cop
MacLean was armed with a five-shot automatic shotgun as
well, capable of bringing down a horse.

By now, Keogh was even more worried. Not only had he
still not heard any word from Mehdi, but they'd been walking
for a good half-hour through the forest and there was still
no sign of their quarry. MacLean was confident that they'd
be coming up from the river on this path, since it was the
only one that led directly out of the woods, and that they
wouldn't have made it this far by now, but Keogh wasn't
so sure. Amanda Rowan would be doing her utmost to hide,
which meant keeping off obvious paths like this one, and
in a forest this size, with all manner of animals living in it,

the dogs were going to have a hard time picking up their scent.

The only bonus was that, from what Keogh had heard, MacLean had some experience of hunting people in this kind of terrain, and not in the course of his police work, either. As well as being a copper, MacLean looked after the boss's country estate in the nearby Cairngorms, and some pretty unpleasant things happened up there. Rumour had it that the boss kept young women imprisoned in the cellars of his manor house, where they were sexually abused, sometimes for weeks on end, before being killed and buried in the grounds. The women were mainly foreign prostitutes working illegally in the country, so they wouldn't be missed, and Keogh wasn't sure if it was just the boss himself who abused the girls, or whether his contacts in the criminal and business worlds were also involved. What he did know, however, was that the previous year, one of the women had escaped and been found by a group of hikers up from London, and it had been up to MacLean and his brother to hunt the five of them down before they raised the alarm. They'd done it too, eliminating both the woman fugitive and all the hikers, with the help of their mother (she, apparently, had been the one who'd hanged the last hiker to be murdered, a female teacher from London, in an effort to make her death look like a suicide). Keogh was hoping that MacLean could manage the same thing again tonight, although he also hoped that Amanda had split from the kids. He didn't want their deaths on what was left of his conscience.

He turned to MacLean. 'How much further on do you think they'll be? They've had two and a half hours to cover the ground.'

'They'll be cold and wet, and there's a kid with them, so they'll be slow,' growled MacLean in his thick Highlands burr.

'But, even so, we ought to run into them in the next fifteen minutes.'

'If they came this way.'

MacLean glared at him, his strange, round baby face looking almost demonic in the watery light of the moon. 'They'll have come this way. If they'd gone along the river, they'd have been in Tayleigh by now, and I'd have heard about it.' He patted the phone in his pocket. 'Don't worry. Even if they try to hide, the dogs will pick them up. They're trained to go after people, not animals.'

Keogh looked down at the two wiry-looking Dobermans and was pleased they weren't after him. 'Why don't we let them off the lead now? See what they pick up?'

'Don't worry. I trained these two myself. When they get a scent, we'll know about it.' Without breaking stride, MacLean examined the map by torchlight. 'There should be a waterfall coming up soon, and a few hundred yards east from that, there's a house.'

Keogh tensed. 'A house? I thought you said this wood was deserted.'

'It's the only house in the forest, and you'd have to know how to find it.'

'Well, if they get there and raise the alarm, we're finished.'

'We'd better make sure they don't get there then,' said MacLean, as the two dogs stopped and began growling. He turned to Keogh and grinned. 'What did I tell you? They've got the scent.'

Twenty-eight

Amanda knew she had two options. She could either follow the single-lane track that led up from the house to the Tayleigh Road, or continue along the footpath through the woods.

As she left the house, she chose the footpath because it offered more hiding places and was, in her opinion, a less likely route for her pursuers to take. Amanda was a fit woman and she moved easily through the forest at a run, breathing in the fresh, cold air. Progress was a lot faster without the two girls in tow. In reality she'd had little choice but to take them with her for the first part of the journey, but she was glad they were no longer with her now, knowing they'd be far safer staying in the house.

For her own part, Amanda was terrified. She couldn't believe she'd been targeted by a highly organized gang who seemed determined to kill her. When she'd found out from DCS Mike Bolt that they'd identified a suspect in the Disciple case, and that he was on the run, she'd been nervous, but not unduly so. There was no reason why he would follow her up here, or even have a clue where she was living. That information, as far as she was aware, was only known to the investigating team, and to one trusted friend whom she'd known for close to twenty years, and who would never betray her. And yet these men had found her, and she could only assume that they were somehow connected to the Disciple case.

The problem was, she couldn't understand why they wanted her. They obviously thought she knew something, but what? Amanda knew nothing about The Disciple that wasn't already known to the police.

Unless . . .

It hit her for the first time. A possible motive for her abduction. Something that truly was worth killing for. Amanda felt a coldness enveloping her as the thought took hold, because she knew that if she was right, then this was the end. She was finished.

But how could they know? How could they possibly know?

Amanda stopped running, telling herself to calm down. There was no way anyone could know about *that*. She shut her eyes and took some deep breaths, absorbing the silence of the forest.

And that was when she heard it.

The sound of dogs barking. Big dogs. Hunting dogs, probably. Not the kind of dogs that people took for walks.

And the barking was getting closer.

Twenty-nine

Jess stood in the darkness at the foot of the bed, staring down at her sister.

Casey was fast asleep, with her head to one side, the position she always slept in, her blonde hair cascading down over her shoulders. Her mouth was ever so slightly open, her breathing coming in soft gasps, and she looked so peaceful that Jess didn't have the heart to wake her.

It seemed strange that, even though they weren't related by blood, Jess loved her so completely. But she did. These days, Casey was the only family she had left. Jess rarely thought about her biological family. On those few occasions that she did, it made her guts wrench and filled her with a cold dread. There were memories there that were far best forgotten, whatever the counsellors she'd spent so much time seeing in those early years might have said. All her love had gone into her adoptive family. The people she considered her real parents. They'd been the ones who'd taken her in – a damaged, hard-faced young girl whose innocence had long since gone – and brought her up as one of their own, showing her a love that she'd never experienced before.

And now Mum and Dad were gone too, and it was just her and Casey left. Two sisters against the whole world.

'I'm going to keep you safe,' she whispered in the heavy silence of the room, resisting the urge to reach out and touch the soft skin of her sister's face, even though she desperately wanted to. Jess knew this was no time for sentimentality. For the next few hours she had to remain strong. If they stayed here, help would come eventually. She was sure of that. Amanda seemed like the kind of person who could get herself out of most situations – she had the kind of confidence about her that good teachers had, or politicians on the TV. She'd be back with help.

She had to be.

Turning away from the bed, she headed back into the kitchen. She was hungry and thirsty, and although there was no food in the fridge, she could at least grab some water. She found a glass and went over to the kitchen tap, staring out of the huge hole in the window where they'd broken in earlier as she poured herself a drink.

Which was when she heard the barking.

Jess froze. Amanda had told her there weren't any other houses around, so who could be out here in the middle of a forest at this time of night with their dogs? Because there was more than one of them and they were making a hell of a noise.

Fighting down a rising sense of panic, Jess searched the kitchen drawers, her movements frantic, until she found a large kitchen knife. She picked it up gingerly, immediately feeling sick. Holding a weapon like this brought the darkest moments in her life rushing back, and for a second she thought she was going to faint. She let the moment pass, telling herself she needed to be brave, for Casey's sake as well as her own. Her grip on the handle tightened and she lightly touched the blade. It wasn't sharp but it would do. She thought about trying to find a weapon for Casey but knew that she would never be able to use it. Casey couldn't hurt a fly. Their best bet was to hide and hope for the best.

But, as she hurried back through the hallway towards the room where Casey was asleep, Jess was startled by a loud knocking on the front door. Four quick raps, a pause. Then another single rap.

Wondering if this was some kind of trick, she crept over to the door.

'It's me, Amanda,' hissed a voice on the other side. 'Let me in, for Christ's sake.' She sounded breathless and scared.

Jess unlocked the door and Amanda came barging through. 'They're coming,' she explained frantically as Jess relocked the door. 'And it sounds like they've got dogs.' They faced each other and Amanda's gaze fell on the knife in Jess's hand.

'I know. I've just heard them.'

'They've got guns and there are at least three of them. We can't stay here. We've got to go.'

'Where? If they've got dogs, they'll catch us.'

'We need to distract them.' Amanda looked as if she was thinking hard, and Jess was glad that she was here again. 'There was meat in the freezer, wasn't there?'

'I don't know. I didn't see.'

'Go and check. Now. I'm going to see if they've got a microwave.'

At that moment, Casey appeared in the doorway, rubbing her eyes, dressed only in the Buzz Lightyear dressing gown that was far too small for her. 'What's going on?' she asked, looking nervous as she saw the urgency in Jess and Amanda's expressions.

'We have to leave,' Amanda told her. 'And you need to be very quiet.'

'But I can't go out like this. I'll be cold.'

'Your clothes are probably dry by now, babe,' said Jess. 'They're on the radiators down here. Why don't you go and put them on as quickly as possible, okay?'

Casey nodded and ran off to find her clothes. 'Don't turn any lights on, whatever you do,' Amanda called after her, then grabbed Jess roughly by the arm. 'Go and get the meat. We've hardly got any time.'

Jess remembered seeing the freezer in a utility room off the kitchen, and she went to it now, conscious that the dogs' barking seemed to be getting closer.

The freezer was about half full, with ready meals on one side and packaged meat on the other. Jess grabbed a couple of packs of frozen sausages and ran back into the kitchen.

'Right, I've found the microwave,' said Amanda. 'Give that here.' She grabbed the sausages and flung them inside, switching the microwave onto full power to heat them up. 'Now, make sure Casey's ready, for God's sake. We haven't got much time.'

Trying hard to ignore the pounding of her heart, Jess ran back into the hallway where Casey sat in a T-shirt and pants, trying to pull on a still-damp sock. 'I can't find my shoes,' she said, her voice breaking with fear. 'And I can hear dogs. Are they coming here?'

Casey was scared of dogs. She had been ever since the age of six when, while out with Jess at the local park, she'd leaned down to pet a terrier tied to a fence and it had bitten her hand and refused to let go. Jess had had to prise the dog's jaws open with her bare hands to make him release his grip, and finally he had, although he'd also bitten Jess in the process. When the owner, a huge woman with a sour face and a whole brood of kids, had come over, she'd tried to blame Casey for the dog's behaviour, even though Casey was standing there crying her eyes out. But Jess had stood up to the woman, taking photos of her and her scraggy hound and threatening to report them both. The woman had tried to grab the camera but Jess had cut her down with a glare that said that if she tried anything, it would be worse for her, and the woman had backed off.

'It's okay,' Jess told her sister soothingly now, trying to keep the ice-cold fear out of her voice as she helped Casey to get one sock on, then the other. 'We're going to be leaving in a moment, and Amanda's getting some food ready for the dogs, so they won't be interested in us. And your shoes are over here.' She retrieved Casey's brand-new Van pumps from a radiator in the single bedroom on the ground floor. They were still wet, as was every other item of Casey's clothing, but there was nothing that could be done about that now.

'Where are my jeans?'

Jess looked round frantically, conscious that every second they wasted brought the men hunting them closer. 'We'll get them in a moment.' It was taking every ounce of mental strength to stop the fear weighing her down. She didn't want to die. God, she didn't want to die. Not here, in this cold, dark place, hundreds of miles from the home where she'd been raised. And, more than anything else, she couldn't bear the thought of them hurting Casey.

'Keep strong,' she told herself, as she helped Casey on with her shoes, noticing that her hands were shaking. 'Keep strong. Keep strong. Keep strong.'

The microwave bleeped, and through the open door of the kitchen, Jess saw Amanda pull out the steaming packs of sausages, juggling them between her hands before chucking them on the kitchen floor and wrapping them up inside the wet clothes that Amanda and she had been wearing when they'd first arrived. 'Right,' said Amanda, catching her eye. 'We've got to go. Right now.' She jumped up and ran past them to the front door.

Jess didn't need telling twice. Pulling Casey to her feet and ignoring her complaint that she hadn't got her jeans on yet, she clutched her sister's hand and followed Amanda out through the front door and into the cold night air.

Even as they sprinted across the empty driveway and towards the thick laurel hedge that bordered the front of the property, they heard the sound of the dogs arriving at the back of the house, and barking wildly as they stopped near the back door. Worse, Jess could hear the sound of footsteps coming from round the side of the house as someone approached the front.

Amanda must have heard the footsteps too because, motioning them to follow, she forced her way into the laurel hedge, immediately disappearing from view. Holding Casey in front of her, Jess threw the knife she was still holding into the hedge, then swung round and threw herself and Casey backwards into the thick greenery, ignoring the pain as the branches tore her skin, before landing on her back, her shoulder blade pressed painfully into a knobbly root sticking out of the dirt.

They were just in time. Through the tiny gaps in the leaves, Jess could see the bottom half of a man dressed in dark clothing. A barrel of a shotgun was visible just in front of him as he walked round the front of the house, moving slowly, barely ten yards away from them. Jess held her breath, putting a hand over Casey's mouth and holding her absolutely still. If they made even the faintest sound they'd be discovered – and then they'd be dead.

But it seemed the man hadn't heard them. He kept moving round the house before disappearing from view. A few seconds later, Jess heard voices coming from round the other side of the house, but she couldn't hear what they were saying.

A few seconds later, they heard a male voice with an English accent call out loudly: 'If you're in there, come out. We only want to talk to you. If you stay where you are, then we're going to let the dogs on you, and you're going to get hurt. Understand? You *will* get hurt.'

'The dogs have picked up the scent of the meat,' whispered Amanda, invisible amidst the laurel a few feet away. 'We need to move while we've got a head start.'

Jess still didn't see how they could outrun the dogs, because as soon as the men realized they weren't inside the house, which would only be a matter of a couple of minutes, they'd be after them again. But she also knew there was no point staying put so, releasing her grip on Casey, she rolled over, retrieved the knife, and crawled through the dirt, forcing aside the laurel roots, whispering for her sister to stay right behind her.

Coming out the other side, Jess turned and pulled Casey through, and Casey cried out as her stomach scraped against a low-lying branch.

'Sshh,' hissed Amanda, putting a finger to her lips, her eyes flashing with fear and anger, and then she turned and began running through the trees.

Casey's face crumpled up as she fought back tears and Jess lifted her to her feet and held her close. 'Quiet baby,' she whispered in her ear. 'Be brave for me. This won't last much longer, I promise.' Grabbing her hand, Jess took off after Amanda, who didn't look as though she planned on waiting around. Jess went as fast as she could with an exhausted ten-year-old in tow, but knew it almost certainly wasn't fast enough.

They were back in the woods again now but, close by, Jess could see a single-track road that led down to the cottage.

And then she saw something else.

Headlights, appearing through the trees on the horizon.

And they were coming this way.

Thirty

Today 19.35

Tony Hansen had had enough of his wife. He and Jackie had been married for twelve years now, and he reckoned that for most of the last ten of them she'd been driving him insane. It was the constant nagging. She nagged him about literally anything: his haircut; his job; his clothes; the way he left the toilet seat up when he peed in the middle of the night. At first he'd tried to react to her complaints by modifying his behaviour (when she'd told him she hated his flowery shirts, he'd stopped wearing them), but all that happened was that she'd start on about something else, and slowly it dawned on him that his wife was never going to be happy unless she was picking holes in him about something.

The fact was, he'd have divorced her years ago, but then she'd got pregnant with Jody (Christ, he'd hated that name, especially for a boy, but Jackie had been adamant and he knew better than to argue), and now there was no way he could leave her. He was trapped in a loveless marriage, and there was no way out of it. He'd tried to make things better by buying the holiday cottage up here in the country. They both liked walking, and wanted to encourage Jody, who was now six, to enjoy the great outdoors. In fact, when he was up here amidst the forests and hills, Tony was at his happiest. Even Jackie's nagging seemed to slip effortlessly off him like the morning mist over the nearby river.

But right now she was driving him mad. She'd wanted him to drive up here via the A9, but he'd chosen the A93 instead, because the A9 had major roadworks between Dunkeld and Pitlochry. Unfortunately, it had taken him longer than he'd thought, and Jackie had been giving him trouble about it ever since. This was their first time away from Jody in over a year. They'd left him with Jackie's mother while they spent four days up here cele-brating (and he used the term loosely) their anniversary. They'd originally wanted to head for the Canaries for a bit of sun, but it seemed too far for such a short space of time and, anyway, money was scarce now that Tony had had to take a ten per cent pay cut at work – another thing she'd nagged him about, as if he had a choice in it.

The car had thankfully descended into a truce-like silence as he drove down the hill towards the cottage on the final leg of their three-hour journey. They'd picked up a curry at the only takeaway in Tayleigh and Tony had some beers in a cold box in the boot. He was finally thinking about properly relaxing. They'd get the heating on, watch a bit of telly. God forbid, maybe even have sex . . .

'Look, Tony. The lights are on in the cottage.'

Disturbed from his reverie, Tony looked up and saw the sloping roof of the cottage through the trees. Jackie was right. The bedroom light was definitely on, and there could be no innocent reason for it either. They never left the lights on when they left, and they no longer had a cleaner, or even a neighbour who looked after the place.

'Can you see, Tony? Can you see?'

'Aye, course I can see.'

'I think we should call the police.' Jackie fumbled in her pocket for her mobile.

'Let's take a look first,' he said, slowing down as he got nearer the cottage. He could see now that the lights on the ground floor were on as well.

'But what if it's burglars and they're still there? Come on. You need to call the police.' She tried to hand him the phone but he didn't take it.

'And tell them what? That the lights are on in our cottage and they shouldn't be? We need to see what's happened first.'

'I don't like this,' Jackie announced warily as he drove into the driveway and stopped, switching off the engine.

'Ah shit, we've been burgled,' he said, seeing the broken kitchen window. 'God knows what they were after. There's nothing there.'

'I knew we should have got a bloody alarm. What did I tell you? The place is too bloody isolated.'

But Tony was looking up at the bedroom window. 'Christ Almighty. There's someone moving up there. They're still here.'

'Let's go,' said Jackie fearfully as he fumbled for his keys, suddenly wishing he hadn't turned off the engine. 'Come on, come on.' She shook his arm as if this would speed him up, her eyes wide with panic.

Behind her, a shadow moved outside the passenger door and the next second there was a deafening bang, very close.

Tony shut his eyes instinctively, and when he opened them a split second later, his face had been sprayed with a warm liquid, and Jackie was tottering in her seat, with a large chunk of the side of her head missing. One eye was gone, and the other was open and staring sightlessly into the distance. Blood and pieces of brain covered the whole of the car's interior, and Tony knew that that was what was covering his face too.

Jackie fell sideways and slumped in her seat. Dead. Gone. Finished. Outside, the man who'd fired the fatal shot was standing beside the bonnet aiming his rifle at Tony. Tony couldn't see his face, and didn't want to.

Dropping the keys, he yanked open the driver's door and jumped out, moving surprisingly fast for a man who was a good three stone overweight. But he was never going to make it. He heard the second shot ring out, felt a huge pressure on his back, as if someone had dropped a rock on it, and fell forward onto the driveway, hitting it face first.

Moaning more in shock than anything else, still unable to process the fact that his wife had just been murdered, he rolled over onto his back as the man with the rifle came round the front of the car and stood over him.

'What did you have to turn up here for?' said the man, in a tone that was more annoyed than anything else. He had a hard, expressionless face, with two thin scars running across it like train tracks, and straight away Tony knew this was a man who was never going to show him any mercy. As if to prove the point, the gunman pushed the end of the barrel against his cheek.

Flinching from the heat of the metal, Tony raised a hand and tried to cry out, knowing it was useless, and thinking in his last moments that he was going to miss Jackie, and that perhaps she hadn't been so bad after all.

Then the shot rang out.

Keogh turned away from the driver's corpse, unable to believe how badly wrong things were going. Two more civilians caught in the crossfire. Five dead in all, now, and one of his men missing. And still no sign of Amanda Rowan. The dogs were in the house but, though they'd found a pack of sausages wrapped in wet clothes, which must have been left to attract them to the scent, there was no sign of either her or the two kids. Either they were hidden extremely well in the house or, far more likely, they were gone.

He looked back across the woods, scanning them for any sign of movement, but they were utterly still.

'You're round here somewhere, Amanda,' he whispered into the darkness. 'And when I find you, I'm going to make you pay for this.'

Thirty-one

Jess covered Casey's ears and pulled her close as the third shot rang out, its retort reverberating through the trees like a thunderclap, making them all flinch.

They'd stopped in a small clearing twenty yards from the single-track road and about a hundred yards up the hill from the house where, barely five minutes earlier, they'd been sheltering. Jess's mouth was bone dry and she felt sick. 'What do you think just happened?' she asked urgently.

'I think the car that just drove down belonged to the owner of the house,' whispered Amanda. 'I think he must have disturbed the men who are looking for us.'

'And they just killed him?' The full force of the danger they were in hit Jess like a sledgehammer.

'I'm going back for the owner's car.'

'What do you mean? You're going to steal it?'

'You heard what just happened. The guy didn't even get a chance to get out of his car. The keys are probably still in there.'

'You can't go back there.' Jess thought of the three shots, and wondered if the little boy who owned the Buzz Lightyear dressing gown was one of the dead.

Amanda's expression was determined. 'It's our only chance. You two don't have to come. You can wait here. When you hear me drive up, come out onto the side of the road and I'll pick you up.'

It struck Jess then that she didn't trust Amanda enough to rely on her to stop once she'd got the car on the track, especially if there were armed men and dogs chasing her. 'I'll come with you.' She looked down at her sister. 'Casey, you stay here and wait for us, okay? We'll just be a couple of minutes.'

'I don't want to,' said Casey, looking terrified. She was still clutching her jeans in her hands like some kind of comfort blanket. 'What if something happens to you?'

'Nothing will. I promise.' Jess wasn't at all sure she believed what she was saying. In many ways going back to the house was madness, but she wasn't prepared to let Amanda go back on her own and, at least if anything did happen to them, the chances were that the men wouldn't go after Casey.

She stroked her sister's head. 'We'll be two minutes. Put your jeans on, and when you hear the car, get over to the road, and check it's us before you show yourself. Okay?'

Casey nodded and Jess pulled away from her, blew her a kiss, and followed Amanda as they raced back through the trees, not daring to look behind them, and all the time she was praying she was doing the right thing.

They slowed up when they reached the laurel hedge and followed it until they reached the entrance to the driveway, moving as silently as possible. Amanda looked round the corner of the hedge, then turned and motioned for Jess to follow her. From somewhere in the house, Jess could hear shouting. It sounded as if the men were trying to get the dogs to stop doing something, but she couldn't quite make out the words. They were close by, though, and Jess felt her legs shaking as she and Amanda crept onto the driveway and made their way towards the back of the car. The body of a man in a dark tracksuit lay on its back near the driver's door, a pool of blood forming on the ground round his head. Jess turned away quickly.

'Go round the other side and get in,' whispered Amanda as she turned towards the driver's side.

Jess continued round towards the passenger door, keeping as close to the car as possible, thankful that it was a concrete rather than a gravel driveway, so that her approach wasn't quite as audible. Suddenly she saw a tough-looking guy appear in the kitchen. The light was on in there and she could see him clearly, only a few yards away. He had scars on his face and he was carrying a rifle and looking down at something at his feet. Then he turned and looked out in Jess's direction.

Jess froze where she was, praying he wouldn't notice her, because if he did, she was dead.

For what felt like a long time but was probably only a couple of seconds, the man stayed where he was, looking out, then he turned away. 'Come on, they're not here,' she heard him call out to whoever was in there with him, his voice carrying through the broken kitchen window. 'They must have made a dash for it.'

Creeping forward quickly, Jess opened the passenger door, flinching when she saw a woman lying with her back to her in the passenger seat, a great chunk missing from the top of her head. The windscreen and dashboard were covered in gore and thick splats of blood, some of which were still dripping, and a horrible smell of shit hung heavily in the air.

Amanda was leaning in the other side of the car, searching frantically for the keys. 'I can't see them,' she hissed. 'Are they over your side?'

Jess looked on the floor, trying hard to ignore the corpse in the seat. She couldn't see them anywhere, and when she looked back up, the scar-faced man was no longer in the kitchen. A shadow appeared through the frosted glass panel in the front door, and she heard the sound of the dogs' paws scrabbling against the woodwork.

Fear surged through her. 'We've got to go,' she whispered desperately. 'They're going to see us any second . . .'

'Hold on,' hissed Amanda. 'Give me one moment.' Turning away, she crept quickly over to the driver's corpse while Jess stared at the door, waiting for it to open, racked by indecision.

'I've got them.' Amanda lifted up the keys and jumped back in the car. 'Get rid of her and get in quick,' she added, motioning towards the woman's body as she shoved the key into the ignition with shaking hands.

A day ago the idea of handling a freshly murdered corpse would have been impossible to imagine for Jess. But now her survival instinct kicked in and she grabbed the dead woman by the collar of her lurid pink tracksuit top and yanked her out, dumping her on the driveway before jumping in the passenger seat just as the front door to the house flew open, and the scar-faced guy appeared in the gap, the rifle held out in front of him, the dogs already pushing past him as they made a dash for the car.

At the same time, Amanda switched on the engine and threw the car into reverse.

'Duck!' screamed Jess as the man raised the rifle and pointed it at straight at them. Without waiting to see whether Amanda followed her prompt, Jess threw herself down in the seat as the car accelerated backwards. A shot rang out and in the same instant the windscreen exploded, raining glass down on her as she squeezed her eyes shut and covered her head.

A second shot rang out, then a third and a fourth, and the car mounted a bank as it came hurtling out of the drive. As Jess opened her eyes again she saw Amanda crouched uncomfortably in her seat, eyes level with the dashboard as she yanked the wheel round, and the car fell back onto the road.

They were now temporarily out of sight of the gunman and they both sat up in their seats, Amanda craning her head round as she reversed the car wildly up the hill.

'Don't forget Casey!' yelled Jess. 'For Christ's sake, don't forget my sister!'

'I won't, I won't. Just hold still and keep your head down.' Amanda had her foot flat on the accelerator. The car was wobbling all over the place and she was going as fast as she could in reverse, but it wasn't fast enough and there was no room to turn round, although for the moment they were just about outrunning the dogs. And now they were coming up towards the bend in the road close to where Jess reckoned Casey would be. If they could get round that and out of sight, then they might just have a chance of escape.

And then, as she looked back down the hill, Jess saw the scar-faced gunman come into view again. In one movement, he crouched down, took aim with the rifle and opened fire, letting off shot after shot.

As Jess ducked back down, she felt the car spin out of control. Amanda was yanking the wheel this way and that but it didn't seem to be doing any good, and suddenly they were leaving the road. The car swerved wildly and hit a tree before coming to a halt, facing back down the hill.

'Out! Out! Out!' yelled Amanda. 'Out your side!' She gave Jess an angry shove as another shot rang out, its impact making the car shake. Smoke was rising from the bonnet now and it was clear the car was going nowhere.

'What about Casey?' yelled Jess.

'Just go!' No longer willing to wait, Amanda scrambled over her and yanked the door open.

The two of them rolled out together and scrambled into the undergrowth as another shot whistled past somewhere not that far over their heads. Using the bushes as cover, Jess leapt to her feet, still clutching the knife she'd taken from the kitchen, and looked round desperately for any sign of her sister. But she couldn't see her anywhere and didn't dare call her name, in case it alerted their pursuers to her whereabouts. She could hear the dogs racing up the hill towards them, coming close now.

Amanda yelled at her to run and took off herself into the trees without looking back but, for a long second, Jess stood where she was, cursing herself for not staying with Casey, knowing that she couldn't let the dogs catch her sister's scent. She had to distract them. 'I'm here! I'm here!' she called out as the dogs – two lean, powerful-looking Dobermans – raced into view.

Knowing she had their full attention, Jess turned and sprinted into the darkness of the woods, running faster than she'd ever run in her life, knowing that it was never going to be fast enough, but praying that Casey at least would make it out of here in one piece.

She could hear them right behind her now. Closing in for the kill. Could hear their hot panting breath only feet away.

Swinging round, she held out the knife as the closest dog leapt through the air towards her, jaws open wide. The knife connected with the dog's chest and it let loose a strange gasping howl as it impaled itself right up to the hilt on the blade, the momentum of its leap sending both the dog and Jess crashing to the ground. Warm blood poured onto her chest from where she'd stabbed the dog, and she just had time to see its eyes roll back in its head before the second Doberman was on her, sinking its teeth into her knife arm.

Jess yelped in pain, trying and failing to retrieve the knife, kicking out wildly at the dog as its teeth tore her flesh. With a huge, desperate effort, she tried to fight her way to her feet, but the dog's grip was too strong, and already she could see the shadows of the men who were hunting her on the road.

But she wasn't going to go down without a fight and she kept up her struggle with the dog, trying to gouge at its eyes, even as she saw a man approaching her at a run in the periphery of her vision, a gun with silencer attached in his hand, the weapon outstretched in front of him.

It was over. She'd tried everything to survive but – when it had come down to it – she'd failed.

Taking a deep breath, she clenched her teeth against the impact as the shot rang out.

Thirty-two

Scope took in the whole scene in the space of a couple of seconds. The girl – pretty, mixed race, no more than eighteen, tops – fitted the description of the older of the two kids on the canoeing trip. She was sitting on the ground staring up at him, her mouth open in shock, the confusion written all over her face as she tried to work out who on earth he was. Her left forearm was bleeding and she was clutching hold of it with her free hand. Two dead Dobermans lay next to her – one she must have killed herself; the other he just had.

Thirty yards away, just visible inside the tree line, were shadowy figures some distance apart. Scope had counted three of them and they'd stopped, clearly having heard Scope's shot, and were crouching down.

Panting from the exertion of running the last half-mile in the direction of the gunfire, Scope leaned down beside the girl, keeping his gaze firmly fixed on the shadowy figures. 'How many of them are there?' he whispered.

'I don't know,' she whispered back, her voice surprisingly

calm given the fact that she'd been bitten quite badly. 'But they've got guns, and they're trying to kill me.'

Scope had three shots left. If they were going to make a dash for it, he was going to have to use those shots to hold off the girl's pursuers and give them a few seconds' head start, which might be enough now that it sounded as if there were no more dogs with them. But as he took aim at the nearest figure, one of the men called out excitedly to the others. 'There's the young one!' he bellowed in a rumbling Eastern European accent.

'Grab her, and keep her alive!' someone else called back, his voice carrying through the darkness. This time the accent was English.

'No! My sister!' the girl next to Scope screamed.

The next second, the powerful beam of a torch swung round towards them, temporarily blinding Scope. This time he didn't hesitate, aiming his pistol towards the light and pulling the trigger twice in quick succession, before grabbing the girl and yanking her to her feet. 'Move!' he hissed, cracking off his third and final shot from the hip, and hearing the tinkle of glass as the torch shattered, plunging them back into welcome darkness.

'My sister!' the girl screamed again, resisting Scope's efforts, but her voice was drowned out by a succession of shotgun blasts. Scope remembered giving the girl a shove and her taking off into the gloom, holding onto the kitchen knife she'd killed the first dog with, and then he felt a sudden, very hard, impact in his side and his legs went from under him. 'Run!' he managed to yell, and then he hit the ground with a hard thud that tore the wind right out of him.

Everything was happening extremely fast for Keogh. First he heard the shot ring out from somewhere inside the woods

– only twenty, thirty yards away. Even though he was half deafened from all the shooting he'd been doing, he knew straight away that the shot had come from a pistol, and one with a suppressor attached. He could no longer hear the barking of the dogs either.

For a split second he wondered if the shooter was Mehdi. After all, guns with suppressors were unheard of in a remote place like this, but there was no way Mehdi could have found them back here. Not wanting to take any chances, Keogh crouched down at the edge of the tree line, motioning for Sayenko and MacLean to do the same, but Sayenko appeared to be looking at something further up the hill on the other side of the road.

Keogh was just about to tell him to pay attention when Sayenko pointed towards whatever he was looking at. 'There's the young one!' he shouted.

Knowing the usefulness of having one of the fugitives as a hostage, particularly a kid, Keogh yelled to Sayenko to get hold of her alive, hoping like hell he had the energy to catch her.

Almost immediately, a female voice called out in alarm from inside the trees. Keogh didn't catch her exact words, but he distinctly heard the word 'sister'. Holding his rifle in the crook of his arm, his finger still poised on the trigger, he switched on the Maglite torch and shone it into the undergrowth, trying to catch sight of whoever was in there.

He caught movement twenty yards in, but then two shots rang out in rapid succession, passing between him and MacLean, who was crouched down with his shotgun next to the abandoned car, five yards away. As Keogh dodged behind a tree, swinging round the rifle as he hunted for a target, a third shot hissed through the trees, and the torch bucked in his hand as the light shattered, plunging the world back into a heavy, impenetrable gloom.

That was when MacLean opened up with the shotgun, its retorts cracking across the night air. Dropping the torch, Keogh put the rifle to his shoulder and leaned out from behind the tree. He saw movement – shadowy figures partially screened by bushes, running further into the woodland – and opened fire until he'd run out of bullets.

He thought he saw one of them fall and hoped it wasn't the target, Amanda Rowan, because if she was dead, he was dead too. But there was little time to worry about that now.

Motioning for MacLean to follow, Keogh started into the darkness.

Casey sprinted for her life through the big dark wood because she knew the horrible bony man with the bald head like a skull, and the big gun, was after her.

He'd seen her in the bushes beside the road, where Jess had told her to wait for them to pick her up. She'd seen the car crash, heard the shots, and didn't even know whether or not Jess was still alive. She was thinking that she couldn't lose her sister, not after everyone else. It was like God was trying to do everything he could to hurt her, even though she'd never done anything wrong before.

Then the man had shouted something and started coming up the road after her, waving the gun, a horrible look on his face like one of the zombies in Jess's Call of Duty 3 game she'd got last Christmas, and then just after that she was sure she heard Jess shout something, but she couldn't be sure what, and then she was running, because she really didn't know what else to do.

And she was continuing to run, even though her shoes were hurting, and the brambles kept scratching her face, and she was more scared than she'd ever been in her life. This was worse than the worst nightmare. It was worse than being attacked by the faceless monster with the werewolf claws that she'd always been convinced lurked beneath her bed ready to tear her to pieces and eat her head the moment she shut her eyes and fell asleep. Because the people doing this were grown-ups. Grown-ups were meant to look after children. Her mum had always told her that you had to be careful of strangers. That strangers might want to hurt you. But Casey had never believed it. The grown-ups she knew, even Lily's mum back home in London who didn't say much and never looked very happy, were always really nice.

But these men . . . These men wanted to kill her.

She sneaked a look over her shoulder for a moment, but couldn't see the bony man with the bald head. If she could keep going a bit longer, then she could hide somewhere and he wouldn't be able to find her. She'd always been good at hiding, and now she could no longer hear the dogs, they wouldn't be able to sniff her out and hurt her. But her legs were tired, and her tummy ached, and she didn't know how much longer she could keep going. She needed Jess here to help her. Jess would know what to do.

Casey turned back round so she could see where she was going and spotted the branch hanging out in front of her one second before she ran straight into it with an angry smack.

She cried out – she couldn't stop herself in time – and fell backwards onto the ground. Her whole face was agony, but her nose especially. It was like someone had smacked it with a hammer. She tried to sit back up, trying desperately not to cry, but her vision suddenly went all blurry and she had to swallow to stop herself being sick.

That was when she heard it. The sound of heavy, rasping breathing.

And it was getting closer.

Thirty-three

Scope was hurt but he could still move.

He could hear the sound of movement in the foliage behind him as the men who'd opened fire approached and, on the other side of him, no more than ten yards away, he could see the silhouette of the girl he'd rescued from the dog, partly concealed by a tree. But she wasn't running, even though she'd be coming into the sights of the gunmen any moment now. She was looking back towards the road. From what Scope could gather, she'd been split up from her little sister, and wasn't going to leave without her which, though a pretty laudable thing, was also the equivalent of committing suicide.

She was dead if she stayed where she was. And so, he knew, was he. His left side ached where he'd been hit but, when he ran his hand down there, there was no blood. Instead, he felt the satellite phone he'd taken from the dead gunman back at Jock's place. It was still in his jacket pocket, but its casing was now badly cracked, where it had clearly taken the force of the shot and somehow deflected it. He took it out and, seeing that it was cleaved pretty much down the middle, left it on the ground.

He didn't dwell on his good fortune. There was no time. Lifting himself as silently as possible to his feet, and using a thick bramble bush as cover, he took off at a sprint further into the woods, conscious of the sound of the leaves crunching beneath his feet as he ran in a crouching zigzag to put off the shooters, motioning angrily for the girl to follow him.

A shot rang out, then another. Then a third. All of them were close by but Scope was eating up the ground quickly, and out of the corner of his eye he could see the girl running alongside him, a few yards away, also trying to keep low as the shooting continued.

But it was sounding further away now.

'I can't leave my sister!' cried the girl as she ran, her face contorted with emotion.

'Where was she?' Scope called across without looking at her.

'We left her when we tried to get to the car. We were going to pick her up.' She began to slow her pace as she talked.

'Keep running,' snapped Scope. 'They're still only just behind us.' The shooting had stopped now, but he knew their pursuers wouldn't be giving up that easily.

'I'm tired,' complained the girl. 'And we're running away from where we left Casey. She's my sister, and she's only ten years old.'

Scope suddenly saw a picture of Mary Ann as a ten year old in his mind. He and Jennifer had had a photo of her at that age on the mantelpiece in the lounge in her school uniform, her long dark hair in matching pigtails, a big grin on her face. His daughter.

His dead daughter.

'I'll find your sister,' he said, without breaking pace. 'But we need to put some space between you and them. Has she got a phone?'

'No,' said the girl breathlessly. 'None of us have. We lost them in the river when the boats were overturned.'

'What's she look like?'

'Blonde, pretty. No, she's beautiful. She's so damn beautiful.' The girl looked as if she was going to break down.

'What's your name?'

'Jess.'

There was a narrow gap in the trees up ahead as they met a path and, as the two of them emerged onto it, they paused briefly. Scope turned to her, feeling in his pocket for his own mobile phone. He knew he needed to part with it because it implicated him in what had happened here, and therefore the killing of the gunman back at Jock's place, but he had no choice if he was going to help these kids get out of here.

He checked it, but there was no signal. 'Okay, Jess, follow this path upwards until you get to the road,' he whispered, handing her the phone. 'Keep to the edge so you can get out of sight if you need to, and keep moving, whatever you do. As soon as you get a signal, dial 999. Understood? Now go. I'll try and distract them.'

They could both hear the sound of movement coming up from behind them. It would only be a matter of seconds until they were back in the sights of the gunmen. Jess nodded. 'Find her,' she said, then turned and started running up the gentle incline, until seconds later she rounded a corner and was swallowed up by the forest.

The sound of pursuit was coming closer now. Scope could hear their footfalls in the trees, some distance apart as the men fanned out, and he moved across the path and into the thick wall of pine trees that bordered it on the far side, weaving between them until he found a spot from which he could no longer be seen. Grabbing a thick branch from the deep carpet of pine needles on the ground, he waited a few seconds until a big shadowy figure appeared on the other side of the path, stepping onto it carefully as he slowly looked round. Scope didn't have a very good view of him, but he could see he was well over six foot tall, and was holding a shotgun.

Scope dropped the branch onto the ground. Not too hard, because he didn't want to make what he was planning too obvious, but not too softly either, because he wanted to be heard.

And he was heard all right. The gunman immediately cocked his head, then motioned to someone else out of sight. He was already pointing the shotgun in the direction where the noise had come from when Scope took off, making as much noise as possible, running roughly parallel to the path in the opposite direction to the one the girl had taken. He heard shouting behind him and then a shot rang out, passing a good few yards behind him.

Keeping low, he continued his sprint, knowing he could outrun them, but knowing too that it was unlikely Jess could. He had to buy her time. A second shot rang out. This time it ricocheted off a tree, only a couple of yards to his left. Stealing a rapid glance, he saw that he'd strayed too close to the path, and the gunman was running down it, not quite keeping pace but not needing to, suddenly only about fifteen yards away.

Scope did a rapid turn further into the trees and sprinted for his life, half expecting to take a shot in the back at any time.

But no shot came, and a minute later he was back deep within the forest. Slowing up, he risked a glance over his shoulder, saw no one there, and turned in the direction of the river. He'd done what he could, and risked his life, to buy time for a girl he'd never met to escape from pursuers who were after her for a reason he'd probably never know. Now he was going to double back and try to find her sister somewhere in one of the biggest, loneliest forests in the country.

He no longer had any bullets in his gun. He had no means of communication. In reality, getting involved in all this was madness. Yet, Jesus, it felt good.

And if he could find that little girl, it would make it all worth it.

If he could find her . . .

Thirty-four

Last night

Mike Bolt sank his first pint of the week before the barman had even come back with his change.

It tasted that good.

It was just after 6.30 on a chilly Friday evening, and Bolt was in the bar of his local pub, The Pheasant, just down the road from the loft apartment in Clerkenwell that had been his home for more than seven years now. The place was full, but mainly with the local after-work crowd, and Bolt only recognized a couple of faces. He tended to get in the pub a couple of times a week, and he knew a few of the locals well enough to chat to, but they were acquaintances, not friends. He didn't really have friends as such, not even among those he'd worked with in the Force down the years. Everyone was an acquaintance. He liked to think that it suited him just fine like that, but deep down, he knew it didn't. The fact was, he was afraid of getting too close to people – a reaction, he supposed, to what had happened to his wife, Mikaela.

He thought of Mo Khan, who would be back home with his wife and kids, while he was sitting here alone downing pints of lager, waiting to spot someone he knew well enough to snatch a conversation with. Mo often told him that his own life wasn't all fun and laughter. 'Sometimes I'd give my right arm for a few minutes of peace and quiet' was one of his typical refrains, delivered while rolling his eyes at how frenetic his existence was, but Bolt knew that Mo wouldn't change a thing about his own life, and was only saying these things to make him feel better.

'Needed that, eh?' said the barman as he returned with the change. He was a young Polish guy called Marius with big tattooed arms, who Bolt occasionally saw doing weights in the gym. 'Must have been a hard week.' He looked at the yellowing bruise on Bolt's left cheek where he'd been struck by Leonard Hope during his escape four days earlier, and which still hurt like hell even though nothing was broken.

'Hard enough,' answered Bolt, ordering a second pint. He didn't think Marius knew that he was the SIO on the Disciple case, even though it was currently the most high-profile murder investigation in the country. He'd only worked behind the bar for about three months, and Bolt tried to keep his personal and professional life as separate as possible. Those people who knew him in here were aware that he was a senior cop, but they never questioned him about it, which suited him just fine.

But Marius the barman was right. It had been a hard week. Leonard Hope's name and photo had been all over the news, and yet four days on from the discovery of evidence at his home that inextricably linked him to the Disciple murders, he'd still not been arrested. Nor had there been even a single sighting. It was almost as if he'd never existed, a situation that was unheard of in these days of blanket media coverage and security cameras on every corner.

The fact that they'd come so close to catching Hope didn't help either. It made them look incompetent, and none more so than Bolt himself who, it was reported in the papers, had got to within a yard of Hope, only to lose him when the suspect had turned and knocked him out with a killer punch. The coverage was lurid, and though not entirely true, it had had the desired effect. It had made Bolt look stupid, and he'd wondered several times in the intervening days how long he was going to last as the head of the inquiry.

The realization that he might be ousted from it frustrated him more than anything else about the whole case. It was unfinished business now. He had to be the one who brought down Hope, especially after what they'd found in his loft. A small tin box hidden under the floorboards had revealed a number of items of jewellery belonging to the female victims, some of it bloodstained. Alongside them in the box, in a clear plastic freezer bag and wrapped in clingfilm, had been the left-hand little fingers of the first three female victims. Even more gruesome had been the film footage found hidden away in a file on Hope's PC. There were three separate films taken at each of the first three murder scenes. They were all very short and concentrated on the torture of the female victims by the man wielding the camera. Bolt had managed to sit through all the footage – seven, interminably long minutes in total – and the horror of it would stay with him for the rest of his days. He'd become used to the savagery of his fellow human beings, having been involved in far too many murder investigations over the years, but he'd never become immune to it, and he'd never come across anything like the extreme sadism that Leonard Hope exhibited. It was for this reason that Bolt wanted to stay involved in this case. He wanted to be the man who read that bastard his rights.

But they had to find him first. And right now they didn't have a single lead to go on.

In the last few days, a conspiracy theory had emerged in the press that there were two killers in the Disciple murders: Leonard Hope, and a second man who'd helped him escape from the police. There was at least some evidence to back this up. According to Hope's mobile phone records, the last call he'd received had been while he was driving home to where Bolt and Mo were waiting to arrest him. The call had come through at almost exactly the same time he'd started driving erratically in an effort to shake off the surveillance team following him, almost as if the caller had been warning him that he was being tailed by the police. Hope had then made a call to the same number five minutes later, lasting about thirty seconds, which was when Bolt had seen him on the phone while he was being chased. To add to the mystery, the number in question turned out to belong to an anonymous pay-as-you-go mobile that had only been switched on for the very first time four minutes before the call to Hope had been made, and had been switched off three minutes after the second conversation. It hadn't been switched on since, and so far they'd drawn a complete blank in finding out who it was that Hope had been speaking to.

Bolt was keeping an open mind on the two-killer theory. It certainly looked as though Hope had been warned that he was under surveillance, which would suggest a second conspirator and, more worryingly, someone connected to the police inquiry. It would also have made it far easier for The Disciple to target couples rather than individuals if there were two of them, rather than one. But Bolt was still far from convinced, and the reason was simple. In the last three days, the inquiry team had turned Hope's life upside down, and in that time they'd been unable to find a single piece of evidence suggesting he was working with someone else. They'd checked all of Hope's phone records going back more than three years and, with the exception of that last phone number, they'd traced every person he'd talked to who was still alive (there hadn't actually been that many), and in the process eliminated all of them as potential suspects. There was nothing on his computer to suggest an online friendship with a kindred spirit (and the film footage didn't show any accomplice), and none of his neighbours or work colleagues had ever reported seeing him with anyone they couldn't readily identify.

Leonard Hope had, it seemed, been the classic loner.

Bolt took a big gulp from his second pint, tired of worrying about the case. Up until today, he'd put in fourteen-hour shifts since Hope's escape and, realistically, there was little more he, or the inquiry team, could do, which was why he'd let most of them go at 5.30 and told them not to come back until Monday morning. There was still the matter of the unidentified DNA sample found at the Rowan/Hanzha murder scene – the one that matched the DNA found on Beatrice Magret's body fifteen years earlier. The results for that were expected in the next twenty-four hours but, even if it was a match with Leonard Hope's DNA, which Bolt assumed was likely, it wasn't going to help them catch him.

The second pint was going down fast and pretty soon he was going to have to make a decision. Grab a takeaway from either the Thai place or one of the local Indians, and settle down at home in front of the TV with a bottle of decent red wine, or make a night of it here, get some food at the bar, and hope that somebody turned up interesting enough to chew the fat with for a couple of hours.

He was still mulling over the alternatives, and the second pint was sitting empty on the bar, when his mobile rang. It was DS Dan Grier, who was in charge of the skeleton crew manning the Disciple inquiry incident room overnight, and Bolt picked up straight away. He'd told Grier only to call him if he had something important, and Grier was the kind of guy who knew not to waste his boss's time.

'Sir, I think you need to get down here right away.' Grier's voice was grim.

Bolt slipped off his stool and moved away from the bar. 'What is it?'

'We've got reports of a body over near Maidenhead. They think it's Leonard Hope.'

Thirty-five

'Jesus Christ,' said Bolt, as he and Mo Khan stared down at the ruined corpse of Leonard Hope. 'I'm glad I hadn't got round to eating dinner tonight.' The two pints of lager he'd drunk in The Pheasant sat heavily in his stomach, making him feel nauseous.

'I have to say, it's not a pretty sight,' said the DI from Thames Valley CID, a big round man called Joe Ruckley, who was standing to Bolt's right, and whose face was far too cheery under the circumstances.

Leonard Hope lay on his back in a small culvert, partly concealed by brush, about five yards from a path that led down to a road around thirty yards away. The area was partially wooded and there were no buildings nearby. Hope himself was naked, except for a pair of grey boxer shorts. A ring of halogen lamps had been set up round his body to illuminate his many injuries, a significant number of which appeared to have been inflicted by deliberate torture. There were round burn marks the size of fifty-pence pieces all over his torso where a blowtorch, or something similar, had been applied to the skin. Both his nipples appeared to have been burnt off and, where his right eye should have been, there was little more than a charred lump of flesh. There was also a single stab wound to his neck that looked to have severed his carotid artery and was almost certainly the cause of death. It was difficult to tell how long he'd been dead for, or how long he'd lain here (although Bolt didn't think it could have been that long, because there were no signs that any animals had been at him), but the body in front of them was definitely that of Leonard Hope.

'There are also burn marks to the groin under the boxers,' said Ruckley matter-of-factly. 'Three of them. One to the end of his wanger that's pretty much sealed the whole thing up down there, and one each to the bollocks. There's not much left of either of them, and what there is just looks like a couple of half-melted Maltesers. Do you want to take a look?'

Bolt swallowed. 'Thanks for the kind offer, Joe, but I think we'll take your word for it. Unless you want to see, Mo.'

'I think I can picture it well enough in my head,' said Mo. 'Far more than I want to.'

Bolt turned back to Ruckley. 'So what have we got so far?'

'The body was found by a dog walker at about two thirty this afternoon. The doctor took the body temperature at four p.m. He reckoned he'd been dead for between twenty-four and thirty-six hours at that point. As you can see, he was definitely killed elsewhere. Whoever did it put his pants back on him for some reason, then brought him here, but made no real attempt to hide the body. It's possible they were disturbed, but probably more likely they just dumped it and left. Obviously, he was tortured for some time before he was killed. The doc reckoned some of those burns could have been done quite a few hours apart, so the killer went to town on him, then finished him off with a stab wound to the throat.' Ruckley shrugged. 'That's pretty much it so far. We're going to do a fingertip search of the area tomorrow, and SOCO have been over the scene taking samples, but we haven't turned up anything useful yet.'

Bolt frowned. 'And the doctor was sure it was twenty-four to thirty-six hours he'd been dead?'

Ruckley nodded. 'Adamant.'

'So that means the earliest he died was four a.m. yesterday morning, which is a full two and a half days after he went missing. We need to know what he was doing during that time, and who he was with.'

'Do you go for that second killer theory they're bandying around in the papers?' Ruckley asked him.

Bolt took another look down at the body, no longer feeling any hatred for Leonard Hope. Now he just looked pathetic lying there, pale and mutilated; it was clear that, one way or another, he'd paid the price for the terrible things he'd done. 'I don't know what to think,' he said, turning away. 'Thanks for your help, Joe. It's appreciated.'

'Can we move the body now? The pathologist is waiting for it, and I want to get home for my supper. The wife's cooking meatballs. I just hope to God she hasn't burned them. I hate being reminded of work when I'm at home.' He chuckled at his own joke.

Bolt didn't join in the laughter. 'Sure,' he said. 'It's all yours. Enjoy dinner.'

He motioned for Mo to follow him and they walked back in the direction of their parked car, and away from the bright glare of the halogen lamps. Mo looked tired and frustrated. The case, it seemed, was getting to him too, and he'd seemed uncharacteristically down when Bolt had phoned him at home – where he'd been watching a movie with his wife and youngest two kids – to tell him the news. Bolt had told him he didn't need to come out to view the body, but he'd insisted, which was Mo all over. He had an almost annoying sense of duty.

'Do you think that guy's always a joker like that?' asked Mo, when they were out of earshot of the dozen or so officers and mortuary attendants still at the scene, and away from the lingering smell of decomposing flesh.

'Probably. You know what it's like. For some people, it's just the best way of dealing with it all.'

Mo grunted. 'He just gets on my nerves.'

They walked in silence back to the car. 'So what do you think?' Bolt asked him.

'There wasn't a second killer working with Hope,' said Mo, leaning against the car. 'We've never found any evidence linking him with someone else; all the missing trophies – the fingers, the items of jewellery – were found at Hope's home. It was Hope who was spotted by Richard Oldham loitering alone outside the Morris murder scene the day before they were killed; and there was only one killer at the Rowan/Hanzha murder scene.'

'Who we know about,' Bolt pointed out. 'There might have been another killer upstairs who Amanda Rowan didn't see when she disturbed the murder of her husband and his mistress.'

'It seems unlikely though, doesn't it? If there were two killers, they could easily have ambushed and trapped her upstairs.'

'As it happens, I agree. But that leaves us with an even bigger problem. Who the hell murdered Hope?'

They were both silent for a minute. Bolt was thinking. 'Someone helped Leonard Hope escape,' he said at last. 'He never left the area on foot. We'd have caught him if he had. And he didn't steal a car because none were reported stolen.

So someone must have whisked him off, probably in the back of a car, and it's got to have been the person he was on the phone to.'

Mo nodded. 'That's the theory that makes the most sense. Then he goes to ground, probably with the person who took him. They looked after him for a couple of days, then, for whatever reason, decided to torture and kill him, and dump his body out here in the middle of nowhere.'

'But how did the person know Hope was being tailed?'

'The only way would be if you already knew the police were onto him.'

The inference was obvious and it troubled Bolt. 'You think it's someone from the inquiry?'

'Well, no. What would be the point? Everyone on the inquiry team's trying to catch the killer, so why risk your career to help him escape?'

Bolt sighed. 'There are over a hundred people on the team. All of them knew for three days that Leonard Hope was a suspect. I know we swore them all to secrecy, but some of them would have talked to friends, family and particularly other cops. So there are probably a couple of hundred people at least with access to that information.'

'But we're still left without a motive,' said Mo. 'Why would you help him escape? There's just no reason for it that I can think of.'

'It could be a vigilante thing. Maybe it was a cop who didn't think Hope was going to get the treatment he deserved in prison. I mean, let's face it, whoever killed him really wanted to make him suffer. He must have died in absolute agony.' Bolt was surprised to realize that the thought of Hope dying in agony pleased him.

Mo shook his head. 'I don't buy the vigilante angle.'

'Why not?'

'Because most cops I know are professional, and detached enough not to take everything so personally. How many of them get so wound up in a case that they can't think straight, and end up being prepared to risk their career, their pension, and twenty years behind bars just to make sure a man who's going to go to prison for the rest of his life anyway dies in agony? And even if there was one prepared to put a plan like that into action, he couldn't have done it alone. It requires organization, and real balls, because there's no guarantee he'd have been able to get Hope in a car with him.' Mo shook his head again. 'I'm sorry, boss, but there's no way it was some Dirty Harry-style cop.'

When he put it like that, it didn't make much sense to Bolt either. 'But someone helped him. Someone who hated him enough to burn his balls into Maltesers with a blowtorch.'

Once again they were silent for a few moments. Bolt took a deep breath and looked up at the night sky. It was a clear night but the stars were obscured by the thick orange glow of London to the east and the lights of planes as they queued up in a long, sweeping semi-circle for their approach into Heathrow Airport, the low rumble of their engines providing a constant background noise. He was stuck, and it irritated him. Worse, Leonard Hope's death was only going to increase the pressure on him. Now it looked like they'd never find out exactly what had happened.

'Shall we head back to town?' said Mo, shivering as a gust of cold wind blew across the road, then opening the car door. 'We need to get in touch with the victims' next of kin and let them know that they're not going to get their day in court.'

'Jesus,' sighed Bolt, opening the passenger door. 'What a pig's ear.' And then, as Mo started the engine, a thought struck him. 'The victims' next of kin,' he said aloud. 'Now they'd have a real reason to hate Leonard Hope.'

'Sure they would, boss, but none of them knew Hope's identity before we announced it, and that wasn't until after he was already on the run.'

'What do we know about Ivana Hanzha's family? You know, George Rowan's mistress. I heard word that her old man's one of those Russian oligarchs. Someone with a hell of a lot of money and good contacts.' As SIO on the case, Bolt hadn't had to deal with the next of kin, but now he was beginning to wish he had.

Mo sat forward, looking more interested now. 'His name's Vladimir Hanzha, and we haven't gone into his background too much. I mean, it's not as if he's a suspect or anything, and from what I gather his daughter's been estranged from him for the last five years. But, yeah, the word is he's a bit of a shady character, like a lot of those guys. I still don't see how he could have got hold of Leonard Hope, though.'

'And maybe he didn't. But we're running low on leads, and he's got to be worth talking to. I'm going to call Sam Verran.'

Sam Verran was a former colleague of both Bolt's and Mo's in SOCA, the Serious and Organized Crime Agency. A career cop with only a year to go until retirement, he was an expert in Russian and Eastern European crime networks, and the extent to which they'd impinged on the UK organized-crime scene. He knew all the key players, and quite a few of the not-so-key ones as well, and if anyone could give them a lowdown on Ivana Hanzha's old man, it would be him. And if he couldn't, then it meant the old man was clean.

Bolt hadn't spoken to Sam Verran since he'd left SOCA, which was close to two years back now. They'd promised to remain in touch but, as was so often the case, they hadn't, which was a pity because Bolt had always liked him. He hesitated for a moment, vaguely embarrassed to be calling Verran at 8.30 on a Friday night because, if he remembered rightly, he hadn't responded to Sam's last email about a SOCA reunion drink. But only Verran could give him the answers he needed, so he didn't hesitate for very long.

Verran answered after the second ring. 'Well, well, well,' he said in a strong Essex accent. 'The wanderer returns. I thought you'd retired and moved abroad, I haven't heard from you in that long.'

Bolt chuckled, getting comfortable in his seat as Mo pulled away from the kerb. 'You know how it is, Sam. Work never stops, does it?'

'How's it going on the Disciple case? I've seen you on the TV taking a lot of flak from those media assholes, as if they could do any better catching the guy. Any news on him yet?'

'Nothing right now,' said Bolt, who didn't want to tell Verran about Leonard Hope before he'd spoken to his boss in Homicide and Serious Crime Command, 'but we'll get him eventually.'

'So, what can I do for you, Mikey-boy? I'm assuming this isn't a social call.'

'Not entirely, no. I was wondering if you could give me some info on Vladimir Hanzha.'

'Ah yes. His daughter was one of The Disciple's recent victims, wasn't she? She was the one killed along with her lover at his place. The wife disturbed them.'

'That's right. My colleague – you remember Mo Khan, don't you?'

'Course I do.'

'Well, he's been hearing rumours that Vladimir Hanzha's involved in some dubious dealings, and I thought, who better to talk to than my old mate Sam Verran to find out if they're true.'

'But what's he got to do with the Disciple case?'

'Nothing as far as I know,' said Bolt, deflecting the question. 'I just need some background.'

'Fair enough. To tell you the truth, I don't know anything about Hanzha for sure, and he's not under active investigation, but you're right, there *are* rumours and, off the record, I reckon there's some meat to them. The point is, though, he's got big money, big connections, and a very big team of lawyers, so you've got to be very careful. The official line is he's an entrepreneur who arrived in this country in the late 1990s with the equivalent of about ninety million in sterling in his pocket, which he made from the sale to Exxon of a natural gas company he owned back in Russia. Since then, he's invested in a number of companies and projects in the UK and overseas – commodities, property, a couple of big holiday resorts. Even through the midst of the worst recession since the 1930s, he's managed to double his personal wealth to a hundred and eighty million. He donates money to charities; he counts a number of big businesspeople, a few lords and ladies, and even a couple of politicians as his friends; and because he's not one of the big billionaire oligarchs, he's managed to keep a fairly low profile.' Verran paused. 'That's the official line.'

'And the unofficial one?'

'That he's a gangster. Back in Russia, the previous owner of the gas company that Hanzha sold was found face down in a swamp riddled with bullets, just after he sold his shares to Hanzha at a knockdown price, and there are more than a few tales of people who crossed him back then ending up dead. Since he's been in the UK, there haven't been any killings that could be linked back to him, but a few years ago a British businessman who'd had a dispute with him disappeared one day, and hasn't been seen since. The businessman also had disputes with a few other people, so there was no way of proving it had anything to do with Hanzha, but there was another incident about a year ago when a South African bloke who'd shafted Hanzha on a deal involving a cobalt mine in Congo ended up shot along with his wife at their house in Cape Town. Again, nothing you can prove, but I'm one of those people who doesn't believe in smoke without fire, and I always think that any man who employs an army of bodyguards, like Hanzha does, has got something to hide. There are other rumours too – that he's involved in money laundering, that he's connected to a major Asian illegal betting syndicate, all sorts – but you get the picture.'

'Yeah, I do. We also heard he was estranged from his daughter – the one who got killed. Do you know what that was about?'

'Off the record . . .'

'This is all off the record, Sam. I promise.'

'It's lucky I trust you, Mike. Even if you do only phone when you want something. Anyway, I've heard Hanzha has a bit of a temper, and he used to knock the girl's mother about. They divorced a long time back but she was the only one of the three kids – the other two are boys – who sided with the mother. As far as I know, she doesn't – didn't – speak to her father or her brothers.'

'He sounds like a really nice guy.'

'He's an arsehole, and a rich arsehole as well, which makes it even worse; but, as far as SOCA are concerned, he's not top priority. There are plenty out there who we know for sure are up to no good, and they're the ones we're after right now. Maybe we'll get round to him eventually, but I wouldn't hold your breath.'

'I won't,' said Bolt, who'd long ago got used to hearing stories of major criminals operating with impunity.

'You still haven't actually told me what this is really about,' said Verran, a knowing tone in his voice. 'What do you think Hanzha really has to do with all this?'

Bolt knew he was going to have to give his old colleague something if he wanted to get any more information from him. 'Okay, and this is definitely one hundred per cent off the record, but we think it's possible that some harm might have come to Leonard Hope.' He ignored Mo's sideways frown and continued. 'We're certain he got help escaping from us when he was under surveillance, but we reckon that whoever helped him might then have killed him.'

'So he's dead.'

Bolt didn't say anything.

'Come on, Mike. You've known me long enough to know I won't shout my mouth off.'

'Yeah, he's dead. His body was dumped in a wood out near Maidenhead and he'd been badly tortured.' Again, Mo gave him a frown, but Bolt just shrugged.

'Well, by the sound of things, whoever did it was performing a public service. I can't see too many tears being shed for a sick bastard like him.'

'As it happens, Sam, I agree with you. But right now we're stuck for a motive. We're looking at the vigilante angle, and what I wanted to know from you was whether you thought that Hanzha would have the capability to snatch Hope from under our noses, and whether he'd go to all that effort to avenge his daughter. At the time, no one outside the Force knew we were onto Hope, so it had to be someone with good connections.'

Verran was silent for a few moments as he pondered this. 'It's possible, I suppose. Like I said, Hanzha's got good connections and plenty of money, which is a pretty effective combination. I also know he's got a bloke working for him called Frank Keogh, who's an ex-copper. You might have heard about him. He was a firearms officer who shot a gang member a few years ago and ended up getting done for manslaughter.'

'Yeah, I do remember something about that. I remember thinking at the time it was a real injustice.'

'It was. They just needed a fall guy. Anyway, it looks like Keogh's gone over to the dark side, and the thing is, he's still got some contacts in the police force, so there could have been a leak. The problem you've got though, Mike, is proving anything. Even if Hanzha *is* responsible, and I'm not at all sure he would be, given he hasn't spoken to his daughter in years, there's no way he would have been involved himself.'

'The torture was personal. It wasn't a professional job. Whoever did it wanted Leonard Hope to die in a huge amount of pain. I'm thinking he'd *have* to have been involved.'

Verran sighed. 'I honestly don't know, Mike, but what you need to take into account is that Hanzha has operated under the radar for fifteen years in the UK without so much as a single arrest, which tells you that he knows what he's doing. Even if he was involved, you're not going to prove anything against him. And to be honest, most people will be thinking good riddance to bad rubbish.'

'I still want to talk to him, and I'm going to want to talk to this guy Keogh who works for him as well. Do you know where Hanzha's based?'

'He's got homes all over the place, but he spends a lot of his time in London, and at a country estate he's got up in the Cairngorms.'

'Thanks, Sam. You've been a big help.'

'Yeah well, don't tell anyone where you got your info from.'

'Course not. You know me. Listen, while I'm on the phone, fancy a trout fishing trip some time?'

'Sure, that'd be good,' said Verran, but he sounded non-committal.

'I'm serious. How about next weekend, or the one after? I could do with a break.' Bolt realized, almost with surprise, that he was desperate for some time away from the job and London, and Verran was good company, and single and childless like himself, having been divorced for close to ten years.

'Ah Mike, I'd love to, but I've got myself a girlfriend now and she might not take too kindly to me disappearing off for the weekend, especially as I don't get a lot of time off either.'

'How long's that been going on for, then?' asked Bolt, hiding his disappointment.

'Close to a year now. We're even talking about moving in together, although that's going to be a bit of a shock after all these years on my own.'

'I'm glad for you, Sam,' said Bolt, and he meant it, even though the news gave him an empty feeling in the pit of his stomach. 'Maybe sometime in the spring then?'

'Sounds like a plan,' said Verran, in a way that was clear to both of them that it would never happen.

'So you reckon Vladimir Hanzha had something to do with it, then?' said Mo, when Bolt came off the phone.

Bolt nodded. 'Someone murdered The Disciple,' he said. 'And you know what? Whoever did it probably deserves a medal. But that doesn't detract from the fact that I want to know who it was and why.'

'Can we at least wait until Monday before we talk to Hanzha? I've got plans this weekend.'

'Sure,' said Bolt, thinking he was clearly the only person who didn't. He stretched in his seat, trying to get himself comfortable, and put in a call to DS Dan Grier back in the Disciple incident room.

'I was just about to call you, sir,' said Grier when he picked up. 'We've just had the results in for the DNA found at the Rowan/Hanzha murder scene.' Something in his voice didn't sound quite right.

'And does it match Leonard Hope's DNA?'

There was a pause down the line before Grier replied. 'That's the thing, sir. No, it doesn't. It wasn't Hope's DNA at the murder scene, which also means he's not the man who killed Beatrice Magret in 1998.'

Bolt frowned, trying to process this new information logically. 'So either the Disciple killings *were* the work of two men – Leonard Hope and the man who killed Beatrice Magret all those years ago—'

Grier finished the sentence for him. 'Or Hope didn't kill George Rowan and Ivana Hanzha at all.'

Thirty-six

It was just before 10.30 p.m. and Bolt was sitting in his open-plan loft apartment with his feet on the coffee table and a glass of Rioja in his hand, when his mobile rang again.

It was DS Grier. 'We've got confirmation that Leonard Hope couldn't have been involved in the Beatrice Magret killing,' he said. 'He was serving in the army in Germany when it happened, and he wasn't on leave.'

'I guess we expected that.' Bolt let out a deep breath. 'Have you managed to track Vladimir Hanzha's whereabouts?'

'Yes. He's at his Scottish estate. He flew up there yesterday.'

'I need to organize a plane ticket up there. I want to speak to him, and I want to speak to Amanda Rowan as well.'

'Already done, sir. You and Mo Khan are on the twelve thirty p.m. flight out of Heathrow, getting to Aberdeen at one fifteen. I've organized a press conference for nine tomorrow morning to announce the news about Leonard Hope's death, so that should give you plenty of time. That's what you wanted, right?'

'Absolutely,' said Bolt. 'Thanks a lot for that.' He made a

mental note to keep an eye on Grier with a view to recommending him for promotion. The guy was still young but, unlike too many detectives of his age, he got things done with maximum efficiency and minimum fuss.

'So, what do you think, sir?' asked Grier. 'Are we back at the two killers theory?'

'Well, there are definitely two killers. The question is whether or not they were working together.' He'd spent the whole of the remainder of the drive back home discussing this with Mo Khan, who'd changed his mind about his weekend plans now that the case seemed to have been blown wide open. Mo was also now convinced that The Disciple was actually working with someone else because, as he'd pointed out, it was simply too coincidental for there to be a murderer at the Rowan household not connected to Leonard Hope, who also knew The Disciple's complete modus operandi. Bolt could see his point, but he still wasn't entirely convinced, which is what he told Grier.

'If there were two killers in the house on the night that George Rowan and Ivana Hanzha were murdered, then I still don't understand how they didn't manage to kill Amanda Rowan, or how she didn't at least *see* both of them. From what I can remember of our interview with her, she said she went upstairs, discovered the freshly murdered bodies of her husband and his mistress in the end bedroom, and was then confronted by the killer, who appeared from the bedroom at the other end of the landing. I was in that house afterwards. I saw the layout. If there were two killers, they could easily have trapped Amanda – it wouldn't have taken any planning at all. But they didn't, and that's what I can't work out.'

'But what's the alternative?' asked Grier. 'That the man who attacked Amanda Rowan was a completely different killer, who somehow knew The Disciple's MO?'

'I don't know what the alternative is, Dan,' said Bolt, who'd already been down this road with Mo. 'I'm just telling you I'm yet to be convinced. That's one of the reasons I want to talk to Amanda Rowan again. I want her to go back through her movements that night, just in case we've missed something.'

'Do you want me to let her know you're coming, or are you going to do that?'

Bolt yawned, weariness beginning to overtake him. 'I'll sort it out, don't worry. Thanks again for your help on this. I appreciate it.'

Ending the call, he finished his wine and got to his feet. Sky News was on the TV in the background, the sound turned down low. There was no word yet on the discovery of Leonard Hope's body, but that would come soon enough. He debated having another glass of the Rioja. It was good stuff, bought on the recommendation of the woman who ran the wine shop just down the road, and red wine always had a way of relaxing him, however hyped-up he was feeling. In the end, though, he decided against it. He had an early start tomorrow and a long day, and he wanted a clear head. Although there was no real urgency to the trip now that Leonard Hope's body had been found, Bolt was keen to talk to Vladimir Hanzha, and get an idea of the man, even if he wasn't going to admit anything. He was very keen to speak to Amanda as well because, the more he thought about it, the more he felt there was something wrong with the Rowan/Hanzha murders.

Something he and everyone else was missing.

Thirty-seven

Today 19.48

Jess felt sick. She'd lost Casey. She'd lost her little sister – the last member of her family still alive – and now Casey was somewhere in this endless forest, alone and terrified. What if she'd been caught by one of the gunmen? Worse, what if they'd killed her? Oh Jesus, she couldn't even bear to imagine that. It would finish her if anything happened to Casey. Finish her just the same as if someone put a gun to her own head and pulled the trigger.

And yet here she was, sprinting further and further away from where she'd last seen her sister, the bloodied kitchen knife in one hand, the mobile phone she'd just been given in the other, as she tried to reach the road and a place where she could get reception and call the police before the other gunmen caught up with her. She prayed that the man who'd come to her rescue a few minutes earlier would find Casey, like he promised he would. She wondered who the hell he was. He'd looked like a nice guy, good-looking in a rugged yet friendly way; the type of man you could rely on in times of trouble. And, by God, she was relying on him now.

She couldn't feel any pain in her arm where the dog had bitten her, even though the skin was all bloody and mangled, but her lungs felt as if they were going to burst and she wondered how much further the main road was. She was running parallel to the path that the stranger had told her to take, keeping well within the tree line. It was a good few minutes since she'd heard the last shot ring out, and it had been some distance away. The stranger had said he was going to try to lure the gunmen away from her, and she guessed that he'd been success-ful. At least she hoped so, since she had absolutely no way of knowing for sure.

Have faith, she told herself. Have faith. Casey will be all right. You'll be all right. You have to believe this.

She slowed up a little, conscious of the noise of her panting, and risked a look over her shoulder into the gloom of the forest. There was nothing there. Relieved, she stopped for a few moments and bent down with her hands on her knees, trying to get her breath back.

And that was when she heard the noise coming from directly behind her.

Jess felt her heart leap and she swung round fast, clutching the kitchen knife tight in her hand, ready to lash out.

'It's me,' hissed Amanda, jumping backwards and almost falling over in the process. She too was holding a knife she'd left the house with.

For a long moment Jess just stared at her. To her surprise, she wasn't relieved to see her at all. In fact, it annoyed her that, after all that had happened, Amanda hardly looked to have broken a sweat. Even her hair, wet and bedraggled a couple of hours earlier, seemed to have bounced back to life. 'Jesus, what do you think you're doing?' she said at last, making no move to lower the knife. 'You scared the shit out of me. I could have stabbed you.'

Amanda eyed the bloodstained blade. 'I didn't mean to scare you but I heard running and I hid behind a tree just in case it was one of them. When I saw it was you, I came out. I was just about to say something when you turned round.' She looked at Jess's bleeding arm. 'I didn't mean to leave you. I'm sorry.'

'Forget it, I'd have done the same,' said Jess, although she wasn't sure she would have done.

'What happened to the dogs?'

'I stabbed one. The other had hold of me –' she motioned to her arm which was now suddenly beginning to hurt like hell – 'but then this guy appeared out of nowhere with a gun and shot it.' She paused, still panting. 'I thought he was going to shoot me too, but he helped me escape and even gave me his mobile phone.'

Amanda looked puzzled. 'Do you think he was police?'

'I don't know, but he was on his own. He's gone back to look for Casey.'

'He'll find her, I'm sure.'

Jess glared at her. 'How do you know he'll find her? She could be dead already.'

'They wouldn't kill her.'

'You said you didn't even know who these people are, so how can you be so sure?'

'There's no reason for them to hurt her. She's nothing to do with any of this.'

'She's a witness to the killings,' said Jess.

Amanda looked hurt. 'God, I'm sorry for what's happened,'

she said quietly, putting a hand on Jess's good arm and moving in close, as if she was going to give her a hug.

But Jess didn't want any sympathy from this woman with her nice hair and educated accent. She just wanted Casey to be okay. She pulled away roughly as Amanda tried to embrace her, her face coming way too close, and took a step backwards. 'We need to keep moving,' she said. 'They won't be far behind us. As soon as I get reception, I'll call the police.'

Amanda stared at her for a long moment, and there was something in her expression that Jess didn't like.

Then, knowing that every second they delayed put them in more danger, Jess turned and ran into the trees, checking the phone in vain for some reception, all her thoughts still dominated by one person, and one person only.

Casey.

Casey lay still on the cold ground, not daring to move in case she disturbed all the dead leaves around her. Her head ached from where she'd hit the branch, and already a big, swelling bruise was sticking out. She didn't care about that, though. It wasn't even making her cry. In fact, she was making no sound at all, because the horrible thin man who looked like a zombie and kept clearing his throat, was standing just a few yards away. Only a thick tangled bramble bush kept Casey hidden from him. All he had to do was walk a couple of steps this way and look down and he'd see her.

He was leaning against a tree and smoking a cigarette, and he'd been there for what seemed like ages. He was dressed all in black and he was holding a very big gun down by his side, and he looked really angry. Casey was so scared and so cold that she had to really concentrate to stop herself from shaking. In her head, she kept praying to God, asking him to make the thin man go away. Jess had told her after Mum had died that there was no God, but Casey didn't believe her. Of course there was a God. Who else made everything? Someone had to have done it to begin with. But she had to admit God wasn't very nice sometimes. He'd killed Dad and he'd killed Mum, and now he'd sent these horrible men out here to kill Uncle Tim and Auntie Jean, and now maybe even her and Jess.

But still she kept praying in her head, knowing that she just had to keep quiet for a little bit longer and it would all be all right. The horrible man looked as though he was bored of searching for her now. Soon he'd go away, then she'd keep running until she found the edge of the wood. It had to end somewhere. She'd never before been in a wood this huge and empty with no people around anywhere. All of Scotland seemed to be like that, just miles of empty space, and though she liked her new home, and the kids at her new school who'd all been really nice to her, she missed the noise and bustle of London.

But of course she might be going back there, now that Uncle Tim and Auntie Jean were . . . She couldn't say it. Even to herself. Her face crumpled as she thought of them then and she almost started to cry. She'd really liked Uncle Tim and Auntie Jean. She'd miss the stories her uncle used to tell her at night of the places he'd seen in the world when he'd been in the Merchant Navy and the people he'd met. She'd miss the way Auntie Jean would hug her really, really close and stroke her hair, and tell her what a beautiful girl she was . . .

She scrunched up her eyes and forced back the tears. She was a big girl now. She had to be brave.

The horrible man dropped his cigarette on the ground and stamped on it, all the time looking round with his big nose in the air, as if he was trying to smell her out.

Behind her, Casey could hear the faint rustling of leaves. Something was moving.

Very, very slowly she turned round, terrified of what she might see.

And had to stifle a gasp.

It was a baby deer, and it was standing next to a tree just a few feet away, looking over at her with big, dark eyes.

For just a couple of seconds, Casey forgot all her terror as she stared in wonder at it, amazed that it didn't run off. She'd only ever seen deer in Richmond Park and they always seemed to be a long way away, but this one was so close she could almost lean over and touch it.

And then the horrible man let out a sharp, hacking cough and the deer tensed, then bolted, scattering dead leaves.

Casey looked back quickly, just in time to see the horrible man swing round fast, eyes narrowing as he pulled the trigger on his big gun.

Behind her, she heard the deer fall. Then she squeezed her eyes shut as she heard his footsteps coming towards her.

Sayenko lowered the gun, and walked over to the bush, peering over into the darkness. The deer – one of those small, rat-like ones you get in this country – bucked a couple of times on the ground, then lay still. Sayenko cleared his throat and spat a lump of phlegm against a nearby tree. He'd thought it was the little brat he'd been chasing, and was immediately disappointed. It annoyed him that he was out here running round after her when what he should have done was shoot her the moment he'd seen her. As far as he was concerned, there was no point in letting any of them live, especially when they'd seen their faces, but Keogh had yelled at him to take the brat alive. No doubt he wanted to use her as a hostage to try to get the others out into the open, but now she'd escaped and was beyond the reach of any of them. Like everything else today, it had been a fuck-up, and that was the fault of this idiot, Keogh.

Sayenko didn't like having to work with anyone he didn't know and trust, and with good reason. This whole thing should have been easy. Three of them with guns, and all they had to do was grab an unarmed girl in the middle of nowhere, jab her with a needle, then chuck her in the trunk of a car and drive away. Sayenko knew if he'd been there, rather than keeping watch in the village, it would have been a different story. Once in Moscow, he and two other gunmen had grabbed a journalist out of her car at some traffic lights in the middle of rush hour, shot dead her two bodyguards, and still got out of there without any problem. Yet the three men he'd been working with today had failed completely, and now here he was, running around these woods, trying to find someone who was surely long gone by now.

Sayenko decided he wasn't going to carry on this chase any longer. He'd go back and find the others, which wasn't going to be easy, as the satellite phone they'd given him didn't have their numbers programmed in. But he'd worry about that in a minute. First, he needed a piss.

He glanced round briefly just to check that he was definitely alone before placing the gun carefully on the ground (he remembered only too well the story of a guy in the army who'd tried to take a leak with a pistol in his hand and who'd shot off the end of his cock when it had gone off by mistake).

Then, with a deep satisfied breath, he unzipped his trousers, relaxing for the first time that night.

Casey was holding her breath. She couldn't believe that the horrible thin man was standing on the other side of the bush, almost right above her. She could see his boots underneath it, no more than three feet away, could hear his harsh breathing. She could see the gun on the ground too.

She knew he was going to pee. She'd heard him unzip his flies. His wee was going to land on her too if she lay where she was, which would be absolutely disgusting.

She had a chance to run while the gun was out of reach. And she knew she was going to have to do it too, because if she stayed where she was, she was going to have to breathe soon – and then he'd hear her for sure.

Almost without thinking about it, she leapt to her feet, seeing the shock on the horrible man's face, then she turned and bolted into the darkness, knowing she was running for her life, that one mistake and she'd end up like that poor deer.

Sayenko leapt backwards with a startled growl. He couldn't believe he'd almost been standing on the little blonde brat without knowing it, and for a couple of seconds he didn't even react.

But then his training kicked in and – with an angry roar – he charged through the bush. He was quick over short distances, and with his long legs he gained on her rapidly, then reached out with one arm, yanking her backwards by the collar of her jacket and throwing her roughly to the ground, before slamming his knee into her back, enjoying the terrified sound she made as he picked her up.

Thirty-eight

'I can't believe he killed my dogs,' said MacLean, staring down at the two dead Dobermans at his feet, his pudgy face dark with rage. 'I spent months training them. What a fucking waste.'

'Who the hell was he, though?' said Keogh, thinking that right now dead dogs were the least of his problems. 'He just came out of nowhere.'

MacLean leaned down and inspected one of the dogs with a gloved hand. 'He shot this one in the neck, and he had a silencer on his gun.'

'He must have used Mehdi's gun, which is why I can't get hold of Mehdi. Do you think he's police?'

'No way. If the police were involved, there wouldn't just be one man, and he'd have shouted a warning before pulling the trigger. There are all kinds of rules about that sort of thing. You of all people should know that.'

Keogh ignored the jibe. 'Did you get a look at him?'

MacLean shook his head. 'He was too far away, and he didn't fire back when I was chasing him down the path.'

'Maybe he's trying to conserve his bullets.'

'Or maybe he's run out of them.'

'Let's hope so,' said Keogh, looking about him. The forest was dark and silent, the only sound the wind rustling through the leaves.

'We need to get hold of Sayenko,' growled MacLean. 'Why'd you send him after the wee bairn? It's just wasting time, and I'm telling you we don't have an awful lot of that left. With all the shooting, sooner or later someone's going to dial 999, and then we're going to be caught out here. And I'm not going to have that. Understand?'

'All right, all right,' said Keogh, trying to stay calm. 'I thought Sayenko could grab the girl as a hostage, but I wasn't banking on some unknown gunman shooting at us.' For the first time he seriously considered abandoning the op, getting in his car, and driving as far away from here as possible. He had money stashed away. He could head to Europe or Asia and lie low for a while. But he dismissed the thought almost immediately. The boss would track him down and exact revenge. 'We can still salvage this,' he said. 'We'll get hold of Sayenko, then we'll go after the other two. Where do you reckon they're going to head for now?'

'They'll go the same route they were always going to go. Out of the woods up to the road, then I reckon they'll cross country, go over the hills, and double back through the valley. I doubt if they'll try going to Tayleigh by road but, if they do, we've got Ma watching the road now, so we'll know about it.'

'So we're going to have to chase them across country? How exposed is it out there? Will we be able to locate them easily enough?' Keogh didn't like the hint of desperation he recognized in his own voice.

MacLean put down his shotgun and took the Ordnance Survey map out from inside his jacket. 'Shine a light over here, can you?'

The light in Keogh's torch had been shot out by the mystery gunman, but he still had a mini-Maglite attached to his key ring and he shone it onto the map.

'See, this is the path they'll take,' said MacLean, running a gloved finger through an area of white on the map lined with elevation contours that looked uninhabited. 'There's a farm here, about a mile and a half from the road, which they'll pass on that route, and if I were them, when I got there I'd stop and ask for help.'

'How long will it take for them to get there from here?'

'At least an hour, even if they're going fast.'

Keogh smiled for the first time in a while. 'That should give us plenty of time.' He took out the satellite phone and dialled the number of the handset he'd given to Sayenko, wondering if he'd managed to get hold of the little girl.

If he had, then Keogh would have no choice but to tell him to kill her.

Thirty-nine

Unarmed and alone, Scope moved as swiftly as he could through the trees. He didn't know this area of the forest very well, but he'd been on a run nearby a couple of months earlier, and remembered the chalet-style holiday cottage, close to where he'd heard all the shooting a few minutes earlier, and rescued Jess from being attacked by the dog.

He doubled back on himself, approaching the cottage from the north in a wide circle designed to keep him well out of the sights of the gunmen, in case they were continuing to look for him. He passed east of the cottage, giving it a wide berth, before trying to pick up the trail of Jess's sister, Casey. But the problem was, he wasn't a tracker. He'd found Jess earlier because he'd followed an established path and the protracted gunfire had pinpointed her exact location. But there was no gunfire or established path here, and he didn't dare call out to her. Casey didn't know him and, after all that had happened to her today, there was no way she'd respond to his calls. Also, Jess had said that one of the gunmen had gone after her, and was probably still in the vicinity. It was also possible that the other two weren't far away either and, now that he'd run out of bullets, Scope didn't want to attract any undue attention.

He stopped for a moment to get his breath back. He must have run at least four miles since he'd left the river, on top of a fast ten-mile kayak, and a fight that had almost cost him his life, and he was exhausted. He also had to make a decision about which way to go. The track that led from the cottage up to the B-road that snaked its way into Tayleigh was about two hundred yards to his right, and from the distance he'd travelled up the hill from the cottage, he guessed he was roughly level with the spot where Jess had abandoned the car she'd been in. That meant he was probably also about level with the place where Casey had entered the forest on this side of the road. She'd have been running for her life and panicking, so would probably have tried to get as far into the woods as possible, which meant running in an easterly direction. That, then, was the direction in which he'd head.

As his breathing slowed, he turned and was just about to start running when he heard it.

The sound of a phone ringing.

Stopping dead, he looked in the direction it was coming from and saw and heard movement coming from deeper in the woods. A second later, a tall, shadowy figure came into view no more than thirty yards away, and Scope could just make out the figure of a child walking closely alongside him. The man was pointing a gun down towards her shoulder and, as the phone rang again, he fumbled for it in his pocket.

Casey shivered in fear. The gun was resting against her neck, and her back really hurt from where the horrible man had jumped on her. She wished she'd stayed where she'd been now, even if it had meant the man weeing on her, because now she'd been captured, and she didn't know what was going to happen.

The horrible man's phone was ringing and he fished it out of his jacket, grunting and cursing to himself in a foreign language she didn't understand.

'Yeah,' he said in a growly voice.

Casey looked up at him. He wasn't looking at her any more. He was busy listening to the voice on the other end of the phone, and his gun was no longer resting on her shoulder.

'Sure, I've got her,' he said. 'What do you want done?'

She couldn't quite hear what the man he was speaking to was saying, but she was sure she heard the word 'kill' and it sent a huge shiver up her spine. She knew then that if she stayed where she was, then she was going to die right here.

Without even thinking about it, Casey grabbed the end of the gun and pulled as hard as she could. The man was so busy talking he wasn't paying attention, and to her amazement the gun came free from his hand.

He shouted out and went to grab it back, but she was too quick, throwing it away as far as she could before turning, ducking away from his clawing hands, and sprinting into the trees, all in the space of a couple of seconds.

Sayenko couldn't believe the little brat had caught him out like that, or that he'd been so careless as to have let his finger drift away from the trigger. And Christ, she was fast, darting away from him into the trees.

'What the hell's going on?' snapped Keogh, who'd heard his curses. 'You've still got her, haven't you?'

Sayenko ignored him as he ran over and grabbed the gun. Then, keeping the phone to his ear with his shoulder, he turned and took aim at the fleeing figure, using both hands to steady the gun. She was wearing a dark jacket and she'd already covered a decent amount of ground, but Sayenko was an excellent shot. Squinting a little, he looked down the barrel, moving it ever so slightly until the middle of her back was in his sights.

Then he fired a single shot, the suppressor masking most of the noise, and the brat fell.

'Bang,' he said down the phone, and turned away, fumbling in his pocket for another cigarette. 'Now we've got one less witness to worry about.'

Scope saw it all happen from barely twenty yards away. The whole thing had taken a matter of seconds. As the tall, thin guy had been talking on the phone, he'd been creeping nearer, yard by yard, taking advantage of the fact that he was distracted. But then the girl had made a sudden break for it and the guy had shot her, just like that.

Scope had thought about charging the gunman when the guy had had his back to him, but he'd left it just a second too long. And now the little girl was dead and the gunman was saying down the phone that they – whoever *they* were – had one less witness to worry about. There was a triumphant tone in his voice that set Scope's teeth on edge.

For a moment, he was too numb to move. It was hard to believe he'd just witnessed the murder of a child. The shock was physical in its intensity. It made his legs weak and his heart surge as his system filled with adrenalin. Then, as the gunman replaced the phone in his jacket and lit a cigarette, the anger came. It wasn't the hot, passionate anger of someone who loses all sense of reason; it was far colder and harder than that. It was anger that cut through steel, anger that was utterly focused in its intensity. It was the anger of killers, and it was what Scope had felt when the twenty-year-old dealer who'd got his Mary Ann hooked on smack had been on his knees begging for his life. All humanity had left him then. He'd put five bullets in a guy barely out of his teens and, even as he'd left him lying there, bleeding out his last breaths, that cold anger had still pulsed through him.

Taking a deep breath, Scope began to creep closer to his quarry, conscious of the silence in the air.

The gunman took a deep drag on his cigarette and started walking in the direction of the track, the pistol dangling idly by his side.

Ten yards separated them, but for Scope it was at least five yards too far. The gunman was a good shot and cool under pressure. If he ran at him, he'd be cut down before he got there – there was no question of it. And if he moved any faster than he was going now he risked being heard, and already the gunman was increasing the distance between them.

Scope controlled the anger. He'd get this bastard, and he'd make him pay for killing that little girl if it was the last thing he ever did, but right now it was going to have to wait.

But then the gunman took another drag on the cigarette, and was suddenly hit by a coughing fit. He bent over double, trying to bring it under control and, as he did so, Scope took his chance and sprinted at his back, hoping he couldn't be heard above the noise.

The gunman spat on the ground and, as he stood back up again, he must have heard Scope's rapidly approaching foot-steps, because he swung round fast, a surprised look on his face, and instinctively raised the gun.

Barely two yards away, Scope dived straight into him, knocking his gun to one side, and sending the two of them crashing to the ground. The gun went off with a loud pop and the gunman gasped as he landed on his back with Scope's weight on top of him, and broke into a second coughing fit. Making full use of his advantage, Scope punched him twice in the face, grabbing his gun arm by the wrist at the same time and giving it a twist. The gun went off again as the gunman fought to hang onto it. Even in his current state, he was putting up surprisingly strong resistance, but then Scope sat up on top of him, and used his free hand to rain blows down on his face with every ounce of strength he could muster, driven on by the thought that the bastard had just murdered a child, and the adrenalin that seemed to course through every sinew and muscle of his body.

The gunman grunted as his nose broke and blood splattered his face, and his body seemed to go slack. His grip on the gun loosened and Scope paused just long enough to pluck it from his hand, then leapt to his feet, panting from the exertion of the violence. Below him the gunman rolled from side to side on the ground, seemingly dazed by Scope's onslaught, his face already beginning to darken and swell.

Scope pointed the gun down at his chest. 'Who are you?' he hissed in the darkness. 'And what do you want here? Tell me now or I'll kill you.'

The gunman finished coughing, rolled to one side, and spat blood and phlegm into the dirt. 'Fuck you,' he grunted.

Scope stiffened, the cold anger he was feeling enveloping every other thought. 'No,' he said, pulling the trigger. 'Fuck *you*.' He shot him once in the belly, feeling too much pleasure at the spasm of pain that passed across the gunman's features, then once in the chest, finally finishing him off with a third bullet just beneath his left eye.

Afterwards, he stood rigid for several seconds staring down at the man he'd just killed, waiting for the anger to subside. He knew he was going to have to check the little girl to see if she was still alive, even though he felt sure she wouldn't be. There was no way she'd have got more than a few yards into the undergrowth, and the gunman had seemed confident that he'd finished her off with the shot, but he was going to have to look, however hard it might be.

A vision of that little boy back in Afghanistan staring up at him with the gaping hole in his throat tore across his mind, and he took a deep breath and closed his eyes.

Which was when he heard it. The faint crunch of leaves underfoot.

His eyes flew open and he saw two shadowy figures a few yards apart, approaching him quietly through the trees, some fifteen yards distant. There was no question they'd seen him. Not only that, it looked like they'd identified him as an enemy. They were both holding rifles and, even as he watched, the closest of the two put his rifle to his shoulder and took aim.

Scope leapt for cover as the first of the shots rang out, scrambling behind a tree. A chunk of bark flew off as a round struck the trunk, only a few inches from his outstretched leg, and he rolled over on the ground so he was temporarily out of sight and, knowing he only had a few seconds to put some distance between himself and the two gunmen, he leapt to his feet and took off into the foliage, keeping low.

No more shots rang out and, as he ran, keeping to a straight line and using the thick undergrowth as cover, knowing he was going fast enough to outrun them, a sudden thought struck him.

He'd just run past the exact spot where Casey must have been shot. He remembered it well enough, even though he hadn't actually seen her fall.

But there was no body there now.

Forty

'Jesus Christ, what the hell's going on?' said MacLean, looking over towards Sayenko's corpse from his position behind a beech tree about ten yards away.

Keogh was standing behind a second tree nearby. His ears buzzed from the gunshots and his shoulder ached from the recoil of the rifle as he looked beyond the corpse to where the man who'd just killed Sayenko had disappeared. He'd almost had the slippery sod as well. One more second and he'd have got him in his sights and blown a nice big hole in his heart, but then that big oaf MacLean had made a noise and that had been it. The target had bolted, moving far too fast and purposefully for an amateur.

'I don't know,' he said, trying to keep his voice quiet, even though the buzzing in his ears made it hard to hear himself. 'Maybe he's something to do with Amanda Rowan. A bodyguard, someone like that.'

'If he was her bodyguard, where was he when we tried to snatch her?' grunted MacLean dismissively.

It was a good point, but Keogh was completely at a loss as to any other explanation. He wasn't a cop: MacLean was right about that. So who the hell was he?

Keogh motioned to MacLean and together they slowly approached Sayenko's corpse, crouching low in case the stranger was waiting to ambush them.

'Cover me,' whispered Keogh, slinging his rifle over his shoulder and quickly searching the corpse as MacLean stood above him, looking round carefully. There were bullet holes in Sayenko's belly, heart and head, and it was obvious that they'd been delivered by someone who knew how to use a gun. Even at a range of just a few feet, if you're not good with firearms, you won't make as precise hits as Sayenko's killer had.

Keogh took out Sayenko's sat phone and a spare magazine he had for his pistol, then got slowly to his feet. For the first time on this op – in fact, for the first time in a long time – he felt truly nervous.

'So, what are we going to do about this fellah?' asked MacLean.

Keogh sighed as they stepped back into the cover of the trees. 'I don't see how he's going to raise the alarm. Not after he's just committed cold-blooded murder. Our best bet's to keep to the original plan, pick up Amanda Rowan, give the bitch a well-deserved kicking, then get the hell out of here with her.' He took one more look into the gloom, wondering if the stranger had rescued the little girl (and, in a small way, hoping he had), then turned away, knowing that they were fast running out of options.

Forty-one

Today 15.45

Bolt opened the window of the hire car they'd picked up at Aberdeen Airport and breathed in the fresh clean air as he and Mo drove along the A95, a thick wall of pine forest on one side of them, and a long sweeping loch with bleak, tree-dotted mountains rising up into a pale blue sky on the other.

It was rugged, dramatic scenery, and a far cry from the city where Bolt spent so much of his time. This was only his second visit to Scotland – the first had been a two-week family holiday to the Western Isles when he was a boy, and it had rained pretty much the whole time – but, looking at it now in all its silent, natural beauty, with virtually no other traffic on the road, he promised himself he'd come back at some point and do some fishing – even if it was on his own, now that his old fishing buddy Sam Verran had got himself a girlfriend.

'This is where all those hikers got killed last year, isn't it?' said Mo, doing a great job of breaking the mood.

Bolt remembered the case well enough. Two young couples

had come up from London for a weekend of hiking, and had been reported missing a few days later. All four bodies had been found in the house they'd rented for the weekend. Three had suffered stab wounds while the fourth – a teacher called Ashleigh Murray – had been found hanging in the living room. The local CID had concluded that the deaths had been a case of murder suicide, with Ashleigh Murray as the perpetrator, but the case had been racked by controversy ever since, with Murray's family pushing hard for a full review by a separate police force.

'That's right,' he said. 'I always thought there was something weird about that case. A woman primary school teacher, well liked by her colleagues, and with no history of mental illness, who reportedly has a great relationship with her husband, goes mad with a knife and kills him and two other people, then kills herself. I don't buy it. I never did.'

'Me neither,' said Mo. 'You know why? They never explained the injuries to the lower leg of the female murder victim. Remember? She had deep cuts consistent with being caught in an illegal hunting trap, as well as the stab wounds, but there was no sign of a hunting trap anywhere round that house.'

'You know a lot about the case.'

'I just remember, it all seemed wrong. Do you know what else?'

'Go on. Surprise me.'

'The cottage where the bodies were found was less than two miles from Vladimir Hanzha's country estate.'

Bolt *was* surprised at that. 'Really?'

'Really. Do you reckon that's a coincidence?'

Bolt frowned. 'God knows. The thing is, there are too many coincidences around this whole case.'

'Exactly, but I've got a strong feeling that our Vlad's not going to shed much light on things.'

'I think you're right, but at least we've got a good excuse for going to see him. Any grieving parent would want to know that their child's killer's been found, even if he is dead.' So far, the Disciple inquiry team hadn't announced the discovery of Leonard Hope's body. They'd been told from above to keep it quiet for at least another twenty-four hours. Bolt wasn't quite sure why, but he guessed the Brass were still trying to come up with a way to announce it that didn't make the Met look like a bunch of incompetents for losing him in the first place. Either way, it had meant that the press conference that Bolt had chaired that morning had just turned into another bout of hostile questions about the hunt for Leonard Hope that he'd been unable to answer properly, but at least it meant he and Mo could get Vladimir Hanzha's reaction to the news of the demise of the man who'd killed his daughter first-hand.

'He doesn't know we're coming, does he?' said Mo, as Bolt slowed the car to turn up the well-kept private road that led to the estate.

'No, and if he's not in, we'll wait. We know he's up here somewhere.'

As it happened their luck was in. When they arrived at the ornate wrought-iron gates and introduced themselves through the intercom, they had a wait of less than a minute before the gates opened automatically and they were allowed to drive inside. A plainclothes security guard who looked Russian checked their warrant cards, then directed them down the left-hand fork of the road that led them a further two hundred yards through carefully manicured gardens, before they came to an impressive-looking, three-storey Georgian country house, the size of a small hotel, with turrets at either end and an imposing clock tower in the middle.

'How the other half lives, eh?' said Mo as they parked the car at one end of the driveway next to a brand-new crimson Ferrari and got out.

'And I bet you we pay more taxes than him,' said Bolt, taking a moment to bask in the afternoon sunshine before walking over to a flight of steps wide enough to hold a wedding party that led up to the front door.

Before they got there, the door opened, and a big man in an open shirt and suit trousers appeared. He was in his mid- to late-fifties, with a thick head of curly grey hair and a slight forward stoop, without which he probably would have been about Bolt's height at six foot four. He was beginning to run to fat, and his face was jowly and grizzled, but not without a degree of charm, and Bolt reckoned that a decade ago he probably would have been a pretty good-looking guy. Even if he hadn't seen a photo of Vladimir Hanzha, he would have known straight away that this was him. He looked exactly as you'd expect a dodgy Russian oligarch to look, and Bolt was surprised that he'd chosen to greet them personally rather than send someone else. Men like him usually had a fairly sizeable entourage.

'DCS Bolt,' he said in a booming voice, coming down the steps. 'I recognize you from the press conferences.'

They shook hands and Bolt wasn't surprised that Hanzha tried to crush his in some kind of Vulcan death grip. 'Pleased to meet you, Mr Hanzha,' he said simply, not reacting to the pain as the Russian released his hold. 'This is my colleague, DS Mo Khan.'

Hanzha gave Mo a curt nod and made no attempt to shake his hand. 'Come inside,' he said, addressing Bolt. 'You must have come a long way. Can I get you a drink of anything?'

They both declined and followed him through a grand, richly

carpeted foyer with animal heads and expensive paintings of traditional country scenes mounted on the walls. Bolt noticed the head of a huge stag with antlers several feet long that looked newer than the others.

'I shot that one,' said Hanzha, his tone matter-of-fact, as if he did such things every day.

Bolt didn't comment. He'd never considered hunting animals with a big gun particularly impressive, and was one of those people who thought they looked better alive in their natural environment than decapitated and stuffed in a rich man's house.

Hanzha led them down an adjoining hallway, past an indoor swimming pool, separated by a floor-to-ceiling glass window, and into a spacious, traditionally furnished living room with views out towards the mountains in the distance. They sat in chairs next to an unmade fire, Bolt and Mo opposite Hanzha.

'Let me start by expressing our condolences for the loss of your daughter, Mr Hanzha,' said Bolt.

Hanzha sighed deeply and his expression tightened. 'We didn't get on well, me and Ivana. She was headstrong, like her mother. But I miss her.' He nodded slowly, as if this was the first time he'd admitted this to himself. 'I miss her.' For a few seconds he didn't speak, then he looked at them both in turn. 'So what brings you all the way up here to see me?' he asked.

'We have some news regarding our prime suspect, Leonard Hope,' Bolt told him.

Hanzha's expression darkened. 'Tell me,' he said, leaning forward in his chair, suddenly very interested.

'We found his body yesterday. It had been dumped in countryside west of London.'

'It showed signs of extreme torture,' put in Mo, watching Hanzha closely.

For the first time the Russian smiled, but there was no humour in it. 'Good,' he said. 'I hope the bastard died in plenty of pain.'

Bolt nodded. 'Yes, he did.'

'So the hunt for The Disciple is over. It cannot bring my daughter back. She is with God now. But at least some kind of real justice has been served. I was worried he would end up in one of your prisons, watching television in his cell, taking drugs, living out the rest of his life in comfort.'

'I don't think our prisons are that comfortable,' said Mo.

Hanzha grunted dismissively. 'They are a lot nicer than Russian ones. Russian prisons are real prisons. The prisoners actually suffer there.'

'The point is, Mr Hanzha, there are still unanswered questions,' said Bolt. 'The foremost of which is: who killed him.'

'You're the detective, Mr Bolt. That's for you to find out, isn't it? I'm just a businessman.'

'Someone helped Leonard Hope escape our surveillance team. We suspect whoever helped him then killed him.'

'You have a Frank Keogh working for you,' said Mo. 'Can you tell us what he does?'

Hanzha turned in his seat and glared at Mo, a barely suppressed anger in the expression, almost as if Mo was the one responsible for the death of his daughter. 'Why are you asking about people who may or may not work for me? What has this got to do with anything?'

'It's just a simple question, Mr Hanzha,' said Bolt, knowing he had to be careful here.

'Tell me why you ask.'

'Because he has a conviction for manslaughter, has links to organized crime, and we believe he may have had something to do with Leonard Hope's disappearance.'

'And do you have any evidence to back up this claim?'

demanded Hanzha, sounding as if he genuinely didn't believe a word of what Bolt was saying.

Bolt didn't have a scrap of evidence, but he wasn't going to admit to that. 'We can't discuss that. We just need to know whether or not he works for you.'

'And I can't discuss that. You want to continue this conversation, you talk to my lawyers. I thought you were coming here to keep me informed of progress on the case to find my daughter's killer, not question me about affairs that have nothing to do with any of this.'

'Mr Hanzha, we're just trying to find out what happened to Leonard Hope,' said Bolt, attempting to smooth things over.

'Listen to me, both of you.' He pointed a finger at them. 'I have no idea who killed Leonard Hope, although I am glad he's dead. He brutalized my daughter. Raped her, tortured her. Painted signs on the wall in her blood.' He gesticulated angrily with his hands. 'I hope he rots in Hell for all eternity.'

'I have no doubt he will,' said Bolt.

Hanzha got to his feet. For him, the interview was over.

Bolt and Mo followed suit. They both knew there was no way they were going to get anything else out of him now, but that didn't matter. Bolt had already heard what he needed to.

'I heard that there were two killers,' said Hanzha, as he led them back through the house. 'That's what some of the newspapers have been saying. How do you know it wasn't the other killer who got rid of Hope?'

'The two-killer theory is a line of inquiry,' Bolt told him. 'But we're not convinced of it yet. If there is a second killer, we'll find him and bring him to justice.'

Hanzha let out a vaguely derisive grunt. 'If there is a second killer, I am surprised that, between them, they didn't manage to kill the woman who disturbed them murdering my daughter. What was her name again?'

'Amanda Rowan. It seems she's a very resilient woman.'

'Very,' said Hanzha, and there was something malicious and sceptical in the way he spoke the word. 'Almost unbelievably so.'

Bolt frowned. 'What do you mean?'

Hanzha shrugged. 'I'm just very surprised she got away. That's all.'

They were at the front door now. Hanzha opened it and stepped to one side.

'Thank you for your time, Mr Hanzha. Once again, let me reiterate how sorry we are for your loss.'

'You came a long way just to tell me that.' Something in his expression seemed to dare Bolt and Mo to accuse him of wrongdoing.

But Bolt simply nodded and turned away.

Neither he nor Mo spoke on the way back to the car. It was only when Mo had started the engine that Bolt turned to him. 'Did you notice what Hanzha said?'

Mo smiled. 'Course I did. I've been a detective a long time, boss. His problem is that he's too arrogant. "Painted signs on the wall in her blood." That's what he said, wasn't it?'

'Exactly. We never released that information. The only way he could have known about it is if he had someone on the inside.'

'And if he had someone on the inside, he could easily have organized Leonard Hope's abduction and murder.'

'He did,' said Bolt. 'There's no question of that. No one else could have pulled it off, and he's got the resources.'

'But you saw him in there. The guy's as hard as rock. He's

not going to admit a thing, and you can bet he kept a long way from the whole affair.'

'That's as may be, but someone tortured Hope, and if we can lift some of the killer's DNA from his corpse, we might strike lucky.' But Bolt wasn't at all sure he believed it. So far, SOCO hadn't managed to secure any DNA from the murder scene that would point a finger at Hope's killer, and once again he felt the familiar frustration that had haunted him throughout this whole inquiry.

He and Mo were silent as they drove through Hanzha's perfectly manicured lawns and out of his grand estate.

Finally Mo said: 'Even if we know Hanzha was responsible for Hope's murder, that still doesn't tell us what the DNA of a separate killer was doing at the Rowan house. Someone else was involved in the murder of George Rowan and Ivana Hanzha, but who?'

Bolt sighed. 'I still think we're looking at this the wrong way. It was odd what Hanzha was saying about Amanda Rowan, wasn't it? You know, talking sarcastically about how resilient she was.'

Mo looked startled. 'You don't think she did it, do you, boss?'

'No, but I'm beginning to wonder if she knows more than she's letting on. Now seems a very opportune moment to pay her a visit.'

It was only a few minutes after the two detectives had left that Keogh called Vladimir Hanzha to tell him that the Amanda Rowan snatch had gone wrong.

Hanzha could barely contain his anger. This should have been an easy, straightforward job, but Keogh had managed to make a mess of things. Hanzha had warned him to make good his mistake or face the consequences but, in reality, he'd already decided to rid himself of the scar-faced Englishman. Keogh had worked for him for more than three years and, although he'd always been a loyal and competent employee, he knew far too much about his boss for Hanzha to allow him to retire in peace. Keogh was going to have to disappear, especially now that the police had his name.

It didn't surprise Hanzha that the police had suspicions that he was behind the abduction and murder of Leonard Hope. They would never prove it, though. The authorities in the UK were soft and tied up with all kinds of rules and regulations. A man with enough money and cunning could always stay one step ahead of them.

He put down the phone and walked back through the house, staring out of the window at the grounds of his estate in silence. For years he'd given his estranged daughter little thought, but since her murder she'd rarely been out of his mind, and he wasn't quite sure why. It wasn't as if he missed her – they hadn't spoken in so long he had to work hard even to remember the sound of her voice. But she was still *his* daughter, and someone had taken her from him. Such an act made him lose face, and a man like Vladimir Hanzha couldn't afford to lose face. He wanted revenge on those who'd crossed him.

And by the end of tonight he was going to get it.

Forty-two

The wind blew hard across the exposed hills as Jess and Amanda trudged upwards towards the first of the rolling peaks.

Jess was shattered. Her legs felt like lead and her breathing was coming in short, hollow rasps. Once again, she checked the phone the stranger had given her. Once again, there was no reception. Pausing for a moment, she turned and looked back towards the long winding road as it disappeared into the distance. Behind the road, the forest spread like a great black carpet as it arched down towards the river. Casey was in there somewhere, lost and alone. The thought made Jess's heart lurch. She felt sick that she was leaving Casey to fend for herself, and furious that she couldn't get a phone signal, however high she climbed. What was wrong with this place? It was like the fucking Stone Age . . .

'Are you okay?' asked Amanda, stopping a few yards above her.

Jess put her hands on her hips and lowered her head, trying

to get her breath back. 'I just need a couple of minutes, that's all. Then I can keep going.'

'It's not that much further to the top. Then it's all downhill into Tayleigh.'

'I need a signal on this phone. There must be somewhere round here I can get one.'

Amanda came down and stood beside her. 'We should be able to get a signal at the top of the hill and, even if we can't, we'll be in Tayleigh in just over an hour if we move fast.' She paused and put a hand on Jess's shoulder. 'Look, I know you're worried about Casey, but she'll be okay.'

Jess moved away from her. 'How do you know?' she demanded.

'Because it's me they seem to be after. You know, if you want, you can wait here. I can take the phone, and as soon as I get a signal, I'll call for help.'

'No, it's okay,' said Jess. There was no way she was going to give up the phone to anyone, not when it was her and Casey's lifeline. She sat down in the long grass behind a gorse bush, feeling a wave of exhaustion.

Annoyingly, Amanda sat down next to her. 'Casey's not your real sister, is she?' she said.

'She's totally my real sister,' snapped Jess. 'Not by blood, maybe, but she means everything to me.'

'I'm sorry. I didn't mean it like that. It's just, you know—'

'My skin colour.'

Amanda nodded. 'Yes, that's what made me say it. I just wanted to talk, that's all.' She gave Jess the kind of earnest, patronizing look that a couple of the younger teachers at college liked to give her, as if the fact that she was mixed race made her somehow special, rather than just like everyone else. It annoyed her when they did it, and it annoyed her now.

She sighed. 'I was adopted at seven. Before that, I had a shitty childhood – more shitty than someone like you could imagine. Then I had a happy childhood until first my mum died, then my dad. Casey moved up here, and I stayed at home in London. That's it. My story. Satisfied?'

Amanda turned away, hanging her head down between her knees. 'I'm sorry I asked,' she said.

Jess didn't bother replying. She had no desire to be this woman's friend, not after everything she'd brought down on them.

There was a silence before Amanda spoke again. 'I didn't want any of this, you know. I just want to be happy like everyone else. I drifted for a lot of my life, got involved with the wrong sort of men, and then finally settled down and married a man who said he truly loved me. Only it turned out I wasn't enough for him. He takes a lover, brings her to our own home when I'm not there, and ends up being murdered along with her, and I walk in on the scene. I almost get killed . . .' She lifted her bandaged arm. 'And now, three weeks later, having been forced to leave my home forever, I end up being hunted by men I've never even seen before. And the worst thing is, I have no idea why they're doing it.' She took a deep breath, letting it out slowly. 'No idea at all.'

Jess softened. She'd never been any good at staying angry with people, whoever they were. 'I didn't mean to snap,' she said.

'It's okay. I know how hard it is for you, I really do. I've lost my husband and my home. Everything I ever strived for.'

'You don't have kids?'

Amanda shook her head wistfully. 'Sadly not. We tried. It just didn't work out for us.'

'I'm sorry,' said Jess, who'd always wanted kids. Four in all. Two of each.

'That's just the way it goes sometimes,' Amanda said with a shrug of her shoulders, but there was disappointment in her voice.

Neither of them said anything for a few moments, but then Jess felt a sudden need to speak. 'I saw my birth mother murdered,' she said, not really knowing why she was telling this complete stranger her dark secret, when she'd rarely spoken about it to anyone. 'I was six years old.'

Amanda stared at her. 'Jesus.'

'I was upstairs in bed and I heard my mum arguing with her boyfriend. They were screaming at each other, like they often did, then I just heard my mum gasp and cry out. I can still remember the exact sound she made now.' Jess paused, shutting her eyes tightly, remembering the terror of that night. 'I was really scared, but I went into the lounge anyway, because I wanted to see if my mum was okay, and there he was standing over her, and he had his hands round her neck, and he was squeezing and squeezing. I could see my mum's face. It was turning blue and her eyes were sticking out like they were on stalks, and she was making this horrible, rasping sound. He didn't even hear me come in. He was just looking down on my mum the whole time with his face screwed up with this expression of just total rage . . .' She stopped, the memory hitting her like a blow to the head. 'I didn't know what to do. I was standing there watching, because I think I was so shocked. Then, the next thing I remember, I ran in and grabbed his arm, yelling and trying to stop him, and he turned and looked at me, and there was this total hate in his eyes, like he was possessed by the devil or something. He punched me in the face. I remember that. It didn't even hurt, it just felt like this massive shock, and then I was flying backwards. I think I must have been out cold for a bit because the next thing I knew he was gone and my mum was just lying there.' She frowned, aware of how cold and factual she was making it sound, clinical almost, when in reality it had been anything but. 'She was dead. I tried waking her up. I shook her. I cried. But she was gone, and eventually I went to the neighbour's flat, knocked on the door, and told them what had happened.'

Amanda swallowed audibly. 'I don't know what to say,' she whispered.

'You don't have to say anything. I told you because, before tonight, it was the most scared I'd ever been. Casey's only a few years older now than I was then, and I know she's going to be just as scared out there, and it makes me feel so bad that I'm not there with her.'

'Come on then,' said Amanda, getting to her feet. 'Let's get to the top of this hill and see if we can get a signal.' She helped Jess up and they continued their uphill trudge.

Five minutes later they'd reached the peak. It was bare and craggy with patches of heather and ferns dotted about, and the wind was even stronger. Jess knelt down behind one of the heather patches and checked the phone. It was showing a single bar and she felt a surge of excitement as she immediately dialled 999.

The phone rang twice before being picked up at the other end. But the line was cracked and virtually inaudible. Jess could just about make out the operator's voice, but it was so faint she couldn't tell if it belonged to a man or a woman. 'Hello? Hello?' She shouted into the phone as a gust of wind blew hard across the peak, all but drowning out her voice.

The phone bleeped three times and went dead, and Jess dialled a second time, her fingers shaking as she found the call button. 'Come on, come on,' she whispered.

The phone bleeped again. Now it wasn't even connecting, and when she checked the signal, it read No Service. She cursed angrily, holding it up and moving it around, trying desperately to get some kind of reception.

But it was no good. Somehow they'd lost it, and on the top of a fucking mountain of all places! Jess felt the tears come then – tears of frustration, anger, and sheer, blind grief.

'It's okay,' said Amanda, coming over and putting out her arms. 'It's okay.'

This time Jess allowed herself to be held and cried into her chest while Amanda stroked her hair in silence.

But Jess wasn't the type of girl to let weakness take her for long, and after a few seconds she moved out of the embrace and wiped her eyes. 'Come on,' she said. 'The sooner we get to Tayleigh the better.'

Amanda nodded. 'I think there's a farm somewhere in the next valley. Maybe we can get help there.'

They looked at each other for a long moment, just a few feet apart, and Jess felt a bond begin to form between them.

Then she turned away and started walking, not daring to look back towards the darkness of the forest, nor wanting to dwell on the fate that might have befallen her beloved Casey.

Forty-three

Casey found it totally by accident. She'd been walking and running for miles through the forest, ever since the horrible man had tried to shoot her, which seemed ages ago now.

She'd been running away from him after she'd broken free while he'd been on the phone, and she remembered tripping up because she was going so fast at just the same time when the horrible man had fired his gun at her. She'd fallen flat on her face and had just lain there, thinking that she should pretend she was dead like they did in films sometimes, because he hadn't hit her with the bullet and that maybe if he thought she was dead, he'd go away.

And he had too, but then almost straight away Casey had heard the noise of fighting going on behind her, and more shooting. So she'd got scared again and had got up and started running.

But she'd had no idea where she was going, or where the woods would end. And all around her there'd been lots of strange noises: rustlings in the bushes and the hooting of owls, as though they were warning someone of her presence. Shadows moved in the trees too, and Casey imagined there were all kinds of horrible creatures lurking about, like werewolves and vampires, looking for lost people like her to feed on, even though she was old enough to know that werewolves and vampires didn't really exist.

But now she'd found the end of the forest. She'd come to a quiet road with hills rising up on the other side and, even better, a little house tucked away behind a hedge with its lights on.

Casey was shy about ringing on the bell, even though it was a pretty place with a brightly painted front door, and lots of plants growing up the walls, and best of all, smoke from a fire rising out of the chimney. She didn't know the people who lived here. They might not let her in. And she didn't want to have to talk to anyone about what had happened to her today. She just wanted to forget about it. She even thought about lying down and going to sleep in the shed she could see behind the gate in the back garden, and waiting until morning. But it was cold, and she was tired and hungry, and maybe the people who lived here would call the police, and then the police could come and rescue her and Jess, and the other lady, Amanda, who all the bad men were after.

The curtains were drawn so she couldn't see inside, and she stood staring at the front door, which was painted bright red, for quite a long time before finally she got the courage to ring the bell.

After a few seconds, she heard footsteps moving slowly inside the house, then an old man's voice asked: 'Who is it?'

'It's me, Casey,' said Casey, leaning in close to the letterbox. 'I'm lost, and I need to call the police. Could you let me in, please?'

262

The door opened a few inches behind a chain and a white-haired man in glasses with a friendly face, who looked a bit like Liz Warren's grandad, stared down at her.

'Hi,' she said.

'Gosh, you poor wee thing, you look frozen,' said the man in his Scottish accent. He took the chain off the door, opening it wide so that a big breath of warm air wafted out over her. 'Come inside. Come on, come on.'

Not needing a second invitation, Casey hopped through the door and the old man closed it behind her. 'Whatever happened to you, wee bairn? Tell me while you get yourself warm in front of the fire.'

He led her through into a comfy sitting room. The TV was on, showing an old-looking drama, and there was a big, roaring fire blazing away with a chair next to it. He ushered her into the chair and she sat down with a smile, basking in the heat of the flames. Briefly, she told him what had happened to her today, still unable to quite believe it all herself. She didn't even cry when she told him about Uncle Tim and Auntie Jean.

The old man had a kindly face, and he nodded as she spoke, saying things like 'Oh dear' and 'Poor wee thing', but she could tell by his expression that he didn't entirely believe her. 'It's all true, I promise,' she told him when she'd finished. 'We need to call the police. Jess is still out there. She might be hurt.'

The old man smiled. 'Don't worry. I'll call the police. Now you look very hungry. Would you like something to eat?'

Funnily enough, she wasn't hungry at all. Just thirsty. 'Do you have any Diet Coke?' she asked, because she was only ever allowed it as a special treat.

'Och no, I don't drink that stuff,' the old man scolded. 'I could make you a cup of tea, though.'

'Water's fine, please,' said Casey, hiding her disappointment.

He got to his feet. 'You wait there. I'm going to call the police, then I'm going to get you a drink.'

Casey watched him go, feeling safe for the first time that night.

In the kitchen, the old man replaced the phone receiver in its cradle, before pouring a glass of water from the tap for his surprise, but very welcome, guest.

In fact, he couldn't believe his luck. This beautiful, innocent little thing was like a gift from God.

The old man's name was Ronald Dewey, and it was nine years since his release from prison. In that time, he'd kept his nose clean and, although he would be on the sex offenders register for the rest of his life, he was now categorized as at low risk of reoffending. In fact, he'd almost forgotten about the beauty of little girls, since he saw them so rarely these days, and it had been almost two decades since lovely, sweet Morag. But now, seeing little Casey brought all the memories flooding back, and he felt a hot flush washing over him.

Nobody knew she was here. She'd said so herself. If the story she'd told him was true, and there were a bunch of lunatics in the forest killing indiscriminately, then no one would ever suspect old Ronald of being responsible for her disappearance. Even if she'd made it all up, the fact was that she was alone, and had clearly wandered a long, long way from her family.

He knew it was wrong. He knew he shouldn't do it. He was happy here and had no desire to go back to prison. And he loved children. He really did. But Casey was such a nice, polite thing that it seemed such a terrible waste not to enjoy what she was offering, even if she wasn't aware of what that was yet.

No. He couldn't waste this opportunity.

He went back into the lounge with the water and gave it to Casey. 'The police are on their way,' he told her, hoping she'd heard the call he'd pretended to make from the kitchen, 'but it's going to take them a while. We're a long way from the nearest police station.'

'Thank you,' she said sweetly, drinking from the glass, which she held with both hands.

'Would you like to lie down and have a rest while you wait for them?' he said, only just managing to keep the growing sense of excitement out of his voice. 'You look very sleepy, and there's a spare bedroom where my granddaughter stays sometimes.'

'What's her name?'

'Eleanor,' he lied.

She smiled, showing lovely white teeth. 'That's a nice name. Is it warm up there?'

He smiled back. 'Oh yes. It's lovely and cosy. I always keep the house warm.'

She put down the empty glass. 'Do you really mind if I go to sleep? I don't want to be rude but I am very tired.'

'Of course not. Come on, I'll show you to her room.'

He led the way up the stairs, keeping his breathing steady, and opened the door to the spare room, switching on the light.

'It doesn't have any pictures on the walls,' said Casey, the first hint of concern in her voice. 'Doesn't Eleanor like pictures?'

'We're going to be getting her some soon,' he said, looking into the stark, lifeless room that he hadn't used in years. It smelled of damp and stale air. 'She hasn't been for a little while, but the sheets are clean.' He forced another smile. 'Go on. In you go.'

Hesitantly, she stepped inside, and went over to the bed,

looking down at it. 'Maybe I'll come back downstairs if that's okay,' she said, turning back towards him.

'No. I think it's best you stay here for now,' he said, and before she could answer back, he shut the door and turned the key in the lock.

Now she was his.

Forty-four

Today 16.40

There was no sign of Amanda Rowan at her house. Bolt had already called the landline and got no answer, but when he tried her mobile, the automated message said it was switched off. He then called his contact in Highlands CID, DI Sally Miles, who told him that a liaison officer had been sent over to give her the news that Leonard Hope's body had been found, and that Bolt was going to be paying her a visit, but she hadn't heard back from him. The liaison officer was a DC Andy Baxter and Sally gave Bolt his number, but then when he called that one, there was no answer either.

Bolt left a message asking Baxter to call him back urgently, before pocketing his phone. 'Christ, what is it with the people round here? Ninety per cent of the time you can't get reception, and when you do, no one picks up their bloody phone.'

'Well,' said Mo. 'Should we wait for her?'

They were standing outside the front door of Amanda's rental cottage at the edge of a pretty little village backing onto fields about twenty miles southwest of Inverness. If she'd wanted to get away from it all, she couldn't have picked a better place.

'No, let's head back up to our hotel. We can come back later.' Bolt put a note through her door asking her to call him, then he and Mo walked back to the car. A local man walking his dog along the road stared at them as he passed. Two strange men in suits, one of whom was Asian, were always going to stand out. There was a pub that looked more like a church hall about fifty yards down the road, and Bolt thought about stopping and grabbing a drink – after all, it was the weekend, and he could do with a decent pint – but he decided against it. Maybe he'd down a couple later on, back at the hotel where they were billeted for the night.

Somewhere in the distance came the distinctive retorts of gunfire.

'Someone's out hunting,' said Mo.

Bolt wasn't really listening. Once again, he was turning over the case in his mind. 'You know,' he said eventually, 'something's not been right about the Rowan/Hanzha killings from the beginning. First off, there was no trace of Leonard Hope's DNA at the murder scene, but there was DNA from a different, as yet unidentified, killer. Secondly, there was footage of every murder scene on Hope's computer except for the Rowan/Hanzha one.'

'So, what are you saying, boss?'

'I don't know, that's the problem. I mean, I know there are plenty of similarities with the Hope killings as well.'

'The fact that the killer used the same MO makes it likely it's him.'

'And yet it isn't, is it? It was a different killer.'

'But we've already covered this. There could have been two Disciples working together.'

'But if Vladimir Hanzha was the man behind the kidnapping and murder of Hope – and we reckon he is, right?'

Mo nodded slowly, clearly yet to be convinced. 'Right.'

'Then the two-killer theory doesn't hold up. Remember, there was never any evidence of a second killer found anywhere – not on Hope's footage of the killings, not in any of his phone records. The only place it was ever found was at that one murder scene.'

'So you're saying the killer of Ivana Hanzha and George Rowan might be someone completely different, and unconnected to The Disciple?'

'It's got to be a possibility, hasn't it?'

They stood facing each other over the car. 'I guess so,' said Mo. 'Are you thinking it's some kind of copycat killing?'

Bolt shook his head. 'No, I don't think it is. I'm thinking that maybe – and it is still a maybe, because I've got nothing to back this up with – it was just meant to look like the work of The Disciple. Which means we should try and look at it in a different way. Who had the motive to kill either Ivana Hanzha or George Rowan?'

'Someone might have killed Miss Hanzha to get at her father,' said Mo. 'He's a controversial figure, and I'd say he must have plenty of enemies.'

'I bet he has too, but it seems an awfully complicated way of doing it. Far easier just to shoot her in the street. And, anyway, they'd been estranged for years. I reckon she's the least likely of the two targets.'

Mo shrugged. 'We didn't dig up anything much on George Rowan. He's got no obvious enemies. As far as we could tell, he's just a boring banker.'

'But one with quite a lot of money, and quite a lot of assets.'

'He's worth a couple of million, I think. Maybe three, if you include the house.'

'What about life insurance policies?'

'We never checked. There didn't seem much point at the time.'

Bolt nodded. 'Exactly. Why would we, when we all thought it was the work of The Disciple? But I think it's worth checking now, don't you?'

'You think there's going to be a policy?'

Bolt thought about it for a moment. 'Yes,' he said. 'I do. And I'm willing to bet that the beneficiary's going to be Amanda Rowan.'

Forty-five

Today 21.23

Tired, and not sure what else he could do, having covered miles in the last hour on his hunt for Casey, Scope finally made his way back to the Tayleigh Road. God only knew what had happened to the poor kid. He'd doubled back on himself, gone in circles; stood listening to the sounds of the forest for several minutes at a time, trying to detect her presence. And all without coming across the slightest sign of her. He was beginning to wonder now if he'd been mistaken about her body not being where he'd thought it had fallen.

But maybe it was possible that she had got away after all, which meant that Scope was going to have to try to hook up with Jess and make sure she was all right. He hoped she'd managed to find a spot with phone reception so she could call for help, but he knew how poor the coverage was round here, and he could hear no sound of sirens across the night air.

The road was dark and silent, but Scope could see the faint glow of a light ahead and he quickened his pace. If this was a house, he was going to have to raise the alarm. He didn't want to, because it meant that he'd have to wait around to answer questions which, given that he'd killed two men tonight, meant that he'd almost certainly be arrested, and potentially charged with murder. In the end, neither killing had been self-defence. He'd shot both men when they were presenting no threat to him or anyone else. Scope was no expert in ballistics, but he guessed that from the angle of the bullet entries and the position of the bodies, it would be possible to tell that he'd stood above them to deliver the fatal shots, which wasn't going to reflect very well on him, particularly with his past. But he had no choice but to call the police. Two young girls were out here, alone, terrified, and in mortal danger, and if he didn't do all he could to help them, he'd never be able to forgive himself.

The light was getting closer now and he could see that it came from a cottage set back behind a high hedge. Immediately, he broke into a jog and, as he reached it, he saw that there was a car in the driveway and lights from both floors. He unscrewed the suppressor on the gun he'd taken from the man he'd just killed, slipped it into his jacket pocket, and put the gun itself out of sight in the back of his jeans. The magazine contained three bullets, and he wasn't going to get rid of it until he was sure that Jess and Casey were both safe.

He went up to the door and rang the bell.

There was no answer, so he gave it ten seconds, then rang again.

Still no answer.

Cursing silently, he listened at the door, and heard the faint sounds of a TV coming from somewhere inside.

This time he banged hard on the door knocker, then opened up the letterbox, listening again to discern if there were any signs of a human presence inside.

But there was nothing.

Stepping back from the door, Scope took a deep breath. It was possible there was no one in there and they'd left some lights and the TV on to give the impression they were at home and deter burglars, but if so they'd gone some way over the top, which left him with a straight choice. Did he keep walking, or did he break in and use the landline they were bound to have inside to dial 999?

The windows on the cottage looked new, and the front door looked solid. Even if he wanted to get in, he might not be able to without causing all kinds of damage and taking a lot of time.

Sighing, he turned away.

As soon as Casey had stepped inside Eleanor's bedroom, she'd felt uneasy. It smelled really funny and there was no kids' stuff anywhere. And then when she'd asked to come back downstairs, the old man had suddenly looked a lot less friendly, and had locked her inside the room.

Running over, she banged on the door and started yelling: 'Let me out! Let me out!' She'd always hated being stuck in enclosed places, and now she felt really frightened. But it didn't do any good, and finally she stopped, not knowing what to do, or why the old man was suddenly being so nasty to her. She bet he hadn't called the police either.

Casey could hear movement on the other side of the door – someone shuffling around – and she wondered what the old man was doing. Mum had always taught her to be polite, so she thought that maybe if she asked really nicely he'd take pity on her. 'Please can you let me out?' she said, leaning close to the door. 'I'll be really good, I promise.'

She heard the door being unlocked on the other side and she

grinned. See, being polite could really work. She stepped back as it opened, and her grin immediately disappeared.

The old man was dressed in a pair of stripy pyjama bottoms and an old vest, and there was a strange look in his eyes. It was as if he'd been taken over by something evil, and was having to do what it told him to.

'It's okay, wee lassie,' he said soothingly. 'I just thought it would be nice for us to talk.' He shut the door behind him and locked it.

Casey took a step back, then another one. 'Can we go down-stairs, please?' she asked, her voice shaking, because she was trapped in here now and she didn't know what to do, and the old man was bigger and stronger-looking than she'd initially thought. And there was that look in his eyes . . .

He followed her further into the room. 'Why don't we sit down on the bed? I can tell you a story and help you sleep.'

He reached out a hand, but Casey darted away in the direction of the bedroom's only window.

'Little bitch,' the old man hissed, and grabbed her from behind, pulling her back.

At that moment, the doorbell rang.

Casey let out a gasp of relief that was stifled straight away when the old man clamped a hand over her mouth. She struggled in his grip with all the strength she had left – but she was so tired, and she couldn't seem to manage to get away from him.

'Stop moving or I'll put a knife in you,' the old man hissed. 'I'll stab you and cut you up and bury you in the woods.'

Casey stopped struggling, trying to work out what to do. He didn't have a knife – not on him, anyway – but he did have the key. If she could get hold of that, she might be able to run outside and find out who was ringing on the doorbell, and get them to rescue her.

The doorbell rang again, followed a few seconds later by a loud banging on the door knocker, and Casey could feel the old man stiffening as he tightened his grip over her mouth. It was obvious he didn't know who it was, and was scared himself, which gave her just a little bit of hope.

They stood in the middle of the room, waiting to hear if there'd be another knock or ring, but there was none, and Casey could feel the old man relaxing his hold on her.

Suddenly she wriggled free of him and ran for the window, pulling back the curtains and hammering on the glass. She couldn't see a thing in the darkness, but prayed whoever it was who'd been at the door was still there.

But then the old man was on her, dragging her backwards and throwing her on the bed. For a moment he stood over her, his eyes full of rage as he clenched and unclenched his fists.

'You little bitch,' he said quietly. 'Now I'm going to make you very, very sorry you did that.'

Scope was standing by the car belonging to the house's occupants, an ancient Land Rover Defender, wondering whether there was some way he could hotwire it, when he caught a glimpse of movement from one of the upstairs rooms. A curtain was jerked back and a face briefly appeared in the gap before disappearing again. It all happened so quickly Scope didn't get a good look at it, but he had a feeling it belonged to a girl.

For a couple of seconds, he stared up at the window. But the curtains were closed now. Was it possible that the occupants were simply scared of opening the door at night, and one of them had just pulled back the curtains to check whether or not he'd gone? But he knew from experience that people in these parts tended to be pretty hospitable. Unlike a lot of places, they didn't turn their back on those in trouble, but tended to stop and help. They were also inquisitive.

Slowly, carefully, Scope walked back to the front door, keeping to the shadows so he couldn't be seen, and very gently lifted the letterbox and listened. The TV was still on, but there was still no movement from inside. Then he heard what sounded like a man's grunted curse coming from somewhere upstairs, followed by something else. A girl's cry?

Moving fast now, he climbed over the wall into the rear garden and circumnavigated the house until he reached the back door. Unlike the front door, it wasn't new, but it still looked pretty solid. Scope gave it a hard kick just below the handle, but it wasn't budging. He was in a hurry now, knowing that the kick would have been heard inside. Looking round, he saw a large stone plant pot the size of a bucket with a bay tree sticking out of it, and tugged the tree free. Full of soil, the pot was heavy, and he had to clutch it in his arms as he charged forward and hefted it with all his strength into the wood, just below the handle.

The door opened with a loud bang, and Scope fell inside after it, landing on one knee in the kitchen as the pot upended its contents on the floor. He was on his feet in an instant, the gun out of his waistband and back in his hand as he raced through the cottage until he found the staircase. He took the stairs two at a time, remembering that the window where he'd seen the movement was on the right. There were three doors at the top of the stairs, but only one on the right-hand side. He grabbed the handle but the door was locked, so he took two steps back and launched a ferocious kick, sending it flying open, before racing into the room.

A white-haired guy in his late sixties was standing beside a single bed, dressed in a white wife-beater vest and a pair of pyjama bottoms. His face was red and he had an expression of guilt written all over it. The reason was simple enough. Sitting on the bed was a blonde girl of no more than ten, wearing a coat and blue jeans. The coat was hanging half off her shoulder, her hair was a mess, and she looked terrified. This, Scope knew, had to be Jess's sister, Casey, and it was clear what had been about to happen. He thrust the gun back in his waistband, hoping Casey hadn't seen it, then advanced on the man.

'Listen, I can explain,' said the guy, putting up a hand and backing away from Scope. 'It's not what it looks like.'

'Yes it is,' said Scope, letting fly with a left hook when he was within range.

The punch connected perfectly with the guy's chin and he flew backwards, his head striking the wall with a hard smack. Scope watched as he slumped to the floor, unconscious, feeling a cold anger that someone could do this to a young, defence-less girl who'd come here looking for help. He turned to her and, seeing that she'd stiffened and looked ready to make a run for it, he smiled. 'It's okay,' he said. 'Your sister Jess asked me to come looking for you. Your name's Casey, right?'

The little girl looked up at him with a suspicious expression, which didn't surprise Scope, given what she must have been through today. 'Who are you?' she demanded.

It was imperative he got her to trust him, which meant telling her the truth. 'My name's Scope. I work for the canoe company you rented the canoes from.'

She nodded slowly, as if she was thinking through this information. 'Is Jess okay?' she asked eventually.

'Yes. I helped her escape from the bad men, then gave her my phone so she could call the police.'

'What about Amanda? Is she okay?'

Scope frowned. 'I didn't see anyone else. Who's Amanda?'

'She was being chased by the bad men too, and she jumped in Auntie Jean's canoe, and that's when it all started.'

'So it's Amanda that the bad men want. Do you know why?'

Casey shook her head. 'No. She said she doesn't know either.'

This was interesting, thought Scope. At least now he knew why the gunmen were here, and who they were after.

'Scope's a funny name,' said Casey.

He shrugged. 'It's kind of my nickname. No one calls me anything else.'

'Do you work for the nice man in the hat?'

'Yes. His name's Jock.'

'That's right. I remember him saying. Can you tell him we've lost the canoes?'

'Don't worry about them. In fact, don't worry about anything. You're safe now.'

'That's what *he* said.' She nodded in the direction of the guy in the pyjama bottoms. 'He locked me in here and tried to hurt me.'

'I know he did.'

'But I don't know why. I didn't do anything to him.'

Scope sighed. It broke his heart to see a young child's innocence taken away from her in such a cruel manner. 'Some people are just nasty,' he told her. 'But always remember, there aren't very many of them. Most people are good. I promise you that.'

The man in the pyjamas started moaning and rubbing his head, although his eyes were still closed.

'What are you going to do with him?' asked Casey.

'I'm going to make sure he can't do you any more harm. Then I'm going to call the police and get them here as fast as possible. You just stay where you are.'

'Can I go downstairs? It smells funny in here.'

He smiled. 'Of course you can, but stay in the house. Those other bad men might be out there somewhere.'

Casey said she would, even managing to give Scope a small smile in return, and got up off the bed.

Scope waited until she'd left the room, then hauled the guy to his feet. He was a big guy, but one who was well out of shape. He still looked dazed and it was possible he was concussed, given how hard he'd hit the wall. Scope didn't care. As far as he was concerned, someone like him deserved everything he got. He half dragged, half carried him from the room and down the stairs. The guy's moans were becoming louder and more pronounced now, and Scope could tell from the way he was tensing in his grip that he was regaining strength.

'Where are you taking me?' the guy asked in a spaced-out tone.

Scope ignored the question as he manoeuvred him out through the back door. He'd spotted a coal shed next to the fence a few minutes earlier, and he dragged the guy over to it now, pleased to see that the door locked with an outside bolt.

'What are you doing?' asked the guy as Scope released the bolt, and this time his tone was indignant and he began to struggle.

Scope punched him in the gut and, as the guy doubled over, he drove a knee into his face, before flinging him into the darkness of the shed. The man landed on a pile of coal, holding his bloodied nose with both hands, an expression of angry surprise on his face, as if he knew what his rights as a criminal were and couldn't believe that someone had had the temerity to infringe them.

That was when Scope felt the cold rage grip him. He clambered inside the shed, grabbed the guy round the neck with gloved hands, and began squeezing.

The guy made a desperate choking noise, but Scope squeezed even harder. He wanted to kill this man. For a few dark seconds it was as if nothing else mattered. Once again an image of Mary Ann flashed across his mind. Mary Ann when she was Casey's age. She'd had the same blonde hair, and had been a cute, beautiful, innocent kid, just like Casey. And Scope had no doubt that this man would have killed Casey to cover his tracks and avoid detection. Maybe even have put his hands round her neck, just like Scope was doing now.

The guy's eyes were bulging, his face darkening to the colour of wine, and he was grabbing uselessly at Scope's arms. But he just didn't have the strength to even begin to break the grip.

And then a voice in Scope's head told him to stop what he was doing. The man beneath him was a pervert. He might well have killed Casey but, in the end, he had no proof of that. He couldn't simply murder him. He was better than that.

He released his grip, and the guy slid down the pile of coal, choking and coughing. Livid red marks were already appearing on his neck, but Scope hadn't finished with him yet. He might not deserve to die, but he didn't deserve to be treated with much in the way of mercy either.

Scope leaned his face in close to his. 'I'm going to leave you here until the police turn up. If you make a noise or try to get out – in fact, if you do anything at all, I'm going to come back here and finish throttling the life out of you. Do you understand?' The guy didn't immediately respond, so Scope grabbed him by the chin, forcing him to look into his eyes. 'I said: do you understand?'

'Yes, yes . . . I understand,' he gasped.

'And if you say a word to the police about those marks on your neck, or where you got them from, you're a dead man.'

The guy nodded wildly – he could see Scope meant it – and Scope let him drop onto the coal pile before backing out of the shed and bolting the door behind him.

He knew now he had to call the police, even though it was going to leave him with some pretty inconvenient questions to answer. The thought of being charged for the murder of either of the two men he'd killed today scared him, although less than he'd thought it would. In the end, he'd done the right thing, and if these kids survived because of his actions, it was worth suffering for. He tried not to think about how long he might have to spend behind bars if he was found guilty.

When he got back inside the house, and had found the land-line, the first call he made was to his mobile phone, hoping that Jess might answer. But she didn't. He hoped that wasn't a bad sign.

Taking a deep breath, he made his second call, dialling 999.

As soon as the operator answered at the other end, Scope told her that there had been a series of shooting incidents in the Tayleigh area and that the police should send out armed response teams as soon as possible. 'Is this the first call you've had about the shooting?' he asked.

'Yes it is,' she answered, sounding sceptical. 'Can I have your name please, sir?'

But Scope continued talking as if she hadn't asked the question, telling her that there were multiple victims involved, and at least two perpetrators who were still on the loose. 'There's also a young girl of ten who's with me at a cottage on the Tayleigh Road, about five miles south of the town. She's shaken and tired, but otherwise unhurt.'

The operator wanted more details but Scope was tiring of the conversation, especially now he knew that Jess had yet to call the police and wasn't answering the phone he'd given her.

So he wrapped things up by telling the operator he was calling from the cottage's landline, reiterated the need for the police to get here as soon as possible, and hung up.

He turned to see Casey standing in the doorway watching him. 'Have the police found Jess yet?' she asked.

'Not yet, no.'

'I'm scared for her.'

So was Scope. 'I'm going to need to go and find her and make sure she's all right,' he said as calmly as possible. 'The police are on their way now but I want you to wait here for them, okay?'

'On my own? What about that horrible man?'

'I've locked him in the shed. He can't get out.'

'But what if he does?'

Scope smiled at her reassuringly. 'He won't. I promise. I've made sure he's in no position to hurt you.'

Her eyes widened. 'You haven't killed him, have you?'

He laughed. 'Of course not, but he knows what I'll do to him if he does anything to you. You'll be fine. The police may take a little while – they've got a long way to come – but when they get here, you tell them everything that happened, and they'll look after you.'

'You'll find Jess, won't you?' She looked at him with real hope in her eyes.

'I'll do everything I can, I promise.'

And he knew he would. Even though it meant risking everything.

Forty-six

Today 21.35

'One million three hundred and twenty thousand pounds.' Mo Khan whistled through his teeth. 'It's a lot of money.'

Bolt nodded. They were talking about the life insurance payable on the death of George Rowan. 'Add that to roughly one and three-quarter million pounds in other assets, and you've got a tidy amount of money. Worth killing for.'

They were sitting in the small, old-fashioned bar of their hotel in Inverness – the only two in the place, aside from an ancient barman who was reading the paper. A clock ticked far too loudly in the room and, for a Saturday night, the place was worryingly silent, although after the foul meal the two of them had had, Bolt wasn't surprised. He was now on his second pint of the evening as he and Mo continued to toss around their theories on the case.

'But I'm still stuck,' said Mo, taking a drink from his orange juice and lemonade. 'How could she have set it all up? How could she have hired a killer – a man we know was responsible for the sexual assault and murder of a young woman fifteen years ago? I mean, it wasn't like she could advertise, and she's hardly the type of person who moves in those kinds of circles. And how could she know the MO of The Disciple? She doesn't know anyone on the inquiry.'

'That's my problem too. It still doesn't make sense. The problem is, none of it does.'

'There's something else as well. Amanda Rowan was attacked by the killer at her house. She was caught on film on the house's CCTV camera. It even shows the killer slashing her with the knife, an injury requiring – what? – two dozen stitches. And her neighbour witnessed the killer chasing Amanda through her home. How do you fake all that?' He shrugged. 'It's impossible.'

Bolt nodded slowly. Mo's reasoning seemed sound, but still his doubts persisted. Earlier he'd re-read Amanda Rowan's statement of how she'd discovered the bodies of her husband and Ivana Hanzha, and it threw up unanswered questions. 'I know, I know,' he said to Mo, 'but there are still things bugging me. According to Amanda Rowan, when she got home that night she heard a sound, which she described as 'a faint, sudden gasp, like air escaping from a tyre'. She reckoned it was the sound of someone – either her husband or his lover – dying, and clearly it was coming from the bedroom where the bodies were found, because we know they weren't moved afterwards.' He frowned. 'So the implication is that the killer was still in the process of murdering the couple when Amanda arrived home, which means he was still in the room with them. According to Amanda's statement, she called out a couple of times to let her husband know she was back, then proceeded up the stairs towards where the sound had come from. Now, you've been in the room where they were murdered. It was the end bedroom.' Bolt paused.

Mo nodded. 'That's right.'

'But if you were the murderer and you were going to ambush her, or even if you were just going to try to hide and slip out unnoticed, you'd stay put, wouldn't you? Which is in the room along with the victims. So that, if Amanda had gone into the room where the bodies were lying to investigate, you could simply stand behind the door and ambush her. That way, you get three victims for the price of two, and no annoying witnesses.' Bolt threw up his hands. 'I mean, surely the last thing you'd do would be to creep along the landing to the other side of the house, and hide there. I remember those floorboards. They creaked like crazy. And yet, according to Amanda's testimony, that's what he must have done, because he tried to ambush her from the other end of the landing and, by doing so, he allowed her to escape. It just doesn't make sense. Nor does the fact that, having completely messed up his ambush, he chased her all the way to the next-door neighbour's house fifty yards away and, rather than stopping then, he risks everything by actually chasing her *through* the neighbour's house. We always said that's not how The Disciple operated, didn't we? And yet that's exactly what happened.'

Mo looked puzzled. 'So you're saying it's a set-up, boss? That somehow the whole thing was faked to make it look like The Disciple's work so that no one would think of looking closer to home for a motive? Because it still leaves us with all those other issues we talked about. Like, where did she find a murderer from? And how did she know The Disciple's MO?'

Bolt sighed. 'I'm not saying it was a definite set-up. But I've thought through all the possible scenarios – we both have – and none makes sense. George Rowan and Ivana Hanzha died for a reason. Amanda had at least three million pounds' worth of motive, as well as the knowledge that her husband was cheating on her and might well have left her for this other woman.'

'She'd still have been left with money, even if they'd divorced.'

'But a hell of a lot less. Fifty per cent of the assets, tops, and none of the life insurance. So probably a maximum of three quarters of a million, which is less than a quarter. And she'd have had the humiliation of everyone knowing that her old man had gone off with another woman.'

Mo shrugged. 'But it could still be the work of The Disciple.'

'Except there's no way there were two killers at the scene. If The Disciple had been there along with the killer of Beatrice Magret, Amanda would never have made it out of there in one piece.' Bolt shook his head. 'This killing wasn't the work of The Disciple. I'm convinced of it.'

'But the MO, boss? If that's the case, how did the killer know The Disciple's MO?'

Bolt sat back in his seat and stared up at the ceiling. 'God knows,' he said at last.

Mo put down his pint of orange juice and lemonade. 'I've always thought I liked cases like this one, when it's not your run-of-the-mill murder involving some low-life who you catch five minutes later because he didn't even make an attempt to cover his tracks, but where it's actually complex. But in reality I hate this case, because I get the feeling we're never going to get to the truth, and that someone somewhere is laughing at us.'

'You're right,' said Bolt, taking a big gulp from his pint, grimacing at the hint of sulphur in the flavour. They obviously didn't clean the pipes very often in this bar. 'I'd really like to have another chat with Amanda Rowan. I don't like the way she's suddenly gone AWOL.' He'd been trying to get hold of her every hour since they'd stopped by her house, and he'd now left three messages on her landline phone, and two on her mobile. All to no avail.

Mo opened his mouth to say something, but stopped when Bolt's mobile rang. It was on the table in front of him, vibrating angrily. He picked up, not recognizing the number, and was immediately greeted by the gravelly tones of DI Sally Miles of Highlands CID.

'We've had reports of a series of shootings in the Tayleigh area,' she told him. 'That's about twenty miles southwest of here and close to where your witness Amanda Rowan's been living.'

Bolt straightened in his chair, surprised. 'Is she involved, do you know? We've been trying to get hold of her for the last six hours and we've had no luck whatsoever.'

'I honestly don't know. So far, we've only had one 999 call from a cottage a couple of miles south of Tayleigh. It wasn't big on details and it's yet to be verified, but we're taking it seriously. There are a couple of uniforms in Tayleigh on duty but we're keeping them back until armed response arrive.'

'How long's that going to take?'

'We've got one unit up here that we're scrambling but the rest of them are going to have to come from Aberdeen.'

'Jesus. How long's that going to take?'

She gave a deep, smoky laugh that was devoid of humour. 'A good wee while. They've got a long drive ahead of them. We're trying to get a helicopter organized from Glasgow as well, but I haven't got confirmation of that yet. Another thing. We haven't been able to get hold of Amanda Rowan's liaison officer, Andy Baxter.'

Bolt's jaw tightened. 'When was the last time you had any contact?'

'He called to say he was on his way down to see her at fifteen twenty. We haven't heard a thing since.' She paused. 'And it's not like him, either. I know Andy. He's reliable.'

Bolt got to his feet and Mo followed suit. 'We're on our way down to Amanda Rowan's house,' he told DI Miles.

'I'm telling you all this out of professional courtesy, sir, but I'd appreciate it if you don't go charging right in on this. We're rendezvousing at Tayleigh nick. We'll meet there.'

Bolt told her he'd be there as soon as possible and ended the call.

'What's going on, boss?' asked Mo.

'I don't know,' said Bolt. 'But whatever it is, it's not good.'

Forty-seven

Jess was shivering with cold; her legs were so stiff she could hardly bend them, and her forearm was burning like crazy from the dog bite, when Amanda called out from up ahead, her voice only just audible above the biting wind.

'I can see lights,' she said. 'We're almost at the farm.'

They were walking along the ridge of a rolling, heather-clad hill that ran into a wide, twisting valley, with a stream running down its centre. Amanda was leading the way and seemed to be trying to keep to a narrow path that was little more than trampled grass. As Jess rounded the corner and caught up with her, she saw a cluster of farm buildings laid out below them a few hundred yards away. There were lights on in the main house, and a car parked outside.

'This is the place I was talking about,' said Amanda, giving her a relieved smile. 'We should be able to get help here.'

'Thank God,' said Jess, keeping up with Amanda as they made their way down the hill.

As they reached the first of the outbuildings, a big wooden

barn that smelled of hay and manure, Amanda stopped and listened.

'Is everything okay?' whispered Jess, stopping next to her.

Amanda nodded. 'We've just got to be careful, that's all. If any of the men chasing us know the area, they might know we'd come here.'

'The only one I heard speak had an English accent.'

'Maybe, but they knew enough to cut us off in the forest.'

It was a good point, and suddenly Jess felt nervous again. For the last hour and a half, as they'd got further and further from the forest, she'd begun to feel safer. But now she realized that this wasn't over. Not by a long way. As long as Casey's okay, she thought. As long as she's okay.

They were both silent for a few seconds. Jess could hear the noise of animals grunting and moving about inside the barn but, aside from the wind, which was stronger here, there was no other sound.

Amanda motioned her to follow and they crept quietly across the driveway in the direction of the house, passing the entrance to the barn where a group of cows stared out at them with dull-eyed expressions. The night was clear and the sky full of more stars than Jess had ever seen in her life. You didn't see stars like this in London. In fact, you hardly saw them at all and, even after everything that had happened, she couldn't help gazing up at them in wonderment.

They kept to the shadows, stopping again behind a tractor to listen out for anything suspicious. By this time, Jess was getting desperate. She was exhausted and thirsty, and desperately in need of the toilet. The curtains were drawn at the front of the house, but the light that glowed out from behind them was so inviting she was tempted just to knock on the door.

But Amanda was more careful. She listened at one of the

front windows for a second, then made her way round the side of the house. The curtains weren't drawn on the side windows, allowing them a view straight into a comfortable-looking living room where an old lady, in a floral dress and cardigan, with her grey hair tied back in a tight bun, sat watching TV with a cup of tea in her hand. She had the ruddy, cheery face of someone who's spent much of her life outdoors and enjoyed every minute of it and, though she must have been close to seventy, she was well built and looked as if she could handle herself. As they watched, she took a sip of the tea and settled back in the chair to make herself comfortable.

Jess and Amanda grinned at each other as they went round to the front door and knocked hard.

There were a few moments of silence and then a voice came from behind the door, asking who was there in a strong Scottish accent.

'Please could you call the police for us?' asked Amanda, leaning in close to the door. 'We've been attacked, and we're lost.'

The door opened a crack, revealing two separate chains, and the old lady's face appeared in the gap, appraising them both carefully. 'What do you mean, you've been attacked?' she asked. 'I don't think I've ever heard of anyone being attacked round these parts.' Her tone wasn't unfriendly, just surprised.

'It was by some men in the woods. I don't know who they are, but we only just managed to escape.'

The old lady looked at them both in turn and Jess exaggerated her shivering in an effort to gain some sympathy for their plight. 'I'm not sure what to do,' the lady said. 'My son and his wife are out, and I'm on my own here.'

'If you could just dial 999 and tell the police that we're here, that's all we want.'

'All right, I'll do that, but I can't let you lassies in, I'm afraid. Not when I don't know who you are.'

Amanda told her that was fine, and the woman shut the door and disappeared from view. Jess was disappointed. She said: 'Can't we just ask to go inside and warm up?'

Amanda shrugged. 'We could, but I don't think she'll let us, and you can hardly blame her.'

'She said she'd never heard of any attacks out here. You'd think she'd be more trusting of us.'

'Well, maybe if we both put on our best sad, vulnerable faces, she might take pity.'

'I already did that. It didn't work.'

Amanda smiled. 'You need to try harder, Jess. You give off this tough, don't-mess-with-me vibe, but I bet you're a real sweetie underneath it. Show your inner sweetness and I'll try to show mine.'

Jess was about to respond, but then she saw the smile die on Amanda's face. It was immediately replaced by a look of intense concentration.

'What is it?'

'I think I can hear a car.'

Jess listened. They were sheltered from the wind by the farmhouse and, after a couple of seconds, she too picked up the sound of a car coming from some way away. It was difficult to know whether it was coming closer or not, but it put Jess on her guard.

The door opened again and the old lady looked out at them. She seemed more relaxed now, her face creasing into a kindly smile. 'I've called the police, and they're on their way from Tayleigh. They shouldn't be too long.'

'Thanks ever so much,' said Amanda, flashing her a winning smile back.

'Please, do you mind if we come in and use your toilet?' asked Jess, desperate to get into the warmth of the house.

'Well, you look like nice wee lassies, and since I know the police are coming . . .' She removed the chains and opened the door to let them in.

As Jess stepped inside after Amanda, she caught the sound of the car again. It sounded closer.

'I wouldn't answer the door again unless you're sure it's the police,' said Amanda as the old lady shut it behind them. 'And if anyone else does turn up, we'd really appreciate it if you didn't tell them we're here.'

'Don't worry, lass. I can see you're scared about something. You can explain it all to the constables when they arrive. In the meantime, you can sit in the kitchen out of sight if you want.' She turned to Jess. 'The bathroom's at the end of the hall.'

Jess smiled and thanked her before hurrying down the hall, past a narrow staircase leading up to the next floor. As she passed the kitchen, a pleasant waft of freshly cooked food made her mouth water. For a second, she was reminded of home. Her mum had loved cooking. She'd make something different every night, and it was always tasty, and in all those years of growing up, Jess had never really appreciated it. Now that she lived with a foster family, who tended to exist on takeaways and ready meals, she realized how much she missed real home-cooked food.

And how much she missed her mum.

Forcing this new, unwelcome thought out of her mind, Jess found the bathroom, which was basically just a toilet and sink, and sat down and relaxed a little for the first time in hours. She could hear Amanda and the old lady talking as they went into the kitchen, and she wondered if they were going to get fed before the police turned up. She hoped so, and immediately felt guilty. Casey was out there somewhere, scared and alone, and here she was thinking about her stomach. She thought about the strange man who'd appeared out of nowhere and rescued her from the dog, risking his life in the process. He'd had a gun but he wasn't a cop. He'd also told her he'd find Casey. She trusted him to do so, even though she knew nothing about him, and it made her wonder if she was just deluding herself.

'You've done everything you can,' Jess whispered to herself as she washed her hands in the cold water of the sink and went back into the hall, but she wasn't sure she believed it.

She heard the old lady laughing from the kitchen, and there was something comforting and familiar about the sound that put a smile on her face, and gave her just that tiniest chink of hope that everything was going to be all right.

And then she saw it. A small dark patch on the carpet, just outside the cupboard under the staircase. For a second, Jess didn't realize what it was, but as she took a closer look, her heart suddenly started beating faster and she had to stifle a gasp.

It was blood. Fresh blood.

Frowning, she looked up and down the hall. In the kitchen she could hear Amanda talking with the old lady, but she couldn't make out what they were saying, although it all sounded perfectly normal. Jess took a deep breath. She really didn't want to look inside the cupboard, terrified of what she might find, but she knew she had no choice. Something was bleeding in there.

Slowly, very slowly, she bent down and opened the door. It made a clicking sound and a light came on inside revealing a sight that made Jess groan aloud.

Two bodies – those of a man and a woman, both middle-aged

– were hunched up and lying on top of each other in the narrow space. The man was on the bottom and his face was turned towards Jess, staring sightlessly at her like one of those paintings where the eyes follow you round. He had a large hole in one cheek that was leaking blood onto the floorboards. The woman had dyed blonde hair that was matted with blood and her face was buried in the man's back.

Jess wanted to throw up. Even though she'd seen too many dead bodies today, this sight was the worst of the lot because it was so unexpected. Straight away, she knew that these two were the people who lived here, which meant this was a trap.

Closing the door as quietly as she could, she stood back and took a deep breath.

Then felt the cold metal of a gun being pushed against the back of her head as a voice hissed at her not to move an inch or she was dead.

Forty-eight

Scope had no idea which way Jess – a girl who didn't know the area – would head, but concluded that there was no way she'd stick to the road. It was too exposed. This meant, in all likelihood, she'd try and head up the hill away from the road and make her way down into the valley that he knew eventually wound its way into Tayleigh.

There'd been an old Ordnance Survey map at the house where he'd rescued Casey and he'd spent a couple of minutes perusing it before he'd left. There was a farm in the valley en route and, if she had any real sense of direction, she'd be heading towards it. Even if she didn't, and went the other way, it was a good starting point for him to begin looking for her. His plan was to park at the farm, check that Jess hadn't arrived there, then head back through the valley on foot, since there was no road he could use, and try to locate her that way. He'd found a torch in the house and he still had the gun and three rounds of ammunition, so he was as prepared as he was ever going to be.

A long rutted track, with cattle grids at various intervals, led down to the farm. The hills rose up on either side of him, stark and bleak, and it struck him that the gunmen might have had the same thought as him, and be using the farm as a starting point for cutting off Jess and Amanda's escape if they chose to come this way.

He switched off the lights on the borrowed Defender and, when he was a hundred yards short of the farm, pulled up on the verge and cut the engine, concluding that it would be safer to continue his journey on foot.

Jess experienced a pure, unrelenting terror like she'd never felt before as she was manoeuvred down the hallway towards the living room, with the gun pressed hard against the back of her head. The gunman told her not to look round, and she didn't, but then she saw Amanda being pushed out through the kitchen doorway just ahead of her by another gunman, who had an arm round her neck and a gun pushed into the small of her back. She immediately recognized him as the scar-faced man from the house where they'd originally taken shelter.

What really scared Jess was the fact that he hadn't bothered to disguise himself, even though he had one of those faces that was utterly memorable, which meant that he didn't care if she saw his face, because there was no way they were going to let her live.

Her legs felt weak and she thought that at any minute she might collapse. She kept telling herself to be strong but it wasn't working. She was trapped, and at the mercy of men who thought nothing of killing innocent householders and stashing them in a cupboard like discarded rubbish. And soon she'd be joining them. At that moment, she wished desperately that she believed in God. But she didn't, and never had. No

God would let someone kill a mother in front of her young child, but that was what had happened to her, and it had been a hard lesson burned indelibly into her soul.

When they got to the living room, the gunman holding Jess threw her onto the sofa in the corner next to Amanda.

Jess was tempted to lie there with her face buried in the cushion and simply wait for someone to put a bullet in the back of her head, but she forced herself to turn round and sit up, clinging to a tiny hope that she could somehow talk her way out of this. The man who'd been holding her was tall and powerful-looking, with a pudgy baby face that looked out of place on such a big body, and small round eyes set too far apart. There'd be no mercy from this one, she knew that. Her own eyes drifted towards the gun in his hand, with the long silencer attached. It was such a small thing, really, and yet she'd seen all too vividly today the terrible damage it could wreak.

The older man with the scarred face was standing above Amanda, and he turned to Jess, something close to pity in his expression. 'I'm sorry you had to get caught up in all this,' he said in an English accent. 'You were just unlucky.'

Jess was clenching her teeth so hard they hurt. But there was a question she had to ask. 'My little sister . . . The blonde girl. Where is she?'

The scar-faced man shook his head. 'I don't know. She escaped.'

Jess felt a flood of relief that made her shake. If nothing else, at least Casey was okay.

'Who was that man who helped you?' demanded Scarface.

'I don't know,' said Jess. 'Honestly.'

'Have you ever seen him before?'

She shook her head, unwilling to tell them that he worked

for the canoe operators, just in case they tried to get him later. She owed the stranger that.

'Do *you* know who he was?' he asked Amanda, pointing his gun down at her.

Amanda shook her head. 'I never even saw him,' she said.

'You've been a real pain, Amanda,' Scarface told her, something close to respect in his voice. 'If you'd just come quietly, you'd have saved a lot of lives.'

The comment made Jess bristle, reminding her of Tim and Jean, and the havoc Amanda had wrought on her and Casey's lives in just a few bloody hours.

'I don't even know why *you* want me,' said Amanda, looking up at him. She looked scared, but still in control, and she wasn't shivering like Jess was. 'I have no idea who you are, and I've done nothing wrong.'

The scar-faced man gave a mocking laugh. 'That attitude might work with the police, but it doesn't wash with us. We know what you did.'

'I have no idea what you're talking about.'

'You set up your old man, darling. It was you who had him killed. Now you'd save yourself a lot of pain if you told us who the other killer was.'

Amanda looked totally shocked. 'Look, I don't know where you're getting your information from—'

'We got it from the best source possible. The Disciple.'

'Well, he got it wrong. I'm telling you. I had nothing to do with my husband's death.'

'Come on,' growled the big, baby-faced guy, in a thick Scottish accent. 'The bitch isn't going to admit anything until we start on her properly. When the laird gets his hands on her, she'll talk until she's blue in the face; but, right now, we need to get the fuck out of here.'

'Rory, mind your language,' came a voice from the doorway. It was the old lady. She still had the cheery, grandmotherly expression on her ruddy face, except now she was holding something in her hand. Jess looked down and saw that it was a hypodermic syringe.

'Sorry Ma,' said the big man. 'I'm just keen to get on, that's all.'

'Aye, you're right. We need to move, Keogh,' she said, addressing Scarface as she came into the room. 'Let me give this little jab to our wee lassie and then we can be on our way.'

Jess felt the fear crashing through her in waves. They were talking as though she wasn't there. As if she was totally and utterly unimportant.

Which meant she had to talk fast.

'Please don't kill me,' she said quietly, addressing the scar-faced man, guessing that he was the only one likely to have any mercy.

Scarface gave her an uncertain look. It was obvious he didn't relish the idea, but that didn't mean he wasn't going to do it.

'We could take her with us,' said the old lady, walking round behind Scarface and inspecting Jess from the other end of the sofa with a malicious glint in her eye. 'The laird's been known to enjoy some dark meat. He might appreciate the gift.'

Jess was so scared she couldn't move. She had no idea what the old lady was talking about but she didn't care. Anything that kept her alive for a little bit longer was good enough for her.

'No,' said Scarface emphatically. 'She doesn't deserve that. Let's just finish it.'

'Please,' said Jess, her voice barely a croak.

'I'm sorry,' said Scarface, turning away. 'Do it, MacLean. And be quick.'

Out of the corner of her eye, Jess saw Amanda stiffen in her seat as the old lady bent down towards her with the syringe. Amanda turned and stared up at the big baby-faced man as he raised his gun and pointed it down at her. She looked in his eyes and saw nothing there, and in that moment she suddenly believed in a God who'd be there for her when she died, and a kind of heaven where she'd see her mum and dad again, and even her real mum . . .

And then she shut her eyes as the shot rang out.

Forty-nine

But Jess didn't die.

She heard the sound of glass breaking behind her, followed by a grunt of surprise, and, as her eyes opened, she saw the big, baby-faced guy falling backwards onto the floor, dropping his gun in the process.

Everything happened very fast then. A second shot rang out and it was clear from the renewed sound of breaking glass that it was coming from outside, giving Jess a sudden surge of hope. But the scar-faced man – the one called Keogh – was already diving out of the way, knocking the old lady over in the process. At the same time Amanda leapt to her feet, keeping low to avoid any more shots from outside, and made a break for the door. Immediately, Keogh's arm whipped out, snake-like, grabbing her by the leg and yanking it backwards, sending her sprawling. He was on top of her in a second, shoving the gun into the side of her face before dragging her to her feet, and forcing her round so she was facing the window and acting as his shield. Keeping well hidden behind her, he then retreated towards the front door, switching off the main light in the process, leaving the room only dimly lit by a single lamp in one corner.

For a second no one was taking any notice of Jess. The big man was groaning on the floor in front of her, and she could see that his face was covered in blood. But he was a long way from being dead. One big, gloved hand reached out, patting the carpet as he tried to locate the gun. Before Jess had time to react, he'd found it, his fingers gripping the handle as he started to sit up, his eyes open and alert, even though there was a bloody hole in his cheek where the bullet had struck him.

Jess had a sudden nightmarish thought that this guy was invincible, like Jason out of the old *Friday the 13th* films – that, whatever happened to him, he would survive and keep hunting her down until she was dead. But then her instincts took over and she leapt forward off the sofa, punching him as hard as she could in the face with one hand, and using the other to try to wrestle the gun from his grip.

The gunman clearly hadn't been expecting an attack because he fell back, his head hitting the floor with an angry thud. The gun clattered out of his hand and Jess reached over and grabbed it by the barrel, a surge of hope rushing through her.

But then suddenly her head was yanked back by her hair with such force that she felt her neck crack, and the next second her face was being slammed into the carpet and the old lady's voice hissed very close to her ear.

'*Bitch. Now you die.*'

As soon as Scope fired the two shots he moved out of sight of the window. He knew he'd taken out the first one with a head shot, because he'd seen the way he'd gone down, but he didn't think he'd hit the second guy – the one with the scarred face – because, just after the second shot, the main light had gone off inside the room.

He would have preferred not to have opened fire when he did, because he only had a decent view of the big guy. The scar-faced one was partially obscured by a half-pulled curtain. Scope had approached the house carefully – really just a routine reconnaissance, not expecting to see anything untoward – but then, having identified the two gunmen inside, he'd still been in the process of formulating a plan for taking them out when the big guy had raised his weapon and aimed it at one of the two women on the sofa. Even though he couldn't see either of their faces, he recognized Jess by her short black hair, and he'd fired on instinct.

But now he had a real problem. One bullet left, and at least one gunman still alive.

He moved back round towards the front of the house, keeping to the shadows, before sheltering behind a parked car with a view of the front door.

Almost as soon as he'd positioned himself behind the car, the door flew open and the scar-faced gunman appeared, holding an attractive woman in her thirties in front of him. Scope assumed this must be Amanda, the woman Casey had told him they were after. The gunman held a pistol to the side of her head, and he spotted Scope straight away.

Scope aimed the gun at him, two-handed, but the guy was keeping well hidden behind Amanda, who looked understandably terrified. As Scope watched, the scar-faced man walked sideways, crab-like, away from the door, still using her as a shield. When he was level with Scope, about fifteen feet away, he stopped and took a quick look over his shoulder to check there was no one behind him. Then, satisfied that

Scope was alone, he poked his head out a little from behind Amanda.

'Drop the gun,' he demanded.

Scope knew there was almost no chance he'd be able to take the gunman down with a clean shot. It was dark, his target was well hidden, the pistol wasn't accurate over distance and, in the end, he was too out of practice to rely on his shooting skills. But he wasn't going to disarm himself voluntarily either, knowing this would be as good as sentencing himself to death. 'I don't think so,' he said.

'Drop it or I'll shoot her. Right here. Right now. Do you want to be responsible for that?'

'I won't be responsible. *You* will be.' Scope's voice was deadly calm, giving no hint of the tension he was feeling inside. One mistake and he was dead. And if there was another gunman in the house, he was dead anyway.

'I'm going to count to three,' said the scar-faced gunman, sounding equally calm. 'Then I'm going to kill her.' As he finished speaking, he slipped from view behind Amanda.

She was looking at Scope, the expression of fear frozen on her face. Her mouth was open, as if she desperately wanted to say something but just couldn't quite get it out.

Who is she? thought Scope. What's she done, that these people want her so badly? She looked like anyone else – an ordinary woman, with painted nails and a pretty face – caught up in a situation far outside of her experience and control. He mouthed the words 'it's going to be okay' to her, but her expression didn't change.

'One.'

'You're not going to kill her. You need her alive. Otherwise you'd have killed her already. So, why don't you just let her go, turn round, and you have my word I won't try and stop you.' He paused, hoping he was right in what he was saying. 'It's over. I called the police half an hour ago. They'll be here any minute. Leave while you still can.'

There was a pause, as if the gunman was contemplating Scope's words, but it was impossible to tell because Scope couldn't see him properly. Amanda was still staring at him, and Scope knew without a doubt her life was in his hands. And yet he was trapped. He could try and shoot the gunman in his gun hand, but the chance of success was twenty per cent at best, and the price of failure would be death. If he dropped the gun, he died. If he stayed as he was now, the gunman might very well kill Amanda, and he'd probably die anyway in the ensuing firefight.

Standing there under the cold and clear night sky, Scope suddenly felt terribly alone. The tension was loud in his head, like a steadily increasing drumbeat, and out of the periphery of his vision, he saw the pistol shake ever so slightly in his hands.

'Two,' said the gunman.

Jess's nose was bleeding. She could feel the wetness on her face. The pain was sharp and intense, going right back into her head but, rather than slowing her down, it acted as a focus. She knew she was fighting for her life, but she also knew that the woman she was fighting – though amazingly strong for her age – was beatable. She had to be.

They rolled across the carpet, struggling in a brutal embrace. Jess had lost the gun when the old lady had smashed her head into the floor, but she'd managed to knock it out of range as she'd torn herself out of her grip and smacked her hard round the face.

But now the old lady had the advantage. She'd somehow

managed to get on top of Jess, her knees pinning down Jess's arms, her meaty hands round her neck, squeezing. The old lady's eyes blazed with a cold fury that came right up from her dark heart, and it seemed to give her the strength of someone half her age.

Jess couldn't breathe, and bright dots were appearing in her vision. She was so exhausted she didn't know how much strength she had left to fight, but she wasn't prepared to give up yet. A vision of Casey – beautiful, sweet Casey – burned itself on her mind, and she knew that she couldn't die, because she owed it to her sister to look after her. So, calling on her last reserves of energy, she forced one arm out from under the old lady's knee, grabbed her nearest boob above the dress, and gave it a savage twist, pulling at the same time.

The old lady let out a shriek, her grip on Jess's neck easing temporarily, and Jess managed to free her other arm. Sitting up in one sudden movement, she punched the old lady in the side of the head, then scratched her down the face, drawing blood, lost in a sudden elation of violence.

The old lady fell off her and Jess pounced, smashing her knee into her ample chest, still punching and scratching, not really thinking about what she was doing. Knowing this was all about survival. That, and revenge.

'Please stop,' cried the old lady, the rage gone from her eyes. She looked vulnerable and scared now, her face a bloody mess, the skin already swelling and darkening where Jess had struck her.

But it was too late for mercy. Jess struck her again and again. It was as if all the anger she'd ever felt for every terrible thing that had been done to her: the murder of her birth mother; the untimely deaths of the couple who'd taken her in; the savagery of these people she'd had the terrible misfortune to have run into today – it was as if all that anger was pouring out of her gut like a volcanic eruption.

The attack probably only lasted a few seconds before Jess's conscience got the better of her, and she stopped, but the old lady was no longer moving beneath her. Her eyes were closed, and for a shocked moment Jess wondered if she'd killed her. But then she let out a moan and, feeling a flood of relief, Jess jumped up. She had to get out of here.

As she looked round, she saw the big gunman – the one with the baby face who'd been about to shoot her – lying on his side facing her, the gun in his gloved hand. He looked in a bad way. His gun hand was shaking and his eyes were unfocused. Blood dripped steadily from the hole in his face onto the carpet. But it was clear he wasn't finished yet. With what looked like a huge effort, he lifted the gun so it was pointed at Jess's belly.

She leapt out of the way just as he fired, the shot hitting the wall somewhere behind her.

He followed her with the gun, ready to fire again, but luckily his movements were slow and, without thinking about it, Jess sprinted for the half-open front door as a second shot rang out, missing her. She pulled open the door so hard that it slammed against the living-room wall, and then she was through it, seeing Amanda and Scarface out on the driveway in front of her, barely registering the sight before she heard the third shot and felt something hard and painful bang into her leg.

As the scar-faced gunman counted three, both Scope and Amanda visibly stiffened, and Amanda let out a small cry that tore at Scope's heart, her eyes wide with fear.

But nothing happened. No shot rang out.

'I said: fucking drop it. Last chance. Or she dies.'

Scope swallowed; even in the cold, he felt a bead of sweat forming on his brow. He suddenly felt very tired. 'You're not going to kill her,' he said firmly. 'Just walk away. This is over. I'm not dropping my gun.'

For a long moment, the three of them stood there, rigid as statues, as if they'd been caught in a freeze-frame. It was a classic Mexican standoff, but one that both Scope and the gunman knew couldn't last. As if to confirm the fact, way off in the distance, its sound carried by the wind, came the wail of a police siren. There was no question that, out here in such a lonely, isolated place, the siren was meant for them.

Something was going to happen, thought Scope. It had to. His finger tightened on the trigger.

And then a shot – muffled, thanks to the suppressor – rang out from inside the house. It was followed almost immediately by a second, then a third.

Scope couldn't help it. He glanced towards the house as Jess came sprinting out the door.

Which was when the scar-faced gunman appeared from behind Amanda and fired at Scope, the shot coming so close to his face that he felt its heat as it passed. Resisting the instinctive urge to fire back and use his last bullet, Scope dived down behind the car, as the gunman let off a second round that passed right through it, exiting the driver's side window in a noisy shower of glass.

Keeping down by the driver's side door, Scope moved a couple of steps to the left and peered up through the back window. The gunman was trying to pull Amanda backwards, at the same time waving his gun in his direction, while trying to keep half an eye on Jess who was staggering towards him, clutching her leg. Then, in a sudden movement, Amanda broke free from the gunman's grip and grabbed for his gun.

Reacting fast, the gunman shoved her out of the way, so there was a few feet between them, and swung round again so he was facing the car Scope was sheltering behind.

But Scope was fast too. Leaping up from behind the boot, he had a split-second advantage over the gunman, who'd clearly expected him to appear from a different spot, and he used it to take rapid aim and pull the trigger.

The shot took the gunman somewhere in the upper body. He managed to loose off a round himself, which only just missed Scope, but then he staggered backwards, clutching a spot just below the shoulder of his gun arm, a surprised look on his face.

There was a moment's pause as Amanda, who was standing a few feet from the gunman, waited for Scope to fire a second shot, but he shook his head, mouthing that he was out of bullets. Amanda didn't hesitate. Before the gunman could recover, she leapt forward and punched him in the side of the head, the force of her blow knocking him to the ground, although he still continued to keep a grip on his gun.

Over to his right, Scope saw movement in the doorway of the house. A figure was emerging, moving very awkwardly, and Scope immediately recognized him as the big gunman he'd shot. The lower half of his face was almost entirely obscured by a curtain of blood, and he had to lean against the doorframe to support himself. But he too still had hold of a gun and he was trying hard to lift it so he could shoot at the two women.

'Run!' yelled Scope. 'My car's up the track. Take it!'

Amanda let fly with a ferocious kick to the head of the scarfaced gunman that actually shunted him a foot or so along the concrete, then turned and took hold of Jess, who was still clutching her leg. They set off up the driveway clinging together like a couple in a three-legged race, but moving at a surprising speed thanks to the adrenalin that must have been pumping through them both.

Hearing Scope's shout, the big man at the door turned his gun towards him and pulled the trigger. But the shot was way off and he was clearly so weak that, when the gun kicked in his hand, it almost made him lose his footing and fall over.

Meanwhile the gunman lying on the ground was leaning round facing the direction of Amanda and Jess, aiming his gun at their fleeing figures.

It was a bad mistake. Knowing he had to take his chance, Scope charged across the courtyard, keeping low to avoid giving the big guy a target. The scar-faced gunman heard him coming and turned round, raising his weapon, but he was way too slow and, without breaking stride, Scope kicked the gun out of his hand, before hitting the deck himself as a shot rang out from the doorway. He rolled over on the concrete, grabbed the gun in both hands, and took aim at the big guy, who was balancing precari-ously, shifting from foot to foot, looking as if he might fall at any second, the gun hanging from one gloved hand as if it was a huge weight.

Scope took his time, then fired a single shot, hitting the big guy in the chest. The gun dropped from the man's hand, clattering on the steps, and he fell to his knees. Scope waited, not wanting to fire again so he could conserve what bullets were left, and a second later the big guy toppled onto his side, his head hanging from the bottom step, and stayed still.

Scope lay where he was for a few seconds, gun pointed towards the door, wondering if there was anyone else in there he needed to deal with. But all was silent and eventually he got to his feet. Looking behind him, he could just make out Amanda and Jess in the darkness, rounding a corner on the track and disappearing from view. The sight pleased him. They were safe now. So was Casey. He'd done what he had to do. Now he was going to have to face the consequences of his actions.

The scar-faced gunman moaned on the ground. 'Who the fuck are you?' he hissed through gritted teeth.

Scope walked round so he was standing above him and pointed the gun down at his head. 'I'm a man who doesn't like to walk on by. You killed a friend of mine. You tried to kill innocent people, including kids. I was never going to stand by and let that happen.'

'I bet you think you've done a really good deed, don't you?' There was a mocking tone to the gunman's voice as he spoke, and a thin smile formed on his face, causing the scar tissue to ripple.

'I saved lives.' He looked towards the front door. 'Who else is in there?'

'No one. There was only me and MacLean. He's a copper too. Can you believe that?' He started to laugh but it turned into a choke. 'I've never been shot before,' he continued after he'd recovered. 'It's funny. It doesn't actually hurt that much.' He moved his gloved hand away from the wound and inspected it.

The entry wound was small, and Scope knew it wasn't going to be fatal. It crossed his mind to shoot him there and then, but the anger that had been driving him on all night was beginning to fade now. In the distance, he could hear the Land Rover he'd come in starting up.

'That woman,' hissed the gunman. 'The one you've just saved. Amanda Rowan. Guess what?'

Scope didn't say anything.

'She's a killer. She killed her husband and my boss's daughter. Her and someone else. That's what we wanted her for. To find out who her accomplice was. And now you've let her go scot-free, and no one's ever going to be able to prove a thing against her. Thanks to you, she's going to get away with murder.'

'How can you be so sure she did it?'

'The murders were meant to be the work of The Disciple. You know, that serial killer who's been slaughtering couples down south.'

'I've heard of him.'

'Except we know for a fact that The Disciple never killed Amanda Rowan's old man or my boss's daughter, because we spent two days torturing him, and he admitted everything except those two murders.' He coughed and spat on the flagstones before carrying on. 'It was all a set-up. I almost admire the bitch.'

Scope rolled his shoulders back, trying to ease the tension in them. 'I was just trying to save the kids,' he said.

The gunman groaned. 'Christ, it was all such a mess. We were just meant to snatch her and that was that. No one else was meant to get hurt. I didn't want to kill any kids. I'm not an animal.'

'Tell it to the cops,' said Scope. 'I'm not interested.'

'No way. I'm not going back inside. I spent too long there.' With a huge effort, he sat up, using one hand for support.

Scope had already killed twice in cold blood tonight. He didn't want to have to do it a third time. Instead, he kicked the gunman in the face, knocking him onto his back, his head hitting the flag-stones as he cried out in pain, closing his eyes.

Scope patted him down to confirm he didn't have any more weapons, then left him there, confident that he was no longer any threat, and walked over to the farmhouse door. It was time to call the police and give them the latest on what had happened. The thought worried him. If the scar-faced gunman was right, and Amanda Rowan was a killer, then Jess was still in danger, which meant that he needed to get the police to intercept them. He could hear faint sirens in the distance, above the sound of the wind. Christ, what a night it had been. And yet, if he'd had his time again, he wouldn't have done anything differently, even if it did mean he'd soon be under arrest and on his way to a police station.

Whether he came out of it again a free man was anyone's guess.

He stopped by the body of the big guy and looked down at him. He had a round, pudgy baby face and he looked young, definitely under thirty. What a waste of a life, he thought, even if he had brought it on himself.

He bent down to pick up his discarded gun and stopped, frowning.

Because it wasn't there.

Fifty

'Are you okay?' asked Amanda over the noise of the Land Rover's engine.

Jess nodded weakly in the passenger seat. 'I think so.' She didn't want to look at her leg but she forced herself to. She knew a bit about entry and exit wounds from watching too many seasons of *CSI*, and she could see that the bigger hole where the bullet had exited her leg was only a couple of inches from where it had gone in. 'I'm not sure how much damage the bullet did,' she said, 'but it's bleeding a fair bit.'

'We'll get you help soon.'

'Who was that guy? The one who helped us?'

'I don't know. He's the one who got involved earlier, isn't he?'

'Yeah. That was him.' Jess took a deep breath. 'God, I can't believe I almost got killed back there.' She began shaking in the seat. She'd been hit by a car once while walking home from secondary school. It had been her own fault. She'd been texting someone and had walked right out in front of it. Luckily, it had only struck her a glancing blow and, having convinced the driver she was okay, she'd limped home, only to go into complete shock as she'd put the key in the lock, almost fainting on the doorstep. She had that exact same feeling again now, and it made it difficult to think of anything else. And yet something was bothering her.

'We'll be in Tayleigh soon,' said Amanda. 'Then we can get you to a hospital.'

'What did they mean back there about you killing your husband? I thought it was The Disciple.'

'Of course it was The Disciple,' said Amanda, giving Jess a smile that looked way too condescending.

'So why have so many people been chasing you then?'

The smile disappeared. 'I told you. I'm just a normal woman trying to get over the death of my husband, who wants to be left alone. That's all.'

As they drove through the darkness, Jess stared at her, thinking. 'It's just I can't understand why they'd say all that stuff unless they were really sure of it.'

Amanda sighed. 'Look, it doesn't make any difference. They were still wrong.'

They fell silent for a few moments and Jess decided to let it go. All she wanted now was to be reunited with Casey, and put this whole nightmarish episode behind her.

Amanda took a deep breath, then another, before slowing the car.

'Are you all right?'

'I think I'm going to be sick.' She pulled up at the side of the road, got out and staggered round the front of the car before bending over in front of a gorse bush, her hands on her knees.

Jess turned away, feeling nauseous herself. It was still almost impossible to come to terms with everything that had happened today. Her step-aunt and step-uncle were dead. So were many other people. Casey was still missing. And the whole thing centred round one person.

Amanda.

The door flew open fast and, before Jess could defend herself, she felt strong hands clamped round her neck, squeezing hard. She tried to struggle but it was as if all the strength in her body was sapping rapidly away and, as she was pushed back into the seat, her vision already blurring, she found herself staring into Amanda's eyes. But they were different now. The expression in them was cold and determined.

Jess tried to struggle. She grabbed at Amanda's arms, tried to get a grip on them, but they didn't seem to move, and she was choking now, unable to breathe, feeling as if her lungs were going to burst.

Her last thought was that this was such an unfair way to die, after all she'd been through, at the hands of a woman she'd grown to trust, and then her eyes closed and she lost consciousness.

Fifty-one

Scope stood at the open front door to the farmhouse, keeping out of sight of anyone who might be inside, listening hard. He could hear a barely audible moaning coming from one corner of the front room, but nothing else.

He remembered there being two gunmen in the forest earlier, just after he'd killed the one who'd shot at Casey, and he'd now killed them both. But someone had taken the big guy's gun. There was no doubt about that. Scope had checked all round his body and there was no sign of it. But if there was a third gunman inside, then why hadn't he taken a shot at Scope when he'd had his back to him?

But the gun was gone. So someone had taken it.

He looked back towards the other gunman, but he was still flat out on his back on the concrete.

Slowly, he crept round the front of the farmhouse and looked through the side window. The room appeared empty but he could just make out a pair of stout legs in a floral dress poking out in front of the sofa. The rest of the woman's body was obscured by the sofa, but it was obvious she was the one whose moans he could hear. He continued further round until he was staring into the kitchen and the hallway beyond. But again it was empty.

Knowing he couldn't leave an injured woman on her own, Scope crept back round and very slowly pushed open the front door with the barrel of the gun, standing off to one side, just in case there was someone there planning to ambush him. Then, when the door was fully open, he took a cautious step inside, keeping his finger tight on the gun's trigger.

He now had a view all the way down the hallway to the end of the house. Confident that there was no one hiding there, he looked round, his gaze falling on the old lady lying on her back. She was a big woman of about seventy with her grey hair tied back in a large bun, and Scope was sickened when he saw that her face was a mass of bruises. Her nose was dripping blood down one cheek and it looked as if it was broken.

'Jesus,' he said under his breath, lowering the gun and crouching down next to her. 'It's going to be okay,' he told her, lifting her arm and establishing that she still had a strong pulse. 'I'm going to call an ambulance.' He gave her hand a gentle squeeze.

Her eyes flickered open and she looked up at him, managing a weak smile.

'There's another one in here,' she said quietly, her voice a hoarse whisper, the accent local. 'He's out the back, and he's got a gun.'

Scope nodded and stood up, taking a step towards the door, the gun raised again now.

He heard movement behind him, as if the old lady was sitting up, and some deep-seated instinct caused him to turn round.

He just had half a second to process the fact that she was

sitting completely upright, holding the missing gun two-handed and pointing it directly at his upper body, before she pulled the trigger.

Only the fact that he was already reacting and diving to one side saved his life, but the bullet still caught him somewhere in the midriff with a ferocious jolt, as if someone was driving a baseball bat into his ribs, and he fell backwards against an armchair, already aiming his own weapon and pulling the trigger before he even had a chance to think about it.

Scope's shot was a lucky one. It caught the old lady in the mouth, sending a fine cloud of blood over the sofa behind her. At the same time, her gun discharged, the bullet ricocheting off the floor and disappearing somewhere behind Scope, and then it slipped from her fingers and her head tilted back until it came to rest on one of the sofa cushions, leaving her staring upwards at the ceiling.

For a full minute, Scope didn't move. He'd killed a number of times before, not just in the heat of battle, but also in cold blood, when he'd been avenging the death of his daughter. He'd never, however, shot an old woman, and he was having difficulty coming to terms with what he'd just done. It was surreal. Here was an elderly local woman in a print floral dress, her face battered and bruised as if she'd been the victim of a brutal crime herself, and then, just like that, she'd tried to kill him.

She'd come close, too. He put his hand on his shirt where he'd been hit and felt the wetness of the blood, before finding the exit wound on the left-hand side of his upper back, just below the shoulder blade. It had left a big hole in his jacket, and he was bleeding heavily. Slowly, taking a deep breath, he stood up, flinching from the pain. It felt as if a couple of ribs had been broken, but thankfully he could still move, although God knew what his insides were looking like. Often it was impossible to tell the seriousness of a gunshot injury for some time after it had been inflicted.

Still clutching the gun, he staggered into the hallway, spotting a telephone on a chest of drawers next to the staircase. He lifted the receiver and, after only the briefest hesitation, dialled 999, trying hard not to think about the fact that he'd killed five people that night, and that apart from Jess and Casey, who were still far from safe themselves, there was no one out there who could say whether or not he was one of the good guys.

Fifty-two

Ignoring the moans from the back of the Land Rover, Amanda checked the phone she'd taken from Jess and saw that at last they had a signal, even if it was just two bars.

Slowing the car down, she glanced over her shoulder at Jess, who was tied up in the back, her mouth covered with a filthy rag to stop her crying out. It hadn't been hard to overpower her, especially as Jess was in a weakened state anyway. Luckily for Amanda, whoever owned this old Land Rover Defender had left some interesting bits and pieces in it, including an array of tools, a couple of very new Stanley knives and, best of all, some duct tape. It was almost as if he was planning a kidnap himself.

Jess's eyes were open but they weren't really focusing on anything, and it was obvious she was in no state to free herself.

Amanda turned back to the road and punched a number she knew by heart into the phone.

It was answered on the third ring. 'Where the hell are you?' demanded her lover. 'I got here more than an hour ago and you haven't been answering your phone.' He sounded worried, which pleased her. She liked to feel she had power over him.

'It's a long story,' she said wearily.

'Tell me.'

So she gave him a brief rundown of everything that had happened since she'd left her house at four p.m. that afternoon for her walk.

'God Almighty,' he said incredulously when she'd finished. 'Are you serious?'

'I'm afraid so. I don't know how the people chasing me found out about George and Ivana, but the fact is they did.'

'I found out on the way up here that the police found The Disciple's body yesterday night, and it showed signs of severe torture. I also heard that Ivana Hanzha's old man may be some kind of gangster,' he continued, sounding stressed. 'This could be a real problem. He could be after us for years. Do they know about me?'

Typical, thought Amanda. After all this time together, he was still more interested in trying to save his own skin than caring about what happened to her. 'No,' she said. 'Your secret's still safe.'

'What do we do now?'

'I don't think these people will risk coming after me again. Not after all this. My feeling is that whoever's responsible will let it go. Then, we've just got to keep our heads down, and when the inheritance money comes through, we'll take off abroad somewhere a long way away.' Or I will, thought Amanda, because she was beginning to conclude that he was more trouble than he was worth. And, in the end, even after everything that had happened between them, she could never trust him entirely. 'In the meantime, we've got a problem.'

'Christ. What now?'

'One of the girls I escaped with – the older one, Jess. She knows about us. I've got her trussed up in the back of the car now.'

'Why don't you just kill her and dump the body? You don't want to be caught with her, do you?'

'I can't. I've got no gloves, and my DNA'll be all over the place. You should know the problems of DNA after your fuck-up back at home.'

'Does anyone know she's with you?' he asked, ignoring the jibe.

'The guy who rescued us at the farm. He saw us leave together. We're in his car now. But the last time I saw him, he was in a fight with two of the gunmen, so it's possible he's dead.'

There was a long pause while he thought this through.

'Look, I've got an idea,' said Amanda. 'She's injured. She got hit by a bullet. I'll just say she collapsed, and that I couldn't get her into the car, so I made her comfortable then went off to get help. No one'll ever suspect anything, even if they can't find her. They'll think some other gunman came and took her. All we have to do is make sure she disappears. You're at my place now, are you?'

'That's right.'

'Good. Stay put. I'll drop her off with you, then drive to Tayleigh Police Station, and tell them all about what happened to me. I'm going the back route and avoiding Tayleigh, so I might be about half an hour.'

'How old's she?' he asked, an undercurrent of interest in his voice.

Amanda had a flash of contempt for him then, knowing he was never going to grow out of his twisted habits. 'Seventeen, and very pretty,' she said coolly. 'Looks a bit like Jessica Ennis. You'll like her.'

Fifty-three

Mike Bolt parked the hire car on the road outside Amanda Rowan's cottage, and he and Mo Khan got out. A full police cordon had been set up over an area of close to ten square miles on the other side of the river, where the shootings were alleged to have occurred, but the village of Sprey, where Amanda rented her cottage, wasn't part of it, and DI Sally Miles had reluctantly given the two of them permission to come here in an effort to locate her.

So far, there was no proof that Amanda was involved. In fact, so far there was no proof that a series of shootings had even occurred. There'd been a second 999 call half an hour earlier from a farm three miles northeast of Tayleigh, reporting further shootings, including possible fatalities. But the caller had already been identified as the same individual who'd made the first 999 call from a house two and a half miles away, and since there'd been no other calls, there was still a great deal of confusion about what, if anything, was happening.

When Bolt and Mo had left Tayleigh's tiny police station twenty minutes earlier, only one armed response vehicle had turned up, and the locals were still waiting for further reinforcements to arrive by helicopter from Glasgow and road from Aberdeen, before they were prepared to venture out to the farm, even though the 999 caller had claimed to have been shot and wounded himself. This, Bolt knew, was the way they had to do things these days. Thanks to the incredibly tight rules of health and safety, everything had to be done exactly by the book. Risk assessments had to be taken, and the police would only intervene when it was considered as safe as possible, even if it meant innocent people bleeding to death in the meantime. Nobody liked it, least of all longstanding career cops like him and Mo, who remembered all too well the days when an officer would be allowed to intervene, regardless of the risk to himself.

Amanda Rowan had still not responded to Bolt's messages, and he'd tried her landline again ten minutes earlier without success, but he'd got sick of hanging round the police station and, if Amanda turned up at home, he wanted to be waiting for her. She had urgent questions to answer about the deaths of her husband and Ivana Hanzha, and Bolt was certain that if a series of shootings had occurred tonight, they had to be something to do with her.

As they stepped inside the front gate, Bolt could see that the lights were on behind drawn curtains on the cottage's first floor.

'Well, someone's in,' he said, stopping halfway up the garden path that led to the front door.

'Or they've been and gone, and left the lights on,' suggested Mo.

'Maybe.' Bolt pulled out his mobile and once again dialled Amanda's landline. The phone rang for thirty seconds and went to voicemail, but he didn't leave a message. He turned to Mo. 'What do you think?'

Mo stared at the door. 'It's possible she's in there under duress. When did you leave the first message for her on the landline?'

'Hours ago. After we left Vlad's place.'

'It was daylight then and when we first came by, the curtains weren't drawn. Which means she's picked the message up.' He looked at Bolt. 'Or someone else has.'

'I don't like this.'

'Me neither. Shall we take a look round the back?'

Bolt nodded, and they walked slowly round the side of the cottage. There was a small driveway at the back that led onto a single-track road, and a newish-looking Alfa Romeo was parked there, out of sight of the neighbours' houses.

Bolt walked over to it, careful not to make too much noise on the gravel, and felt the bonnet.

'Still warm,' he whispered to Mo. 'Do you remember if Amanda drove an Alfa Romeo? I don't remember seeing one when we went to their house after the murders.'

Mo shrugged. 'I honestly can't remember.'

Bolt looked at the back of the cottage. The curtains were drawn there as well. 'Can you do me a favour and get onto Grier, see if he's still up, and ask him to run a check on these plates urgently?'

As Mo slipped into the shadow of an old potting shed to make the call, Bolt approached the cottage and listened at the glass. It was silent inside, but he maintained his position for a good minute, and then he heard the sound of a toilet flushing somewhere inside, followed by the sound of footsteps coming closer. Someone was coming into the room closest to where he was standing. Whoever it was cleared his throat, and it was definitely a 'he' by the sound he made. Then the room descended into silence once again.

So there was a man in Amanda's house, and one who wasn't prepared to answer the phone. Bolt decided it was definitely time to bring in reinforcements if they were available.

And it seemed they might be because, as he crept back towards the potting shed, he heard the distinctive sound of distant rotor blades. Turning, he saw two sets of red and white lights in the night sky a couple of miles away, heading in towards Tayleigh. The cavalry had finally arrived.

He turned back to Mo and, as soon as he saw Mo's face, Bolt knew there'd been some kind of breakthrough. The excitement was written all over it.

'You're not going to believe this, boss,' he whispered when they were both in the shadow of the shed. 'The Alfa Romeo's only registered to our esteemed clinical psychologist, Dr Thom Folkestone.'

'Jesus Christ,' said Bolt, his voice loud in the silence as, suddenly, for the first time, everything in this whole complex inquiry made sense.

Fifty-four

Amanda Rowan had always thought of herself as a good person, but also one who'd made some wrong choices. And one of those wrong choices was Thom Folkestone.

She'd first met him at university twenty years earlier. Thom had been a real charmer: good-looking; witty and intelligent; interested in philosophy. Amanda had been attracted to him immediately, although it hadn't been until the second year that they'd started dating. Theirs was an intense relationship. Everything about it was full-on: the sex; the drug taking; and, of course, the arguments. Nothing and no one else seemed to matter when they were together. The whole world was just the two of them.

It had been fun – God, it had been fun – but there'd always been something unhealthy about their feelings for each other. During one of their more intense rows, Amanda had smashed a wine glass against the wall and tried to slash his arm with it. But Thom had been too fast, and he'd twisted her wrist viciously until she'd been forced to let go of the glass. He'd slapped her too. Hard round the face.

What followed had been one of the most savage, brutal and amazing bouts of lovemaking Amanda had ever experienced. Thom had had this way of tapping into her dark side, and bringing it further and further into the open and, in the end, it had only been a matter of time before they'd started talking about jointly inflicting pain on someone else. At first it was just that. Talk. What would it be like to kill a girl? Possess her, use her, then simply discard her, like a used toy. Thom had justified it using the Nietzschean philosophy he was so into, with its core belief that the weak were always going to be devoured by the strong. That was simply the way of the world and all she and Thom would be doing was following the path that nature in its wisdom had intended. If she wanted to go on seeing him, he told her, then she was going to have to be a participant, not just a passive observer. And she'd wanted Thom so badly, she hadn't turned and run when she'd had the chance. He was like a drug to her. An addiction she couldn't shake.

And then they'd chanced upon a young French student called Beatrice Magret. The year was 1998 and Amanda had been twenty-two years old. Beatrice had been hitchhiking as Amanda and Thom had driven past her on the way to Glastonbury festival. They'd picked her up, got chatting, and had decided to stop in some isolated woods en route for a joint and a late picnic. They'd smoked a hell of a lot of dope together and time had just seemed to run away from them. Thom had suggested a threesome and Beatrice, as stoned as they were, had agreed.

But Thom had got carried away and had started hurting Beatrice. Amanda had joined in, holding her down while Thom had finished her off.

Afterwards, she'd been in shock. They'd killed someone. Thom had told her not to worry about it, that this was nature's way of natural selection – the strong ridding the world of the weak. But the guilt had preyed on Amanda and she was hugely relieved when it turned out that the police had no leads.

She'd also forced herself to leave him and break her addiction, and they'd ended up going their separate ways.

It would be many years before Amanda saw Thom again. By that time she was married to George, another relationship that had already run its course, thanks to the fact that there was no prospect of him providing her with children. She'd contacted Thom through Facebook, found out that he was single, and they'd arranged to meet for a drink in London. She knew in her heart that seeing him was a bad move, but she seemed unable to stop herself and, true to form, the intense relationship they'd had before was immediately rekindled.

Thom wanted her to leave George, but for a while she'd resisted, and it might just have remained an affair had she not found out about George's own affair with Ivana, which was when events took a more lethal turn. Thom came up with the idea of killing them both and making it look like the work of The Disciple, using his inside knowledge of the case.

At first, Amanda had been reluctant, thinking it too risky, but Thom had persuaded her it could be done. After all, had they not got away with murder before? The more she thought about it, the better she liked the idea, and it would serve that philandering bastard George right.

So she'd agreed.

The plan itself was flawless. Amanda had got herself an alibi by travelling to London to see her father for the night, already knowing from his emails that George had arranged to spend the night with Ivana at their home. She'd stage-managed an argument with her father (never a problem given his cantankerous nature) and driven back home early. Thom had already let himself in the back door using the keys she'd given him, having earlier blacked out the CCTV camera so it couldn't record him.

He'd wanted her to take part in the actual murders themselves, but she'd refused, not at all sure she had the stomach for them, and instead timed her arrival for just after they'd been committed.

Thom had been insistent that when Amanda came in the house, she should act as naturally as possible. He wanted her to put all thoughts of what they'd done out of her mind. She had to play the part of an innocent woman right down to the last detail, because that way, when she recounted what had happened to the police, there'd be no way she'd contradict herself. So they'd acted out the whole thing. Her calling out to George as if she was expecting him to answer; the ambush on the landing; her fleeing down the stairs and out through the front door, even the fake tattoo on his left arm. Just to add to the authenticity, Thom hadn't even warned her he was going to cut her with the knife. Although she'd been furious at the time (as well as in a hell of a lot of pain), Amanda had had to admit it had been a masterstroke on his part. As had been the chase, which had totally fooled the police.

In the end, there'd only ever been one hitch, and that was the fact that Ivana had managed to scratch Thom's neck, drawing blood, before he could restrain her properly. Even though he'd done everything he could to clear it up before it contaminated the scene, he hadn't been successful, and the police had managed to get a DNA sample.

Although Amanda didn't like to admit it to herself, she knew it was only a matter of time before the police caught up with Thom, and then her. The problem was that the intense attraction they'd felt for each other all those years ago was still there, which was why she'd arranged for him to drive up to see her tonight, even though they both knew they were taking a huge risk contacting each other at all.

But, as she backed the Land Rover down the track and into the entrance to her rear garden, her heart still thumping from the ordeal of the last few hours, she knew she was going to have to do something about him, and sooner rather than later.

Turning round in the driver's seat, she held up the Stanley knife, using her thumb to expose the blade, so that Jess could see it glinting in the darkness. 'Make another noise and I'll kill you, understand?'

Jess nodded, her eyes wide with fear, and Amanda slipped out of the car, checking her neighbours' windows to make sure no one was snooping on her. There were old people on either side and, although nosy, they tended to go to bed early, which suited her fine. She was annoyed that Thom had parked his car there, though. She'd told him to park out of the way so that no one would know he was here. Her plan was to spend a couple of days in bed with him, then have him slip away under cover of the night and head back down south. Now it was obvious she had a visitor.

She was about to phone Thom and tell him to help her with Jess when the back door to the cottage opened and he stepped out into the darkness.

It had been three weeks since Amanda had last seen him, but the sight of him standing there – tall, broad, hair tousled – sent shivers down her spine. He was her one true weakness.

Thom came over and they embraced, holding each other tight, her head buried in his neck, taking in his smell.

'Are you all right, darling?' he asked.

She sighed, amazed that she hadn't gone into shock yet. She knew she was tough but, even so, the ordeal she'd experienced had taken her right to the edge. 'I think so. I just want to make my report to the police, and come back here and be with you.'

'Have you got the girl?'

'She's in there. Can you deal with her before I get back?'

He smiled. 'With pleasure.'

She opened up the back of the Land Rover and the two of them looked down at Jess, who was shivering on the floor, hands trussed behind her back, mouth gagged.

Thom let out an appreciative murmur and reached out for Jess's legs. 'Now this really is a nice surprise. You've surpassed yourself this time, Amanda.'

The terror was coming off Jess in waves. The woman she thought was her friend had changed into a monster, and there was no one left to help her. She had no idea where she was, just that whatever she'd been brought here for, it wasn't good.

Now she was staring up at Amanda and a big, good-looking man in his thirties. The man was smiling at her, and making a satisfied, grunting noise, as if he'd just been presented with a really good meal. He leaned in, grabbing Jess's ankles, and said, 'Now this really is a nice surprise. You've surpassed yourself this time, Amanda.'

Jess tried to move away from him, but he dragged her out of the back of the Land Rover easily.

Then, as they sat her down on the edge of the vehicle, with Amanda holding the Stanley knife close to her face to prevent her doing anything stupid, Jess caught a blur of movement behind them as two figures approached, running.

Fifty-five

During his days in The Flying Squad, the Metropolitan Police's specialist Armed Robbery Unit, Mike Bolt had been taught that, when ambushing armed robbers, sudden overwhelming force, delivered without any warning whatsoever – be it with fists, guns, or even planks of wood – was by far the most effective means of bringing down men with guns, and could often be achieved without fatalities.

Bolt hadn't wanted to arrest Amanda Rowan or Thom Folkestone before the reinforcements he'd called in from Tayleigh had arrived. With just him and Mo on the scene, there was too much risk of one or both of them escaping. He'd already had a good meal and a couple of drinks that night, and Mo, who was short and stout and preferred detective work to chasing suspects, wasn't the most athletic of coppers, so it would have been far easier to have kept an eye on them from their position behind the shed.

However, as soon as he'd heard them talking about some girl Amanda had apparently brought with her, he'd known they were going to have to do something. As Amanda and Thom had leaned into the back of the Land Rover and he'd heard the muffled cries of someone inside, Bolt had crept out from behind the shed, motioning for Mo to follow, and approached them from behind.

Thom had heard them at the last second, but he'd been too late. Bolt raced forward and punched him in the side of the head, putting all his weight behind it. Thom's head hit the edge of the roof, bounced back, and Bolt grabbed him by the collar of his shirt, swung him round, and drove a knee into his balls, lifting him off his feet.

At the same time, Mo grabbed Amanda round the middle, pinning her arms, while she screamed and struggled violently, almost knocking them both over. Bolt could see she was holding a Stanley knife, with the blade about an inch exposed, and he knew he had to act fast before she broke free. As Thom fell back against the car, his face contorted with pain, Bolt rained blows down on his face, one after another, literally beating him to the ground.

Only when he was lying on his side, coughing up blood and teeth, did Bolt turn round to deal with Amanda.

Mo still had hold of her, but only just. She was stamping on his foot, and trying to drive her head back into his, fighting like a bucking bronco, while he stumbled about, desperately trying to keep his grip.

And then, as Bolt leaned his arm back to throw a punch at her, she broke free and, with a scream of rage, went for him with the Stanley knife.

He moved to one side, dodging her easily, his fist connecting perfectly with her jaw as she turned towards him, sending her flying backwards. She tripped over Mo and landed sprawling on her side on the scuffed grass, the Stanley knife clattering out of sight behind her.

As Mo went over to comfort the terrified girl (a pretty, mixed-raced teenager of around seventeen, who'd been tied and gagged), Bolt walked over to Amanda, who was trying to crawl away. He slammed a foot down into the centre of her back, driving the wind right out of her.

'I don't normally hit women,' he said, ignoring the burning in his knuckles. 'But in your case, I'm happy to make an exception.' He leaned down so his face was close to her ear, feeling the satisfaction of a job well done. 'Amanda Rowan. I'm arresting you for the murders of George Rowan and Ivana Hanzha.'

Fifty-six

Three days later

Scope sat on the edge of the hospital bed, a small bag containing his belongings at his feet, waiting to find out if they were going to let him go.

Two armed officers with Heckler & Kochs had been stationed outside his room the whole time he'd been getting treatment for the gunshot wound he'd received in the farmhouse, and they were still there now. He'd also been interviewed twice under caution by detectives from Scotland's Specialist Crime Division, who'd been very interested to find out the extent of his involvement that night. Luckily, Scope had had time to work on his story. He'd admitted to the killing of the gunman at Jock's house and taking his gun, but claimed that it was self-defence. When pressed as to why he'd not called the police then, he'd claimed that he'd panicked and gone looking for the family who'd hired the canoes, worried for their safety. He'd denied killing the Russian guy who'd shot at Casey because there was nothing tying him to the scene, but had admitted shooting the two men and the old lady at the farm-house. Again, though, he'd claimed self-defence, and whether the detectives had believed him or not, they hadn't actually arrested him which, right now, he was taking as a positive sign.

There was a knock on the door and a tall, broad-shouldered guy in a suit came in. He had the demeanour of authority, coupled with an underlying hardness you sometimes get with certain big city cops who have spent time dealing with the more serious criminals, a look that was accentuated by his short, military-style haircut and the three vicious little scars bunched together on one cheek. Scope liked him immediately.

'Mr Scopeland, I'm DCS Mike Bolt from the Met's Homicide and Serious Crime Command.' He smiled and put out a hand.

'You're a long way from home,' said Scope, getting up to shake it, while trying not to wince from the movement.

'Still hurting?' asked Bolt, sitting down on a chair next to the bed.

Scope didn't sit back down. 'It's on the mend,' he said. 'The bullet passed through without hitting anything too serious, but it did manage to break two ribs, and they're going to take a while to heal.'

'I've had cracked ribs. They hurt. Are you sure you're ready to leave?'

'There's not much more they can do for me so yeah, I'd like to. The question is, am I allowed?'

'Why don't you sit back down for a minute? I don't like having conversations when I'm craning my neck.'

Reluctantly, Scope did as suggested.

'I've been looking at your record, Mr Scopeland.'

'Are you allowed to call me Scope? No one's called me

Mr Scopeland for so many years that sometimes I forget it's me.'

'Okay, Scope it is. I read about your role in the Stanhope Siege.'

'What can I say? Trouble seems to have a habit of sniffing me out.'

'I've heard a lot of people say that. Most of them were criminals.'

'I'm no criminal, Mr Bolt,' said Scope. 'I didn't ask to get involved in the Stanhope Siege. And I didn't ask to get involved in this.'

'You killed three men and a woman, Scope. That's a lot of dead bodies.'

'It was self-defence. Every one of them was pointing a gun at me when I shot them.'

Bolt nodded slowly. 'I'm willing to go along with that. More importantly, so are the Scottish police. Mainly because of the special circumstances of this case. But I ought to tell you that if trouble sniffs you out again, and you end up being discovered surrounded by bodies with another gun in your hand, I don't think any of us are going to be quite as charitable.' He leaned forward in his seat, fixing Scope with his piercing blue eyes. 'Do you hear what I'm saying?'

Scope smiled. He couldn't help himself. 'I hear exactly what you're saying. I'll learn to turn the other cheek.'

'Do that. I'd appreciate it.'

'How are Jess and Casey? No one seems to want to talk to me too much about them.'

'They're both recovering extremely well, but you know what they say about kids and resilience. To be honest, it's the main reason you haven't been charged. Your actions almost certainly saved those kids' lives, and I reckon there would have been a public outcry if you'd been put away for killing the people you did. Suffice to say, and this is off the record, they weren't very nice people.'

'No, I gathered that. Who did they work for?'

Bolt laughed, getting to his feet. 'I can't tell you that, Scope, but both the Met and the Scottish police are building criminal cases against a lot of people. Everyone involved is going to be brought to justice, I promise you that, even though it may take some time.'

'Fair enough,' said Scope, getting up as well. 'I'll check the papers.'

'There are a couple of people who want to see you before you go,' said Bolt. 'They're waiting outside.'

As Scope followed him out of the door, he saw Jess and Casey in the corridor next to a small, slightly overweight Asian guy who also looked like a cop.

Bolt stepped aside as Casey came dashing forward, holding a piece of paper in her hands. She was wearing jeans, a flowery top, and a very big smile. 'Thank you for saving us,' she said. 'I made you a thank-you card.' She thrust it into his hands.

Scope was overcome with a wave of emotion, and for a second he thought he was going to lose it and burst into tears. The picture on the front of the card was of a big stick figure and two smaller figures that were obviously Casey and Jess on either side. 'That's lovely,' he told her. 'Thank you. And I'm glad I had the chance to help you.'

She put her arms round his waist and gave him a big hug, and he felt her warmth against him, bringing back long-ago memories of fatherhood.

'Come on, Case, leave the poor guy alone,' said Jess, prising her sister off him before putting out a hand. 'Thanks from me, too. We wouldn't have made it without you.'

He gave her hand a squeeze. 'You look very well, considering what you've been through.'

And she did. Her right arm was bandaged where the dog had bitten her, and she was on crutches, courtesy of the gunshot wound she'd received, but otherwise she looked largely unscathed. Scope knew from his military experience that the worst of an individual's suffering was on the inside, but something about the positive expression on Jess's face suggested she was going to recover from this.

'I'm going to be okay,' she said. 'We both are.'

Scope smiled. 'I know you are.'

And that was it, really. They said their goodbyes and Bolt escorted Scope to the hospital entrance. Outside it was raining hard, and Scope took a deep breath, suddenly feeling a huge sense of relief. He'd risked everything to do the right thing, and it had worked. And now, finally, he was free again.

'Where are you heading now?' Bolt asked him.

'God knows,' answered Scope, and without another word he walked out through the doors and into the future, a little scared but also excited to find out what it held in store for him.

Mike Bolt watched Scope walk away before heading back into the hospital.

They were still trying to piece together the events of that night and, though it was unlikely they'd ever get the full story, they had a pretty good idea of what had happened.

Vladimir Hanzha, in a bid to avenge his daughter's murder, had arranged the abduction and murder of Leonard Hope, the man known as The Disciple. Bolt was still unsure exactly how they'd managed this, but the most likely scenario was that Hanzha's police contacts had told him that Hope was a suspect and under surveillance, and that Hanzha had sent a team, probably led by Frank Keogh, to abduct him. It seemed that one of the gang had phoned Hope, told him he was under surveillance, and offered to help him escape. Desperate, and realizing he was hunted, Hope had taken the bait and gone with them but, rather than letting him go, Keogh and his men had tortured him on Vladimir Hanzha's orders. Under torture, however, Hope had claimed that he wasn't responsible for Ivana's death and, believing him, Hanzha had worked out that the most likely culprit was the one with the most motive: Amanda Rowan. Having located her in Scotland, barely thirty miles from his country estate, he'd sent his men to abduct her so she could be brought back and forced to tell him who her accomplice was. Unfortunately, the abduction had gone wrong. Amanda had escaped and, by sad coincidence, run into Jess, Casey and their aunt and uncle.

The police strategy now was to try to prove the case against Hanzha, which was not going to be easy. Frank Keogh, the only surviving gunman, was not saying anything, and Hanzha had got himself lawyered up, but there was evidence linking one of the dead gunman, serving police officer Rory MacLean, and his mother Rose, who was also killed at the farmhouse, to Hanzha. Rose was Hanzha's housekeeper (although quite what she was doing armed with a gun was anyone's guess), and MacLean had told colleagues on more than one occasion that he did the occasional bit of security work for Hanzha. It wasn't enough for an arrest or a search warrant, but it did mean that Hanzha was now under active investigation.

Meanwhile, Amanda Rowan and Thom Folkestone had been jointly charged with the murders of George Rowan and Ivana Hanzha, and Folkestone had been additionally charged with the murder of French student, Beatrice Magret, in 1998. So far, no charges over Beatrice had been laid against Amanda, but they could very well follow. Since neither of them was talking, their motive for Beatrice's murder was still unclear. They'd also come perilously close to escaping justice and, even though they were now both in custody, Bolt had a horrible feeling that Amanda in particular might get away with her crimes.

Still, he thought as he wandered back through the hospital, he'd done everything he could and, mercifully, The Disciple case was now closed, which suited him just fine.

Jess held Casey's hand tightly as they sat waiting in the hospital reception area, along with the friendly detective from home, DS Khan, who'd helped rescue Jess from Amanda. She'd been in a state of shock after everything that had happened to her, and on that first night in hospital, she'd had some terrible nightmares. But each day was getting just that little bit easier than the last, and already the whole experience was taking on an almost dreamlike quality, as if it was some kind of movie she'd taken part in.

Casey too seemed to be recovering well, although Jess was worried because she was still trying to find out what was going to happen to them now. She could go back to live with her foster family, but the situation was more complicated with Casey. She'd asked the other London detective, Mike Bolt, whether or not she and Casey could stay together, and he'd said he would do what he could, but that it was in the hands of social services. Then, yesterday, he'd come back and told her that he'd looked into things and because Jess stood to inherit half her adoptive parents' money on her eighteenth birthday, which was only three months away, it was possible that she could buy her own place and they could live together. Jess was hoping they could be together straight away, and she knew Casey thought they were going to be, but if they had to wait three months, then so be it. At least they'd be travelling back to London together, accompanied by the two detectives. It was sad but, after all that had happened, Jess couldn't wait to get out of Scotland.

She leaned forward and kissed Casey on the top of her head. 'Are you looking forward to seeing all your friends again?'

Casey looked up and grinned, her eyes bright and mischievous. 'I'm looking forward to seeing everyone and everything.'

'Yeah,' said Jess, with a smile of her own. 'I know exactly how you feel.'

At that moment the door opened and DCS Mike Bolt walked into the room. A big, imposing figure who immediately made Jess feel safe, he was a reminder that there were still plenty of good people in the world.

'Come on you two,' he said. 'It's time to go home.'